Trading Reality

Also by Michael Ridpath

Free to Trade

MICHAEL RIDPATH

Trading Reality

HarperCollinsPublishers

This book was originally published in Great Britain in 1996 by William Heinemann, an imprint of Reed International Books, Ltd.

HarperCollins books may be purchased for educational, business, or sales promotional use. For information please write: Special Markets Department, HarperCollins Publishers, Inc., 10 East 53rd Street, New York, NY 10022

FIRST U.S. EDITION

ISBN 0-06-017629-6

97 98 99 00 01 RRD 10 9 8 7 6 5 4 3 2 1

For Barbara

Acknowledgements

I received help in writing this book from a large number of people. I should like in particular to thank Anne Glover and her colleagues at Virtuality; Mike Bevan, editor of *VR News*; and Paul Marshall of Maxus Systems International, whose financial software was the inspiration for Bondscape.

I have occasionally used the names of real companies in this book. All their actions are fictitious.

FairSystems, Jenson Computer, Onada Industries, Harrison Brothers, Banque de Genève et Lausanne and Wagner Phillips are entirely fictional companies. Any similarity to any real organisations is accidental.

1

It didn't take much to wipe twenty billion dollars off the world's bond markets. Just a small sentence. A few words transmitted simultaneously on to every screen in every dealing room round the world:

12 April. 14.46 GMT.
Fed Chairman Alan Greenspan warns that US interest
rates are 'abnormally low' and will move up shortly.

The announcement was met by an assortment of cries from around the dealing room, ranging from the hysterical 'Christ, did you see that?' to the angry 'What the hell is he playing at?' to the quietly groaned 'Oh shit'.

I put my head in my hands and counted to ten. I looked up. The message was still there.

The panic started.

People shouted into phones, and shouted at each other. Etienne, Harrison Brothers' head of trading, and my boss, screamed at the futures trader to sell anything he could at any price. The phone boards flashed like discotheques as customers called to sell, sell, sell. Salesmen held their hands over mouthpieces and shouted to their traders, demanding to know what prices they would pay for their customers' bonds. The traders

1

weren't interested. They had their own long positions to get rid of first.

Etienne paused for a moment to look around him. He caught my eye. 'How are your positions, Mark?'

I straightened up. 'Not so good,' I said.

A look verging on triumph flitted across Etienne's face and was gone as he turned to deal with the chaos behind him.

I was furious with myself. Only that morning he and I had argued at the daily meeting about the likelihood of a change in Fed interest rate policy. He had insisted that we should not lighten up our positions, he was convinced that the bond market rally would continue. I had disagreed. I'd planned to spend the next couple of days making sure my positions were fully hedged against a rise in interest rates.

I had made plans, but I hadn't done anything. Now I was caught long and badly wrong.

For the past two years interest rates had fallen month after month. Bond prices had risen month after month. It had been easy to make money; the more bonds you owned, the more money you made. Harrison Brothers had made record profits the previous year from just such a strategy, as had most of the other large American investment banks in the market. But now that the US Federal Reserve had announced that it would be raising interest rates, there would be carnage. Bond prices would fall, and then fall some more as people sold to protect their profits, to hedge their positions, or just through a mixture of fear and panic.

I had seen it coming and I had done nothing. How could I have been so stupid?

'What do we do?' Ed Bayliss looked up at me through the thick lenses of his glasses. He was clinging on to his cup of coffee for dear life. This is the first true market panic he has seen, I thought. Recently out of the training programme, he had been assigned to help me trade the London office's proprietary book three months before. It was an important job: we were responsible for placing Harrison Brothers' own bets in the bond market. Ed lacked experience, but he was bright and learned fast. In normal times I found him extremely helpful. I wondered how he would cope under pressure. I was going to find out.

'Work out how much we've dropped.'

I checked my screens. The initial panic was turning into a rout. The thirty-year US treasury bond, known as the 'long bond', was already off nearly two points. I looked over at Greg, our treasury trader. I knew he had a hundred and twenty million dollar long bond position; he had lost two million dollars on that alone. He was furiously working the phones, trying to sell some of his bonds to other traders in the street. The German, French and British bond markets were also sharply down. There was no doubt that the market had been surprised by this one.

'We're two point four million dollars down on last night's revaluation,' Ed said.

Two point four million! Almost two months' profits gone in ten minutes. I allowed myself thirty seconds to curse my own stupidity, the market, Alan Greenspan, Ed, and my own stupidity again. I needed to get it out of my system. To clear my head. To figure out what to do next.

'What now?' asked Ed, his face wrought with anxiety.

I realised I hadn't answered Ed's question. 'We don't panic,' I said. 'In all this turmoil, some bonds are bound to get out of line. If we see anything that gets too cheap, we pounce.'

That was easy to say, difficult to carry out in practice. We were responsible for looking for opportunities across all the bond markets, and with prices moving wildly in each of them, it was difficult to pin any of them down.

I felt, as much as saw, Bob Forrester at my shoulder. Bob, a big, broad-shouldered American in his forties, was in charge of Harrison Brothers' London office. He had been a trader himself, a very successful one. The announcement on his Reuters screen had sent him rushing down to the trading floor. He looked concerned. He knew exactly how large Harrison's positions had been at the close of business the night before. Even so, he watched the scenes of panic in front of him with disapproval.

'You all right Mark?' he asked in his gruff voice.

I turned to meet his eye. 'We took a bit of a hit,' I answered coolly. 'But there have to be some good opportunities out there. We'll make it back.'

Bob looked at me for a moment. He had been where I was now a dozen times before. 'Good kid,' he said, patting my shoulder, and strode over to where Etienne was exhorting Greg to dump his position. Etienne was given to brilliance on some days, hysteria on others. This was one of the others, and it was infectious. Bob had presence, and that presence was just what was needed to calm the floor down.

To work. I examined the screens full of prices and yields in front of me, looking for opportunities. I tried a couple of ideas, but by the time I had checked each one, the prices had moved. I wasn't getting anywhere.

I glanced over to Ed, who was involved in a similarly fruitless struggle next to me. 'Shall we try Bondscape?'

'What, live?'

'Yes, live. I think we've done enough dry runs. You can't practise for ever. And it's the only way we have of quickly making sense of this market.'

'But we haven't ported the software yet.'

'Sod that. Let's just pick up the computer and plug it in. We haven't got time for any fancy stuff.'

Bondscape was a completely new computer system for analysing the bond markets. It used 'virtual reality', a computer technology that allows a user to feel that he is actually inside a computer-generated virtual world. Bondscape was brilliant. It had been developed by Richard Fairfax. Richard was my brother.

Ed and I went down one floor to Information Services, this year's name for the computer department. There I grabbed one of the computer analysts, and persuaded him to help me physically pick up the Bondscape system and carry it up to the trading room. It was heavy, and there were lots of wires, plugs and bits and pieces, but within ten minutes we had it all plugged in and ready to go. The rest of the trading floor were too absorbed in what they were doing to notice us.

I sat in my chair with the Bondscape computer beside me. I picked up the 'wand', a six-inch pointer with a couple of buttons on the handle. I put on the headset. It wasn't much larger than a pair of sunglasses, but instead of a lens in each eye, there were two liquid crystal displays, like tiny television sets. As I strapped the clasp round the back of my head, I entered a completely new world.

Before me, a landscape of rolling green hills stretched away to brown and then grey mountainsides. The hills were dotted with clusters of buildings of different sizes and colours, and with national flags. The whole landscape was shifting gently. An eagle flapped lazily over a group of tall buildings, halfway up the hillside.

I was looking at a representation of the world's bond markets. The hillside was made up of a series of ridges. Each ridge represented a bond market; the higher the ridge, the higher the yield. The plains in the foreground represented the Japanese market with yields of only four per cent, rising through America, Germany, France and the UK, to Italy towering in the background at a yield of nine per cent. The hillside also sloped up from left to right, with the shorter maturity, lower yielding bonds to the left, and the longer maturity, higher yielding bonds to the right. By looking at the landscape, it was possible to see immediately how the yields in the different markets related to each other.

At the foot of the hills was a clock tower. I waved the pointer in front of my eyes. In my virtual world, I could see a wand move over the landscape. I pointed it at the clock tower, and, with a few clicks, I had moved the time back over an hour to 14.40 GMT, a few minutes before the announcement. I then pressed the fast forward icon and watched.

For the first few seconds, representing the first few minutes of real time, everything was still. Then suddenly the hillside began to heave and buckle. First one ridge, and then another moved upwards, as the whole landscape rose, reflecting the sudden rise in yields and fall in bond prices all round the world.

Something caught my eye. I ran over the sequence again. It

seemed to me that the section representing the French market had moved up more than those around it.

So I pointed to the tricolour, waving precariously on the side of the hill, zoomed down to land beside it, and rewound the simulation. We were back at 14.40 GMT. The German and American markets were along ridges just below me, and the Dutch and British markets were farther up the hill above me. I played the sequence through. As the clock ticked through 14.46, I had the sensation of being suddenly thrust up into the air. The ridges above and below were moving as well, but not as much as mine. In particular, the portion of the French ridge that represented the five-year maturity was moving up fast.

'French five-years are dead cheap, check them out!' I snapped to Ed.

'OK,' he said. A pause. I couldn't see what he was doing in the real world, but I could hear the click of his keyboard as he checked prices on his screen. He pressed the intercom, and got through to Harrison's French bond trader in Paris. 'Philippe, it's Ed in London. What's happening in the five-years?'

Philippe sounded harassed. 'I don't know. It's crazy. There is a big seller through BGL. Why they are selling I don't know. I would buy some if I could, but my position is too big already.'

'Thanks,' said Ed. 'Did you get that?' I heard him ask me.

'Yes,' I said. BGL was a big Swiss bank not known for its sophistication in the markets. They were probably just panicking. 'Now we just have to work out which bonds to buy.'

Each building on the hillside represented a particular bond issue. Once again, the height of the building represented the yield, the higher the building, the higher the yield. The idea was to buy a bond whose yield had suddenly increased in the market turmoil for no good reason.

I rewound the simulation and stood right in the middle of a cluster of buildings in the five-year segment of the ridge. I pressed fast forward again and watched closely. Once again, at 14.46 GMT, I could see, and almost feel, the earth underneath me move upwards. This time, I focused on the buildings around me. They shook, some growing taller, and some smaller. There

6

was one to my right, which had been one of the shortest, but was now thrusting upwards to become several storeys in height, a mini-skyscraper. It had the Renault logo on its side. I pointed to the door and clicked. The words 'Renault 6% 1999' loomed large.

'The yield on the new Renault has shot up. See if you can get some of that,' I said.

'How much?' asked Ed.

'A hundred million francs should do if you can get them.'

'OK.' I heard Ed on the squawk box with the traders in Paris, asking them to buy the bonds for us. Within a minute our order was filled. I watched, entranced, as the building shuddered, and collapsed a couple of storeys. Our purchase had already affected the price of the Renault bonds, and Bondscape had picked it up.

'Done,' said Ed. 'What do we sell?'

My next task was to scour the hillside for bonds that were too expensive. I had to be quick. I didn't want the market to fall further before we had sold something.

'I'll try the eagle,' I said. The eagle was what is known as an intelligent software agent, which can be programmed to search data according to certain criteria. With a couple of clicks, I asked the eagle to find me bonds that had become significantly more expensive in the last two hours.

The eagle flew swiftly a short way up the hillside to circle the Dutch flag. I followed it. It was hovering over a five-year Dutch government bond, which had created a hole in the ground because it had such a low yield.

'OK, Ed, I've found one. Sell the Dutch Treasury seven-and-a-halfs of ninety-nine!'

'Right,' said Ed. Within thirty seconds he had completed the trade.

Encouraged, I continued my search of the landscape. The whole time I was doing this, I was talking to Ed, making sure that the real world tallied with the virtual one.

'Earth to space cadet. Earth to space cadet. Come in please!'

I flipped up the virtual glasses, to see the tall figure of Greg strolling towards me, carrying a cup of coffee. The cuffs of his sleeves were rolled up once to reveal his wrists, and his yellow tie had dropped half an inch to show an undone top button. But he still looked calm and relaxed.

'What are you doing, Mark? Checking out the futures market on Alpha Centauri? I'm a seller, by the way.'

I grinned at him. Originally from New Jersey, Greg had been in London for two years now. We had become good friends.

'Do you want to take a look at Bonds?' I asked him. By that, I meant the US government bond market, where Greg plied his trade.

'Hey, that's a horror movie. Blood and guts everywhere. Haven't you got something with a bit more class?'

'Shut up and put these on. You need all the help you can get.'

Greg sighed. 'You're right there.' He picked up the second set of virtual glasses.

I took him to the part of the mountain that showed the long-term US government bonds. On normal days, this would be a smooth, gentle slope, scattered with similar one-storey bunga-lows. Today it looked more like a Tuscan hill town, a jumble of buildings of different sizes and shapes, perched on a jagged hillside.

'What a mess!' Greg said. I showed him how Bondscape worked. He picked it up quickly. He was able to explain away many of the anomalies with such comments as 'No wonder the nine-and-a-halfs look so expensive. They all got stripped years ago!'

Greg knew the relationships of all the bonds he traded inti-mately. It was by placing himself actually on one of the build-ings representing a bond, and fast forwarding through time, that he was able to see a change in these familiar relationships. 'The eights of Novie twenty-one!' he said at last. He meant the US Treasury eight per cents of November 2021. 'Those suckers just shouldn't be that cheap. I gotta go.' He gave me the head-set, and rushed off to buy some bonds. Knowing Greg, it would be quite a lot of bonds.

I was just about to flip back the glasses when I saw Bob Forrester striding towards me.

'What are you doing fucking around with toys at a time like this?'

I had expected this. I swivelled my chair round, lifted the headset on to my brow, and looked Bob straight in the eye. He liked to be looked straight in the eye.

'Our positions are a mess,' I said evenly, 'and they're getting worse.' Etienne, standing next to Bob, bridled.

Bob frowned, but he was listening. 'Of course they're a mess! The market's shot to hell.'

I pointed to the computer. 'With this system, I can see what the firm's long and short positions are. And they make no sense.'

'What do you mean?' growled Bob.

'For example, one trader is busy buying German government bonds, while another is happily selling German eurobonds. It's crazy. Sure the government bonds are cheap, but the eurobonds are cheaper.' I had overlaid a colour scheme that shaded the buildings blue if Harrison was long, and red if we were short. This had highlighted some ridiculous trading in the hour and a half following Greenspan's announcement.

Bob looked to Etienne. 'Well?'

Etienne looked confused and angry. He knew I was right, but he wasn't going to admit it. He recovered swiftly. 'This thing is dangerous, Bob. In a market like this the best thing to do is to sell anything you can as quickly as you can. You can't afford to spend time mucking around with fancy machines. If the market falls again tomorrow, those positions Greg and Mark have put on will be a problem. A big problem.' Bob was watching him thoughtfully. 'Nothing can beat a good trader's gut-feel, Bob. You know that.'

I was about to open my mouth to protest. With the trades we had constructed we should have been all right if the market moved either way. Then I saw Bob's face, and kept quiet.

'I sure hope you're not just pissing away more money, kid,' growled Bob, and he stalked off.

I re-entered Bondscape's world. Over the next hour or so, I picked out a couple more trades to put on. Eventually, the landscape stopped shifting, indicating that the market had calmed down, and I took off the headset and stretched. 'How much are we down now?' I asked Ed.

It took him a few minutes to do the calculations. 'Still two point one million,' he said, glumly.

I rubbed my face with my hands. Shit! It took a long time to earn two million dollars, and it had only taken an afternoon to lose it. Why oh why hadn't I hedged my positions that morning?

Greg came over and leaned against the desk. 'How much did you drop?'

I winced. 'Over two mill. And you?'

'A touch more. But I'll get it back. I'm long two hundred twenty of the Novie twenty-ones.'

'Jesus! I hope you know what you're doing.'

'I do,' said Greg with a relaxed smile. 'Thanks to that machine of yours. Was Bob impressed?'

'Not really,' I said. 'I think he prefers gut-feel to rational thought. I hope to God those trades we put on work.'

'Don't worry,' said Greg, 'they will.' With that he went back to his desk to tidy up.

'Are you OK, Ed?' I asked.

Ed nodded. He still had a scared look in his eye, but he had coped well.

'That was a tough day,' I said. 'You did well.'

He smiled, and returned to the paper trail of our afternoon's trading.

I stood up, and looked around the huge trading room. There were nearly two hundred trading desks in eight long rows. Bonds, foreign exchange and equities were all traded from the same room. There were no windows, although the walls were lined with a series of glass meeting rooms. At the end of a turbulent day, the floor looked as though a hurricane had hit it. Desks were cluttered with screens, computers, phones and intercoms, and there were bits of paper everywhere. Chairs

10

were pushed haphazardly between the rows of desks, and traders were milling about, stretching, looking for a cup of coffee, chatting.

I headed over to the exit on the far side of the room. I walked past the equity group. Harrison Brothers was mostly known for its expertise in the bond markets, but it felt it had to have a presence in equities. The small group sat underneath a giant ticker-board, like an electronic frieze, giving constant updates on the prices of the thousands of stocks quoted on the New York Stock Exchange. It was irrelevant to nearly all of us, but Bob Forrester thought it gave the place a true American investment-bank look, and besides, it allowed him to keep up with his personal portfolio. It was of no use to the only people for whom it might have had any professional interest, since they couldn't see it; they were sitting directly underneath.

Another Forrester touch was the brown HB logo on every column and wall, there to be picked out by any visiting TV cameras providing those background shots for market reports on the news. The room had to look good.

I stopped at the water-cooler just by the exit and poured myself a cup. The equity group, too, were all winding down after a hard day's work. All of them except one. Karen. She was sitting on her desk, a phone jammed between her cheek and her shoulder, her long legs resting on her chair. Despite the day's excitement, her yellow skirt and white silk blouse had not a wrinkle in them, and she looked as cool as she had at seven thirty that morning.

'Oh, come on, Martin, really? You didn't!' She chuckled down the line. I sipped my water and listened. 'Now, how many of those Wal-Marts do you want?'

She brushed the fine blonde hair out of her eyes, and winked discreetly at me. She turned to a trader who was packing up to leave. 'Jack! Before you go, what's the offer on Wal-Mart?'

2

I looked over the clusters of dark suits gathered around the huge atrium. She wasn't here yet.

The atrium was ridiculous. Waterfalls, smooth sculptures, and whole trees seemed to take up most of the space in the middle of the building, leaving a narrow shell around the outside for people to work in. We had both been invited to a party by Banque de Genève et Lausanne, who were opening new London offices. I usually avoided these things if I could, but Barry, their head trader in London, had been insistent that I should come. I didn't know anyone there, and was happy supporting a black marble column that shot fifty feet up into the air above me, sipping a glass of champagne.

What a day! I had managed to lose over two million dollars. Whichever way you looked at it, that was a lot of money. My year's profit and loss should be able to stand it. In fact, Ed and I were, or rather had been, three million dollars up on the year. But dropping that much money had hurt my pride badly, especially since I had foreseen Greenspan's move and done nothing about it.

Still, in a funny kind of way, I had enjoyed the day. I was facing quite a challenge – to make back two million dollars in a treacherous market. And I was determined to make it all back. I had my reputation to think of, my track record. For a trader, the annual profit and loss is all.

And I had a pretty good track record. I had started trading the proprietary book for Harrison Brothers two years ago. In my first year, I had made eight million dollars for the firm, and that had grown to fifteen million dollars in my second year. Not bad for a twenty-eight-year-old trader. And my salary, and especially my bonus, were beginning to reflect my trading success.

So, how was I going to make back that two million dollars? Bondscape would certainly help. It had given me a tremendous feeling of power. I had been able to visualise the whole bond market, to get right inside it, to see and feel it moving. And I was the only one in the market with that capability. Richard and I had been working on Bondscape for a few months. I had been through several practice sessions, and suggested a number of changes. I had known it would work, but never dreamed it would work that well.

It was a strange sensation. I had indeed experienced an alternative reality. I had always been sceptical that virtual reality provided an experience that was any different from a fancy computer game. But today I had felt as though I were living and moving inside another world, an abstract world of bonds, yields and currencies. What would other virtual worlds be like, I wondered.

A flash of blonde hair weaving its way through the suits caught my eye. 'Hi. Sorry I'm late. God, I need a drink.' She looked round, a waiter was instantly by her side, and she was soon swallowing her own champagne.

'I got here as quickly as I could,' she said. 'It's impossible to get Martin off the phone. I don't know when he gets any work done.'

'He just likes to chat you up, that's all.'

Her eyes twinkled over her glass. 'As long as he does the trades, I don't care. Anyway, I hear you had a good day.'

'That's one way of looking at it. Another is that I dropped two million dollars.'

'Well, Greg was impressed. He says you'll make it back. He told me you were using that virtual reality machine.'

'That's right. Bondscape. It worked brilliantly.'

Karen laughed. 'I bet you looked pretty funny in those little glasses.'

'Oh, I don't know. I think they suit me. In a couple of years everyone will be wearing them.'

'Nerd.'

'Hey! As long as it helps me make that two million back, you can call me what you like.'

'I'm sure you'll make it back. You always do.'

'I hope you're right.' I sipped my champagne thoughtfully. 'How did you cope today?'

'Not too bad. The panicky clients panicked. The sensible ones sat on their hands. Nothing I couldn't handle.' And she did indeed look as if the day's turmoil had had no effect on her at all. 'The atmosphere on the desk is pretty bad though.'

'Why's that?'

'The rumours are they're going to reorganise Equities world-wide. That probably won't be good for London. Everybody's getting pretty defensive. Watching their own backs, looking for exposed areas in other people's.'

'What a team!'

Karen snorted. 'We're just one big happy family.'

'You'll be all right, though, won't you?'

'I should be,' she said. 'My commission is up fifty per cent on last year. But you can never tell.'

She was right. You couldn't tell. Somehow, though, I expected Karen would be a survivor.

'Do you want to play tennis on Saturday morning?' she asked. 'I've booked a court for nine.'

'Oh God,' I groaned. 'Nothing like some early morning humiliation to set me up for the weekend.'

'What do you mean? You might win. You've won before.'

'Yes, twice.'

'This could be the third.'

'OK,' I sighed. 'I'll play.'

14

Karen was a much better tennis player than me. She was a better skier too. And swimmer. She was athletic, co-ordinated, and she liked to win. I just sweated a lot and hit the ball too hard.

A studious-looking man of about my own age hovered at Karen's shoulder. 'Peter! How are you?' she said, holding out her cheek to be kissed. 'Thanks for inviting me.' She looked around her. 'This building is amazing!'

'It is rather good, isn't it,' said Peter. 'Much better than the rabbit warren we're used to.'

'When did you actually move in?'

'Last week. We're still trying to get the phones to work. As you know.'

'Don't I just! It's been a nightmare getting through to you. Oh, by the way, this is Mark Fairfax. He trades the proprietary book at Harrison. Mark, this is Peter Tewson, from BGL Asset Managers.'

I smiled at him. He nodded quickly towards me, and then turned back to Karen. 'You were dead right about Chrysler. It's up over ten per cent since you recommended it.'

'I'm glad it's working out,' said Karen. 'You know, when I hear something, I want to make sure my best accounts hear it too.'

This I knew wasn't true. Karen had researched Chrysler thoroughly before tipping it. But she knew that her clients would be quicker to act if they thought they were the first to hear a rumour.

I let them talk, and watched the crowd, looking for Barry.

A tall, silver-haired man glided across to us. Peter saw him coming, stiffened, and shut up.

'Good evening, Peter, how are you?' said the man in a French accent.

'Very well, thank you, er, Henri,' stammered Peter. 'Henri Bourger, head of our London office. Er, this is Karen Chilcott from Harrison Brothers, and this is, um . . .'

'Mark Fairfax,' I said, holding out my hand.

15

'I was just remarking how wonderful these offices are,' said Karen.

'Thank you,' Bourger replied, politely.

'They look very similar to your New York building. But I think this central space works much better. Was this designed by Fearon as well?'

Bourger's eyes lit up. 'Well yes it was as a matter of fact,' he said, and he launched into a long description of how and why BGL had commissioned Fearon for London. Trust Karen to look up the architect before coming here.

I felt a touch on my elbow. 'All right, Mark? How are you, old son?'

It was the bulky figure of Barry, BGL's head trader.

I winced. 'I've had better days.'

'You're telling me. My lads have been shitting bricks all afternoon.'

I looked around and grimaced. 'Why am I here, Barry?'

Barry laughed. 'Not your scene, is it? Well, it's not mine either. Come here, I want you to meet someone.' He pulled me over towards the far side of the atrium. 'He's our head of trading, worldwide.'

So that's what it was. They were sounding me out for a job, and Barry wanted to show me to his boss before he made the first approach. It was flattering, but I wasn't interested. In my business, Harrison Brothers was one of the best firms in the world. BGL was an enthusiastic amateur with deep pockets, and big trading losses. One day I might cash in my experience at Harrison Brothers for a big ticket elsewhere, but not yet. I was still learning my trade, and enjoying it. The money was secondary.

I was polite to Barry's boss, and we talked for half an hour, neither of us giving much away. When eventually I did break free, I saw Karen standing by herself near the entrance, looking around agitatedly. She was relieved to see me.

'Can we go?'

'If you like,' I said. 'I won't keep you. What's up?'

Karen bit her lip, and didn't reply.

16

I hailed a taxi outside, and we jumped in. 'Barry's going to offer me a job, I'm sure of it,' I said.

Karen didn't respond. She stared out of the window, her shoulders hunched.

I was worried. I hadn't seen Karen like this for several months.

We sat in silence until the taxi pulled up the narrow cobbled mews just off Holland Park Road where I lived. Karen went straight into the bedroom to change. I went up to the large sitting room at the top of the house. It was my favourite room. It was sparsely furnished with a sofa, an armchair, a TV, stereo, a small fridge, and my mother's piano, which I had no idea how to play, but which I couldn't face getting rid of. The evening sun shone in from a large sliding window that opened out on to a tiny terrace. I grabbed a can of Stella from the fridge, and walked out on to the terrace to watch the sun setting over West London. The little town gardens were dotted with the white and pink of cherry blossom. I quickly checked the house next door. No luck. A famous footballer was supposed to live there, but I had yet to see any sign of him.

I had bought the house six months before, helped by the proceeds of last year's bonus, and it was my first. After six years cooped up in small flats in various parts of London, it was wonderful to be able to move up and down stairs between rooms.

It wasn't very big, but I loved it. When I'd bought it, it had been a sickly pudding of orange, black and brown. Lots of velours, lots of dust. Even I hadn't been able to handle that. So the painters had been in, and I was pleased with the result. The place was now light and airy, under-furnished with the randomly assembled pieces from my much smaller flat.

I took a swig of my beer. Things were going well. The house. The job. Karen.

But what was wrong with her this evening? I didn't think I had said or done anything to upset her. She had seemed perfectly fine at the beginning of the party. Whatever it was, I was confident I would sort it out.

I heard her footsteps coming up the stairs.

'Glass of wine?'

She nodded, a barely perceptible movement of her chin. I opened a bottle and poured her a glass. I sat next to her on the sofa. 'What's up?'

She took the wine and stared ahead of her.

I waited.

'I saw him,' she said at last. 'He was there, at the party.'

'Who?'

She didn't say anything, but she bit her lip.

'Who?' I repeated. Then I realised. 'Oh no. Not him?'

She nodded. I took a deep breath. This was trouble. I put my arm round her.

'Did you talk to him?'

She shook her head.

'No, but . . .'

'But what?'

'He . . . looked at me. Like . . . I don't know.' She turned away from me.

I took her hand, and gripped it, and waited. Damn! After all the work I had done – no, we had done, the last thing we needed was for her old lover to show up.

I'd never found out much about him. I didn't even know his name. He was married, and a lot older than her. They had been having an affair for a couple of years, when Karen had given him the choice of her or his wife. She hadn't liked the answer.

They had split up. She'd been distraught. I'd been considerate and friendly. Rather than probe the depths of her pain, I'd tried to take her mind off it. We'd clicked. There was a lot about each other that we genuinely liked. Underneath all that confidence, she was vulnerable, unsure of herself. I never could fully under-stand why, but I found that mystery alluring. Why she liked me, I didn't know for sure either. I think I relaxed her. I was fun, in a safe kind of way. Over the last eighteen months I had won her trust, her confidence, and now, I hoped, her love. She had her own flat in Maida Vale, but a couple of months before she had effectively moved in with me. She hadn't said anything, nothing was discussed. It was just that now she spent almost every night at my house, and little by little, her things were migrating from her place to mine.

We kept it quiet. An open relationship in a trading room would be bound to cause problems somewhere along the line. Only Greg and Ed knew. If there was gossip, none of it had got back to us yet.

And now she had seen him again. As I sat next to her, watching the tension in her face and her body, feeling it in the pressure of her hand, a slow fear began to grip me. I didn't want to lose her now.

At last she sighed deeply. Her shoulders relaxed, and she turned to me with a small smile.

'Oh Mark, I'm sorry to put you through that again. You've been really good to me.' She touched my face. 'And he was a real shit. I don't know what I ever saw in him.'

She reached up and kissed me.

Half an hour later, as we were lying naked on the sitting room floor, with the last of the twilight creeping out of the room, I thought of telling her that I loved her. Love was something we never talked about, never mentioned. But it was a good description for the overwhelming feeling of affection I felt for her right then. But I was afraid. Afraid of something. Not exactly rejection. More the part of Karen I didn't yet know, but which I had glimpsed that evening. Anyway, I didn't want to risk the moment.

She stirred. 'What is it, Mark?'

'Nothing.'

3

I was at my desk by seven fifteen the next morning clasping a cup of coffee and a croissant. I wasn't surprised to see quite a few others in so early. We all had a lot to do.

With trepidation I switched on the computer in front of me. It had a large light grey screen on which I could display a whole range of prices from Reuters and Telerate, and then manipulate them however I liked. Next to it was the smaller, squat Bloomberg box, which provided graphics of the relationship of everything against everything else. As the screens warmed up, I glanced at what the market had done to me overnight.

Well, it had held in New York's afternoon, but come off again in Tokyo. The Renaults I had bought yesterday had opened lower, giving me a small loss on my trade. Still, it was early days. Greg's eights of twenty-one were also down a touch.

I looked across towards him. He had just put down his phone, and was already writing a ticket to record a trade. 'Greg, sorry about those bonds you bought yesterday!' I called over to him.

He turned and grinned. 'Hey, it's the spring sales! They're a quarter of a point cheaper, so I bought another fifty!'

I had to admit, Greg had more balls than me. We both ended up making the same amount in the long run, but my profits tended to come in equal monthly instalments. Greg's came in large dollops, and went in spectacular blow-ups.

Ed came in, surprised to see me in so early. He had dark rings around his eyes, magnified by his thick glasses.

'No sleep?' I asked.

He looked embarrassed. 'Not much. I was on the phone to Tokyo.'

Modern technology means that you can keep in touch with the market twenty-four hours a day. But human frailty means that anyone who tries to deal in the middle of the night often makes mistakes. So I usually sleep, and let the market go its own sweet way.

Bob Forrester came over. 'Well, how did that machine do?' he asked, nodding at the Bondscape computer by my desk.

It was an unfair question, and he knew it. 'It's too early to tell yet,' I said. 'But our positions have real potential. We'll get our money back, I'm sure of it.'

'We'd better. You're a good trader, son. I don't want you wasting all your time on expensive gizmos. You can keep it here till the end of next week, but if you don't have any results by then, I want it off my trading floor. Understand?'

I understood. As he walked away, I turned to Ed. 'OK, let's get this thing powered up. We've two million dollars to make back from somewhere. All we have to do is work out where.'

We donned the little headsets, one pair each, both plugged into the computer. The familiar landscape stretched in front of us. The day before, we had looked for bonds that had temporarily shifted out of line. Now, I wanted to focus on new trends that had been set in motion by the hike in interest rates.

My attention was drawn to the flattening of the slope of the hillside more or less everywhere. It was particularly true in the American section. The difference in yield between US two-year and ten-year government bonds had narrowed from 1.6 per cent to 1.4 per cent. Far from expecting this relationship to return to previous levels, I expected it to narrow further. Before Greenspan's announcement, US interest rates had been too low and there had been a real risk of inflation rearing its head again.

21

Now, the Federal Reserve's chairman seemed determined to raise short-term rates despite political opposition from the Treasury Department. If he stuck with that view, and I thought he would, then short-term rates would rise further, and expectations of inflation in the long run would diminish. Sell two-year government bonds, and buy ten-years.

So, we sold four hundred million dollars of two-year treasuries and bought one hundred million dollars of ten-years.

Now all we had to do was wait.

Later that morning, my brother called.

'I tried Bondscape for real today,' I said.

'Oh yes? How did it go?' I could feel the anticipation in his voice.

'It was terrific! Truly brilliant. It was as though I was actually inside the market, feeling it move.'

'How was the landscape metaphor? Did it work? Or did it just get in the way?'

'No, it worked very well.' I, and the financial software company that was working with Richard, had thought that Bondscape should show graphs of bond yields. Richard had felt that a moving landscape would provide the information more effectively, since it would be in a form that humans could intuitively understand. As usual, he was right.

I described in detail how Bondscape had performed. Richard listened closely for a couple of minutes, but then he interrupted me. 'I'm just leaving to catch a plane to London. I've got a meeting this afternoon. Do you mind if I drop by later on? There's something I want to ask you and Karen.'

I was intrigued. 'Of course, Richard. What is it?'

'It's a bit awkward,' said Richard. 'I'll tell you then, if you don't mind. Where shall we meet?'

'Let's have a drink at the Windsor Castle at seven, and then you can have supper with us. Stay the night if you like.'

'Thanks. I will. See you at seven.'

I was glad I would see him in the evening. I had enjoyed working with him on Bondscape, and I missed the frequent contact. His company, FairSystems, was based in Glenrothes, a New Town in Fife. But despite the physical distance between us, we were close. We always saw each other every month or two, usually in London, although I would occasionally travel up to Scotland to stay the weekend.

I smiled to myself. Bondscape's success under fire had pleased Richard, and I liked to please my big brother.

On the way out, I told Greg I wanted a drink of water. He chuckled, and we loitered by the water-cooler. All was not well on the equity desk.

A wiry man in his forties was standing at his desk, shouting at a much younger woman a couple of spaces along. 'Jesus, Sally! I know those Scottish assholes own Caremark. They'd be crazy not to sell at this price. All you gotta do is get them to sell to me!'

It was Jack Tenko, a burned-out, grizzled old equity trader, who had been sent to London from New York because they didn't want him there any more. His mouth was working furiously on some gum as he stared at the woman.

She was in her early twenties. She had short dark hair in a bob, and glasses. She looked scared. Karen was sitting next to her, talking on the phone, but keeping an eye on what was happening.

'But Jack, they won't tell me what they have in their portfolio. They say they don't give that information away,' the woman protested. She looked close to tears.

'Well, how the fuck do you think I know then?' the older man demanded. 'Get on the phone, and get that stock!'

Sally looked at her phone in misery. She knew if she called the client again, he would be angry. If she didn't, Jack would be. She reached for the phone.

Karen hung up, and held out her hand. 'Wait a minute, Sally!'

Tenko glared at her.

'Jack, you think you know what Sally's client owns because someone told you in a pub at lunchtime. Right?'

'I have my sources,' said Tenko, gruffly.

23

'Well, you know these guys are difficult at the best of times. They only deal with a small list of brokers, and we're not on that list. You can shout at Sally all you like, but it won't change that.'

'Well, she should get us on the fucking list.'

'Maybe she will, maybe she won't,' said Karen. 'But you've got to give her time. And encouragement.'

Tenko glared at Sally and Karen, and turned back to his desk. 'Yeah, well one of you get me some Caremark,' he muttered. 'I've got a big order to fill, and the market's bouncing.'

Greg and I exchanged glances, and left.

We propped up the bar of the Windsor Castle, and tucked into our second pint of IPA. It was a small, old pub in Kensington with three cramped bars and enough genuine drinkers to prevent its warm atmosphere deteriorating into olde worlde charm. Greg had said that he wanted to be introduced to Richard, and so I had brought him along. We had arrived slightly early. We were thirsty.

I saw the tall figure of my brother push into the crowded bar, and waved to him. 'Pint?'

'Yes please,' he said. 'I need it. I've just spent two hours with one of our Japanese customers. God, it was tough. The guy I'm talking to is fine, in fact I quite like him. But his bosses in Japan . . . They just won't negotiate.'

I swiftly procured a pint and handed it to him. He took a long gulp. Looking at us side by side, you could tell we were brothers. We had the same shape of nose and chin. But Richard was five years older than me and three inches taller, at a little over six feet four. He had my father's blond hair and blue eyes, while I had the dark curly hair and almost black eyes of my Italian mother. I was often mistaken for an Italian, and Richard for a Norwegian. He was very good looking, and issued a charm that attracted men as well as women. Certainly a big brother to look up to.

I introduced Greg.

'So you have the misfortune to work with my brother?' said Richard.

'That's me,' Greg answered. 'It's tough, believe me. But for a tight-assed Brit, he isn't so bad. And he gets me out of a hole now and then.' He grinned at me.

'Oh yes?'

'Sure. My second week in London, I almost blew myself up. I was long a billion dollars of a government issue that the US Treasury suddenly decided to reopen during an auction. That means instead of creating a new bond issue to raise money, the government decided to sell eight billion dollars more of an old one,' Greg explained for Richard's benefit. 'The issue I owned. Not surprisingly, my bonds tanked. Red ink everywhere.

'Then this guy pops up, and offers to take up half my position. We sweated it out together over the next few weeks but in the end, we came out whole. So I'm still here, whipping and driving those bonds.'

I was pleased that I had helped Greg out then, even though it had been a big risk to do so. In many places, Harrison Brothers among them, traders compete with each other for glory and bonuses. I suppose my theory is that the markets are difficult enough; you need every friend you can get. And Greg had certainly got me out of trouble a couple of times, too.

'Greg is the second person to use Bondscape in anger,' I said.

'Really? What do you think of it?' asked Richard with interest.

'Oh, it's great,' said Greg. 'All those cute little buildings, and everything. I could play on it all day. I have just one request.'

'Oh yes?'

'Yeah. Couldn't you change it so that there is a nice white beach, some palm trees, maybe a babe or two? I'm sure it would be much more meaningful. You know, blonde means buy, brunette means sell. That kind of thing.'

Richard laughed. 'That would take quite a lot more research.'

'I'd be happy to oblige.' He stood back to let an old man order his half-pint of Guinness from the bar. 'No, seriously, it worked well. I hope you're not going to make this system generally available?'

'I think it will be six months at least before we can put a real system on the market.'

'Good.'

Richard grinned. 'Oh, it's that good, is it?'

Greg smiled and took a gulp of his beer. 'What the hell is virtual reality anyway? I mean, Bondscape is virtual reality, right? What else can it do?'

'You can use virtual reality for all sorts of things. Most of them are more lifelike than the bond markets.'

'Like what?'

'Like medicine. Surgeons can perform virtual operations, and patients recovering from injuries can try out a virtual world before facing the real one. Architects can design virtual buildings, or virtual kitchens and move around them to see what they're really like to live and work in. Engineers can create virtual prototype engines, or cars, and then try to maintain them. And then there are all the military applications.'

'What, guys wandering around a battlefield with those weird helmets on?'

'No,' Richard grinned. 'That's the whole point. You don't need to go near a battlefield. You can create a virtual battlefield for soldiers to drive tanks around, and pilots to fly planes. It's a lot easier. And, what's more, it's cheaper.'

'And what about these arcade games I've seen on TV?'

'Those are virtual reality, too. In fact, entertainment has probably been the most successful application of VR so far.'

'Huh,' said Greg. 'And how does it all work? Do you need some great big machine?'

Richard could see that Greg was genuinely interested, and was happy to tell him more. 'No, not at all. Most systems are similar to the Bondscape one you've used. You need a computer with special software to run the virtual world. Then a head-mounted display with two little screens, one for each eye, earphones to give sound in stereo, and a sensor that tracks where you're looking. So, when you turn to the left, the image you see changes to the view to your left in the virtual world. Special gloves can recreate a sense of touch. With the senses of sight, sound and touch all totally immersed in the computer-generated virtual world, you really are in virtual reality.'

'Cool,' said Greg. He sipped his beer, and a thought struck him. 'So can you make any nice new friends with this equipment?'

'Pervert,' I said.

'No, I think it has lots of possibilities for all those lonely American guys in a strange country shunned by the local talent.'

'You're right,' agreed Richard. 'Virtual sex has plenty of possibilities, most of them truly disgusting. It's called teledildonics, by the way.'

'Gee,' said Greg in his fake innocent-American-in-London voice. 'And what peripheral equipment does that need?'

I glanced at my watch. 'We've got to go,' I said to Richard. 'Karen's cooking supper. Come on.'

We left the pub, Greg heading south, and Richard and I north. It was only a fifteen-minute walk back to my house.

'Nice guy,' said Richard.

'Yes, he is.'

We walked on in silence for a bit. 'I saw Dad,' Richard said.

'When?'

'A week ago. In Oxford.'

'How is he?' Much to my surprise, I found I really wanted to know.

'He's fine. He'd like to see you.'

'Oh.'

Richard didn't push it. He could tell I wasn't going to bend. I had only seen my father once in the last ten years, and that had been at my mother's funeral. I still had no desire to see him again.

Until I was seventeen, we were a typical university family. My father was a fellow at an Oxford college, where he taught mathematics. He was an expert in an obscure branch of topology. He had met my mother when he was twenty-five. She had been a beautiful twenty-year-old student from Milan doing a summer course at Oxford. Apart from a few years at Stanford University in California in the sixties, we had been brought up in Oxford. My parents argued occasionally, great squalls that soon subsided. When provoked, my mother had quite a temper. But she managed to create an atmosphere of love and warmth in our house, a cocoon of security for two adolescents uncertain of their place in the world.

And then one day my father had walked out.

Richard and I had no warning, and neither had my mother. He had fallen for one of his post-graduate students. She was only twenty-four, just a couple of years older than Richard. They moved into a small house together in Jericho, less than a mile away. It devastated my mother. She refused to talk to my father, and so did I.

Six months later she was diagnosed with breast cancer. Two years later she was dead.

I was still angry with my father. I couldn't forgive him, though Richard could. I had inherited my mother's temper; Richard was more tolerant.

We walked on in silence for a few minutes. Richard broke it. 'How's work?'

'Fine,' I said. 'We all made lots of money last year when the market rallied. This year, the market's going to fall and we'll all lose lots of money. Simple really. They should just give us the rest of the year off and keep us out of harm's way.'

Richard laughed. 'So, no mega-bonus this time?'

'I'll get by,' I said. 'They tend to look after their proprietary traders.'

'Well, thanks for your help last year.'

'That's OK. I was glad to do something useful with the money.' Frankly, the bonuses embarrassed me. But if I earned Harrison fifteen million dollars a year, it was hardly surprising they gave me some of it. I just didn't want to get used to it.

'And your boss is keeping off your back?'

'Bob? He's OK. Growls a bit sometimes, but you get used to it. As a matter of fact, he doesn't like Bondscape much.'

'Oh?' Richard sounded concerned. He didn't want his system to pick up a bad reputation.

'Don't worry, Greg and I will prove him wrong. No, I enjoy Harrison Brothers. There are some nice people there: Greg, a guy called Ed who works for me now, several others.'

'Including Karen?'

'Including Karen.' I smiled.

'How's that going?'

'Pretty well. Things are much better now. I think she's finally got over him.'

'Who? The bloke she was seeing before you?'

'Yeah.'

'What was his name?'

'I don't know. She won't tell me. In fact, she won't tell me very much about him at all.'

'Strange.'

'It's not so strange. It's too painful, I think.'

'Hm. Do you know what he did to her?'

I paused. I had asked myself that question many times over the last year. 'I'm not sure he did anything. I think she was just very fond of him.'

I could sense the tension in my voice as I said this. So could Richard. 'Are you jealous?'

I shrugged. 'Perhaps. She saw him last night at a party. It shook her up. I think I had hoped that by now he wouldn't have that much of an effect on her.'

I was jealous, of course. But it was something I had done my best to deny over the last year, and I didn't want to admit it out loud to myself, or to anyone else. I hoped that Karen's love for me would one day match her passion for him. But even as our relationship improved, I feared that it would not.

'Sorry, I shouldn't have asked that,' he said.

'Don't worry, I don't mind.' And I didn't. One of the reasons that I liked talking with my brother was that we often touched on things that were important to both of us, things that were difficult to say to other people.

We arrived home to be met by the smell of spices.

'Hi Richard,' said Karen, offering her cheek. Despite wearing faded jeans and one of my old white shirts, she still managed to look elegant. 'Oh, Mark. Brian's just leaving. He wants to have a word. I think he wants to be paid,' she whispered. 'Would you excuse me, things are bubbling. There's a bottle of Sancerre open, Richard.'

Richard poured out a couple of glasses, and refilled Karen's, while I sought out Brian.

He was packing up his brushes in the guest room. He was a small man, but wiry and capable-looking, and he had indeed proved able to organise the band of thugs who worked for him into an efficient team. He had fallen for Karen's charm, and had been happy to redo bits that she thought were not quite right. She had discovered that he was an ex-con gone straight. I somehow doubted the second part of the statement, but he had done a great job quickly.

'I've left my bill on the kitchen table,' he said. 'I'll pick it up the following evening, if you don't mind. And, er, it will be cash, eh, Mark?'

'Fine,' I said, wondering vaguely about how I was going to get two thousand pounds in cash by the following evening. 'Thanks, Brian. You've done a great job. Good night.'

Back in the kitchen, supper was ready. We sat down to a delicate lamb curry.

'The house looks good,' said Richard. 'A hell of a lot better than the other holes you've inhabited.'

I smiled. He was right. It was a definite step up. 'Of course. Curtains in every room.' Actually, this was a little luxury that Karen had insisted on as she had spent more time in the home. Most of the light bulbs now had shades too.

'What was all that fuss about this afternoon?' I asked Karen.

'I told you everyone's jumpy about a reorganisation. Well, Jack's giving Sally a rough time. I think he wants to fire her, to show that he's cutting costs and headcount. It really annoys me. She hasn't got much experience, but I'm sure she's going to be good in time.'

'She was on Ed's training programme,' I said. 'He says she did very well.'

'Well, I hope she gets a chance to show it,' Karen said. 'Ugh!' she shuddered. 'I can't bear that man. It's all right for you, Richard. If you run your own company you don't have to put up with this kind of stuff.'

Richard laughed. 'Oh, I don't know. There's politics in small companies, too. I can assure you of that.'

'And how is our little company doing?' Karen asked. She called FairSystems 'our little company' because it was just that. Or at least she and I owned 7.5 per cent between us.

'Really well,' said Richard, his face coming alive. 'It's been a struggle, but I think we're nearly there.'

'Uh, nearly where?'

'Remember when you invested a year ago, I said that my goal was to put a virtual reality system on every desk and in every home? Well, I think the technology is almost in place to do that.'

'What, so we'll throw out the microwave and the toaster, and get a virtual reality machine instead?'

'No,' he replied, smiling. 'But in a year's time it'll be possible for anyone who owns a personal computer now to buy a VR system. And within five years, they will have.'

'What's the big breakthrough?' I asked.

'I'm afraid I can't say. It's very confidential. But it will be big.'

'Oh, come on, you can tell me.'

'Sorry. It really is confidential. It goes beyond inside information. What I'm talking about will change the whole virtual reality industry and the way technology affects all of us. And I can't let anyone outside a small circle within the company know about it.'

I was a little put out by Richard's discretion. It wasn't as though I was going to rush out and tell the competition, and he ought to have known that. He ought to have trusted me.

'Oh goodie,' said Karen rubbing her hands. 'So that means our shares will go up again.'

There was a bit of history here. Nearly a year before, Richard

31

had approached me distraught. FairSystems was short of cash, but a flotation on the London Stock Exchange had been planned to raise more money. Suddenly the company's brokers had pulled the float, saying that market conditions were not quite right. FairSystems was left high and dry. The company's prospects were excellent, but all the cash it was making from the growing sales of existing products was being eaten up by new developments.

I did two things. Karen and I between us put in seventy-five thousand pounds to tide the company over for a few months. We invested at a price of fifty pence a share.

I also suggested that Richard call Wagner Phillips, a San Francisco stockbroker that I had heard specialised in small technology companies. Wagner Phillips did an excellent job, and the company floated in November that year on NASDAQ, the American stock exchange for small companies. The shares were issued at a price of ten dollars, and in the first couple of days of trading, moved smartly up to twelve. Given our investment price of fifty pence, or about seventy-five cents, this represented a huge paper profit of about eight hundred and fifty thousand dollars each. Champagne all round.

However, at flotation we had been obliged to sign an undertaking not to sell any of our shares for two years. Nothing happened for three months or so, and then the share price had begun to drift down steadily to today's six dollars. And there were still eighteen months to go before we could sell out.

Richard hesitated. 'Yes, they should go up,' he said, with an attempt at conviction.

Karen's face showed she had heard it all before. And, indeed, we both had. Richard had always said that FairSystems would be worth hundreds of millions if we only hung on. Until then, I'd been inclined to believe my brother. Karen hadn't.

She'd known what she was doing when she had made the investment. She was, after all, an equity saleswoman. And she still had a very handsome paper profit. But eighteen months is a long time in the computer world, and Karen wasn't convinced that FairSystems would be around at the end of it. She had seen

32

lots of high-tech companies come and go in her brief career. I knew she felt like this and I felt guilty for having suggested the idea in the first place.

'It was actually FairSystems' share price that I wanted to talk to you about,' said Richard.

Both Karen and I leaned forward. We were intrigued.

'I've done some analysis of the price movement since flotation, and compared it with a sample of similar stocks whose prices have also fallen. There's something strange about FairSystems.'

'What?'

'Let me show you.'

He fetched his briefcase, and produced some printouts of graphs and statistics. They were difficult to decipher, even with Richard's explanations. It was typical of Richard to do the most thorough statistical analysis of any company's share price I had ever seen.

'So, what does all this mean?' asked Karen.

'It looks as though FairSystems' price has fallen on unusually heavy volume given its shareholding structure.'

Karen looked at the graphs, tables and Greek letters, and nodded her head. 'OK. So what?'

'Well, that's what I'd be grateful if you could find out. I mean, all I can do is look at the numbers. You can talk to your contacts in the market and see if they know anything.'

'Have you spoken to Wagner Phillips?' As FairSystems' broker, they should have been able to explain any strange dealings in the stock.

'Yes. They say it's just the company's bad performance.'

We watched Karen. She was staring at the numbers, thinking. Hard.

'How much cash have you got left?' she asked.

'Well, um, not much.'

'Not much!' I broke in. 'You raised five million dollars six months ago! Has that all gone?'

'Nearly,' said Richard. 'But we're expecting an advance

payment from one of our customers, Jenson Computer. That should tide us over for part of the summer.'

'And then what?' I was exasperated. The bloody company was going to run out of cash again!

Richard shrugged his shoulders.

'What do Wagner Phillips say?'

'They're not much help. They say it's too soon to go to the stockmarket for more money. But they have a possible purchaser for the company.'

'Who's that?'

'They won't say. They say their client insists on anonymity.'

'Well? Are you going to sell?'

Richard looked down at his hands. The outside two fingers of his left hand were missing above the first joint. He seemed to be checking to see if they had reappeared. 'No.'

'No? Richard, you're going to go bust unless you do something!'

'It makes no sense to sell just now, I promise you. Trust me.'

'Yes, well I think you should sell out while you can,' I said. 'Bankruptcy is serious. The chances are your ideas will be lost for ever. People will lose their jobs. We'll lose our money.' For all Richard's intelligence, it seemed to me he was lacking a sense of perspective. He was in a losing trade, and he should cut his losses early. I was a trader, I knew about things like that. Richard was an inventor, and he didn't.

'I know bankruptcy is serious!' said Richard sharply. 'And believe me, I care. Especially about my people. Some of them have stuck with me for five years. They've worked seven-day weeks, and created miracles to meet deadlines. And I'm not about to throw all that effort away. I'll look after them. OK, I know it's going to be difficult, but we'll make it, you'll see. And when we do, your shares will be worth a damn sight more than they are at the moment!'

There was silence. Both Karen and I were taken aback. Richard never lost his temper.

He took a deep breath, and turned to Karen. 'Well? Will you ask around?'

'OK, I will,' said Karen soothingly. 'But it may turn out that people are just selling because they think you're going bust. I'll let you know.'

I made some coffee, and we drank it quickly before going to bed. I was angry with my brother. He was going to lose us all a lot of money through financial carelessness as much as anything else. I had believed in his stories of virtual reality. I still had confidence in his technical ability to achieve all that he had set out to, although I was beginning to wonder about 'big breakthroughs' that he couldn't even explain to his own brother. If only he had had the common sense to hang on to some cash while he'd got it.

I was still angry when Richard got up very early the next morning to catch the plane to Edinburgh. What he said at the door only made it worse.

'Karen is very attractive, isn't she?'

'Yes, she is,' I said, a touch of pride in my voice.

'Be careful of her, little brother.' He turned, and walked out into the empty early morning street.

I was stunned. The patronising git! Karen had put up her life savings to bale him out, and he had squandered them. And it wasn't even she who had got angry with him last night, it was me! I had every right to be cross with him and he had no right at all to talk to me like that about her.

Noisily, I clattered the final debris from the previous night's dinner into the sink and washed it up. But amidst the anger, something nagged, a truth from which I couldn't hide. It made me more furious.

You see, ever since I could remember, my brother had always been right.

4

Karen and I were both busy. Prices were still sliding, but in a slower, more orderly fashion. We were at the beginning of a bear market. That was fine with me, I would adjust my trades accordingly. I made sure all my positions were hedged. For every bond I bought, I sold short a different one. Selling short means selling a bond you don't own. You are allowed to do that in the bond markets; it's very useful. It means that in a falling market, the money you lose on the bonds you own is more than compensated for by the money you gain by buying back the bonds you sold short. That is, if you picked the right bonds in the first place, of course.

Well, it was beginning to look like Greg, Ed and I had picked the right bonds. My two-year ten-year trade was only just beginning to work, but I was feeling more confident. Greg's eights of twenty-one were rocketing up, or at least were falling slower than the bonds he had shorted. But we were both still a long way under water. Bob was still frowning, but he gave us more time.

Karen schmoozed clients. She was out with one on Thursday night, and was due to meet some more on Monday in Paris. She decided to spend the weekend there with a friend with whom she had been on an exchange as a child. The friend had never really learned English successfully, and my French was pathetic, so I wasn't invited. Our game of tennis was cancelled. Never mind. There was a good race meeting at Newmarket I wanted to go to.

Karen got a late flight back on Monday. She didn't arrive home till about ten. I poured her a glass of wine, and we sat on the sofa upstairs.

'Did you have a good trip?'

'Yes, great,' she said enthusiastically.

'How was Nicole?'

'She's fine. She thinks Jacques is finally the right one for her.'

'And what do you think?'

Karen giggled and held her thumb down. 'Too boring.'

'What, not as boring as me, I hope?'

'Oh no, darling, nowhere near as dull. Don't worry. How was Newmarket?'

'Not too bad. Only twenty quid down. I'm taking Greg to Ascot next Saturday. Do you want to come?'

'Sorry. I'd love to, but I really ought to see my mother next weekend. She's being quite insistent. Do you want to come?' She laughed. We both knew the answer. Karen's mother was an overbearing, fussy woman, who worried about everything all the time, especially her daughter. She still lived in the detached house on the outskirts of Godalming where Karen had grown up. Karen's father had walked out on both of them when Karen was twelve, and her mother had not been able to forgive him. Nor for that matter had Karen. It was something over which I could sympathise with both of them, and indeed it was something that drew Karen and me together. I could sympathise with her mother, but I didn't have to spend the weekend with her.

'But you don't have to go on Friday night, do you?'

'I'm sure I can put her off. Why? Have you got other plans?' She smiled. Friday was her birthday.

'I've booked a table at the Café du Marché. You remember that place.'

She nodded, grinning. The last time we had been there, a year and a half before, had marked the transition of our status from friends to lovers. Of course she remembered.

'That's a brilliant idea,' she said, and gave me a quick kiss.

Karen was tired, and we went to bed. She was in good spirits, I could hear her humming in the bathroom. But when we were in bed, and I rolled next to her to stroke her thigh, she kissed me lightly on the nose and said, 'Not now, Mark. I really am tired.'

I lay there, watching her fall asleep, a small smile on her face.

The insistent beep of the telephone woke me. I looked at my alarm clock. Quarter to twelve. Who would ring me at quarter to twelve?

I picked up the receiver. It was Richard.

'I'm sorry to disturb you so late,' he began.

'That's OK,' I said, pulling myself up on to my elbow.

Silence for a moment. I waited to see what he wanted. 'Richard?'

'Look, Mark, would you mind coming up to Scotland this weekend? There's something I need to talk to you about.'

'Oh, um,' I played for time. Scotland was a long way to go just for a chat. 'Can't we talk about whatever it is over the phone?'

'No. I'd rather talk face to face. It's quite difficult. Well, very difficult actually.'

It must have been for Richard to want to ring me. He had dealt with all kinds of stress in his brief career as an entrepreneur, and apart from the cash-flow problem last year, he had never needed me to help him out.

I thought about airports and shuttles. Then I remembered the Café du Marché. And Ascot. I could just make it on Saturday night after the last race.

'Will Saturday night do?'

'Can't you make it Friday?'

I thought about cancelling my date with Karen. But, after all, it was her birthday. It was important to her, to us. I didn't want to cancel. And I remembered what Richard had said about her the last time I had seen him.

'No, it'll have to be Saturday evening.'

'OK, that's fine,' he said, but he sounded disappointed. 'Get the eight o'clock shuttle, and I'll meet you at Edinburgh airport.'

'All right. See you then.' I put the phone down.

Karen stirred next to me. 'Who was that?'

'Richard,' I said. 'He wants to see me this weekend.'

Karen sat up, wide awake. 'What about?'

'I don't know,' I said. 'But he sounded worried.'

'Are you going?'

'Not on Friday,' I said, touching her cheek. 'But I will go up on Saturday, after Ascot.'

'Thank you,' said Karen, giving me a quick kiss. 'I wonder what it is. Wouldn't he say over the phone?'

'No.'

'Sometimes your brother is too mysterious for his own good.'

I lay awake for at least an hour, thinking. Karen lay motionless opposite me. I was pretty sure she was awake also. I don't know which one of us fell asleep first.

We agreed to meet at the restaurant. The Café du Marché is in Charterhouse Square near Smithfield Market. It's not too far from Harrison Brothers' offices, which is why I had suggested it a year before. It's a converted warehouse, all light woods and black-painted wrought iron. It has none of the expense-account heaviness of plush City restaurants, but the food is nevertheless excellent. It had been a good choice.

Karen was coming straight from work. She often worked late; the problem with covering the American equity markets was that she had to hang around in case any of her keener European customers wanted to deal while the New York Stock Exchange was still open.

She arrived half an hour late. She was wearing a thin black Armani suit with a short skirt. Actually, the suit wasn't Armani, it was made by a tailor in Hong Kong she had found on a trip there three years before, but I was the only person who was supposed to know that. She looked good, and she knew it as she weaved towards me, between the small white-clothed tables, followed by the eyes of all of the men and most of the women in the room.

She smiled when she saw me, and gave me a quick kiss.

'Sorry I'm late. Martin was faffing about trying to decide whether or not to buy some Disney. In the end he couldn't get his act together, and just went home.'

'Does he ever do any trades?'

'Eventually. But you have to be patient.' She reached across the table and touched my hand. 'I'm sorry I've been working so hard recently. But with these reorganisation rumours I've got to put the effort in. And they want me to spend more time on the road.'

'Really? Have you got any more trips coming up?'

'Yes. Holland next week. And I'll have to go to Paris again in a couple of weeks' time.'

I was disappointed. I knew there was nothing she could do if her bosses and clients demanded it. I was usually disciplined about leaving my positions at six in the evening, and I suppose I expected other people to be the same.

Karen saw my disappointment. 'Sorry,' she said.

We ordered a couple of kirs. 'I went shoe shopping with Sally at lunchtime. She was pretty depressed.'

'Did it work?' I asked. Buying shoes was what Karen did when she was miserable. She had dozens at home, many of them bought the previous year. She hadn't bought any for several months, I was glad to see.

'I don't know. I think I cheered her up a bit. Jack Tenko has really got to her.'

'Poor woman. It's vital to get a good boss, isn't it? Especially when you're starting out.'

'That's true.' Karen grinned. 'Apparently Ed is full of praises for you.'

I shrugged. 'These young guys are so impressionable,' I said. But I was pleased to hear it.

'So, how was your day?' she asked.

'Not bad. Some of those trades I put on last week are really starting to come right. But I'm probably still one and a half million down on the month, and there's only one week to go.' I hated ending the month down, especially by such a large amount, but it looked inevitable this time.

'Bad luck. Even you can't have a good month every time.' She paused to order.

When we had both chosen, she took a sip of her kir. 'What do you think Richard wants to talk to you about?'

'I've no idea. It must be something pretty important for him to want me to go all the way up there at such short notice.' I was struck by a thought. 'I bet FairSystems has run out of cash already!'

'No!' said Karen. 'Do you really think so?'

'Could be. I'm just not sure he has a good handle on the finances of that place. Well, the stupid bastard should sell out. And I'll tell him that.'

'Yes, do,' said Karen. 'It would be a shame to lose everything after coming so far.'

'It might have something to do with the fall in the share price I suppose. Did you pick up anything in the market?'

'Nothing,' said Karen. 'It's a tiny little company. Most people haven't heard of it, let alone bought shares in it. Wagner Phillips has locked up all the trading in its stock. I called a friend there, but he didn't know anything other than that the price was falling steadily.'

'Yeah, I think Richard's imagining things,' I said. 'He can analyse anything to death. And even if the share price was being manipulated, I don't see what the urgency would be.' I sighed. 'No, I'm afraid it's bankruptcy.'

The meal came. It was good. I ordered an expensive bottle of wine, and raised my glass. 'Happy birthday!'

'Thank you,' she said. 'Thirty.' She shuddered. 'I'm not sure I want to be thirty.'

I kept quiet. I had been careful not to mention which birthday it was.

Karen sipped the wine. 'Mm. This is good.'

'When are you going to see your mother?'

'Not till tomorrow evening. My second birthday dinner. It always seems strange, just me and her.'

'I'm sorry I can't come. I really do have to see Richard.'

'No, don't worry,' she said. 'It's much better if you don't. You'll only rub each other up the wrong way.' She took a sip of wine. 'It just seems odd that's all.'

'Without your father?'

'Yes.' Her voice was suddenly strained.

We both came from families that had split up, and it was a sore subject for each of us. For that reason, we didn't often compare notes, but I had an urge to now.

'Have you ever tried to see him?'

'I don't know where he is. I think mother knows, but she won't tell me.'

'Won't tell you?'

'That's right.' Suddenly, I noticed tears forming in her eyes. 'Of course she denies it. She says he disappeared without trace.'

'But you don't believe her?'

'You know mother,' she said contemptuously. 'She's protecting me. I'm sure of it.'

We ate in silence. Karen sniffed, and somehow managed to blink back her tears. But as she did so her mood changed for the worse. She tensed as she tackled her duck. I had seen this before. I wished I had never brought the subject up. I had been right to avoid it.

'I loved him,' said Karen suddenly. She had controlled her tears, but her voice was low and husky, as though she was holding back something. Sorrow, or anger, or both. 'He was everything to me. Every evening, I couldn't wait till he came home so I could play with him. Even when I was twelve, I wanted to spend as much time with him as possible. I remember once he took me to the office party as his date. I was so proud of him. He was so proud of me. I couldn't believe it when he left me. How could he leave me, Mark? How could he?'

For a second, her eyes looked up at me, tormented, angry, searching for something. It was something I couldn't give her, because they swiftly broke away from mine, and stared darkly into her plate, her face as still as stone. She sat there, rocking backwards and forwards slowly, coiled tight. She made no effort to touch her food. Something was churning deep within her body. It was as though there was a wild, terrible scream bottled up inside, ready to burst out at any moment, releasing all that pain and anger. I had seen her like this before, just after she had been ditched by that man, and it was frightening.

When she was a girl, after her father had left her mother, Karen had been to see a string of psychiatrists. I wasn't sure what they had found, or even if they had been any help; Karen had never given me details, and I had never asked. Then, after she'd been dumped, she'd seemed to me to be on the verge of a breakdown, and I'd suggested she talk to someone again. In the end that someone had been me, and eventually she'd pulled herself back together. I was proud of that, but now I wondered if talking to me had been enough. Seeing her old lover the other day, and talking about her father now, we seemed to be going back to where we had started.

I sat there, silently watching her, praying for the tension to leave her. After five minutes she slowly began to relax. She turned to me. 'Sorry,' she said.

'Will you be all right?' I asked.

'Yes.'

But we ate the rest of the meal in silence, paid the bill and went home.

I sipped the glass of champagne and settled back in my seat. The clouds were breaking up, and I could see the lights of Sheffield far below. Even though the afternoon had been cold and wet, I had that warm inner glow that comes from a really good win.

I had picked up Greg that morning from his flat in Kensington Church Street. It was his first time on a racecourse, and he was intrigued, as much by what interested me in it as anything else. We got to the course in time for lunch, and I took him through the form card. All my attention was on the third race, and a six-year-old hurdler called Busker's Boy. I had seen him race at Fontwell Park in March. He had run a very promising race over two miles, coming fourth only four lengths behind the winner. It had been his first time out after a long absence and his jockey had been remarkably easy on him; he'd had plenty of puff left at the end.

I was looking forward to seeing him run today; his sire, Deep Run, had been excellent on soft ground, and a new young jockey called A. P. McCoy, who seemed to be winning a few races, was riding him. So, I took ten twenty-pound notes and split them between a couple of bookies at the far end of the Tattersalls enclosure. I managed to get 8–1 odds, when the betting finished at 7–1. I always enjoyed that. Greg missed the 8–1, and tried to haggle with a bookie to improve on his 7–1. No chance, so Greg didn't place a bet on principle.

The race was over two and a half miles, and Busker's Boy moved easily over the first mile and a half. With three-quarters of a mile to go he pulled effortlessly away from the field. My heart almost stopped as his jockey slipped over his right shoulder at the last flight, but he scrambled back and horse and rider passed the winning post together, way ahead of anyone else.

I had reinvested three hundred pounds of my winnings in Britain's bookmaking industry, but I had enjoyed losing it, and I still came out well ahead. I left the course comforted by the firm pressure of the wad of notes stuffed in my hip pocket.

Greg was furious. Having seen me win so much, he had sprayed around twenty-pound notes with abandon, with no success. He ended up two hundred pounds poorer.

'Jesus, this isn't a sport, it's a mugging. No way am I ever going to one of these places again,' he complained.

But I knew he would be back. He had enjoyed himself, despite his losses, and he had seen me win. He would come back until he won too.

I had been a keen racegoer since my schooldays. One of my friends was the son of a trainer, and he'd explained a lot of the mysteries of the form card to me, and had also managed to pass on his enthusiasm for racehorses. I liked to bet, but only

44

relatively small amounts. I knew it was a sucker's game, other people had more information, other people made more money. The odds were stacked against the punter like me. But I liked to try to win, to analyse form, to follow a selection of horses through a season, to try to take an educated view of breeding, past form, the going, distance and all the other factors that mysteriously determined whether a horse would win a race. Very rarely did all this analysis pay off, but when it did, as with Busker's Boy, it felt really good.

The fact that Karen usually bet on the jockeys wearing the prettiest colours, and often came out a winner, I put down to an extended run of beginner's luck.

The stewardess doled out a small blue plastic tray of unidentifiable food. She pointed to my empty glass. 'Can I get you another, sir?'

'Yes, please.' Why not? I had earned it.

My mind turned to Richard, and what I would find once I arrived in Scotland. I was pretty sure that he would ask me for ideas to bail him out. I only hoped Wagner Phillips' client's offer was still good.

It was beginning to look as if it had been a mistake to invest in FairSystems, and in particular to allow Karen to. On the other hand, if we hadn't stumped up the cash, FairSystems would certainly have gone bust, and Richard's dreams and achievements would have gone with it.

The worst thing about the whole business was the effect it was having on my relationship with my brother. Despite the five years' difference, we had always been close, always trusted each other, always helped each other out.

But now, for the first time in my life, I felt I couldn't depend on Richard, and that feeling was unpleasant.

The plane landed a little late, at nine thirty. Richard wasn't there to meet me. I wandered through the concourse, the café, the bar and the shops. Not there.

So I telephoned his home. No answer. He must be on his way, then.

45

At ten I began to worry. At ten fifteen I began to think things through. Perhaps he had had an accident. Or perhaps he had forgotten and was working at the factory. It wouldn't have been unlike him to work on a Saturday night.

I rang the factory in Glenrothes. Eventually, a woman answered. She said she was sure that Richard was spending the day at his home in Kirkhaven. He had said he might come in to work briefly on Sunday morning.

Well, there was no point hanging round here much longer. Luckily, one of the car-hire desks was still manned. I hired a Ford Fiesta, and set off on the forty-mile drive to Kirkhaven.

I was tired, and it seemed a long way. North over the Forth Bridge to Fife, and then east to what is called the 'East Neuk', a peninsula sticking out into the North Sea. It is dotted with attractive little fishing villages, one of which is Kirkhaven.

It was nearly midnight by the time I got there. I drove down the steep narrow streets, which were empty apart from a group of three or four drinkers making their unsteady way home. I reached the quay, and saw the squat lighthouse at the end of the harbour wall, silhouetted against the contrasting greys of sea and sky. I could clearly make out Inch Lodge perched on a small outcrop of rock right at the mouth of the Inch, the burn that ran into the sea at Kirkhaven. It was a whitewashed house looking out over the harbour on one side, and the Presbyterian church on the far bank of the Inch on the other. A small boathouse clung to the side of the building. Richard had converted it into a workshop, and spent many nights in there, tinkering and thinking.

I parked the car outside, and got out. The night air was cold and salty, invigorating after my drive. The house was dark. I pushed the bell. No reply. I pushed several more times before trying the door. It was locked.

I was getting cold. I looked around me. Lights were scattered about the jumble of houses on the hill above, but there was no sign of life along the quay. The sea murmured somewhere out in the darkness. Drunks laughed incoherently farther along the quay, and were gone.

I looked up at the walls of the house, glowing a very pale yellow in the light of the half-moon. I was definitely worried now. It seemed more and more likely that he had had an accident on the way to pick me up. I should just make absolutely sure he wasn't here. I walked round the back of the house to the boathouse, Richard's workshop. Ah! The door was open, but it was dark.

As I neared the entrance, I realised that there was in fact a flicker of light inside. It was low and blue. He must be working in the dark.

'Richard?' No reply. I pushed open the door, and looked inside. 'Rich . . .'

5

He was lying on the floor of the boathouse, the top half of his head split open.

I don't know how long I stared at him. A second? Ten seconds? His head was a mess of red and grey and jagged white bone. The bottom half of his face was Richard, flickering in the pale blue light of the computer. His mouth was open, I could see his front teeth.

The mixture of champagne and British Airways supper pushed itself up from my stomach, and I turned for the door. I retched, and spilled it on to the path outside. I gulped for air, but kept retching. I stood up to turn back to look at him, but I couldn't.

I took a couple of deep breaths, and staggered out on to the road. I stopped at the first house, at the end of a stone terrace, and rang the bell. Then I began hammering the big door knocker, and didn't stop until I heard a gruff voice inside.

'Who is it? What d'ye want?'

'I'm Richard Fairfax's brother,' I gasped. 'The man who lives at Inch Lodge. He's dead. I've got to call the police.'

The door opened on a squat, bald-headed man with a pyjama'd stomach sticking firmly out of an ancient dressing-gown. He eyed me suspiciously. He didn't have his teeth in.

'Come in, laddie. The phone's over there.'

I dialled 999 and answered all the operator's questions. When I turned round, the man had been joined by his wife. No teeth either.

'Och, you look a mess. Won't you sit down, now. Let me make you some tea.'

I sat at a kitchen table. 'No, he needs a wee drop of this,' said her husband, and a moment later placed a tumbler half full of golden liquid in front of me. I took a gulp. It hurt the back of my throat, and stabbed the lining of my irritated stomach. I downed the rest.

Moments later, the doorbell buzzed, and a policeman came in. He was a small, thin sergeant with a neat little moustache and darting eyes. He took one look at me, and spoke firmly, but gently. 'Mark Fairfax?'

I nodded.

'I'm Sergeant Cochrane. You said your brother has been murdered?'

'Yes.'

'Where is he?' the policeman asked softly.

'Do you want me to show you?'

Cochrane nodded. We went outside where four policemen were waiting. I led them all round the back of the house to the boathouse. I couldn't go near it. I let them look. Cochrane came out a few moments later. Even in the darkness, I could see that his skin had lost its colour. Beads of moisture were clinging to his moustache.

'I'm sorry Mr Fairfax. It's horrible in there. Let's go back to the MacAllisters' house.'

He took me by the arm, and led me to the neighbours' cottage. The man had pulled on a shirt and some trousers. The woman was fussing round the kitchen. They both had their teeth in. They welcomed us, and let us sit at the kitchen table.

The sergeant asked me quickly when and where I had found the body, where I had come from, whether I had seen anyone, whether I had touched anything. Then he told me to wait until the CID arrived.

I sat at the table sipping cups of tea while Mrs MacAllister fussed over me and stuck her head outside to discuss events with neighbours. Mr MacAllister was taking generous doses of the medicine he had offered me. I didn't touch any more whisky. I wanted to get my whirling brain into some sort of order.

I was numb. I was only dimly aware of what was happening around me, of the bustle in the road outside.

Richard was dead.

It didn't seem real. It seemed like a late-night television film, watched from the hallway into a darkened room.

I was suddenly aware of a figure sitting at the table opposite me. He was crumpled, wearing a bad brown suit and a brown and yellow tie. He had longish dull hair, and a full moustache, which could have done with a trim. Folds of fat hung over his collar, and thrust out beneath his shirt. His bulbous nose was criss-crossed with an intricate design of veins. 'Mr Fairfax,' he said. 'Can I have a word?'

He asked more questions. The same stuff as the sergeant earlier. The questions were asked softly. I think I answered them. All I can really remember is the pattern on that nose.

Finally, he said, 'Do you have anywhere to stay tonight?'

'No. Er, I don't know. I thought I would stay in Richard's house.'

'I'm sorry, son, you can't do that. We need to look over it. But Sergeant Cochrane has fixed up for you to stay at the Robbers' Arms. He'll take you there.'

They found me a room. I shut the door behind me with a sigh. It was on the hill above Inch Lodge. Through the window, I could look down on the house, surrounded by shadows thrown off by the floodlights that had been rigged up around it. There was a jam of cars back along the quayside, many with their blue lights flashing impatiently.

Standing there, alone, looking at Richard's house, the numbness went. My eyes stung with tears, and the sobs came. I threw myself on the little bed. Someone knocked on the door, opened it, and then shut it again quietly.

I cried for a while, huge great sobs, but eventually they

abated. I stood up, took off my clothes, brushed my teeth and crawled into bed. But I couldn't sleep. I couldn't even shut my eyes – whenever I did, I saw Richard there on the floor of the boathouse.

After a few minutes, I stood up and began pacing up and down, throwing glances towards Inch Lodge below. Things had quietened down now. Fewer people were milling about, spectators had gone home to bed.

Disconnected thoughts exploded in my brain. Painful fragments, spinning wildly, smashing into each other. I paced faster and faster round the little room, getting angrier and more confused. My brain was tiring, but all through my body chemicals were pumping furiously, primed by the shock of what I had just seen.

Eventually, I stopped in front of the window, took several deep breaths and then lay down.

The assault on my mind didn't stop, but it did slow. After a long while, the window turned from black to grey. I got up, pulled on some clothes and went outside.

The light came in low from the east, lighting up the cream-, yellow- and white-painted houses of Kirkhaven in a watery northern glow. I walked down the narrow streets, past a masonic temple, and a row of brightly painted shops waiting for the summer tourist trade. My Fiesta was still parked outside Richard's house. Tape flapped in the wind all round it. Two constables stood guard.

'Morning,' I said to one.

He must have known who I was. 'Good morning sir,' he said, and looked the other way, not wanting to face grief at this hour of a Sunday morning. I couldn't blame him.

I stared at the house, remembering the many times I had been here. It jutted out into the tiny estuary of the Inch Burn. Black rocks clustered around its foundations, and the ebbing tide had revealed an expanse of dark yellow sand. The window- and door-frames were blue lines, none of which was quite straight. My brother had bought the house several years before, with the money that our mother had left him. It was a peaceful place, a

51

place where my brother had liked to think, where he had come up with some of his best ideas.

I tore myself away and walked along the quay past the small baked potato and fish and chip shops. The town was virtually deserted. There were a few fishing boats tied up in the harbour, but nobody was to be seen at this early hour.

I followed the harbour wall towards the lighthouse perched on the end, pointing out at the North Sea. Picking my way past lobster pots, coils of thick rope, and an old Maestro, I stopped by a red dredger moored twenty yards from the entrance to the harbour, it's engine chugging gently to itself. The grey sea sparkled in the morning sunshine. Over the Firth of Forth, I could see the low waves of the hills of East Lothian. In front of them were a couple of rocks, one grey, one chalk-white.

I turned back towards Kirkhaven, a crowded little town of pale houses, crammed together on the hillside. The muffled sounds of the sea soon became a lulling, soothing background to the odd cry of seagulls. Every now and then I could hear an old car engine straining to negotiate the narrow winding streets and steep hills of the town. Three church towers rose proudly above the houses; not for nothing was it called Kirkhaven. To the left of the harbour front, I saw the mouth of the Inch, winding its way through rocks and sand between my brother's house and the graveyard of the church opposite. Daffodils lined the bank.

That's where I would bury him. Within sight of his beloved workshop, in the peace of this small Scottish village.

I closed my eyes. Immediately, I saw his body, lying sprawled on the boathouse floor. I opened them. Would I never be able to shut my eyes again?

His left hand had lain open, clutching at something, the stubs of his two missing fingers pointing upwards. Those fingers had become by their absence a totem of our friendship, our dependence.

I was six, Richard eleven. My father was laying a terrace in the garden. I was clambering about on the paving stones, piled five feet high. The pile wobbled. Richard dived over, and

52

pushed me out of the way. He slipped, the stones fell on his outstretched hand. There was nothing the hospital could do with what was left of his fingers.

He had saved my life. Could I have saved his?

Grief often brings with it two strong emotions: anger and guilt. This morning, I felt guilty as hell.

I thought about FairSystems. The company was at the forefront of the most exciting new technology in the world. It had stolen a lead over companies much larger and better funded. With half a dozen other geniuses in America and England, Richard had made virtual reality a reality. I had griped at him for the financial shortcomings of his company, but did that really matter?

I thought about the last time we had seen each other, at dinner at my house. We had parted then on bad terms. I couldn't remember my exact last words to him, but I could remember the tone in which I'd spoken them: anger. Oh God, how I regretted that!

And then, only the day before, I had had a chance to go up to see him, to talk to him, to help my brother who had helped me so much in the past, and I had said no. If I had come, would he still be alive? I had let him down. It would take me a long time to forgive myself.

I owed Richard. I owed him a lot. I would look after what was left of him, his house, his possessions. And I would look after FairSystems.

I was getting cold. I stood up and walked back to the Robbers' Arms. As I entered through a small hallway, a voice called out, 'Morning.'

I paused. A tall thin man with a neat white beard stooped beneath the narrow doorway. He was wearing a jacket and tie. 'Did you sleep all right?' he asked.

'Not really,' I mumbled.

He looked me up and down, and then said, 'Let me get you some breakfast?'

Food suddenly seemed a very good idea. I nodded my head. 'Take a seat in there. I'll be through in a moment.' I sat in the small dining room, and in a few minutes the smell of frying bacon drifted through.

Ten minutes later, the man returned with a cup of tea, and a big plate of eggs, sausages, bacon, tomato, the works. 'Here you are. Get your teeth into that.'

He left me to it. I appreciated his discretion, and quickly cleared my plate.

Although the fresh air and the food made me feel a lot better, my brain was fuzzy from a night without sleep. I went upstairs to my room to use the phone.

It was still only eight o'clock on a Sunday morning, but Daphne Chilcott answered as though she had been awake for hours. Which she probably had. She was the type of woman who is up pruning roses before six.

'Good morning, Daphne. It's Mark. Can I speak to Karen.'

It took her a moment to work out who I was.

'Ah, Mark. How are you? It's a little early don't you think? Karen's still asleep. Perhaps you could telephone again later on.' What she meant was 'What the bloody hell are you doing ringing at this hour of the morning?' but being Karen's mother, she couldn't say that.

'I would very much like to talk to her now, Daphne. It's important.'

'Very well.'

After a moment, I heard Karen's voice, heavy with sleep. 'Mark, what's up?'

'Richard's dead.'

'No! What happened?'

'He was murdered. Last night. At his house.'

There was silence at the other end of the phone. I heard a whispered 'Oh God'. With a jolt, I suddenly realised that I would get no support from Karen this morning, she would need support herself. I wouldn't be the only person grieving Richard, just one of many.

'How?'

I told her. The tears came. I could hear her weeping and sniffing four hundred miles away. 'Karen, Karen. It's all right,' I said uselessly. I heard her try to speak, but she couldn't. The sobs became uncontrolled, as though she was having trouble breathing.

Suddenly, I heard her mother's crisp voice, 'I don't know what you've said to Karen, but it has upset her. Now goodbye,' and the phone went dead.

The old cow! I would call Karen back later, when she had calmed down.

The next call was going to be even more difficult. I dialled the number.

It took several rings before there was an answer. 'Frances Fairfax.'

I didn't recognise the voice. It was a woman's voice, a young woman's voice. I felt cold. This was the woman who had torn my family apart.

'Can I speak to Dr Fairfax?'

'May I say who's calling?'

'It's his son.'

'Oh, Richard. It doesn't sound like you.'

'It isn't,' I said grimly.

There was silence as she fetched my father.

'Mark?' Hearing his voice gave me a jolt. It sounded the same, only different. There was a guttural hoarseness that had not been there before. The voice of a man approaching sixty.

'Hello? Is that Mark?'

'Yes, Dad. Yes, it's Mark.'

'How are you? It's good to hear your voice.' He did sound pleased to hear from me.

There was so much I wanted to say to him. But keep it brief.

'I have bad news, Dad.'

'Yes?' The enthusiasm disappeared. It was replaced by fear.

'Richard's dead,' I blurted.

Silence. 'Oh, no! Um . . . What happened?'

'He was killed.' Silence. 'Murdered.'

'God. When?'

'Last night.'

'How?'

'He was hit on the head. I found him lying in the boathouse. He . . .' The image of Richard's shattered skull flashed back before my eyes. I couldn't continue. I took a few deep breaths. 'I just thought you ought to know,' I finished.

'Yes, thanks for telling me.' My father's voice had suddenly aged another ten years. I wanted to share my grief with him, but it was impossible. Too much, all in one phone call.

'There will be things to sort out,' I said. 'Funeral, the will, that sort of thing. His house. FairSystems. His bits and pieces.'

'Yes.'

'I'll do it.'

'No, it's all right. I can do it.'

'Please, Dad. Please, let me deal with it. I'm here in Kirkhaven now.'

'I'll come up as well.'

'No!' I said sharply. That, I couldn't handle. 'Look, I'll sort everything out, and you can come up for the funeral. We can talk things over then.'

A pause. 'OK, Mark, we'll do it that way if you like.'

'All right then. Goodbye.'

'Goodbye.'

I stared at the phone. I was glad Richard had made peace with my father. We hadn't spoken for ten years. How would he have felt if I had died? More to the point, how would I feel if he died?

Morbid thoughts. Not surprising. After all, someone had been killed. Some bastard had cold-bloodedly murdered my brother! I knew that most murderers were caught. I hoped to God they caught this one.

There was a knock at the door. It was the sergeant from the night before. He looked tired, but his uniform was immaculately pressed.

'Mr Fairfax? Could you come with me to the station, please, sir. It's probably easier to talk there than here.'

That wasn't really true. Kirkhaven's police station was tiny, being not much more than a corral of portakabins. There was plenty of activity. Cars were pulling up, spilling policemen out into the tiny car park. Some wore uniforms, many didn't.

I was ushered into a cramped little office. The crumpled man with the ravaged nose was there, looking even more crumpled. Next to him, rising, as I entered, from the main chair behind the little desk, was a tall, bald man with an impeccable tweed suit, worn just like Sergeant Cochrane's uniform.

'Good morning, Mr Fairfax. Detective Superintendent Donaldson. I believe you have already met Detective Inspector Kerr?' I had, but the name hadn't sunk in. 'Take a seat.'

We all sat down, Kerr perched on an uncomfortable stool.

'I'm in charge of the investigation into your brother's murder,' the big man went on. He had a clear, crisp Scottish accent. Very businesslike. 'First, let me say how sorry I am about your brother's death.'

I nodded. I realised I was going to receive a lot of these awkward condolences over the next few days. Difficult to give, difficult to receive.

'Let me start by asking you a few questions.'

'I've already answered two lots of questions in the last twelve hours,' I said irritably.

Donaldson held up his hand. 'I know, son, but we've got a few more. We're going to find whoever did this. We had nine murders in Fife last year, and we cleared up every one. And this will be no exception. But I need your help.'

I saw he was right. 'OK, I'm sorry. I'll do anything I can to help you catch him. Anything.'

'That's good. Just answer some simple questions for now. The doctor places the time of death within a couple of hours of noon on Saturday. Where were you then?'

'What do you mean where was I?' I protested. 'Surely you don't think I did it?'

Donaldson flinched. The crumpled man, Kerr, leaned forward. 'Of course not, son,' he said in a kind voice, thick with fatigue. 'But most murders are committed by people who knew the victim. That's why we need to eliminate everyone who

57

knew him. We just want to start with you. The Super likes to be very thorough about eliminating people, right sir?'

Donaldson coughed. 'Quite so. Now where were you?'

'At home in London, until about eleven. Then I went racing at Ascot.'

'Did you go with anyone?'

I gave them Greg's name and number. Kerr wrote them down. I also showed them the stub of my boarding card for the eight o'clock shuttle from Heathrow to Edinburgh.

Donaldson took up the questioning again. 'Do you know anyone who bore a grudge against your brother? Anyone at all now? Think carefully.'

I had already thought. 'No one that I know of. He wasn't the sort of person to have enemies.' My voice shook. My eyes stung. I took a breath. 'No, no one.'

Donaldson waited a moment for me to recover my composure. 'Do you know if your brother was worried about anything.'

'Yes,' I said. 'He was. In fact, that's why I came up here.'

Donaldson raised his eyebrows.

'He rang me last week, and said he wanted to talk to me. He didn't say what about. He said it was important, and he didn't want to talk on the phone.'

Donaldson leaned forward. 'And do you have any idea what he was concerned about?'

'No, not really.'

'You must have some idea,' he urged. 'Guess.'

'Well,' I hesitated. 'It might be one of two things. His company might be days away from bankruptcy. When I last saw him he said that he was running out of cash again.'

'Again?'

'Yes. FairSystems had a cash-flow problem last year, and I bailed it out. Or Karen, my girlfriend, and I did. It could have been the same problem again.'

'And would you have helped him out a second time?'

I paused. 'I don't know.' I knew the honest answer, but I

didn't want to say it out loud. I had had no intention of throwing good money after bad. I winced at the thought.

Donaldson was watching me closely. He understood. 'And the second possibility?'

'He thought FairSystems' stock was being manipulated. He had spoken to Karen and me about it. He had all sorts of statistical analyses which he said suggested FairSystems' stock was behaving strangely.'

'Why?'

'He didn't know,' I said. 'He had just spotted a pattern that was inconsistent, and, like a good scientist, he wanted to find out why.'

'Do you have any ideas?'

'No. We checked out the market, and no one had heard anything. I think Richard was imagining it.'

'I see. Do you have his analyses?'

'Yes, I do. At home in London.'

'May we see them?'

'OK. I'll send them to you, if you like.'

'Thank you.' Donaldson looked at Kerr and stood up. 'That will be all for now, Mr Fairfax,' he said. 'You've been very helpful. Please let us know where we can get hold of you if we need to ask any more questions. And if you do have any more thoughts about who bore your brother a grudge, you will let us know, won't you?'

'Of course,' I said, getting up to go. 'Um, will I be able to see Richard's house?'

'Yes of course. But not for a few days. I'd like to give forensics all the time they need. But before you go, please give DI Kerr your girlfriend's name and address, and the address of everyone who you know who knew your brother.'

Kerr led me out, and I scribbled names and addresses on a piece of paper. 'I hope you find him,' I said.

Kerr rubbed his tired eyes. 'Believe me, we'll check out every half-lead you gave us. The boss is thorough. And he does get results. We'll get the bastard, don't you worry.'

'Good.'

There wasn't much point in staying in Kirkhaven, especially since I couldn't get into Richard's house. It was crawling with forensics, and they were crawling slowly, creeping over every scrap of dirt and fluff, leaving a trail of fine grey powder behind them.

So I took the Fiesta back to the airport and flew down to London. It was good to put four hundred miles between myself and the scene of Richard's death. The pain became less acute, less overwhelming. More manageable.

Karen met me at the airport. I pulled her close to me, and held on to her. 'Oh Mark, Mark,' she whispered into my ear. 'I'm so sorry. I'm so sorry.'

She took my hand and led me to her car. We drove home in silence. I couldn't say anything, she didn't push me.

When we arrived, she poured me a large whisky, and sat next to me, holding me in her arms. 'Tell me about him.'

And so I did. Haltingly at first, trying to hold back the tears. In the end I gave up, letting the sobs come as I talked about Richard, picking up on random memories. We talked, or rather I talked, late into the night.

I needed her. My mother was gone, and so, effectively, was my father. Until Richard went too, I hadn't realised how much I had relied on him for all that a family gives: love, continuity, security. Now I was all alone.

Over the next few days, I leaned heavily on Karen, and she supported me. Perhaps she was repaying me for all those difficult times when I had been there for her, right after she had been dumped. Richard's death had clearly affected her too, more than I would have imagined, but she had recovered from her initial shock, and built steel defences around herself. I knew when I talked about him, and cried over him, these defences were tested, but they held. She herself never cried, nor talked about Richard. She just listened.

I stumbled into work on Monday, exhausted from the emotional fatigue of the last forty-eight hours. The last thing I wanted to do was spend the day moping alone at home. I wanted people, distractions.

It was good to be back in the trading room again, to lose myself in prices, yields, spreads and basis points, and to focus once again on the inescapable monthly profit and loss. The month was looking better, but April would definitely end up as a loss, not a profit. I considered a number of possible trades, but didn't have the desire to put any of them on. So Ed and I just watched the positions we had, the Renaults moving ever upwards, and the ten-year treasuries outperforming their two-year brethren.

Everyone was sympathetic, Greg especially so. Ed didn't say anything directly to me, but tried to anticipate my every wish. I caught him watching me with an agonised expression on his face. People left me to my own devices. If I wanted to come to the office, fine. But they didn't expect me to do a proper day's work; they would let me behave how I wished and take their cue from me. I thought I was behaving normally, although I suspect I wasn't. Still, they let me be, and that was what I wanted.

The thoughts that had tumbled around my head the night I had found Richard began to straighten themselves in my mind. The pain of losing him was almost unbearable, but I was determined not to let it screw me up. I knew I was vulnerable psychologically: I had never got over my parents' divorce and my mother's death. But I would do all I could to deal with this new blow.

I felt guilty and angry. The anger sprang from the guilt, as a sort of frustration at my failure to have foreseen and prevented Richard's death. It was also, in a strange kind of way, directed at Richard himself. My big brother, my only protector in the world, had abandoned me, got himself killed over his stupid company. If he had only been more sensible, and sold it like I had told him, he might still be alive. I knew these thoughts were irrational and disloyal, but that knowledge only fed my anger.

My mother could be an angry woman. She would vent her frustration over some minor domestic problem: my returning home for the second time in a day with muddy trousers, my father breaking a jug when washing up, the English summer raining on her every day. When she exploded, it was a phenomenon, a torrent of English breaking into Italian, of tears and gesticulation, even of thrown plates and glasses (always my father's old possessions, never hers). But it went away. Within half an hour she was calm again, and within a day, she was smiling and laughing. Except once. When my father walked out, the explosion lasted for a week, and the anger stayed, festering, until she died.

And then it lived on in me.

I had her temper. It had been a problem, sometimes, at school. I'd got into fights. I'd rowed with girlfriends. So, as I'd grown older, I'd struggled to control it. Trading had helped; I'd soon realised that I would have to ignore my initial impulsive reaction to events if I were to maintain the self-discipline necessary to make money month in, month out. With Karen I had been the model of patience. But the anger was still there. It was just buried deep.

The more I thought about it, the more my anger at Richard's death achieved a focus. The bastard who had killed him. I prayed the police would find him.

The police investigations were thorough. Inspector Kerr showed up at Harrison Brothers' offices to talk to Karen and Greg, and then apparently made the trip to Godalming to talk to the fearsome Daphne Chilcott. Just to eliminate us, of course. I was sure that all the other people whose names I had given the police were also investigated.

There were a lot of phone calls. Sergeant Cochrane rang to say that the police had finished with Richard's house, and I was free to enter it when I liked. The investigation was continuing, although they had very few leads as yet.

I rang the procurator fiscal in Cupar, the local market town, to talk about certificates and forms. To my disappointment, he said that although a post-mortem had been carried out on Richard, he would not be able to release his body for burial in case a future defendant's lawyer later demanded his own examination. Since there was no defendant yet, the funeral would have to wait until one emerged.

Graham Stephens, a solicitor from the Edinburgh firm of Burns Stephens, phoned to tell me the contents of Richard's will. He held eight hundred thousand of the two million FairSystems shares outstanding, or forty per cent of the company. The share price had fallen to four and a half dollars following news of his death, so this stake was technically worth about three and a half million dollars. This was split equally between our father and me. The only other asset of any value was Inch Lodge, which Richard had left to me. Fortunately, the large mortgage on the house that he had taken out three years before to temporarily slake FairSystems' thirst for cash, would be paid off by a life assurance policy.

I didn't really feel as if I was worth nearly two million dollars. Richard, too, had signed an undertaking not to sell his shares within two years of flotation. Besides, it would be impossible to sell that large a stake through a broker. To lock in the money, the whole company would have to be sold. Taxes would have to be paid. And I still wasn't convinced that FairSystems would exist in eighteen months' time, anyway.

On Wednesday, I received another phone call, just after I arrived home from work. It was an unfamiliar voice. It was loud, and forceful and American.

'Is that Mark Fairfax?'

'Yes.'

'Good afternoon, Mark, this is Walter Sorenson. I'm a friend of your father, and I guess I was a friend of Richard as well.'

I had never met Walter Sorenson, but I knew who he was. My father had met him when he was at Stanford in the 1960s. Sorenson had been both a successful physicist and a great college football player, a rare feat, even in those days. He had become a well-respected figure in the computer industry in the 1970s, earning a reputation for himself as a coach for the young geniuses infesting the garages of Silicon Valley. Together with one such genius in the mid-seventies, he had founded a software company called Cicero Scientific and a few years later had sold out at a handsome profit. He now busied himself as a non-executive director of a clutch of growing computer companies that interested him in America and Europe. So, when FairSystems had floated on NASDAQ the previous year, and had needed a credible chairman in a hurry, my father had suggested to Richard his old friend Walter Sorenson.

Sorenson had been happy to take the job. Virtual reality was the hot new technology, and Glenrothes was three-quarters of an hour away from St Andrews and its golf courses.

Richard had told me that he had found him a useful sounding board and source of encouragement. FairSystems could certainly use his experience in the next few weeks.

'I'm sorry to hear about your brother. He was a great guy, and a truly brilliant scientist. The industry will be much poorer without him.' Sorenson's regret, and tribute, sounded genuine. I felt a stirring of pride for my brother. 'I've worked with entrepreneurs in California for twenty years, and I'd say that Richard was up there with the best of them.'

'Thank you. I'm sure he was.'

'As you can imagine, this news has hit FairSystems pretty hard. They don't know whether they're coming or going up there. I've appointed two of the management team, Rachel Walker and David Baker, as acting joint managing directors until we can come up with something more permanent.' Sorenson's tone was businesslike, inspiring confidence in a situation that badly needed it. 'As you probably know, I'm based in the States, but I plan to come over next week to sort things out.'

'Good,' I said.

'You and your father are the two major shareholders now. How well do you know the company?'

'Not very well at all,' I said. 'I mean, I know roughly what they do, but I've never been to Glenrothes. I invested as a gesture of support for Richard, rather than anything else.'

'OK,' said Sorenson. 'Well, I think it'd be good if you could come up to Glenrothes and spend some time with us. Can you manage that?'

'I'd be delighted to,' I said. 'I was thinking of going up to sort through Richard's stuff next week anyway.'

'Good. I'll be in Scotland on Sunday. I'm planning a round of golf at St Andrews. Would you like to join me? It would be a good opportunity for us to get to know each other.'

'OK,' I said, 'I'll see you then.'

I drove up to Kirkhaven on Saturday. I wanted to drive. I felt more secure in the private world of my BMW than crammed into an aeroplane with strangers on either side intruding into my grief.

I had told Bob Forrester that I was not sure how long I would be out of the office. He didn't mind me going; frankly, I wasn't much use there anyway. I left Ed with instructions where to sell our positions if the market moved one way or the other.

The sun fell low over the upper reaches of the estuary as I crossed the Forth Road Bridge into Fife. I passed the rubble of grey boxes that was Cowdenbeath, swung south of Glenrothes, and followed the road running a mile in from the coast to Kirkhaven. I stopped in at the police station to collect the keys, and drove down the narrow streets to the quay, and my brother's house.

I let myself in, and wandered round. The house had Richard's imprint all over it. Neat, functional, with little in the way of decoration. I looked into the kitchen first. It was old and wooden. There was a big old oak table where we had spent long Sunday breakfasts chatting and reading the papers. Outside, the evening sun poured in, reflected off the gently swelling sea. I went back into the hall and down a couple of steps to the sitting room. My eyes fell on the stone hearth, and I winced when I saw the pile of neatly chopped firewood in the basket. The room was furnished with pieces I remembered from our childhood: the grandfather clock, a sideboard, my mother's writing-desk, all salvaged from the house in Banbury Road after my mother had died. I checked the clock. I smiled as I saw the notches I had cut a foot from the base when I was six and had wanted to count the days of my imprisonment by pirates. Now *that* had caused an eruption.

There were several pictures of seabirds dutifully hanging on the walls. Richard had never really been interested in birds, but they were our father's passion, and Richard had spent many frozen afternoons with him, seeking out obscure waders along godforsaken stretches of shore. The pictures had been gifts from our father over the years. I didn't have any on my walls. I had always made my lack of interest in birds perfectly clear.

A few photographs were scattered about; my parents' wedding, my mother looking worn and ill, Richard and me together, Richard walking in the Himalayas with an old girlfriend. There were books and magazines everywhere, most of them to do with computing.

A biography of Bill Gates, the billionaire founder of Microsoft, lay face-down on the sofa. I picked it up. Richard had got as far as chapter three.

Through the window, I could see the Inch Burn, and the tough, squat stone church, with its stubby spire on the far bank. The view was partially obscured by the back of the boathouse. I went into the hallway to look for the key. It wasn't where it should have been, on a hook beside the door. The police hadn't known where to return it. I stuck my head into the kitchen, and saw it on a counter. Grabbing it, I walked outside and round the back of the house to the whitewashed building. I paused by the door, and took a deep breath.

As I entered, my eyes were drawn to the patch of floor, six feet from the door, where I had last seen Richard, almost a week before. The old carpet had been cut up and removed, leaving a patch of bare concrete underneath. I tore my eyes away, and scanned the boathouse. Despite the attentions of the police, it still looked a total mess, a jumble of terminals, computers, circuit boards, dismembered headsets, wires and papers. I knew it was organised chaos. Richard had proudly shown me round a few years before. He'd liked to think amongst this chaos, to scribble furiously on A5 paper, to tinker with his software and hardware. There was a Compaq 486 computer by a window, the keyboard scuffed and dirty from frequent use. I stood for a moment and thought about Richard, sitting here for hour after hour, worrying at some intractable problem that was beyond the scope of most of us to understand, let alone solve. Many of the great computer companies, Hewlett Packard and Apple Computer amongst them, had started in garages. Richard had wanted FairSystems to be different: it had started in a boathouse.

Suddenly, I felt cold. I shivered, and left the small building, locking it firmly behind me. I didn't want to go back in there again.

6

The ball flew straight at the old oak tree seventy yards to my
left, hit it, and bounced back on to the fairway, much to
my relief. I am not a good golfer. My strategy is to hit the ball
short distances in a straight line, aiming for a consistent seven
on each hole, and avoiding excessive embarrassment. It usually
works, until I get overconfident and start trying to hit the ball
too far. That always leads to lost balls, ploughed-up fairways,
and intense frustration. So far, I was doing well. The sixth
hole, and not a single lost ball.

Needless to say, Sorenson was a much better golfer than me.
He was good company, offering tips and encouragement. But he
was hard on himself; every time his big shoulders didn't swing
in perfect time, his wince showed real annoyance. Had I been a
better player, I suspected that the round would not have been
quite so light-hearted.

It was the first time I had met him since childhood. He was
tall, with broad shoulders and a Californian tan. He had a big
face with uneven features, a nose that was not quite straight,
and one bushy eyebrow set off at a different angle to the other.
It was a craggy, handsome face. He had a thick neck but no flab,
and his figure was trim. He looked as if he could still play
football, but his neatly brushed white hair and his expensive
golfing clothes gave him the sheen of a successful modern

American businessman. He had power. Not so much the power of money or of control over thousands of employees, but something much more elemental. It was a physical and psychological power, unused, but there if necessary. In Sorenson, it became charisma.

The setting was magnificent. A fresh breeze blew in from the Tay Estuary, and the grey town of St Andrews was lit up in that clear northern light that I was beginning to get used to. Here, perched on a promontory on the east edge of Fife, lay side by side the great grey cathedral of St Andrews, one of the oldest religious buildings in Scotland, and the place of pilgrimage of that more modern religion, the Old Course. If I hadn't had to concentrate so hard on hitting that bloody ball in a straight line and not making a fool of myself, I might have enjoyed it.

'Tell me about what you do,' said Sorenson, as we walked to where my ball lay. 'Richard said you trade bonds.'

So I told him. For someone not involved in the markets, he picked it up remarkably quickly, and soon had me explaining in detail my ideas about the bond market and how to make money in it. He listened closely and his questions showed that he understood what I was saying.

'You know, your business sounds a lot like mine,' he said. 'Things change fast. Technology changes, the markets change. To succeed, you have to have more than just smarts, you've got to have energy, enthusiasm, a willingness to question the way things are. You can't follow the rules, because the rules change every six months. That's why kids like you and Richard do so well.'

He lined up a tee-shot and hit it hard and to the right of the green. The wind pulled it back, and the ball landed only a few feet short. Sorenson pursed his lips in quiet satisfaction. My own ball had travelled exactly half the distance of Sorenson's. As we walked over to it, Sorenson continued, 'I like working with guys your age. There is no place for someone like me to come up with new technology any more. I don't have the stamina. But the right people, I can help.'

'How do you do it?' I asked. Sorenson was suddenly very

important to FairSystems' future. I was curious to find out more about him.

'Part of it I learned on the football field,' he said. 'To win a football game, you need many of the same skills you need in business. The will to win, teamwork, a mixture of planning and opportunism, and you mustn't be afraid to give the ball to the best guys on the team, and let them do what they can with it. I guess I just learned how to motivate people, starting with myself.'

'How did you start out?'

'When I left graduate school, I joined NASA. In the sixties, it seemed like mankind's future was out there, somewhere in space. Eventually, I realised that was all wrong. The future lay in micro-electronics, in nanoseconds rather than light years.

'A couple of geniuses I knew at Stanford had joined Xerox's Palo Alto Research Center. It was probably the major centre for computer research in the seventies. They had been working on Graphical User Interfaces, which are basically software systems that make it easier for a layman to use a computer. They had some good commercial ideas, but Xerox didn't want to back them. They didn't quite have the courage to start out on their own. So I helped them.

'We called the company Cicero Scientific. It was a hell of a lot of fun. The technology all came from the other two. I just kind of held the whole thing together. We sold out four years later to Softouch for eighty million dollars.'

Wow! Eighty million dollars! You could bet Sorenson had had a good bit of that action. I suddenly realised that the big man walking along next to me was probably the richest man I had ever met.

The name Softouch rang a bell. 'Didn't I see Softouch in the papers a couple of years ago?' I asked. 'Wasn't it in some kind of trouble?'

The enthusiasm left Sorenson's voice. 'It sure was,' he said.

I decided he didn't want to pursue it. I lined up a seven iron and hit my ball cleanly and evenly into a bunker. Bugger! It sometimes took me three shots to get out of one of those.

'Nice shot. You were just unlucky with the wind,' said Sorenson.

I shrugged my shoulders. 'So then what did you do?' I asked.

'Well, I played golf more or less full time for six months, but I couldn't stay away from the business. So I built up a portfolio of interesting companies in America and Europe whose boards I served on. Sometimes I invested in them too. I like to think of myself as a sort of coach. I think I can bring the best out of people. I've seen a lot of successes and failures in my time; I can share that experience.'

I could imagine that Sorenson would be good in that role. He was a good listener, but he also had authority. If he believed that you could do something, you would probably go right out and do it.

'And how does FairSystems line up against all these companies you've seen?' I asked.

He turned towards me. 'I tell you, Mark, it has real potential. One of the best. And virtual reality will be *the* computer market of the next decade.'

'That's what Richard said. I'm not sure I truly believed him.'

'Well, you should have. Most of the breakthroughs in computer technology over the last twenty years have come from getting more and more power on smaller and smaller chips. But you still have to be a computer jock to deal with a computer. That's got to change. You remember I spoke about Graphical User Interface, how people talk to computers? That's where the next great strides will come. And virtual reality is the ultimate user interface. When a person is actually in a computer generated world, can talk to it, point within it, then the computer disappears as a barrier. Computer and user become one. I'm convinced that a whole new range of human activity will become possible. Anything to do with creating something, or any communication between people in different physical locations, will be vastly improved by virtual reality.'

We started walking towards the bunker. 'You hear about all the obvious applications for design, entertainment, training and so on. But the really exciting applications we can't even

71

visualise now, because we haven't lived for long enough in a world with virtual reality. It's the same with all new technologies – electricity, the telephone, the computer – until you've lived with them for a while, you don't know what they will really be used for.'

I looked closely at Sorenson. He wasn't bullshitting me. He really meant it.

I trudged down into the bunker and hacked about a bit. Finally the ball bobbled on to the green.

My thoughts drifted back to Richard. I asked the question that had been on my mind all week. 'Do you know why Richard was killed?'

'No idea,' he said. 'I've been trying to figure that out myself. Do you know if the police have gotten anywhere yet?'

'No. They're asking a lot of questions.'

'Damn right they are. They came to see me yesterday afternoon. I spent hours with them. Do you have any ideas?'

'Well, I know something was on Richard's mind,' I said. I told Sorenson about Richard's anxious plea for me to come to see him. 'Did he call you about anything in the week before he died?'

'No, I don't think so.' Sorenson paused a moment. 'I don't think we spoke all week. I know he was worried about the cash position at FairSystems. So was I. I still am, for that matter. But I didn't get the impression there was a particularly urgent problem.'

'What about FairSystems' share trading?'

'No, he didn't mention that either. I guess the shares have been falling because investors are worried about the risk. And that makes some sense to me. Mind you, there's not much I can do about it. I can't sell my shares until two years after flotation. Not that I hold many anyway, just enough to keep my interest up.'

FairSystems' future worried me, too. 'Now Richard has . . .' I hesitated, 'gone,' I said finally, 'won't FairSystems fall apart?'

Sorenson rubbed his chin. 'It could, but I hope it won't.'

'But Richard was behind most of the technology, wasn't he?'

'To some extent, especially in the early days,' said Sorenson. 'But there's a lot more to FairSystems than just Richard. He worked very closely with a girl called Rachel Walker. Rachel has just about every FairSystems development in her head, and she has good people working for her. And then much of the technology isn't FairSystems' at all. Richard was excellent at putting together technical partnerships. There's a whole array of technologies that go into a virtual reality system. What FairSystems does is pull them all together.'

I listened intently. Sorenson went on. 'One of Richard's greatest skills was motivating people like Rachel and bringing in all his technical partners. That's what will be difficult to replicate. But we'll try.'

Sorenson took a long putt, and winced as it came to rest an inch short of the hole. My ball went in in two, and we moved on to the next tee. I was pleased with myself. My game hadn't fallen apart completely yet.

'I'm looking forward to seeing the company tomorrow,' I said.

'It'll be interesting to see what you think. Don't underestimate Rachel. She's brilliant. She knows as much about VR as anyone else in the world.

'She's running the company jointly with a guy called David Baker. He's more of a businessman. I rate him. He's got a Harvard MBA, but he's hungry, know what I mean? He wants FairSystems to go places. And he's signed up a pretty impressive client list for such a small company.'

'Do you think the combination will work?' I asked.

'In theory they should complement each other perfectly,' said Sorenson, chipping his ball on to the green. 'In practice, I don't know. I just don't know.'

'Shouldn't we just sell out? Richard told me he'd been approached by a buyer.'

'That may be the right decision. Personally, I'd like to see what state the company is in before making up my mind. But there's one problem.'

'Oh? What's that?'

'Your father.'

'My father?'

'Yes. He doesn't want to sell.'

'He doesn't want to sell? Why not? We should get out while we can.'

'He's adamant. He feels that FairSystems was so important to Richard that it would be wrong to sell. He says Richard didn't want to sell out, so he doesn't think we should.'

'Can't you persuade him he's wrong?'

Sorenson stopped by the next tee, stood up straight and looked at me. 'Geoff told me that you and he haven't spoken to each other for ten years. And after what he did to Gina, I guess I can understand that. Maybe.' He sighed, and looked out to sea for a moment, as if searching for something. 'But you and your father are FairSystems' two biggest shareholders. If you two have differences of opinion about what you want to do with the company, as chairman, I have to insist that you resolve them. The company doesn't need that uncertainty hanging over it.'

His eyes locked on mine, and he said slowly, with absolute authority, 'Mark. You've got to talk to him.'

I held his gaze for a moment. He was right.

'OK,' I said, and sliced my ball into the rough.

The sun shone off Detective Superintendent Donaldson's bald pate, as he sat bolt upright at the old oak table in Richard's kitchen. Kerr slouched next to him. We all sipped mugs of tea.

'We've made some progress with our inquiries,' Donaldson was saying. 'We'd like to ask you a few more questions in the light of what we've discovered.'

'Go ahead,' I said with interest.

'We've found the murder weapon. Your brother was killed by a blow from a firewood axe, probably whilst he was turning to look at his attacker. We found the axe in a hedge in a lane just off the road to Glenrothes.'

'Oh, right. I remember Richard chopping wood when I came to stay with him last winter,' I said.

'Would you be able to identify the axe?' asked Donaldson.

I thought for a moment and shook my head. 'No, I really can't remember what it looked like.'

'Never mind. We're pretty sure the murderer was someone your brother knew. There are no signs that the door was forced. The front door, and a number of surfaces in the kitchen, were wiped clean. This suggests that your brother let the murderer into the kitchen, and then took him out to the boathouse.'

I was listening carefully.

'It probably wasn't premeditated,' continued Donaldson. 'The axe was just the nearest weapon to hand. If the murder was planned, then the killer would have brought his own weapon. There are no signs that anything was stolen, although we can't be completely sure about that.'

'Any fingerprints?' I asked.

'No,' said Donaldson. 'As I said, all the surfaces in the kitchen were wiped down with a cloth. So was the axe. No footprints either. Nor any fibre evidence.'

'Do you have any suspects?'

Donaldson frowned. 'Patience, son. A murder investigation takes time. A lot of officers, a lot of time. But we'll get there.'

I looked appropriately chastened.

'Now, we've learned that Mr Fairfax had an argument with one of his colleagues, David Baker, on Friday, the day before he died. Apparently, Baker was so angry he stormed off home immediately afterwards. You mentioned that your brother spoke to you about problems at FairSystems a couple of times over the last few weeks?'

I nodded.

'Did he ever mention David Baker?'

'No. I hadn't heard of him until Walter Sorenson mentioned him a few days ago.'

'So he gave no indication that Baker had anything to do with whatever was worrying him?'

'No, none at all.'

'I see,' said Donaldson. He referred to his notes. 'And what about BOWL?'

'BOWL?'

'Yes. It stands for the Brave Old World League. It's a group of activists who believe that new technology will ruin society. They are particularly upset about virtual reality.'

'I think Richard did mention something about some people like that,' I said. It had been during a conversation several months before. I struggled to remember more about it. 'Hadn't one of his people joined them? Doug? Dougie? Something like that.'

'That's right,' said Kerr. 'Doogie Fisher worked for FairSystems until last year, when he joined BOWL. It's quite a secretive organisation – more like a network, really – a group of individuals in Britain and America. Most of them seem to be disillusioned technical people; at any rate, they seem to know a lot about computers. They are prepared to use violence to achieve their ends. A couple of months ago, there was a spate of letter bombs sent to virtual reality companies in the UK. None caused any damage. We think that Doogie, or one of his colleagues, was behind it.'

'And you think this Doogie might have been involved in Richard's death?'

'It's a possible line of inquiry,' said Donaldson. 'But you can't tell us anything about him?'

I shook my head. I wanted to help. I wished I had listened more closely when Richard had spoken about BOWL. But I hadn't. It had seemed so far away then. So remote from my everyday life.

'We've followed up your brother's suspicions about manipulation of FairSystems' shares,' Donaldson continued. 'The Stock Exchange are looking into it now, and they are consulting with the authorities in America.'

'Oh really? Have they found anything?'

'They're still gathering data. But to go back to the evening when Richard Fairfax asked you to look into FairSystems' share price. Did you?'

'Yes. Or rather Karen did.'

'Karen Chilcott. Your girlfriend?'

'Yes.'

'And she discovered nothing?'

'That's right. FairSystems is such a small stock that it's only really traded by one firm, Wagner Phillips. When she checked with a friend of hers there, they didn't know anything. It seemed to us that there was nothing funny going on.'

'I see,' said Donaldson. 'Have you traded in FairSystems shares yourself?'

'No. At least not since the company went public.'

'You haven't sold any?'

'I'm not allowed to. Not for two years.'

'Do you know anyone else who has been involved in the shares?'

'No. Just Karen. And she operates under the same restrictions as me.'

'And does she have any contacts who are involved in Fair-Systems shares?'

'Of course not!'

'Calm down, Mr Fairfax. Just answer the questions.'

'Let me save you some time,' I said, successfully controlling my temper. 'I had no inside information about FairSystems at all. I know virtually nothing about the company. Neither does Karen. In fact, she knows even less than me. So we would have had nothing to tell anyone, even if we had wanted to. In any case, why should we? The shares went down, not up. What would be the point of getting anyone to buy them? If we'd told someone to buy, they'd have lost money.'

I looked from Donaldson to Kerr, and back to Donaldson. His grey eyes held mine. I knew what I said made sense, and so, I could see, did he.

'All right, Mr Fairfax. But we may have to make some more inquiries.'

I relaxed. He believed me. And I did want to help. In a way I was pleased he was asking difficult questions. 'That's fine with me,' I replied.

'Thanks for the tea,' he said, getting up to leave. 'By the way, make sure you don't touch anything in the boathouse. There are a lot of technical papers there that we want to go through with Rachel Walker later this week.'

'Fine,' I said, and saw them out. The last thing I wanted to do was go back in there, anyway.

7

I drove fast to Glenrothes. The more I thought about it, the less likely it seemed to me that Donaldson's suspicions of insider trading would lead anywhere. To be an insider trader you need to have inside information. I had had none, until perhaps Richard had hinted that FairSystems was running out of money again. But that had been only a few days before he'd been killed. Karen had known nothing either.

I was still a little nervous. In the City, even a hint that you have been involved in something dodgy doesn't do your reputation any good. I hoped Donaldson wouldn't ask too many questions.

I thought about strange movements in share prices. From what little I knew, they were usually moves up, just before a takeover was announced, as people with inside knowledge bought shares in anticipation of the announcement. But Fair-Systems' shares had moved down not up. Despite Richard's theories, I saw nothing mysterious about that.

I arrived at Glenrothes just before lunch. The town sprawled beneath three low hills. It was ringed with industrial estates, each containing blocks of rectangular, windowless metal factories. Grey cloud hung low overhead. There was very little movement, noise or smoke. Whatever machinery there was, was humming away quietly to itself under those metal cocoons.

Richard had told me a little of Glenrothes' history. It had been set up as a New Town in the 1940s and had grown with miners flocking from the west of Scotland to exploit the giant Rothes coal pit. This had turned out to be unworkable, and had been closed down after only a few years. Since then the town had enthusiastically embraced the concept of Scotland's 'Silicon Glen', and had managed to attract large sums of foreign investment, much of it in high-technology industries. The biggest employer was the American company, Hughes Electronics.

FairSystems' factory was in the midst of an industrial estate just like all the others. When a big local computer company had gone bust three years earlier, Richard had been able to rent its facility cheaply from the local development corporation.

It was a large, rectangular grey metal box, bigger than most of those surrounding it. The company logo was placed at various points round the exterior, an orange rising sun with the word *FairSystems* running across it. The only windows were clustered round the front of the building.

I pulled into the car park, and walked across the tarmac past a newly planted garden in front of the factory. Scrawny young trees poked up from scantily planted flowerbeds. On two sides were similar featureless factories, and on the other was some wasteland stretching towards a small hill grazed by cows.

Inside, the reception area was brightly decorated. The receptionist had very short red hair, and was wearing a simple black dress. I saw a chunky copy of *Anna Karenina* lying opened on the chair next to her behind the desk. When I said my name she gave me a sympathetic smile. She asked me to take a seat and wait for Mr Sorenson.

So I sat down and waited. I was curious to see the factory. It had played such an important part in Richard's life, and probably his death.

The receptionist was staring out of the doorway, looking bored.

'Carry on with your book,' I said. 'I don't mind.'

She smiled guiltily, and picked it up. She read a paragraph or two, and then looked towards me.

'Mr Fairfax,' she began nervously.

'Yes?'

'I'm really sorry about your brother's death.'

I smiled weakly.

'So are all of us here,' she went on. 'He was a good man. We all liked him.'

I was getting used to receiving condolences. But her sincerity was obvious, and suddenly touching. My eyes stung, and I swallowed.

'Thanks,' I said simply.

She smiled quickly and went back to her book.

Two minutes later Sorenson rushed into the reception area, followed by a man I didn't know. 'Mark. I'm glad you could make it. Good day yesterday, wasn't it? Boy, that's a great course.' He held out his hand and I shook it. 'I'll be tied up for most of the day, today, so I won't be able to show you round. But that's probably a good thing. So David, here, and Rachel will give you the tour.'

David Baker held out his hand. 'Welcome to FairSystems, Mark.' His accent was a strange combination of mild Scottish with an American intonation. He was in his early thirties, medium height, thin, with his dark hair plastered back over his head with oil. His small eyes peered at me down a long, pointed nose. He wore an Italian-looking suit, and brown shoes. A Hermès tie was held in place with a silver tie pin. Red braces peeked out beneath his jacket. He looked out of place in this grey Scottish factory. But then I probably looked that way, too, in my City suit.

'I'm really sorry about your brother. He was a great friend of mine. It was a terrible shock. No one here can quite believe it.'

'Thank you,' I said, politely.

There was an awkward pause. I was getting used to these, too.

'Right, well, come upstairs,' David said. 'I thought you might like to have a chat with Rachel Walker and myself first. Then I can show you around the factory, and take you on to Willie Duncan, our finance director.'

'I'll catch you later,' said Sorenson. 'I'll be in Richard's office if you need me.'

We moved out of the daylight, and into the factory. We were in a long corridor. There was glass on both sides, and through it I could see a jumble of plastic and electronics, with men in bright blue overalls moving about. Posters of VR systems covered the walls; the orange FairSystems logo was much in evidence. A radio played pop music somewhere in the distance. We walked up some stairs to a similar corridor, but this one was lined with more familiar office spaces. The carpets were light grey, and most of the furniture was black, although there were the odd flashes of blue or orange plastic. It was a world turned inside out. The external walls had no windows; all the internal walls were glass.

David showed me into what looked like some kind of conference room. There was a large screen against one wall, and a computer with a headset, 3–D mouse and keyboard next to it. A long oval table stretched the length of the room, and a side table held two more computers. Embedded in the ceiling was a series of tiny cameras, pointing down at the seats below.

'This is our board room,' David explained. 'We use it for demonstrations. You can even have a virtual meeting here with half the people in the room, and the rest at other locations. It's not always practical, but it looks flashy. Have a seat.'

I sat down on one side of the table and David sat on the other. He placed a smart leather folder on the table. Inside was a gleaming white pad, and some business cards. He handed one to me.

'These are old,' he said. 'It should say "Managing Director". Rachel will be here in a moment.' He looked quickly at his Rolex just to confirm that Rachel was, in fact, late.

'I thought you and Rachel were joint managing directors?'

David looked at me suspiciously. 'Oh, that's right. But I'll handle all the business side of things. Rachel has a great technical brain,' he said, 'a great technical brain.' He managed to make it sound as if this was an unfortunate state of affairs, and would explain why Rachel could not use her brain for anything useful.

Just then the door opened and Rachel ambled into the room carrying a cup of coffee in a plastic cup. She pushed long frizzy brown hair out of her eyes, and offered me her hand.

'Hi. Rachel Walker. How are you?' She had a pleasant soft Scottish accent and a low husky voice.

'Mark Fairfax. Nice to meet you,' I said.

She sat down at the other end of the table to David Baker, and pulled out a packet of Marlboro. She began to light one, and then looked over towards me. 'You don't, do you?' she asked, nodding at the packet.

I shook my head.

'I didn't think so,' she said. 'I can always tell.'

I realised now where the huskiness in her voice came from.

David coughed. Whether to express disapproval of the cigarette, or to attract my attention, I didn't know. 'How much do you know about FairSystems?' he began.

'Not much. Richard told me a bit. I read the placing document, but that was a few months ago. And I have used a system.'

'That was Bondscape?'

'Yes. I was impressed.'

'It's good,' said Rachel matter-of-factly.

'But assume I know very little.' This was in fact the truth. I wished I had listened harder to what Richard had had to say about his company and about virtual reality. I was all ears now.

'Fine, let me tell you something about us,' said David. He clicked a remote control, and slides appeared on the screen behind him. He made a professional presentation. He talked about FairSystems' history, its market, its products, forecasts for the virtual reality market, and gave an outline of the company's strategy. I listened very closely, following every word.

It seemed absurd, David in his carefully ironed cotton shirt, his cuff-links and Hermès tie, making a slick presentation to me, a twenty-eight-year-old trader. But it was a wise thing to do. I was now the single largest shareholder in FairSystems; my half of Richard's forty per cent stake, together with my existing 3.75 per cent, made almost twenty-four per cent. I was important to the company and to David himself, and I was getting the red-carpet treatment to justify it. It was an excellent effort.

When he had finished, David smiled at me. 'Any questions?'

'Yes,' I said. 'I've heard a lot about all the different applications for virtual reality, and FairSystems seems to be involved in most of them. But sales are only, what, three million pounds? Is there really such a large market out there?'

'Definitely,' said David. 'Right now, the only major spending on VR comes from the US military, followed by those machines you see in arcades. That will change. Once the technology is there at the right price,' at this he paused to look tellingly at Rachel, 'and people are used to the concept, no one knows how big the total market will be. But it will certainly be numbered in the billions.' He flipped back a few slides to a virtual portrayal of an office block in Frankfurt. 'It's always going to be cheaper to build a virtual building, try it out, and improve it, rather than build a real one and live with the mistakes.'

I nodded. He had a point.

'Anything else?'

I had a hundred questions about the business, but for the moment I thought it was more important to find out about the people. 'Yes. Could you tell me something about yourself? How do you come to be working for FairSystems?'

David's face became serious; his career was a very serious topic.

'Certainly. I'm an economics graduate from LSE. I spent several years on the fast-track management programme at IBM.'

'Was that in sales?' I interrupted.

David smiled. 'Sure. I've been at the sharp end selling to dealers. But I was also responsible for developing strategy, project implementation, production-marketing interface, divisional resource allocation, as well as some high-level general management responsibilities.'

I didn't understand any of that. A salesman then.

'But I found IBM stultifying. I could see which direction the company was going, so I went to B-school. Harvard.' A pause for the impact of this to sink in. 'My goal was always to become an entrepreneur. So, when I left Harvard, and I saw the opportunity to join FairSystems, I jumped at it. I'm a natural entrepreneur, a money-maker. Richard and I made a good team. There's no doubt that he'll be badly missed, but I can take this firm a long way.'

Rachel blew smoke towards the ceiling. David and I turned towards her. She looked impassively back.

'Any more questions?' David asked, hopeful for a chance to explain his talents further.

'No, thank you. That was very helpful,' I said. 'Do you have a hard copy of the presentation?'

'Here you are.' David pushed one over to me. 'Now, perhaps I can show you the factory?' David gestured towards the door, and Rachel got up to leave.

The computer world is not the only one with slick salesmen. We have them in the bond markets, too. I did not want my view of FairSystems to be entirely determined by David Baker.

'Just a moment,' I said. 'I wonder if it would be possible to talk to Rachel? Perhaps she could show me round.'

David frowned. 'Rachel's our top technical person. She's very busy right now. Right, Rachel?'

We both turned to Rachel.

She paused for a moment and looked me over. Through her round glasses she had deep, brown, intelligent eyes. She was making some sort of assessment of me, and it made me uncomfortable that I had no idea what it was.

Finally, she sat down and said, 'No, that's all right, David. I'd be happy to talk to Mark.'

We both turned to look at David. He paused, couldn't immediately think of any way of keeping me in his grasp for the afternoon, and reluctantly gave up. 'Fine,' he said. 'Drop by when you've finished, won't you, Mark?' He smiled and left the room.

Rachel stubbed out her cigarette. She was sitting upright in her chair, poised but relaxed. 'What can I tell you?'

I guessed she was about my age, but I felt very little empathy with her. Like David, I was clean-cut in my City suit; she was wearing a baggy grey jumper over black leggings. She wore no make-up and her hair kept drifting in front of her eyes. I had been told that she had a great technical brain, and, looking at those eyes, I could believe that she was frighteningly clever. I was scared of asking her any questions about FairSystems because of the inevitability of them seeming stupid.

I pulled myself together.

'An impressive presentation,' I said.

'Ah ha. David's a good salesman,' said Rachel.

She paused. It looked as if she wanted to say more. I waited. She lit another cigarette, took an initial puff and blew smoke towards the ceiling in the same dismissive way she had done during David's presentation. 'It's a shame he can't program a calculator. Let alone a computer.'

I leaned over the table. 'Well, I can't program a computer either,' I said slowly but firmly, 'but I am very interested in FairSystems and its future, and I pick things up quickly. So tell me about the company.'

Rachel grinned. It was a surprisingly wide, warm smile, but in a moment it was gone. 'Sorry. He gets up my nose sometimes. It's not his fault. We're just different people. Do you want to have a look around?'

'Yes, please.'

'I'll show you the assembly areas first. We buy in most of our components. What we do here is put them all together to build a system to our design and specification.'

We went downstairs and into the large area I had noticed before. There was no obvious production line as such. Fair-Systems was not yet at the stage of mass-producing machines. To the untutored eye, the production floor seemed to consist of groups of young men, and some young women, strolling around, fiddling with the bits and pieces strewn all over the place. Rachel sorted out the areas of activity for me. The first section was where circuit boards were assembled. They were fascinating, each one a tiny, bustling city of roads, bridges and buildings on a bright green field. Most of the power lay not in the boards, but in the little integrated circuits, or 'chips' – thin wafers of silicon, some containing millions of transistors, more computing power than had sent man to the moon.

Next to it was a section where the headsets were put together from miniature circuit boards and tiny liquid crystal displays. Then came the assembly of the computers themselves, and finally a complicated array of testing equipment to make sure the whole thing worked. There was no noise of working machinery, just the ubiquitous babble of a radio.

I met the production manager, Jock, a forty-year-old who looked as though he had been on some factory floors in his time. He seemed intelligent and capable.

'One good thing about being located in Glenrothes is that we can get some excellent people,' said Rachel. 'There are whole families who work in the electronics industry, and the recession brought some very good people on to the market. They're reliable and they work hard.

'Take a look at this,' she continued. She pointed to a cluster of electronic equipment: an ordinary-looking computer, a terminal, a headset not much bigger than a pair of sunglasses, an electronic glove and a mouse. Everything had the orange FairSystems logo stamped on it.

'This is our current system. As you can see, many of the components are made by other people.' She tapped the grey plastic casing of the computer. 'This is just a standard IBM PC. It takes the messages it receives from the headset, the glove and the mouse, does all the millions of calculations necessary to create a virtual world, and transmits the results back to the devices. And it has to make these calculations twenty times per second.'

'That sounds like a lot of number crunching.' I picked up the headset. It was the same model I had used for Bondscape, and weighed only a few ounces.

'That's our own design,' said Rachel. 'We call it "Virtual

Glasses". But once again it's made up of components from other manufacturers. The liquid crystal displays, which generate the images in each eye, are made by Horiguchi Electronics in Japan. The sound system is from Crystal River of California, and this,' she pointed to a small black plastic cube embedded in the headset, 'this is a head tracking system, which monitors where the user is looking. It's made by a company called Polhemus, from Vermont.'

She then showed me the electronic glove, and a '3–D mouse', which was not a particularly lifelike model rodent, but a small plastic gizmo that fitted comfortably in a hand, and could be used to point things out in the virtual world.

'Now, let me take you up to Software.'

On the way to the stairs we passed a door that opened into a kitchen. Three or four people sat round the table in the centre of the room chatting while they ate burgers out of polystyrene containers. What really impressed me, though, was the row of fancy vending machines. They sold drinks of all types, hot and cold, chocolate, crisps and chips, and even hot-dogs and burgers.

Rachel saw me pause. 'A dietician would have a heart attack over some of the people here. This is the fuel that keeps them going all night. Personally, I think it's all crap,' she said wrinkling her nose.

'So what keeps you going all night?' I asked.

Rachel gave me a look that suggested I was crazy, or a pervert, or both, and climbed the stairs.

Software turned out to be a room about half the size of the production floor, but it looked very different. There were about fifteen smooth black desks, each manned by a programmer with his computer. So much for the paperless office – it was everywhere: printouts, newspapers, food wrappers, cuttings, photographs, and dozens of little yellow stickers. But each programmer ignored the paper around him, and stared at his screen in total concentration. The effect was spoiled by a group at one end of the room who were laughing loudly as they tried to hit a cup, perched on a filing cabinet, with a frisbee.

'What are they doing?' I asked as innocently as I could.

'Uh, it's a wee bit difficult to explain,' said Rachel, embarrassed.

One of them saw my suit and the game stopped.

I looked round the room. I suppose I'd expected rows of regulation nerds, stunted twenty-two-year-olds with acne, glasses and greasy hair. Well, there were some of these, but what struck me was the diversity of people. Most were in their twenties, but there were a couple of schoolmasterly types in their forties. There were two or three Asians. Some wore T-shirts and jeans, but others wore ties and hung jackets on the backs of their chairs. There were no women. The overall atmosphere was relaxed, and with the exception of the frisbee throwers, hard-working.

On the far wall was a window. It was about six-feet square, and blue and white curtains hung on either side. Through it I could see a wild moorland, with dark mountains rising up in the distance. Sheep grazed in the foreground.

'Nice view,' I said.

'Good, isn't it?' Rachel said. 'It's amazing how much of a difference it makes. It's a screen left over from a demo we did a year ago. They change the scenery every week. I think that's the Isle of Skye. You've got to admit, it looks better than whatever is really on the other side of that wall.'

She turned back to face the room. 'This is where FairSystems' real strengths lie,' she said, a touch of pride creeping into her voice. 'Creating a virtual world requires a number of steps. First, you describe the shape of an object, such as a chair, in terms of mathematical formulae and coordinates. Then you add textures to the image, such as fabric, leather or wood. But then you need software to calculate what the chair will look like when either it, or the viewer moves; this is the essence of virtual reality. We've developed our own simulation manager that does this, and does this very well. It's called FairSim 1.

'As you can imagine, virtual reality uses up an awful lot of computer processing power. Whenever we want to try something new, it's always lack of computer power that stops us.

There is a whole range of trade-offs a programmer has to make when he is designing a world. He can recalculate the world thirty times a second, which will give the appearance of motion as smooth as television, or he can give his virtual objects realistic textures, or accurate light shading, or precise shapes, or realistic three-dimensional sound, or he can provide a wide field of vision for the user. But he can't do all this all at once. FairSim 1 makes intelligent choices amongst these trade-offs in real time as the system is running. It makes the most of whatever computer power is available to it. It's quite simply the best package in the world.'

Rachel made the last statement matter-of-factly, with no hint of arrogance. She obviously believed it.

She caught the eye of one member of the group which had been throwing the frisbee. He stood up and came over to us. He was tall and very thin, and he walked fast. He had long dark hair, and wore black jeans and T-shirt.

'This is Keith Newall, our chief chip designer. Keith, this is Mark, Richard's brother.'

'Good to meet you. Man, I'm sorry about Richard.'

I smiled.

'Keith used to work for Motorola in California. That's why he talks funny. But don't let it deceive you. He comes from Kirkcaldy.'

'Thank you for that introduction, Rachel,' said Keith, speaking rapidly, his Adam's apple bobbing up and down. He had a barely distinguishable Scottish accent; like David Baker's, it was tinged with American. 'Sorry about the frisbee. That's Matt Gregory, Chief Executive Officer of Chips with Everything.' He pointed to a young man with a sparsely furry face, twiddling the offending frisbee round his finger. 'He likes to play when he comes here. But don't worry, he won't hurt you. He's afraid of suits.' This all came out in a breathless rush.

'Have you told him about FairRender?' he asked Rachel.

'Go ahead,' she said.

'We've just completed a new graphics chip for our next generation of machines. It's very exciting. Let me show you.' He led me over to a large computer screen, plastered with yellow sticky bits of paper. He sat down and clicked his mouse button rapidly. He whisked me through a series of highly complex drawings so fast that it looked like an early animated film. All the while, he was talking about z-buffers, cache-based texture processing, massive parallelism, and Gouraud-shaded polygons, plus a lot else. He gave one final click of the mouse, lent back in his chair, looked up at me and said, 'So, what do you think?'

I thought a bit, nodded, and said, 'Very nice.'

'What do you mean, "very nice"?' exclaimed Keith. 'This is fucking brilliant!'

Rachel laughed. 'Actually, it is quite good. This wee chip represents a totally new way of generating the images you need for virtual reality. It's much better than any of the competition. At the moment, generating a virtual image requires huge amounts of data to be stored in the computer's memory whilst it's doing its calculations. This slows things down. With Fair-Render we can perform all the calculations directly on the chip without storing data in memory.'

'So?'

'So, we'll be able to create virtual images many times faster than anyone else. And we have the patent to the process.'

'That,' I said, smiling at Keith, 'is fucking brilliant.'

'Now, let's look at what we do with all this stuff,' said Rachel.

She led me over to a big man with a tangled black beard, his gut covered by a white T-shirt declaring 'I'm lost in the Myst'. God knows what that meant.

'Hi Terry,' she said.

Terry looked up. 'Now then, Rachel. How's things?' He had a broad Yorkshire accent.

Rachel turned to me. 'Terry's working on a project with one of America's leading retailers. Look.'

I looked over Terry's shoulder. The screen was filled with an image of the fashion department of a clothes store. Terry pressed some keys, and a slinky black evening dress was highlighted. 'This one costs five thousand quid. Want to try it on, Rachel?' asked Terry.

'Sure.'

The screen cut to an elaborate fitting room. There was an image of Rachel wearing the low-cut gown. She walked up and down in front of mirrors, her reflection showing the dress from every angle. Her figure was stunning, at least on the computer. I couldn't stop myself glancing quickly at the baggy jersey next to me. Rachel caught my glance and blushed. It was an attractive sight, a red glow spreading up from her neck to her pale cheeks.

'This will be used as a marketing gimmick,' she said quickly, recovering her cool. 'But in five years' time when we all have these in our homes, who knows, this may well be how we buy our clothes.'

'We've developed body-mapping techniques that can accurately reproduce an image of a real person from any angle,' Terry said. 'Do you want to see me in a bikini?'

I just caught a glimpse of Terry's hairy stomach drooping over a little lime green number, when Rachel pulled me away. 'He's very good, that Terry, but he is weird.'

There was something creepy about a programmer dressing and undressing beautiful women on a computer all day. And then dressing himself up in a skimpy bikini. Very creepy.

Rachel showed me what some of the other programmers were working on. One was developing a three-dimensional representation of an oil well, and another a system that would help sufferers of vertigo get over their fear of heights.

'Try this,' she said, pointing to a jumble of metal and electronics. It was a ski-training system.

I hesitated a moment, and then did as she indicated. I put my feet carefully in the ski-boots, which were fixed to specially designed metal plates, and donned a headset. Suddenly, I was on a ski-slope. All around me were mountains, sky, sunshine, and crisp white snow. I pushed off with real ski-sticks, and immediately I was hurtling down the mountainside. I could hear the swish of snow in my ears, and, strangest of all, my feet picked up the judder and jerks of snow underneath my skis. I tried a turn, my legs felt the shock of the impact, and of course the angle of the view changed. I was disoriented for a moment, but within seconds I had adjusted to the new world I was in. Of course the mountainside did not look totally realistic, and I couldn't feel the mixture of sunshine, chill and wind on my face that is the essence of skiing, but it was a great sensation. And when I wiped out it didn't hurt a bit.

It would be a terrific way to learn to ski, or simply to brush up on old skills before heading out to the slopes. I really wanted another go, but something in Rachel's expression put me off asking. Reluctantly, I followed her towards a small office at the end of the room.

As Rachel was leading me out, a door to our left opened suddenly. A boy of about twelve stumbled out, rubbing his eyes. He was thin, with a soft pale face, and large eyes that were red from lack of sleep. He was carrying four empty pizza boxes. He almost stumbled into Rachel.

'I'm just getting rid of these,' he said. Then he smiled tiredly. 'It's a great hack. We're almost there.'

'Good, Andy,' said Rachel. 'Did you get any sleep last night?'

'Not yet,' mumbled the boy. Then he noticed me for the first time, and pushed shut the door through which he had just come. It had a small sign on it: 'Project Platform. Keep Out.' A large skull and crossbones had been taped to the door underneath the notice.

'Who's that?' I asked, as Andy staggered off with his pizza boxes.

'That's Andy Kettering. He's probably the brightest programmer we have. And he's not quite as young as he looks. I think he's twenty-three.'

'And what's Project Platform?'

Rachel looked at me for a moment, hesitating. Finally she said, 'That's a confidential project we're doing for a third party. Only five people in the company know anything about it. Well, four I suppose, now Richard isn't around.'

I was intrigued but I let it drop. I followed Rachel into a small glass office. It was obviously hers. The desk-top was a litter of plastic coffee cups. There were at least three ashtrays scattered round the small room, each one full of cigarette stubs. Two empty bottles of Valpolicella stood guard over the wastepaper basket. Papers were carefully stacked in three neat piles on one corner of her desk, and her computer hummed gently to itself on the other. She, too, had a window, but no curtains this time. It showed a grey city in the early morning mist, a large river running through its centre.

'Glasgow?' I asked.

'Ah ha.'

I watched a lone ship make its way up the Clyde.

'Richard did a lot of work in his boathouse in Kirkhaven,' Rachel said. 'He kept some important stuff there. I wonder if I could come round and pick it up?'

'Certainly. Or would you like me to bring it in?'

'No, don't bother. Most of it is actually in his computer, so I'll download his files.'

'OK. When do you need it?'

'As soon as possible.'

'How about this evening?'

'I can't make that,' said Rachel. 'I'll be here most of the night. I can come round early tomorrow morning, though. Half past seven, if that's OK?'

'That's fine.' I wondered when she slept. Whether she slept at all.

We were silent for a moment, standing awkwardly by a small conference table.

This was the woman who had worked closely with Richard for years. She knew all FairSystems' secrets. I badly wanted to ask her whether she knew anything about Richard's death.

'Do you have any idea who might have killed him?'

It was the wrong question to ask. She looked at me, face pale and expressionless. She bit her bottom lip.

'No,' she said.

I paused a moment. 'He wanted to see me about something just before he died. Do you know what that might have been?'

Her face was still impassive, but I could tell it was a struggle to keep it that way. 'I don't want to talk about him. OK?' Her voice was firm.

'OK,' I said. I was irritated, but I supposed she had a right to deal with her grief in the way she chose.

We both stood by the small table. The awkwardness remained. 'Was there anything else?' I asked eventually.

She looked me straight in the eye. 'Are you going to sell FairSystems?'

I wasn't prepared for that. I didn't answer. I didn't know the answer yet.

Rachel saw right through me. 'People here are talking about it. They think you'll take the money and run.' They could be right I thought. Rachel's dark eyes were fixed on mine, probing, accusing. I looked down. 'We all worked hard for Richard over the years. His death has been a shock to everyone here; some people have taken it very badly. But we all know what he was trying to do, and we want to see it through. For his sake. It's all we can do.' Her face was taut. She was fighting to control her emotion, and she was succeeding. 'Richard said he would never sell out. I hope you understand that.'

My mind was filled with a jumble of thoughts. Guilt that I had considered selling Richard's company, concern that the last thing the workforce needed now was further demoralisation.

I just said to Rachel, 'Yes, I understand.'

'I know you work in a bank,' she continued. 'I know that money is important to people like you. But this company represents more than just profits and losses. It's Richard. Everything he cared for, everything he believed in.

'The future of virtual reality can be determined right here in Glenrothes. We're so close to making Richard's vision a reality. Don't destroy it, it's too important.' Her voice was full of contempt. She wasn't pleading with me, she was telling me.

I nodded, not wanting to commit myself to Rachel, feeling guilty as hell.

'I'll take you to see Willie,' she said.

8

Willie Duncan had a small circular face, soft, wrinkleless skin, and a shock of curly red hair. His eyes peered nervously through round wire-rimmed glasses. As I entered, he cowered behind the files and loose papers covering his desk.

Rachel was right. I felt on surer ground with Willie than I had with the others. He dealt in numbers, in profits and losses. When you are a trader, you can't hide from your profit and loss. Bad trades show up as losses, good trades make profits, excuses are irrelevant. In my mind, the only real measure of FairSystems' value was its profitability, if not at that moment, then at least in the year or two to come.

Scottish chartered accountants have a fearsome reputation, but Willie was certainly not fearsome. And he had none of the raw intelligence of Rachel, nor the polish of David. But he did seem to have a good grasp of FairSystems' numbers. Everything was consistent. Everything added up.

And it all added up to a problem.

All of the money raised from the flotation of FairSystems on NASDAQ had been spent on a number of essential research and development projects, and on Wagner Phillips' fees. A total of five million pounds. Since cash was running low again, spending had recently been placed under tight control. The company was shipping products to customers, but only at the rate of three hundred thousand pounds per month. The monthly losses were between one and two hundred thousand pounds. There was only two hundred thousand in the bank.

Fortunately, Willie's forecasts showed five hundred thousand pounds to come in from Jenson Computer over the next three months, with possibly significantly more to follow towards the end of the year.

'What do these relate to?' I asked, pointing to the Jenson payments.

'Och, it's some project Richard and Rachel were working on.'

'Project Platform?'

'That's right.' Willie was clearly surprised that I knew the project name. 'Do you know about it?'

'Not really,' I said. 'I passed the project room just now. Do you?'

'Oh, no.'

'Then how do you know about these payments?'

'Well, since last summer I've insisted on doing regular cash-flow forecasts for the business. So Richard gives me the timing and size of expected payments.' He interrupted himself. 'I mean "gave".' He paused, while he tried to collect himself. 'I'm sorry, it's just impossible to believe what's happened,' he said haltingly. He looked so upset, I almost wanted to reach over and pat his hand. But he pulled himself together. 'About three weeks ago, he told me to expect these payments from Jenson Computer.'

'And what about those possible payments later on in the year?'

'He said they could be very large. Or they might not happen at all. It all depended on how Project Platform turned out.'

Project Platform was obviously vital to the company. I would have to find out more about it.

'If there are no more Jenson Computer payments after the summer, what happens then?'

Willie rustled through his papers. 'We run out of cash in September.'

'Are you sure?'

'Well, we might run out in August if we're unlucky.'

Three months. It certainly looked precarious to me.

I asked for more numbers – breakdown of sales by customer, debtors outstanding, information on margins, research and development expenditure by product, stock positions, the lot. Willie had all the numbers and they all showed the same thing: every month more cash went out of FairSystems than went into it. I knew that small companies usually have a poor idea of what their true financial position is, and Willie was actually doing quite well. But, as he passed me each set of numbers, he writhed in anguish. He was literally wringing his hands.

'It doesn't look good, does it Willie?' I said.

'Och, no. Once we've spent the Jenson money, then there's not much to rely on.'

'Can we cut R & D any further?'

'I don't think so. You can ask Rachel if you like, but in the last few months we've slowed right down on new projects, apart from this Project Platform, that is. The cash is needed to finish what we're already working on. If we stand still, then we'll quickly lose our revenue.'

He was right. A company like FairSystems was nothing if it stopped developing new products.

I pulled out the balance sheet. 'There are no borrowings. Have you tried all the banks?'

'Oh, yes. All the Scottish banks said no. I've tried half a dozen English banks, and they weren't interested. Nigel Young from Muir Campion is on our board. Muir Campion is one of the oldest Edinburgh merchant banks. He's tried all his contacts and drawn a blank. You see, there's no security and no profits.'

I did see. 'So, when do we start making money?'

Willie looked embarrassed and shrugged.

'Surely this company must make profits some time?' I said.

'Richard said we would make a lot of money next year.'

'And did you believe him? Did he have numbers?'

'No, he didn't have numbers,' said Willie. 'But he seemed

very confident. I like to see numbers as much as the next man, but somehow I believed him.'

I didn't hide my scepticism. Trust me. That is what Richard always said, and that is what people always did, be they Karen and me, or Willie here. But eventually he had to come up with the goods or the bills would not get paid, and the electricity would be switched off.

These spurious Jenson Computer payments that might come in later on in the year were typical. I doubted they would ever materialise, and I wasn't going to put any faith in them. I just hoped we could rely on those payments due in the next three months.

Willie could see what I was thinking. He wrung his hands again.

But we still had till August. When Richard had called me that night, I had suspected that the company had a much more urgent cash-flow problem, something that would hit in days, not months. FairSystems' problems were big, sure enough, but they weren't that immediate.

'Richard called me a few days before he died,' I said to Willie. 'He wanted to talk to me about something urgently. Have you any idea what it might have been?'

Willie thought for a moment and shook his head. 'I can't think of anything. It was nothing he spoke to me about.'

'It wasn't a cash crisis, then?'

'I don't think so. As you see, we still have two hundred thousand in the bank. It's not much, but it'll keep us going for a few months, especially when we get the Jenson payments in.'

'How about trading in FairSystems' shares?'

'Could be,' said Willie. 'He did ask me for information on our shareholder register. But that was three weeks ago.'

That would have been just before Richard had first spoken to Karen and me about his suspicions.

'Nothing since then?'

Willie thought a moment. 'No.'

'OK,' I said. 'Can you show me what you showed Richard?'

'Certainly. But I don't think it will be very helpful.' Willie pulled a file out of a cabinet behind him, opened it up and passed it over to me. 'This is the shareholders' register.'

Some of it was self-explanatory. The major individual share-holders of the company showed up clearly. There was a total of two million shares outstanding. Richard's stake was still shown intact at eight hundred thousand shares or forty per cent of the company. After dividing this stake up, I was the largest shareholder with 23.75 per cent, followed by my father with twenty per cent. The other individual shareholders named were Walter G. Sorenson III with four per cent, Karen Chilcott with 3.75 per cent, Rachel Walker with 3.5 per cent, David Baker with two per cent, and William Duncan with one per cent. There were about five hundred more shareholders, but these were all identified by 'Wagner Phillips nominees', and then a number.

'What are all these?' I asked pointing to the numbers, which went on for ten pages.

Willie explained. 'As you know, we sold the shares to the public on NASDAQ last November,' he began. 'Do you know about NASDAQ?'

I nodded. It was I who had suggested that Richard try NASDAQ when his British stockbroker had shied away from sponsoring a flotation on the London Stock Exchange. NASDAQ specialised in trading the shares of fast-growth com-panies. Microsoft and Genentech had been just two of their success stories. Over the years it had begun to trade foreign shares as well, often of companies that had too short a track record to trade on their own domestic stock exchanges.

'Well, the share registration system works differently in the US to the UK,' Willie continued. 'The original shareholders at flotation show up on the register under their own names. All those who bought stock in the public offering hold it through a nominee account with their broker, which in this case is Wagner Phillips for just about everybody.

'Now, some of these are employees of FairSystems who bought stock during the offering.' Willie pointed to a cluster of holdings with similar numbers. There were about twenty in all;

quite a good take-up, since there were only fifty employees then. 'They all add up to about two per cent.'

'And the others?'

'Those are all Wagner Phillips' customers.'

'How can we find out who they are?'

'We can ask Scott Wagner,' Willie said. 'He's coming up here next week. If you're here, you can see him with me. But somehow I don't think he'll tell us anything. Don't worry, though. If anyone builds up a stake of over five per cent, they have to file with the Securities and Exchange Commission in the US to make the information public. These shares seem to be distributed widely. Look, no one holding is more than two per cent.'

I took his word for it. I wasn't too pleased that so much of the company was owned by five hundred numbers; I would have been a lot happier to see names. Still, if that was the way the system worked, so be it. There was nothing there to suggest to me that anything strange was going on. I doubted it had told Richard much either.

I looked at my watch. It was already half past five, but there was still one important area I wanted to cover.

'Are there any legal issues outstanding? Any problems with patents, anything like that?'

'That's a nightmare,' said Willie, 'especially as far as software goes. We use a very good firm in Edinburgh that checks our patents. Burns Stephens.' That was the firm who had handled Richard's will, I remembered. 'They charge reasonable rates too. They think that the patent on our new lightweight headset is pretty good. But basically we can't rely on patents to do anything more than slow down the competition.'

I shrugged. That must be the same for all computer companies, I thought.

'No other legal problems?'

Willie looked uncomfortable again. I hadn't spent that much time with him, but I could already read him easily.

'Willie?'

He didn't hesitate long. 'There is one possible legal problem, but it looks like it won't come to anything.'

'And what's that?'

'It's an accident in California. A seventeen-year-old boy named Jonathan Bergey was playing with one of our systems all evening. After he'd finished, he got on his motorbike to ride home. He missed a sharp bend, crashed into a tree, and died in hospital a few hours later. This all happened three months ago. His father's lawyer contacted us, claiming that he crashed as a result of being disoriented by the VR machine. It had me worried, but we received a letter from the father himself two weeks later saying he was dropping the claim. It was quite a relief. American litigation can cost millions.'

'I didn't know we did much in entertainment.'

'We don't. This was a trial we were running with Virtual America, an American amusement arcade company. We only have twelve prototypes out there.'

A near miss indeed. 'Are we insured?' I asked.

'I'm working on it,' said Willie. 'It's difficult to get cover, as you can imagine. There are no VR accident statistics for the actuaries to get their teeth into. But I have a broker looking into it. They haven't been able to turn up a single VR-related accident yet, apart from possibly this one in California.'

I shook my head. This business was a minefield. It made trading bonds seem tame indeed.

Before leaving the factory, I dropped in to see Sorenson. He was in Richard's office, talking to David Baker. He beckoned me in.

David passed me at the doorway. 'Interesting day?'

'Very interesting,' I said. 'Thanks for that presentation.'

'No trouble,' he said, and left.

Richard's office was glass encased, and functional, like the others, with a smooth black desk-top and a computer. Like Rachel, Richard had a small screen window. It was turned off. I wondered what he had chosen to display there. The rest of the wall was taken up with photographs from the early days of FairSystems and before. Weird VR rigs, with long metallic arms attached to the headsets, and wires everywhere. In most of the pictures, the user was Richard, but in one or two, Rachel's dark curls pushed out from underneath the bulky helmets.

Sorenson was wearing a short-sleeved shirt, open at the neck, and well-pressed trousers. It wasn't a suit, but he looked tidier and more businesslike than I ever did. Papers were piled neatly in front of him, next to a brown, well-travelled briefcase.

'So, Mark, what do you think?'

'It's an interesting company,' I said. 'Fascinating. It has some very impressive products.'

Sorenson smiled. 'No, Mark. Tell me what you really think. You're a major shareholder in this company, and you don't work here. You're independent. I'd like to know your views.'

He was sincere, and I was flattered. So I told him.

My mind had been working hard all day processing the information thrown at me. It was all a whirl, but a familiar type of whirl. This was much like the trading problems I came up against every day. A lot was at stake. There was a whole array of different questions to consider, some quantifiable and some unknown. And a decision was required.

I knew how to solve problems like this. Divide the problem into a series of factors that would affect the ultimate outcome. Assign the appropriate level of significance to each factor. Consider what the downside was and how likely it was to occur. Quantify the upside and the likelihood of that occurring. Weigh the two against each other, being very careful to identify and then ignore any emotional considerations that might sway the analysis. Take a decision. And then act on it.

This approach had served me well in the past and I fell naturally into it now.

'The first question to consider is the long-term potential of the company,' I began. 'Even allowing for bias from the people here, I believe this truly is enormous. The world virtual reality market will be worth billions of dollars one day, and right now FairSystems is one of the two or three leading companies in the field. So far no large company has really committed itself to the technology, but even if one did, one of the easiest ways of achieving this would be to buy a company like FairSystems.'

103

Sorenson was listening, closely. Encouraged, I went on.

'No one seems to know for sure which applications will really make the most use of virtual reality. But FairSystems is involved across a range of different uses. It'll almost certainly be well placed to take advantage of any opportunities once they emerge, from whichever direction they come. And its customer list is impressive.

'The problem is the short-term. FairSystems has yet to find a customer that will take more than one or two systems at a time. Last year it shipped a hundred systems at forty thousand dollars each. This year it hopes to ship two hundred, but at only twenty-five thousand each. Somewhere, demand will kick up to the point where the company sells thousands, not hundreds of systems, and then the cash will roll in. But that's got to be very soon indeed, or else there won't be enough cash to keep going.'

'So, what do we do?' asked Sorenson.

'It's difficult,' I said. 'In the hands of a company with deep pockets, FairSystems could be a very valuable asset. A rich parent could fund the cash shortfall for however many years it takes before the market really explodes. But, on its own, with access to the stockmarket difficult, and no bank interested, the company is very vulnerable.'

It wasn't really FairSystems' or Richard's fault. I knew that high-technology companies in America often found themselves in this predicament. And some of them went bust. Others were able to gain access to cash through the myriad of venture capital funds in the US, or through NASDAQ. But there was only so much money that Americans would invest in dreams, and, naturally, they preferred their dreams to be located in Silicon Valley rather than Silicon Glen.

'So?' said Sorenson.

Leaving aside emotional considerations, the correct decision wasn't really that hard to see.

'We sell.'

'Hmm,' said Sorenson. His eyes studied me closely, assessing me. 'You certainly have picked up a lot about the company.' He thought for a moment. 'Have you spoken to your father yet?'

'Not yet,' I said. 'I was going to talk to him tonight.'

'OK. You do that. And I'll have a word with him myself. Then we can discuss it again tomorrow.'

As I drove back to Kirkhaven, I mulled over the day at FairSystems. The more I thought about it, the more I felt that the analysis I had given Sorenson was the correct one.

Leaving aside emotional considerations. As a trader, I had trained myself always to leave emotion out of my decision-making. It was one of the most basic rules. It was what I had accused Richard of not doing before he died.

But I was not looking forward to calling my father.

The sky cleared as I approached Kirkhaven along the road that skirted the sea a mile inland. Two white clusters of houses, St Monans and Pittenweem, hugged the coastline to my right, beyond a lush green patchwork of fields, grazed by black and white Friesians. I could see why Richard had lived here. The factory in Glenrothes was modern and functional, but grey and claustrophobic. This, though, this was a place to think, to let ideas roam far and wide, to make those seemingly accidental connections that can only come from a mind that is both relaxed and awake. The fresh salt breeze, and the weak but persistent sunshine provided the clear air and clear light that good ideas need to grow and develop.

I rang my father as soon as I got in. It was the first time I had spoken to him since telling him about Richard's death.

'How are you, Mark?' he asked. It might have been my imagination, but his voice seemed to have aged again over the last week.

His question was a genuine one. But I couldn't bring myself to tell him how I really was. The day of intense concentration in Glenrothes had pushed the pain and anger and guilt to one side for a few hours. Now it came flooding back.

So I gave the easy answer. 'Fine,' I said. 'How are you?'

There was silence for a moment. 'I'm finding it very . . . difficult, Mark,' he said.

I felt an urge to talk to him, to commiserate, to discuss

Richard. But the barriers were too big, and I didn't have the energy to cross them. I didn't even know whether I wanted to cross them.

I brought the conversation back to the reason I had called. I wanted to get it over with. 'I saw FairSystems today, Dad.'

He caught the seriousness of my tone. 'Yes?'

'It's not good. The company's going to go bust, if not during the summer, then probably in the autumn.'

'That can't be right. What about all that technology? All those new products?'

'It'll never survive long enough to make the most of them. There's very little cash left. And it's losing money every month.'

'I don't believe it. There's got to be a way.'

'There is, Dad. Sell.'

'No, Mark, we can't.' My father's voice was stronger now. Firm. 'FairSystems was the most important thing in the world to Richard. In a way, the only important thing. We have to see it through for him. He refused to sell out only a few weeks ago. We can't cash in now, just because he happens to have died. We have to hang on for another year or two, to give him a chance to realise his goal.'

He sounded like a schoolteacher disciplining a naughty schoolchild. I didn't like it. I had spent the day trying to get to grips with a very complex situation, and I thought I had done pretty well. I wanted the same from him: a cool discussion of the facts, followed by a sensible decision. I clenched my teeth, controlling my anger.

'If we don't sell, there will be nothing left. I know the shares are down to four and a half dollars, but if we market the company properly we can probably get more for it than that. Maybe eight. That's over three million dollars for your stake, Dad.'

That shut him up, but only for a moment. 'It might make financial sense. But if Richard didn't want us to sell, I'm not going to, and neither should you.'

I bit my lip. I didn't like being told what I should do by my father. He had lost the right to do that ten years before.

'What does Walter think?' he asked.

'I don't know. I told him my views. He said he'd talk to you later on tonight. Then we'll discuss it tomorrow. He's quite keen that we reach agreement, since we're the two largest shareholders.'

'All right. I trust his judgement. I'll talk to him tonight. But I'm not going to change my mind.'

'OK. Well, bye, Dad.' I put the phone down.

I was angry. It clearly made sense to sell. And I didn't like my father telling me what to think.

I stood up, took a few deep breaths, and looked out of the sitting room window at the burn running down to the sea.

Of course, what was really making me angry was that my father was right. The defences I had put up against those 'emotional considerations' crumbled and they came flooding in. My father and Rachel wanted to hold on to the company. I didn't owe my father or Rachel Walker anything, but I couldn't hide from the reason they didn't want to sell.

Richard.

The guilt returned. Our row before he died. My refusal to come to his aid when he had asked for it. Dad was right, FairSystems was all that was left of Richard, and I was proposing to get rid of it.

But if I didn't, it would go bust, and then there would be nothing left anyway. And that would be stupid.

I rang Karen. It was good to hear her voice. I told her about FairSystems and the mess it was in. I told her about my decision to sell, and my argument with my father. It helped to talk about it.

'So, what do you think?' I asked her.

'I don't know,' she said. 'You're right, it is difficult. I mean, for Richard's sake, it would be nice to keep the company, but if there isn't going to be a company, then there isn't much point.'

'I'm glad to hear some common sense for once,' I said, relieved.

'But I don't think you can just ignore your feelings for Richard,' Karen went on. 'You can try, but it won't work. You have to do what you think is right. No one else can tell you what to do; not me, not your father, not Sorenson. Trust your own judgement. I do.'

'Thanks. That helps.' And it did.

'How are you coping?'

'OK.'

'Is it difficult being up there?'

'Yes, it is. In a way, it feels good to be surrounded by all Richard's things. By his life. But it makes his death more real. Unavoidable.'

'Do you think it's a good idea to stay in his house?'

'Yes, I do. I've got to face up to the fact that he's gone. I can't hide from it.'

'I suppose you're right,' she said. 'Be strong. I miss you.'

'I miss you too.'

I put the phone down, and looked around me. What I had told Karen was true: it was good to be in Richard's house. It hurt, but it was the right place to be.

I was slumped in an armchair in Richard's sitting room. The room was basically the way I had found it. The copy of *Hard Drive* was still lying face down on the sofa, Bill Gates' teenage face staring petulantly up to the ceiling through huge glasses. I still felt awkward in Richard's house. I had tried not to disturb anything; I kept all my stuff in the spare room upstairs.

An old writing-desk stood next to the window. He had inherited it from our mother. I had no idea where she had got it, probably from a second-hand furniture shop in Oxford. It hadn't quite crossed the line from being simply old and beaten-up to being an antique. A few more years.

Curious, I began to look through the drawers. I discovered all kinds of little things that I wanted to dawdle over. Not much in themselves, just reminders of him. Letters from an old girl-friend, his thesis from Edinburgh, an exercise book from prep school.

I came across an instruction leaflet for the MITS Altair 8800 microcomputer. It was covered with notes in Richard's scrawny handwriting. Dad had brought the computer over from

America in kit form, and Richard had spent hours in his bedroom putting it together. At that stage in his life, it all had had to be done in secret. Richard was a cool kid, and he couldn't let his street credibility be damaged by too close an association with computers. At fifteen, Richard was good-looking and witty, and was becoming very popular with the local schoolgirls. He made the most of it. I smiled when I remembered the look he gave me when I offered to show one of them his new computer. His popularity never quite recovered.

I suddenly felt very tired. I sank back into the armchair, holding the leaflet loosely in my hand. I stared ahead, my eyes unfocused.

Why had Richard died? What was the point of his life? Why had he put all that effort into FairSystems for it only to go bust months later? Why had it fallen to me to sort out this situation?

I had no answers. There was no point in answering these sorts of questions. I didn't have the emotional energy to do more than ask them.

I needed to get out. I changed into jeans and a jersey, grabbed a ten-pound note, and set off for the pub.

The Inch Tavern was only a hundred yards or so farther up the burn. It was warm and cosy. It had low beams, brass knick-knacks, an open fire, and a welcoming atmosphere. There were about half a dozen men and one woman spread along the bar, indulging in a general conversation about someone called Archie. Whoever he was, he roused strong passions.

The barman was a big man with a beard and a heavy check shirt over a light jersey. That seemed to be a bit of a uniform in Kirkhaven: two men at the bar wore a similar outfit, with thick warm trousers. I assumed they were fishermen. All of them, including the barman, had big round shoulders. Strong men.

'What can I get you, Mr Fairfax?' the barman asked.

For a moment I was surprised he knew my name. But, of course, the whole of Kirkhaven must have known my name. Richard's murder would have been discussed and dissected at this bar for hours on end.

'A pint of IPA,' I said.

109

The barman pulled my pint, I paid and sat down at a small table a few feet from the bar. I took a long gulp.

The conversation had dropped off for a minute to allow everyone to get a good look at me, but it soon started again. As I sipped my beer, and sat back in the warm tavern listening to the unfamiliar rumble of Fife voices chatting about this and that, the depression I had been feeling began to wear off. I, too, began to relax. I tried to let my mind wander.

I thought about Karen. I remembered the first holiday we had taken together, cross-country skiing in Norway the year before. Karen was an athletic skier, and fit. I could see her now, pushing her long legs rhythmically through the glistening snow ahead of me. I thought about her naked in the firelight of a small cabin we had stayed in one night. My heart beat faster as I remembered the passionate intensity of our lovemaking. We had both returned from that holiday exhausted. I smiled at the bubbles in my beer.

I drank down the last of my pint, and went to the bar to get another one.

'I'm very sorry about your brother,' said the barman, as he refilled my glass. 'He was a good man.'

'He was,' I said.

The barman wiped the beer from his hand with a towel and extended it. He had a friendly smile. 'The name's Jim Robertson.'

I shook it. 'Mark Fairfax,' I said.

I lingered at the bar, taking a sip from my pint. 'Did you know Richard well?'

'Just a little,' said Jim. 'He used to come in here for a pint and a drop of whisky once in a while. We would chat occasionally. He had a nice way with him. He used to sit over there and read magazines. You know, science magazines.' He indicated a small table and chair by the window on the far side of the bar. 'For a boffin, though, he was quite human. In fact, he came in here the night before he died.'

'Really?'

'Aye. He was in here with a Chinese man.'

110

'Chinese?'

'Chinese or Japanese. I didnae see them myself. But Annie did.' He nodded to the group at the bar.

The conversation at the bar had died down as everyone listened to Jim and me. The one woman in the room, a middle-aged lady with dyed blonde hair, put down her white wine and interrupted. 'Aye, I did. He was only here a couple of minutes. He came in, saw this Japanese man sitting there, and walked right up to him. He was angry.'

'Could you hear what he said?'

'No, I couldnae hear anything clearly. But he was upset about something. The wee Japanese man looked surprised. And then he was gone. The Japanese man drank up and left soon after him. He looked bothered about something.'

'Had you seen him before?' I asked, interested.

'No, never been in here before. At least not while I've been here.' Looking at her puffy face, and the easy way with which she took her place at the bar, I could imagine that that covered much of the time that the pub was open.

'Can you describe him?'

'Not really. He was youngish. Not a kid, a young man. Apart from that, he looked, well, Japanese. Or Chinese, maybe.'

'What was he wearing? A suit?'

'No. It was casual, but smart, ye ken. A blue jersey and smart trousers. The sort of thing tourists wear round here to play golf.'

'Have you told the police this?'

She let out a tipsy laugh, which was taken up by the rest of them round the bar. Jim explained. 'The polis have been very thorough. I think everyone over the age of two has been interrogated. They asked us all about him.'

'Have they identified him?'

'Not that I know of. But why don't you ask him?' He nodded over to the door where a small neat man with a moustache was walking in. It was Sergeant Cochrane. He wore a blue anorak, and red v-necked sweater, every inch an off-duty policeman.

Cochrane gave me a smile of genuine friendliness. 'So, you've found your way in here, have you? Well, I pity you. A pint of Special, please Jim. Can I get you another?'

'I'm all right with this one, thanks,' I said. 'They've just been telling me about the Japanese man they saw in here the night before Richard was killed.'

Cochrane laughed. 'We've got the sharpest criminal investigation brains in the country right here, round this bar. I'm surprised we haven't had the murderer banged to rights already.'

'How's the investigation going?' I asked.

'It's very difficult for me to say,' he answered. 'Superintendent Donaldson likes to keep things close to his chest.'

'I can believe that. I almost thought I was a suspect myself this morning.'

'Everyone is in Donaldson's mind,' said Cochrane. 'But that's no bad thing in a murder investigation.'

'I suppose you're right. I bet it's kept you busy.'

'It has that. We've spent days interviewing almost everyone in Kirkhaven.'

'Any answers?'

'No one saw anything here. It was raining hard, so people were indoors and no one was looking outside much.' Cochrane took a sip of beer. 'One thing I'm sure of, the murderer wasn't anyone from around here. I know what goes on in my patch, and I'd soon find out if anyone local was involved.'

'Have they identified the man Richard was talking to in here?'

'Sort of. They had a Japanese man staying at the Robbers' Arms that night. Hiro Suzuki. But that's the Japanese equivalent of John Smith. And he didn't leave any address.'

'So you're a bit stuck, then?'

'I don't know about that,' said Cochrane. 'Donaldson still has lots of questions to ask. We can carry on until something turns up. He's very patient, and he has a good track record.'

'So he'll find the killer?'

'I didn't say that, laddie. I didn't say that at all.'

9

I was walking along the stretch of sand beneath Inch Lodge. An empty bottle rolled against the shore, buffeted by the gentle waves. I ran towards it. There was a message inside. It was in Richard's handwriting, but it was impossible to read. It was smudged, and water droplets on the inside of the bottle made the message almost legible, but not quite. I knew the message was important, but try as I might, I couldn't make it out.

Suddenly the wind got up, and the waves became bigger, crashing loudly against the shore. I stretched to seize the bottle, but it was carried out of reach of my fingers by the agitated sea. If only I could read that damn message!

I woke up. I propped myself up on my elbow, and looked around the tiny room trying to work out where I was.

Two things hit me at once. I was in Richard's house, and the noise I could hear wasn't the sea.

I leapt out of bed and over to the window. The noise was coming from the boathouse just below. I could see smoke in the cold night air. And I could just catch a glimpse of dancing orange.

I grabbed my dressing-gown and ran downstairs. I picked up the phone and dialled 999. Then I ran outside to look. The fire had definitely taken hold at one end of the boathouse. I thought

113

about fetching buckets and trying to put it out, but it looked to me as though it was already too late.

Could I save anything? In my mind I ran through what was in there. I had no idea how valuable the jumble of equipment was, or how easily it could be replicated. Then I remembered Rachel asking me about Richard's computer. The information on that was definitely worth saving.

The fire was still at one end of the boathouse. There was a door at the side. Richard's computer was opposite. It shouldn't take me long.

I grabbed the key from the hallway, and ran to the door of the boathouse. The flames were clearly visible now, and were beginning to move along the roof. I unlocked the door. It was dark inside. A jumble of metal and plastic objects were illuminated by the flames. It was hot. I smelled burning wood, and something else pungent.

Petrol. Christ, what was petrol doing in there? If that ignited the whole building would go up.

I thought about stepping back outside. But I could see Richard's computer silhouetted against the window. It was only two strides away.

I took them, swept the screen off the top of the computer, and gave the machine a good yank. One cable popped out, but another attached it to something immobile.

Damn!

The flames were licking along the roof. They had almost reached the rafters above me, although the floor was clear. Suddenly smoke was everywhere, shrouding the computer and the doorway. I coughed but I could still breathe. I stood rooted to the spot for a second, debating whether to run.

It would only take five seconds to free the cabling. God knows how much time had been put into developing what was on that hard disk. With Richard gone, it was probably irreplaceable.

I felt behind the computer for the cable. I pulled. It didn't come out. I felt for screws. If it was screwed in I would never get it undone in time.

No screws, just a wire clip. I knew how they worked, I had one on my machine at Harrison Brothers. I fumbled in the dark and smoke, trying to get a good purchase with both fingers.

This was taking much too long. Click! One side out. Click! The other side out. I picked the machine up off the desk and ran for the door. I tripped over something hard and metallic, and fell, still clasping the computer to my chest.

There was a terrific whoosh, as though a hurricane had just been let into the boathouse. Flames rushed along the length of the roof. The whole structure was on fire. The heat suddenly became intense, stinging my face and my hands. The sound of the flames turned up from a loud crackle to a roar.

I pulled myself to my feet.

I was only halfway up when I felt a heavy blow to my back. It threw me spread-eagled back on to the floor. The breath was knocked out of me. I gulped for air. Instead my lungs filled with smoke.

I struggled to get up, trying to lift my body and the dead weight on top of it off the floor. It was like doing your fortieth press-up, when the thirty-ninth was absolutely and definitely the last you had strength for.

I couldn't do it. I gulped and somehow swallowed air not smoke. My back hurt like hell. The heat was searing, tearing at the exposed skin of my face and hands.

I was only going to live a few more seconds.

I threw my body about on the floor, wriggling and writhing, kicking, trying anything to get myself out from under the beam.

Suddenly, miraculously, I felt the weight on my back ease off just a little. I heard a voice shout, 'Get out will ye!'

I didn't need to be told. I started a coughing spasm that seemed to have no end, and my vision was going black around the edges, but I pumped my legs until I had wriggled out from beneath the beam, somehow got to my feet, and grabbing the computer, threw myself through the open door. Strong hands picked me up and pulled me away from the heat and noise and smell.

I gasped, and felt the cold sweet air work its way into my

lungs. I was laid down on my back, my chest heaving in front of me, my body overwhelmed by the heat, pain, grime and the large doses of adrenalin that were pumping round it.

Jim Robertson's face loomed above me. His beard was black, his hair singed, his face covered in soot and sweat.

'Is he all right?' he asked.

'Aye, he'll live,' said a voice.

I lay my head back on the grass, closed my eyes, and let shock do its work.

The next few hours were a jumble. Fire-engines came, and an ambulance. I was taken to the casualty department of a hospital, and soon found myself in a crisp clean bed. I fell asleep immediately.

I awoke mid-morning, feeling very tired and stiff, but still in one piece. My left hand was bandaged, and it stung. A burn. There were no other bandages on me. Nurses clucked around me, and brought me some tea and toast. I lay there for an hour or so, my strength seeping back. I tried to get out of bed, but I was told to wait until a doctor had seen me.

Finally, she came. She looked a couple of years younger than I. She was busy and tired, but friendly.

'Well, Mr Fairfax, I hear you had a lucky escape,' she said, looking at my chart. 'You should be fine. The burn on your hand should heal in the next few days, and I don't think there is any serious damage to your back. If it gives you any trouble, just go and see your GP. You can leave when you're ready. There's a woman waiting to meet you.'

For a moment I thought that Karen might somehow have heard about what had happened, and made it up to Scotland to see me. I was disappointed when I saw Rachel pacing up and down in the waiting area.

'How are you?' she asked.

'OK, I suppose. A bit shaken.'

'I'm glad you rescued the computer. Thanks.'

She gave me a half-smile. Risking my life for a computer had

116

put me one notch up in her estimation. She had clearly thought I didn't have it in me.

Personally, I couldn't believe how stupid I had been.

'Did you recover all the information?' I asked.

'Ah ha,' she said. 'It's all there. Eight hundred megabytes' worth. If we had lost that, it would have set us back months.'

'Wasn't it backed up?'

'Sure it was. Richard would have backed it up every night. But on to a tape-streamer that he kept beside the machine. That burned in the fire.'

Somehow it didn't surprise me that FairSystems had no proper system for keeping vital information safe.

I squeezed into her car, a bright yellow Citroën 2CV. Rachel drove me all the way to Inch Lodge. There was a group of police vehicles parked outside the house. We walked round to look at the boathouse. The brick walls were still standing, although the whitewash was heavily streaked with black. The roof had disappeared, apart from one charred beam pointing upwards. A police cordon was set up around the building and half a dozen men were picking through the remains, inch by inch.

'Mr Fairfax?' I heard my name shouted and turned round. There was Kerr, followed by Sergeant Cochrane. 'Can we have a word?'

'Yes, fine. But can I look at the damage, first?' I asked.

'Certainly,' said Kerr. 'Just make sure you don't touch anything.'

We went inside the shell of the small building. Everything was black and wet. The plastic casings of the electronic equipment had melted and twisted. There was paper ash everywhere. Some things had survived, especially at the end furthest from where the fire had started. Some of the files strewn all over the floor were charred but still legible in places. A shelf of books seemed still to be intact. The smell of burned wood and plastic was everywhere.

I sighed. Another part of Richard's life destroyed. I gestured to Kerr and Cochrane to walk with me to the house. Rachel followed us.

'Tea?' I asked.

'You look as though you need something a bit stronger,' said Kerr.

He was right. I found a bottle of Richard's whisky, and poured myself a glass.

'Want some?' I asked Kerr.

'Just a wee one.'

Cochrane shook his head.

The whisky felt good. I was shaken and tired, but I wanted to know what had happened.

'Well, it was definitely arson,' said Kerr, sipping his drink. My eyes rested on his red nose, criss-crossed with flecks of blue. 'But so far we haven't found anyone who saw anything. The fire started around three o'clock. Everyone was tucked up in bed. It would have been easy for someone to creep up to the house in the shadows of the rocks along the shore. The tide's been up since then. No footprints.'

'And everything was destroyed in the fire?'

'Not quite.'

He held up an orange folder. It was wet, and black at the edges. But the papers inside were clearly legible. The title of the folder was in smudged black felt-tip pen. I could just make it out.

BOWL.

'Look at the top sheet,' said Kerr.

I did.

27 March

Richard,

VR kills people. Some poor fucker in America wrapped himself round a tree after using one of your machines.
You knew about it, but you didn't tell anyone. You shut the kid's father up.

Well, here's the evidence of the accident. And, unless

you undertake to keep all VR machines away from the public on a permanent basis, we will tell everybody about it.

You have one week to decide.

Doogie.

Attached to the note was a copy of the letter from the Bergeys' lawyer. I passed the two sheets of paper to Rachel.

'Jesus!' she said.

'Interesting, isn't it?' said Kerr. 'Did you know about this accident?'

I explained what Willie had told me about the letter from the Bergeys' lawyer promising to sue FairSystems, and the later letter withdrawing the threat.

'So, this looks like blackmail,' said Kerr.

'It does.'

'Have you heard from Doogie Fisher since Richard died?'

'No, I haven't. In fact, I know nothing at all about him apart from what you and Superintendent Donaldson told me.'

Kerr looked at Rachel. 'Did you know about this?'

She shook her head, still staring at the letter. 'No, Richard never mentioned it. But I'm not at all surprised Doogie would do something like this.'

'Neither am I,' said Kerr taking the folder back. 'We've already had words with Doogie Fisher. It looks like another wee chat is in order.'

'Did you find anything else in the boathouse?'

'Not yet. Most of the papers have been destroyed, but it's amazing what documents we can recover these days.' He scowled. 'We shouldn't have missed this first time round. It was in among a wad of technical stuff. We'll go through every scrap of paper this time, don't worry.'

I thought for a moment. I knew very little about Doogie Fisher, or BOWL, but I wasn't too keen on him publishing details of the motorcycle accident. It wouldn't do FairSystems'

119

reputation any good at all. Indeed, it would be bad for the whole virtual reality industry.

'Can you go easy on this man Doogie?' I asked. 'At least until I've had a chance to talk to him. I wouldn't like him to publish this letter.'

'No way, pal,' said Kerr. 'We've got a murder investigation under way here. I won't let some petty blackmail slow it down. I'm going to have a word with our friend Doogie right now. And don't try and talk to him first.' He looked at me sternly.

'Do you think this might represent some sort of motive for Richard's murder?' I asked.

'It's difficult to see how, directly,' said Kerr. 'But it's clear that your brother and this Doogie were pursuing some sort of vendetta. They could have met at the boathouse to discuss this note, and had an argument that got out of control. Who knows? But I'm going to find out.'

With that, he left, leaving Cochrane to join the group picking through the charred shell of the boathouse.

As I shut the door on them, I turned to Rachel. She was sitting at the kitchen table, thinking.

With all that was going on at FairSystems, I hadn't had time to ask her about BOWL. Suddenly, I was very interested in it.

'So, tell me about Doogie Fisher,' I said, sitting down opposite her.

She stirred, and her eyes focused on me. 'Doogie used to work at FairSystems,' she began. 'I first met him when I was at Edinburgh University. He was with Richard and me in the Department of Artificial Intelligence. He was brilliant. Obsessive. He would work flat out on a problem for weeks on end until he solved it.

'Then he kind of dropped out. He became a full-time political activist. He was involved in all the demos, against the poll tax, against the BNP, or just against the police. When the press talked about agitators from outside an area coming in to stir up trouble, Doogie, as often as not, was one of them. As you can imagine, the university wasn't too impressed.'

'Did this happen suddenly?'

'Oh, no. He'd been a member of the Socialist Workers Party since school. His father was a steel worker at Ravenscraig until he lost his job after an accident. Doogie was convinced it was the company's fault. He broke the legs of the manager he thought was responsible. He did two years for that. He's a bitter man. He hates the way the country is run. He thinks the Tories are out to shaft the workers and the unemployed for the benefit of the English middle class.

'Then, about four years ago, Richard tempted him to join us at FairSystems. He said yes.'

'Why would Richard have done that?'

'Doogie was special, and Richard recognised that. There are very few people in the country with Doogie's intelligence, and his understanding of VR. We needed him. And it turned out very well at first. A disrespect for authority is healthy in programming, and Doogie had lots of that. He was also hard-working, he had a real passion for what he was doing. He threw everything into VR; he would usually work a seven-day week.'

'Just like you,' I interrupted.

Rachel smiled. 'Even worse than me. He became interested in the psychology and philosophy of virtual reality; what it really means to spend long periods of time in a virtual world. And I think some of his conclusions disturbed him. I remember him saying that VR would just become another way for the Establishment to manipulate the masses. Here is a new technology that he believes in, and suddenly it turns out to be just another means of social control. When he originally joined Richard, FairSystems was no more than a small team working on a scientific problem. He began to realise that if it all worked out well, FairSystems would become a large profitable company, just like those that he had always hated. It depressed him. That's when he joined BOWL, the Brave Old World League. Have you heard of it?'

'The police mentioned it. It's a strange name, isn't it?'

'It's from Aldous Huxley's *Brave New World*. In the book, the government controls the proles through the "feelies", a kind of virtual reality.'

121

I could vaguely remember reading the book with its warped view of Utopia. 'And BOWL thinks VR could be used in that way today?'

'That's it.'

'It's a bit extreme, isn't it?'

'A wee bit,' Rachel admitted. 'But for a while now, some quite respected academics have been worried about the effects that modern technology is having on society. You know – children spending their lives playing computer games, sex and violence on TV, that kind of thing. I think BOWL see themselves as anticipating the effects of future technology on all of us.'

'And Doogie joined this mob?'

'Ah ha. And he did it in secret. He passed information to them about what we were working on at FairSystems. Doogie was never very stable emotionally, he was working very hard, and he seemed more and more unbalanced. Some of his work became unreliable. I don't know whether he made mistakes on purpose, or whether he was just falling apart.

'Richard was sympathetic at first, and tried to ease the pressure on him. They had known each other for a long time. But then he discovered that Doogie was passing on confidential information to BOWL. He went apeshit. I've never seen him so angry. You know how patient and controlled he normally was. I suppose he didn't like the betrayal. Anyway, he and Doogie had a huge row, Doogie walked out, and they were bitter enemies from then on.'

'When was all this?'

'Oh, about a year ago.'

'And what's Doogie been doing since then?'

'He's put everything into BOWL. He's become obsessed with the evils of virtual reality, and he picks on FairSystems in particular. Over the last few months, he's led a radical wing of BOWL to more violent forms of protest. We were sent letter bombs. So were a couple of other VR companies. We never proved it was Doogie, but both we and the police knew it was him. He also tried to crack our computer system.'

'Is he dangerous?' I asked. 'I mean, would he do something really violent?'

'You never know with Doogie. I used to like him. He believed in something, you know. But, yes, I think he could.'

'Do you think he might have killed Richard?'

'I don't know,' said Rachel, shaking her head. 'Maybe. He certainly hated him.'

I pondered that for a moment.

'What about that note?'

'Well, it must be blackmail. But he was wasting his time. Richard would never have given in to it.'

I was sure she was right. But there was still something I didn't understand about the note. 'How do you think Doogie got a copy of the letter in the first place? It should have been safe in Willie's files.'

Rachel frowned. 'I don't know. I know he's got hold of sensitive information from FairSystems before, but I thought he did that by breaking into our computers remotely. You know, over the telephone wires. We've tightened our computer security as a result, and I would hope he can no longer get in. Besides, this letter would only have been in hard-copy form, there would be no reason for it to be stored in our computer system. No, either someone gave it to him, or he found some way of physically breaking into the factory.'

'Well, let's talk to him.'

'Doogie?'

'Yes. Do you know where he lives?'

'In a flat in Edinburgh.'

'Good. Let's go and see him tomorrow morning.'

Rachel drove me into Glenrothes that afternoon. I still felt weak from the shock of the fire, and my back ached like hell. But I had promised to see Sorenson, so see him I would.

He was in Richard's office. He offered me a chair, and asked Susan, Richard's secretary, to bring us a cup of tea.

'I heard about the fire,' Sorenson said. 'I also heard you almost got yourself killed. How's the hand?'

'It hurts,' I said. 'But it will heal.'

'Have the police any idea who did it?'

'Maybe. They found a note to Richard from Doogie Fisher. It mentioned the accident in California. He said he would tell the press about it unless FairSystems withdrew VR from the public.'

'Really?' said Sorenson. 'Doogie Fisher was the crazy who used to work here, wasn't he? The guy who joined that bunch of weirdo technology-haters.'

'That's right. Did you know him?'

'No. I became chairman after he had left. But I've heard people around here talk about him. There was that letter bomb that was sent here a few months ago. They never found out who sent it, but Doogie Fisher was everyone's favourite.'

'Well, I think he's Inspector Kerr's favourite for starting the fire.'

'Does that mean they think he might have murdered Richard?'

I sighed. 'I don't know.' I rubbed my eyes with my hands. I was too tired to think that through. Richard's death, Fair-Systems, the fire. They were all a whirl. I needed time to let them settle in my mind.

'You look about all in,' said Sorenson.

I straightened up and smiled feebly. 'I'm OK.'

'Well, I hope they clear it up soon. The sooner the uncertainty ends, the better. I've told David and Rachel to make sure that everyone co-operates with the police on this.'

He slurped his tea. The dainty cup looked out of place in his big hands.

'I spoke to your father last night. I guess you two can't agree on what to do with the company?'

I wrenched my mind back to FairSystems and its future. 'That's right,' I said. 'I want to sell, he wants to keep it.'

'May I make a suggestion?'

I nodded.

'Let's hold off selling the company right now. We still have time. We know we should be able to make it through till September. Who knows, we might get more contracts in the Fall. Apparently, Richard thought there was a chance Jenson Computer might come through with some big orders towards the end of the year. The shares are only at four and a half. Too low to sell. Let's just keep going for a couple of months, stabilise the company, and then see where we are. If nothing else, we'll probably get a better price.'

I looked at him doubtfully.

'Look, we probably will end up selling after all,' he continued reasonably, 'but I think we deserve to give the company a chance as an independent entity.'

I was wavering. Sorenson could see it. 'Of course there is the management issue,' he said. 'Rachel and David don't exactly get on. It doesn't make for the sort of decisive management we need.

'So, I've been thinking. How would you like to be acting managing director? Just for three months. After that, either we sell the company, or we hire someone permanent.'

'Me?' I was stunned. 'I can't do it. FairSystems is a public company. I've never managed any company, let alone a public one.'

'I think you can do it. I was impressed yesterday by your ability to pick up what's happening around here so fast. You're young, you've got initiative, and you can take decisions. Most of the successful small technology companies I've seen are run by men under thirty. A middle-aged professional manager would stop this company dead in its tracks. We need someone who can take risks, and you can.'

'But I know nothing about the technology,' I protested.

'Then find out. Your father says you have a good mathematical brain; as good as Richard's. Use it. Besides, the place is full of people who know the technology.'

It was true, I had excelled at maths at school. But I hadn't wanted to follow my father and elder brother into mathematics and the sciences, so I had concentrated on history instead, to my father's great disappointment.

'What does he think about the idea?'

'Your father? He thinks it's a good one,' said Sorenson. 'I guess he likes the idea of you looking after Richard's company. Seeing it through for him. And he trusts you.'

I thought about Sorenson's offer. It did have some logic to it. But I still had my doubts.

'Let me tell you about another company I was involved with a few years ago,' Sorenson continued. 'Melbourn Technology, a British company based near Cambridge. They made security devices for mobile phones, which prevented eavesdropping on sensitive conversations. The technology was world-class, and the potential market was huge, and growing. But the company was losing money, it had run out of cash, and its venture-capital backers were losing patience. So, they called me in.

'Well, the founder of the company was a highly intelligent fellow, great with the technology, and he wasn't a bad business-man. But he was too cautious, he didn't have the guts to make the big changes required. So I brought in a thirty-year-old I knew from the cellular telephony business in California. He knew nothing about the technology, and he had never run a company before, but he knew the market, and I knew he had what it takes. The venture capitalists raised their eyebrows, but since the company couldn't get any worse, they had nothing more to lose.

'Anyway, this guy opened up a marketing operation in the US, moved manufacturing to Singapore, and within three years had floated the company on NASDAQ at a valuation of a hundred million dollars.' He smiled at me. 'So, you see, it can be done.'

My pulse was racing. There was no doubt that I was excited by the idea of running FairSystems, and Sorenson's support gave me enormous encouragement. But I needed time to think it over. And there was the question of getting time off work.

'Can I think about it?'

'Sure,' said Sorenson. 'But think quickly. Let me know by Friday. There's a board meeting next Monday, and I'd like to be able to confirm you as acting MD there. I'll stay here to mind the store till then.'

10

I parked the BMW in a quiet street in Tollcross, a scruffy residential area of Edinburgh to the south of the castle. The car was standard Harrison Brothers issue, fine amongst the leafy streets of west London, but a mild embarrassment elsewhere. A group of students walked up the road chatting and laughing. I knew the area vaguely. Richard had rented a room round here for a couple of years when he was at the university.

Rachel led me up to a large grey tenement building. We entered the narrow hallway, dodged a bike, and climbed the stairs. Three floors up, we came to a door with 'D. Fisher' printed on a scrap of paper taped underneath a bell. She pressed it.

Doogie opened the door. He was thin, and wiry, the muscles of his bare arms clearly defined. An indecipherable tattoo peaked out from underneath the sleeve of his plain white T-shirt. His light brown hair was cut very short, and his face was lined. Dark brown eyes blazed out of deep sockets, blackened by lack of sleep.

'What the fuck are you doing here?' His voice was loud, clear and Scottish.

'We've just come to say hello,' said Rachel.

The eyes looked me over.

'Who's this guy?' he demanded.

Rachel stepped into the flat. 'This is Mark Fairfax, Richard's brother. He's FairSystems' new MD.'

I was taken aback for a moment by this description of myself. Sorenson must have already told Rachel about his proposal.

'What did you bring him for?' Doogie didn't sound pleased to see me.

'He wants to talk to you.'

'Well, I don't want to talk to him. I've had enough of talking to people. I spent two hours with the police yesterday.'

'I'm here to ask you about the note you sent my brother,' I said.

'Why? You've read it, haven't you?'

'Doogie, I know you're a member of BOWL. And I know you have strong views on virtual reality. I've come here to find out what they are.'

Doogie looked me up and down suspiciously.

'So, will you talk to me?'

Doogie hesitated a moment longer. Then he nodded. He could see I was serious. 'OK. Sit down.' He pointed to an old brown sofa. The flat was basic and spartan. Cheap, soulless furniture. The walls were adorned with posters, 'Stop the Poll Tax', 'Save Steel in Scotland', 'Fight the Fascists'. A mantelpiece framed a blocked-up fireplace. On it was a single photograph of a dour squat middle-aged man with a stick, and his thin anxious wife. Next to it, a desk faced a blank wall. It was the only part of the room that looked inhabited: a computer, papers, two coffee mugs.

'I thought you didn't approve of those,' I said, nodding towards the machine.

'I don't,' said Doogie. 'But in this war, you need to understand the enemy and have access to his weapons. That box has done good service.'

There was a tapping of paws on lino, and a squat, powerfully muscled, brindled dog strolled into the room. It was some kind of mongrel. A tongue lolled out of its jaws, which seemed to be too big for the rest of its body. It saw me, and trotted over. I kept perfectly still, hoping that Doogie would call it off. The dog sniffed Rachel's ankles and then mine.

'Come here, Hannibal,' growled Doogie. The dog pulled away and leaned against his master's legs, panting softly.

I relaxed a little, but kept an eye on the animal just in case. 'So. Tell me why FairSystems should prevent the public from gaining access to our machines?'

Doogie gave me a quick glance, trying to decide whether my interest was genuine. It was. I wanted to know BOWL's point of view. If only to know what made Doogie tick.

'Virtual reality is dangerous,' he said. 'It's a bit like nuclear fission. It's a major scientific breakthrough made by people who believe it will do good for mankind. But it has the potential to do tremendous harm. We can't uninvent nuclear power, but so far we have just about managed to control it. We need to do a better job of controlling virtual reality.'

'But what's wrong with VR? It doesn't kill people. It has all sorts of positive uses.'

'Doesn't kill people?' snorted Doogie. 'What about that kid on the motorbike?'

'You know what I mean,' I said.

Doogie's eyes flicked at mine again, but he could tell my curiosity was real.

'Granted, today's clunky machines aren't much of a threat, but they don't create a genuine virtual reality. You can easily tell you're wandering around in some cartoon world. But soon virtual reality won't seem much different from real reality. And that will be dangerous for all sorts of reasons.

'People will prefer virtual reality to the real one. You've only got to see the spread of pornography on the Internet to see what will happen. I'm no prude, but we're not talking about art, or freedom of information here. We're talking about psychopaths and perverts raping and torturing for half an hour before bedtime. And once these guys have got all juiced up on virtual reality, they're going to start doing the same sort of thing in the real world.'

'But surely that's only a small minority?'

'You say that, but you'd be surprised how many supposedly normal men will rape and torture given the opportunity, especially if there's no social control to stop them. We've all heard how much damage an ill-disciplined army can do to helpless peasants in wartime. The Gestapo had wives and children. These tendencies have been buried deep in men for centuries. It used to be war that brought them out. Now it will be VR.'

'OK,' I said. 'I agree virtual pornography and violence should be controlled. But what about the rest of us? All those good uses we can make of VR?'

'When you spend much of your life in a virtual world, you're losing the essence of your humanity. You're pulled out of the natural world, the environment, the ecological system, the family, the community, into something totally artificial. Society will break down in a whole range of fundamental ways as we stop being people and become pleasure-consuming appendages to computers.' Doogie was talking fluently, the anger rising in his voice. 'But do you know what pisses me off most?'

'What?'

'Who do you think will choose these virtual worlds? It won't be the ordinary user. Oh, no, it'll be some huge corporation like Microsoft, or News International, or else the government. We'll all be brainwashed. Oh, it'll be subtle, but we'll be told what to want, what to think, how to behave. We'll all live in a Silicon Valley/Hollywood world of sickly emotions and flabby pseudo-liberal sentimentality. That's today. In thirty years' time, some dictator somewhere will be controlling our minds in ways Goebbels could only have dreamed of.' He shuddered. 'God. Imagine if Thatcher could have got into all our heads through VR.'

Doogie's eyes were shining. He spat the word 'Thatcher', loading it with all the contempt that you would expect from someone who had spent the last ten years protesting. Yet, he spoke with intelligence and eloquence. It was clear he had thought through all this, and believed it completely. The frightening thing was that it didn't seem so far-fetched to me either. I was silent for a moment.

130

'OK. I can see you don't like VR. But what's all this about preventing the public from gaining access to it.'

'I'd like to destroy every VR machine in the world and stop any more from being made,' said Doogie. 'But that won't happen. VR is with us now, we can't make it go away completely. But if we can restrict its use to professionals then we can try to prevent it screwing up the people. That's BOWL's first priority.'

'I see. And who is BOWL?'

Doogie paused. 'We're a group of people who can see the future and don't like it.'

'Do you have an organisation? A leader?'

'No. We keep in touch.'

I nodded to the computer. 'With that?'

He shrugged.

'And does BOWL believe in violence to achieve its objectives?'

I stared hard at Doogie as I asked this. He held my gaze. His dark eyes were alight. 'That's up to each individual member to decide,' he said.

'And you? Would you use violence to stop VR?'

Doogie was silent for a moment. He turned towards the couple in the photograph on the mantelpiece. 'Sometimes you have to use violence to protect what's yours. What you believe in.' His voice picked up. 'Governments, industry, big companies, they use people, ordinary people. And when they're no longer any use, they throw them on the scrap heap. They've done that for centuries with our bodies. Now they're going to start fucking with our minds. You bet I'll fight that. I'll fight that in any way I can.'

He paused. When he spoke again, he was more controlled. 'Well, you asked me what I thought about virtual reality. Now you know. Are you going to keep your machines away from the public? I still have that letter, you know.'

His dark eyes bore into me, challenging me, mocking me.

'What was Richard's answer?'

'He didn't give me one.'

'Did he talk to you about it at all?'

'No, I didn't hear a word from him,' Doogie muttered. 'But I'm not surprised.'

'You didn't meet him somewhere to discuss it? Kirkhaven, for instance?'

Doogie looked at me scornfully. 'I've just had to put up with this shit from the police, I'm not going to take it from you, too. I didn't kill him. I didn't start the fire.' He paused, and smiled. It was a nasty, twisted smile. 'But, you know what, I'm glad he's dead. I'm glad his evil little company is going under. He gave me all that shit about being a small group of talented individuals pushing back the borders of science. He just wanted to make a shit-load of money just like everybody else. He didn't care that VR would poison our society, screw up the minds of millions.'

Something snapped. I leapt to my feet. 'Don't you dare talk about my brother like that! He was . . .'

Suddenly there was a deep growl at my legs. The dog was on its feet, hackles raised, gums pulled back from its teeth.

I shut up and stood still.

Doogie smiled. 'Stay, Hannibal!' he commanded. 'FairSystems is finished. You'd better face it. Now why don't you two just piss off back to your factory while it's still standing?'

Rachel stood up carefully and left the room. I followed, keeping my eyes on the dog.

'Can you believe that?' I said as we descended the stairs. 'What he said about Richard? The bastard!'

'He's a very angry man,' said Rachel.

'And I don't like his dog much, either.'

Rachel shuddered. 'It bit Keith once. Just nipped him. He's still got the scar.'

'Yeah, well I'll tell you something. There's no way we're going to give in to his demands. He can do what he likes with that bloody letter!'

I looked over at Rachel, hurrying along next to me. 'What are you smiling at?'

'You sound just like your brother.'

We got in the car, and drove off. 'There's one thing I don't understand,' she said.

'What's that?'

'Why Doogie hasn't published the Bergey letter already. He gave Richard a week. Richard obviously ignored him. So why didn't he publish?'

A good question. I didn't have the answer.

'Do you know what really happened to that boy on the motorbike?' I asked.

'No, I don't. The accident puzzled me. We've put huge efforts into testing our equipment. It really shouldn't cause accidents like that.'

'Have you investigated it?'

'No. Once Bergey withdrew his threat to sue, we let it drop. We didn't want to stir anything up.'

'Shouldn't you check it out?'

Rachel looked at me coolly. 'You're not MD yet.'

'Look, if one of our machines killed Jonathan Bergey, we need to know.'

'OK,' she said, reluctantly. 'I'll check it out.'

We drove on in silence for several minutes as I stop-started through the traffic-lights of Edinburgh's suburbs. As my anger subsided, I began to think over what Doogie had said. 'Some of that stuff about the risks of virtual reality makes sense.'

'Ah ha,' said Rachel, looking out of the window.

'What did Richard think about VR?'

'He thought it was a good thing. Richard was an optimist about human nature. He just saw the ways mankind could benefit. Doogie's a pessimist. To him mankind is bad, and VR will make things worse.'

'And you? What do you think?'

'I suppose I'm somewhere in between,' she said. 'Doogie's right, it can do good and it can do harm. My job as a scientist is to increase the breadth of human knowledge. I can't be responsible for what people do with that knowledge. If there is a problem, it's with society, not VR.' She turned to me. 'I'm going to see my brother next week. Do you want to come?'

I was surprised by the invitation, but I knew there must be a reason for it. 'Yes,' I said. 'Do you mind me asking why?'

She smiled. 'You'll see.'

I took the plane down to London that afternoon, leaving the car at Edinburgh airport. I knew I would be back some time soon.

I was still shaken from seeing Doogie. The raw anger, the scarcely suppressed violence, that bloody dog, all combined to give me a feeling of anxiety.

And what if what he'd said was right?

As the plane lifted off the runway, leaving Kirkhaven and Glenrothes behind, I thought about what was happening to me. I was becoming enmeshed in Richard's life, and it was a process that I didn't want to fight. I was intrigued by the prospect of becoming acting managing director of FairSystems, even if it were only for a few months. It would be difficult – very difficult. But it would be a challenge, a chance to prove myself away from the familiar world of trading. I was flattered by the trust that my father, and especially Sorenson, had put in me. If Sorenson thought I could do it, I could do it.

The more I thought about it, the more sense it seemed to make. I was still convinced that the best thing to do would be to sell the company, but clearly I would have to wait three months before I would be able to persuade my father to go along with that. Without his twenty per cent behind me, a sale could be tricky, if not impossible. In the mean time, as managing director, I would have some control over the fate of the company. If it did go down the pan, at least I would have had the chance to do all I could to save it.

And it would be something I could do for Richard.

'Why not?' said Karen. 'It sounds like a good idea to me. I'm sure you're up to it.'

'I'll try to make it down at weekends,' I said.

'Well, it would be great if you could, but it sounds as though it might be tough to get away. Don't worry about me. I'll survive. It's only three months.'

I suppose I had secretly hoped that Karen would throw herself prostrate on the floor, and beg me not to leave her. Even a little regret at my absence would have been nice. Still, she was being understanding.

'How will you swing it at Harrison?' she asked.

'I don't think it'll be a problem. Bob will have to let me go. He can't afford to lose me. I'm sure Ed's up to it, it may even do him good to trade without me around.' I squeezed her. 'Are you OK? You look tired.' She was pale, and her eyes were puffy.

'Do I? I'm having trouble sleeping.'

'Why's that?'

'It's ever since Richard died. I'm not sure what it is exactly. I think when someone that young dies, it just makes you think of your own mortality.' She touched my hand. 'I'm sorry. That's sort of selfish, isn't it? And I know it must be much worse for you.'

'No, that's OK. It's hard for a lot of people. And I did ask.'

We were silent for a moment.

'Work doesn't help,' she said. 'It's doom and gloom in our area. All politics and no business. But I'm trying to keep my head down and write tickets.'

'I'm sure that's the best thing to do.'

'I hope so. It seems to be working. Bob Forrester has said one or two nice things to me recently.'

'Good. You'll be all right. Don't worry.'

'Yes, I suspect I will. I'm worried about Sally, though.'

'She'll be OK,' I said without conviction.

Karen looked pensive, but then brightened up. 'Oh, one funny thing happened. You remember that guy Peter Tewson from BGL Asset Managers?'

'Yes, I think so. He spoke to you at that party?'

'That's right. Well, he keeps asking me out. He says he's got tickets for the ballet next week. I mean, it's difficult to say no. He is one of my top clients, after all.'

I recalled the studious fund manager I had met briefly that evening. I was relaxed. 'Well, don't say no on my account.'

135

She laughed. 'I won't. But he's *so* boring. And he's virtually a child.'

I frowned. That was a bit extreme. 'He's about my age,' I protested.

Karen looked embarrassed. 'You know what I mean. He looks a lot younger than you.' She was only a bit older than me, but she sometimes acted as if the age difference was ten years. It irritated me, and she knew it.

'Well, I'm just glad it wasn't that other guy. You know, the one who ran BGL's London office. He seemed very taken with you.'

'Ah yes. Henri Bourger. Now, he's much more my type.' She grinned slyly at me.

'He has such impeccable taste in architects,' I said.

'I know. That building was extraordinary, wasn't it?' Karen laughed. 'Their building in New York is just as ugly.'

'Well, if I catch you with any Swiss smoothies while I'm away, you'll be in big trouble.'

She smiled, and took a gulp of her wine. 'Actually, it seems almost as if I'm in big trouble now.'

'What do you mean?'

'Harrison Brothers has been crawling with Scottish policemen. They've been asking lots of questions.'

'Really?'

'Oh yeah. They've been checking up on all my customers to see if any of them own FairSystems stock. Or if I've spoken to them about it.'

'I suppose I'm not surprised. They're checking into everything. You are involved in the US equity markets after all.'

'Well, I don't think any of my guys had even heard of Fair-Systems. It's stupid. I mean, I know next to nothing about the company.'

'I told the police that. Maybe now they'll believe me.'

'Yes, well I hope they stop. It doesn't do my name in the market much good to have people asking those sorts of questions.' She sipped her wine. 'When do you plan to go up to Scotland?'

'On Sunday night. I thought we'd spend the weekend together.'

'Oh Mark, I'm sorry. I promised my mother I would see her again this weekend. It was such a disaster last time, I think I owe it to her.'

'OK,' I said, disappointed. I had been looking forward to spending the time with Karen before beginning my three-month stint in Scotland. But I knew better than to meddle in the relationship between her and her mother.

'Come on,' said Karen, nudging me. 'Let me look at that hand, and then let's go to bed.'

After Karen had carefully changed my bandage, we went to bed and made love. It was a bit of a disappointment, less spontaneous and exciting than usual.

That bothered me. Although Karen had been very supportive since Richard's death, I didn't feel quite so close to her. But, I thought bitterly, that wasn't surprising. Richard's death had affected me in all sorts of ways, both consciously and subconsciously. I shouldn't be surprised if it disrupted my sex life as well as everything else. I just hoped Karen would be understanding about that as well.

'So I'd like to take the next three months off. Unpaid, of course.'

I looked Bob Forrester directly in the eye as I said this. He sat in his sofa in a position of relaxed authority, broad shoulders and a wide chest under an immaculately starched and ironed white Oxford shirt. Although he had spent ten years in London, he was American through and through.

He turned to the agitated Frenchman sitting next to him. 'Etienne?'

'I don't like it,' he said. 'The market is horrible out there. We need all the experienced traders we have. I think it would set a very bad precedent if we allowed Mark to go. Soon we would have no one left.'

Forrester turned to me. 'He has a point, don't you think?'

'I wouldn't ask this lightly,' I said. 'This is important to me.

FairSystems is all that's left of my brother. I owe it to him, and to myself, to see it through.'

Forrester listened politely, but he wasn't impressed. He paused.

I knew what he was asking, and I answered him.

'I've received a lot of calls over the last few months. So far I haven't returned them.'

It wasn't subtle, but then Forrester didn't like subtlety. And it was true. I had turned down Barry's offer to join BGL, but I had his phone number should I ever change my mind. There were others I could call too. In the bond markets, news of success spreads quickly. So, too, does word of failure, but fortunately I had had no cause to experience that first hand. My losses on 'Black Tuesday', as the day Greenspan had hiked rates was now called, were as nothing compared to those sustained elsewhere in the City.

Forrester knew my request came from a position of strength. 'OK, three months, and three months only. But I want you back in your desk by August first, or you never come back. And make sure that kid Ed doesn't make any screw-ups.'

'But Bob . . .' Etienne started.

Forrester stood up and moved back to his desk, the signal for us to leave.

'Thank you,' I said and walked out, leaving Etienne to remonstrate in Forrester's office. I knew it wouldn't do him any good. Bob Forrester took decisions and stuck to them.

I told Ed. He took the news with a mixture of fear and excitement. It would be very good for him. It would give him a chance to trade his own book for a bit. I was confident he wouldn't cock it up. He would err on the side of caution, which was the right side to be when you were starting out.

I called Sorenson to tell him my decision.

'That's great to hear,' he said. 'Can you get up here next Monday?'

'I'll be there.'

'Good, we need you.'

I smiled as I put down the phone. I knew he was just trying to encourage me. But it was working.

I wanted to take the opportunity to try to find out more about the price action in FairSystems shares over the last few months. Richard had thought it was important, and Donaldson was taking it seriously, too. Although Karen had been unable to pick up any gossip in the market, there was one other person I could try.

Steve Schwartz sat only a few desks away from Karen. He was American, with curly hair, a big fat stomach, and a couple of chins. He had traded small-cap stocks for Harrison Brothers in New York before coming over to London to do the same thing with small European companies. Although he had been in London for over a year, he still felt unfamiliar with the quaint European way of dealing in small stocks.

I told him what I wanted, and he was happy to help. He enjoyed the opportunity to get stuck into familiar territory. He looked at a copy of Richard's analysis.

'This is fascinating,' he said. 'I've never seen anyone do anything like this.'

'Does it make sense?'

He thought for a moment. 'I guess so. He's checked the price and volume patterns in FairSystems shares against those of similar companies in their first six months of trading. I think what he's saying is there's a ninety-five per cent chance that something outside normal stockmarket behaviour is affecting his shares.' He studied it for a minute longer. 'Huh. Can I keep this?'

'I'll give you a copy.'

'Good. I'd like to try this out on some of my stocks.'

'But is he right? Is there something odd about the trading in FairSystems' shares?'

'According to this, there is,' Steve said, tapping Richard's papers. 'But let's take a look.'

He tapped a few keys on the Bloomberg computer in front of him, and quickly came up with a complicated graph. He sucked through his teeth.

'Jeez. That's weird.'

'What's weird?' I was used to looking at complicated graphs, but of bonds not equities.

'Here, let me show you.' He pointed to the graph. 'OK, the stock did real well in the first couple of days of trading. Up twenty per cent on good volume from ten dollars to twelve. That was November last year. Then nothing until February.' He pointed to a flat line on the graph, which ran along the twelve-dollar line. 'Well, no activity in a stock this size isn't surprising. In fact, it's the norm.

'Then in February the stock begins to slide, see?' The line did indeed begin to fall, from twelve dollars down to six in April. Then it lurched down a further dollar and a half to four and a half dollars. 'Was there any news to cause this?'

'None at all. Until of course Richard died. That will explain the last fall.'

'No, it's the decline from February to April that's odd. The volume figures look strange. See these figures here,' he pointed to a row of bars under the graph. 'Those volumes are high for such a small stock. With this share price action and only one real broker, you would have expected much smaller volumes. Let me check the prints.'

'The prints?'

'Yeah. Here, this screen shows you the size of each "print", that is each trade. Look, they're nearly all just a few hundred shares, or maybe a couple of thousand. And Wagner Phillips is the broker each time.'

'So what's happening?'

He sat back in his chair and stroked his chin. Deciphering price action was his forte. I waited.

'Well, volumes like this mean either that a big holder is selling out to a lot of small buyers, or that someone is building up a stake, buying from a lot of small sellers. Normally, sales by a big holder cause prices to fall, and steady buying from one source causes prices to rise.'

'So there must be a big seller?' I asked.

'Maybe. Looking at this graph, I would guess we're talking

about twenty to thirty per cent being either bought or sold by one individual investor. Who owns that kind of stake?'

I thought. 'At that time, just Richard. And I know he didn't sell any shares. In any case, all the original shareholders signed undertakings at the time that FairSystems went public not to sell their holdings for two years.'

'So if we don't have a big seller, we must have a big buyer.'

'Will that show on the share register? Don't investors have to file with the Securities and Exchange Commission when they've bought a ten per cent stake?'

'Five per cent,' said Steve. 'Technically you're right, but it's easy to hide, especially if your broker turns a blind eye. There's not much the SEC can do about it.'

'And you think Wagner Phillips would do that?'

Steve snorted. 'It would certainly fit their reputation.'

'So how do you explain the fall in price? Wouldn't that sort of buying drive the price up?'

'It's got to be manipulated,' Steve said. 'Wagner Phillips must have forced the price artificially low for their favoured buyer. They're probably scaring their existing customers into selling.'

'Why would they do that?'

'Depends who the buyer is. A favour made, a favour owed.'

'Are you sure that the fall in price isn't just investors suddenly getting scared that FairSystems might go bust?'

'Should they be?' Steve asked.

'Maybe.'

'But there's been no public information to make them think that?'

'No. The only bad news has been Richard's death, but we're looking at the price movements before then.'

'Well, investors might have suddenly got scared. But they would need some encouragement, probably from Wagner Phillips. And these volumes suggest that someone has been buying a lot of stock. No, I'd be willing to bet that your stock is being manipulated for the benefit of one buyer.'

'So how can we find out who the buyer is?'

'Let me make a couple of calls. I'll let you know if I turn up anything.'

'Thanks, Steve.'

'Oh, and why don't you try the gorgeous Karen Chilcott? She's well plugged in to the American markets. You know her, don't you?'

'Yes, I do,' I said, suppressing a smile.

I wandered over to Karen. She was writing a ticket. More stock sold, more commission earned.

'Fucking asshole!' Jack Tenko slammed down the phone. 'Hey, Karen! You got influence with Forrester. Can't you get him to give us a proper trading limit?'

Karen ignored him.

'C'mon Karen! We know he's got his eye on your ass.' A painful wheezing sound came from his chest. Perhaps it was a laugh.

'Jack,' she smiled sweetly at him, 'if I were Bob Forrester, I wouldn't let you trade more than two packs of Smarties a day. Now, can you check those prices, please?'

I glared at Tenko. He shrugged. 'What's your problem?' he said, turning back to his screen.

Sally, sitting between us, suppressed a giggle.

Karen looked up, and grinned when she saw me. 'God, you'd think he'd get tired of it. Anyway, what are you doing here?'

We usually made a point of avoiding contact with each other at work. 'Steve Schwartz said I should come and talk to you, so here I am.'

I explained Steve's theory. She frowned and shook her head. 'I'm afraid most of that technical analysis is just looking at tea-leaves. The stock went down because the company is in trouble. It's that simple.'

'But how did the investors find out?'

'Who knows? Someone met someone at a conference who passed on some gossip. Markets find out these things. That's why they work.'

'But what about the volume? Steve said that was highly unusual. Richard's analysis showed it was strange.'

'I asked around. No one knew anything. Sorry, Mark.'

'Can you try again?'

She smiled and shrugged. 'OK. I'll give it one more go,' and she picked up the phone.

I went back to my desk, and returned a couple of hours later to find out how they had got on. But neither Steve nor Karen had heard anything strange.

I gave Steve my number at Glenrothes. 'Give me a ring if you hear something, won't you?'

'Sure,' said Steve. 'I'm kinda curious myself. Something smells. I'm sure of it.'

Friday was my last day. I spent it looking at the markets with Ed, checking on my existing positions and considering some new ones. Any positions I put on would have to be solid, long-term trades that would survive the market turbulence I was sure was just round the corner.

I tried out Bondscape to get an overview of the market since the crash of three weeks before. It really was amazing to see the market actually move. What most impressed me was the way that a number of relationships that had been shaken out of line after Greenspan's fateful announcement had slowly worked their way back to their pre-crash levels. The Renault building that I had spotted earlier, for example, was back to the height it had started at. That translated into a million dollars' profit for our desk, by the way. It was good money that I didn't want to risk, so we sold our bonds. We had made back over half the $2.4 million we had dropped on that one day. Bob Forrester still had reservations about Bondscape, but he had to admit it was working well so far.

The ten-year two-year treasury trade still had further to go, so I kept the position on, agreeing a level with Ed where he would take it off. I told him to call me if he was stuck, and, if it was an emergency, to talk to Greg. I was worried about Etienne interfering when I was gone.

Greg was intrigued by the news of my new temporary career,

and wished me luck. He promised he would look after Ed for me.

I strolled over to the water-cooler, and poured myself a cup. Karen was on the phone. She caught my eye, and mouthed 'Good luck'. I took one last look round the trading room, and left in time to pack and catch the last flight up to Edinburgh.

So, I began my career as a managing director of a high-technology company.

And I didn't have a clue what I was doing.

11

It would be an understatement to say I was nervous as I parked the BMW in the car park in front of the factory. This was a first day at work with a difference. I was scared, but in some strange way confident. I was determined to work out what made Fair-Systems tick, and then to make it tick better.

The board meeting was at nine. It was held in the high-tech conference room I had seen earlier. The board consisted of Rachel, David, Willie and the two non-executive directors, Sorenson and Nigel Young. Young was one of Scotland's great and good, a director of the distinguished Edinburgh merchant bank of Muir Campion, and a non-executive director of half a dozen other Scottish companies besides. He was tall and urbane, with only a tiny trace of Scots in his plummy public-school accent. Richard had told me that Young didn't really understand, or approve of 'high-tech', and deferred to Sorenson on everything.

The atmosphere was formal. Everyone was wearing suits, apart from Rachel, who was wearing a black jersey, hanging loosely down over black leggings. Sorenson called the meeting to order, and instantly stamped his authority on proceedings.

'This is the first board meeting we have held since Richard was killed,' he began soberly. 'I know his death has been a shock to every single person in this company, not least the people round this table. I'm not going to pay a formal tribute to him. We all knew him well, and I can't begin to express the sadness we all feel.

'But now we have to look forward. Richard had a vision, and it is left to us to achieve it. We have a difficult few months ahead of us, but if we all pull together, we can make that vision a reality.' He paused to let his words sink in. There was silence round the table.

'Now, to the agenda.'

He swiftly dealt with the minutes and a couple of formal resolutions.

'OK, let's move on to the business. How's our product pipeline coming, Rachel?'

'It's coming on fine. We are on, or ahead of schedule on most of the major projects. The new virtual glasses have been successfully beta-tested by customers. There are still one or two problems, but we can easily sort them out. Our new simulation manager, FairSim 2, should be ready for shipment in July. And FairRender, the graphics system, continues to look very exciting. We still have a couple of bugs in the software for it, but once again, nothing we can't sort out.'

I was interested that she had made no mention of the mysterious Project Platform.

'Very good. So your people are still working hard after Richard's death.'

'I'd say they're working harder,' said Rachel defiantly.

'David?'

'We've had lots of calls from customers asking what's happening now Richard's gone. None of them are taking their business away, they're all willing to give us a chance. I've assured them we can continue to deliver a quality product without Richard.'

'Good.' Sorenson nodded his approval.

'The order book is still building, but until we get the price of our product down, we can't expect any really large orders. Ones and twos, that's all.' He didn't actually look at Rachel when he said this, but the inference was clear. Her fault, not his.

'Well done, David. You're doing a good job in difficult circumstances. By the way, I bumped into Arnie Miller last week. He said your presentation was impressive. I think he has a real interest in virtual reality. That's great work. It's tough for a company our size to get exposure to guys at his level.'

Arnie Miller was chief executive of one of America's big three auto manufacturers. Sorenson was right. It was quite an achievement.

'Willie?'

Willie coughed nervously. 'Er, well, you've all seen the forecasts. Unless some sizeable business comes in from somewhere, we run out of cash in August, or maybe September if we're lucky.'

There was silence. It was bad, but we all knew the situation.

'Well, that's the challenge. Let's all keep looking for new business and new opportunities.' Sorenson raised his hand as David opened his mouth to speak. 'I know you're unhappy about our current prices, David, but you'll have to do the best you can. In this business, you never get the perfect product at the perfect price. The world just doesn't work like that. You're doing a good job guys, just hang in there. September is still four months away. Yes, David?'

David was still eager to say something. 'Shouldn't we consider selling the company?'

Nigel Young spoke for the first time. 'It would seem an apposite choice of action in our present circumstances.'

'Yes, it's a fair point,' said Sorenson. 'I've discussed this with the two major shareholders, Mark here and Dr Fairfax. Our view is that we should allow the company to settle down over the next couple of months. If the situation still looks poor, we'll seek a buyer. I know Dr Fairfax's view, in particular, is that we owe it to Richard to try to keep the company independent.'

'I think we also owe it to Richard to prevent his company from going bust,' said David. 'I respect your point of view, and especially Dr Fairfax's, but if we don't put the company up for sale now we might be too late. It can take six months to find a buyer. I'm sure the last thing Richard would have wanted would be for all the people who worked for him to lose their jobs.'

David made his point well. I was a little disturbed to find that I agreed with him.

'Crap,' said Rachel. She was fiddling with her pen agitatedly. I guessed she wasn't allowed to smoke in board meetings. 'That's crap David, and you know it. Richard didn't want to sell, so we don't sell. Simple, right?'

Nigel Young's nose moved up a few degrees at this exchange. David ignored Rachel's comment.

'Rachel, I don't want that sort of language used at board meetings,' said Sorenson firmly.

'All right,' she said. 'Rubbish, then. But I know no one in the company wants to sell out now. We want to see it through.'

'I think you've made your point, Rachel,' said Sorenson patiently. 'Now, shall we vote on it?'

We all looked at David. He didn't rise to the argument. He knew the decision had been made. He voted against the proposal, but graciously. Nigel Young, of course, voted with Sorenson.

'Thank you,' said Sorenson. 'Now, we have just one more item. I propose that Mark Fairfax be appointed acting managing director of FairSystems plc, and be nominated to the board.'

Willie seconded the proposal. That was the sort of thing he was there for.

'Any comments?' Sorenson asked. I knew that he would have already discussed this with everyone round the table, but I was still nervous.

David Baker leaned forward.

'David?' Sorenson's voice was ostensibly welcoming, inviting comment. But there was a note of warning, too.

'What will be the term of this appointment?' he asked.

'Initially, three months,' Sorenson answered.

'Meaning that the appointment will be extended for another three months after that?'

'No, not at all. At the end of the three months we will either appoint an MD on a permanent basis, or the company will be sold, in which case the purchaser would make his own appointment.'

'I see,' said David. 'And in the event of a permanent appointment being sought, there's no reason why internal candidates would not be considered?'

David was setting out his position quite blatantly, I thought. Still, if you don't ask, you don't get.

'No reason at all.' Sorenson had paused just long enough before making this statement to give it all sorts of ambiguity. 'Any other comments? No? Fine. Let's vote then.'

Under Sorenson's heavy gaze, my appointment was unanimous.

'Welcome, Mark,' he said. I smiled politely. 'Willie will deal with the formalities.'

The meeting broke up.

I cleared my throat. 'Rachel, David, Willie. Can I have a word?'

We waited for Nigel Young and Sorenson to leave.

Young nodded politely to me as he left the room. Sorenson paused. 'Well, I'm off for a round at St Andrews,' he said. He clapped me on the shoulder. 'Good luck, son.'

I needed it.

As soon as they had gone, Rachel lit up. Willie sat attentively, waiting to be told what to do. David showed signs of minor irritation. He was an important man with things to do. My first challenge. Five years older than me, an MBA, years of experience in the computer industry, eighteen months at FairSystems. He should have been running the company, not me. That's what he thought and perhaps he was right.

I smiled. 'As Walter said, I'm only here for three months. I know you're all good at your jobs, and I don't plan to interfere. I believe FairSystems has tremendous potential, and I'm going to fight hard to make sure it survives to make the most of it. I'm sure we all want the same thing.'

I looked round the table. Rachel lounged back in her chair, watching me, and took a drag of her cigarette. David sat

149

upright, impassive. Willie caught my eye, and nodded encouragingly. I was grateful.

'I won't be taking any salary for the next three months. I know we need the cash.' Willie relaxed a little at this. One expensive chief executive on board could have been enough to topple the company over, things were so tight.

'Now, I'd like to spend the first few days getting to know in detail how the place works. So, if possible, I'll spend this morning with Rachel, this afternoon with David, and tomorrow morning with Willie. Can you all manage that?'

They nodded.

'Good. I'll use Richard's old office. If you want me for anything, please come and get me.'

David coughed, and shifted in his chair. 'Actually, I've just moved my own stuff in there. You can use my old office if you like. It would make a good temporary base.'

I suppressed a smile. I had expected this. Frankly, I couldn't have given a toss where my office was. I had even considered setting up shop with the programmers so that I could really get an idea of what was going on. But if I didn't care, others did, especially David. He hadn't wasted any time. He must have moved his stuff in over the weekend.

'I'm sorry to inconvenience you, but for appearances I think it's important that I use Richard's old office, don't you?' I smiled at him, polite and friendly.

He stared at me for a moment, making up his mind whether to make an issue of it. He decided not to. 'OK,' he said, gracious again. 'It will be available tomorrow.'

'Thank you, David. All right, Rachel, shall we go?'

I followed Rachel along the corridor. The all-important first meeting seemed to have gone well, but I was sure David would pose problems in the future.

'I'm pleased you're with us,' said Rachel.

'Yes?' I said surprised.

'Yes. Big Wal said a lot of good things about you. Said you were a bit like your brother. And we need someone to hold back David.'

150

Big Wal. I smiled. Not a bad name for Sorenson. 'But it must be difficult for you to have someone thrust in over your head.'

Rachel laughed. 'Oh, no. The last thing I want to do is manage this place. I want to make VR machines. You can deal with all the crap.' We wandered over to a coffee machine. 'Want some?'

'Please,' I said. 'Black, no sugar.'

She pressed a button and the machine whirred and ground until it dribbled black liquid into two cups.

I thought about the board meeting. Sorenson had clearly dominated it.

'What were those meetings like when Richard was there?' I asked.

'Different,' said Rachel. 'You still got the impression Walter was in charge, but he let Richard do most of the running. I reckon he thinks they need a firmer hand now. And he's probably right.'

'He's impressive,' I said.

'Big Wal?'

'Yes.'

'I suppose so.'

'He told me what he did with Melbourn Technology. How he brought it back from the brink of bankruptcy.'

Rachel snorted.

'Wasn't that true?'

'Oh yes, it's true all right. But didn't he tell you what happened to the poor wee guy who founded it? John Naylor?'

I shook my head.

'He ended up with nothing. With less than nothing; the bank took his house.'

'Sorenson told me that they needed new management.'

'Maybe they did. But explain to me why Sorenson grossed over a million from the deal, and Naylor, the man who invented this wonder-product, ended up a bankrupt?

'Sorenson's good, all right, but he's always looking after number one. If I were you, I'd remember that.'

We entered the large software room and wended our way

through the toiling programmers towards Rachel's office. There was silence, just the faint click of keyboards, every head staring at a computer screen. I glanced across to the electronic window; it showed white sand, and palms, with the sea rolling gently against the beach. I smiled to myself – Greg would have approved. Despite this view, the lack of real windows was disconcerting. The walls were probably a lighter shade of grey than the sky, but it would have been nice to have been able to check it for myself.

Rachel shut the door, and we sat at her little table. 'So, what can I tell you?' she asked.

'I'd like to know more about the applications for our VR system. We don't produce all the programs in-house, do we? Who writes the software?'

'This is where Richard's strategy was truly amazing,' she said. 'We're in touch with dozens of software companies, all experts in their particular fields: auto-design, education, military simulation, or whatever. We provide them with the Fair-Systems world-building software, and the FairSystems hardware, and encourage them to design virtual reality applications. Richard persuaded them that virtual reality was just about to happen, and it was just about to happen using FairSystems technology.

'But with Richard's way of working, they all stay independent. We can't afford to buy them. We don't want to, and they don't want us to.'

'So, how do they get paid?'

'Only partly in cash. Mostly they get access to each other's ideas and equipment. There are tiny firms all over the world looking for new ways to use our technology.' Rachel was getting into her stride. 'For example, most of the work on Bondscape wasn't done by Richard at all, but by a company that specialises in financial software, based in New York.

'Within three months there will be fifteen new VR application packages completed. Within six months there will be forty. Bondscape's one of these. Everyone is just waiting for VR systems to be mass produced at an affordable level, and then the market for all these products will take off.'

'And FairSystems will be right in the middle?'

'That's right,' said Rachel. 'We put it all together. We make a lot of money.'

I was impressed. It sounded like a neat, low-cost way of placing yourself at the centre of the coming virtual reality revolution.

'How do you keep in touch with all these people?'

'E-mail. Here, I'll show you.' She turned to her computer, and flashed up a screen full of messages. 'Everyone communicates this way now. It works well, especially when you're working on a computing problem. You can send computer files to each other as well as text messages. The guys out there will often communicate with one another using e-mail, rather than speech, even though they're in the same room. That way they don't interrupt each other's train of thought.'

I looked at the group of programmers outside Rachel's office, tapping away and thinking. Very odd.

'Is Walter on the system?'

'Oh yes. It's often the only way of getting hold of him. I'll get someone to put you on tomorrow, once you can get into Richard's office.'

'Thanks.' I scanned the messages on Rachel's screen. There was one which began 'What the hell is going . . .'

I asked Rachel to call it up. She did so, reluctantly. It was a message from Matt Gregory of Chips with Everything. It had that day's date at the top.

'What the hell is going on with you guys?' it read. 'Now Richard's gone, who do I talk to? Not that arsehole Baker, in case you were wondering. Are you for sale? Are you still making VR machines? What gives?'

Rachel was watching me closely. I laughed. 'Not shy of saying what he thinks, is he?'

'None of these people are.'

'Maybe I should talk to him,' I said. 'On second thoughts, maybe I should talk to all of them.'

153

'Yeah,' said Rachel. 'It can't hurt.'

So I put together a message that was upbeat but credible. I emphasised that things wouldn't change, and that Rachel would still be around at all times to help anyone out. I said I was proud of my brother's company, and I would do everything I could for it. I knew it was a cynical audience, but I hoped I had pitched it right. Rachel seemed pleased with it, so we sent it out over the network. It was exciting to feel myself in the middle of this community striving towards a common goal. Richard's goal.

'You said all we need is for VR prices to fall. When will that happen?' I asked.

Rachel looked away, avoiding my eyes. 'Och, I don't know. A year. Two years.'

I wondered why her answer was evasive. Perhaps she was embarrassed that despite all Richard's promises, there was still a long way to go. But I thought there was more to it than that. 'What are the obstacles?' I asked.

'There are several,' she said. 'The first is raw computing power. Any virtual reality system uses up a lot of processing power. At the moment we use Silicon Graphics workstations to run our fancier systems. For a mass market, we need to develop a system that will work well on a standard personal computer. To do that we have to work out a very efficient way of doing all the calculations involved. FairSim 1 helps, but we need something more.'

'Like FairRender, the new graphics chip?'

Rachel smiled. 'Quite right. Many of the calculations can be done directly on to the graphics chip, freeing up the PC's CPU.'

'CPU?'

'Central Processing Unit. The chip that usually does all the calculations in the PC. Yes, with FairRender, and FairSim 2, we will be able to speed things up enough to create convincing VR experiences on a standard PC.'

'OK, so we're nearly there. What's the delay?'

'Once you have the technology, you then have to mass-produce it and market it. Chips can be very cheap, but only if you

154

make them in vast quantities. Hundreds of thousands rather than a few hundred. Now, it's a big risk for anyone to tool up a factory to make that many chips when there is no market yet. But until that happens, the prices of the chips will remain high because of the low production run. The same applies to other parts of the system, the headsets and so on. And with high prices, you can't increase demand.'

I thought about what Rachel was saying. 'So, how do we get the market going?'

'I suppose that's for you and David to work out.' I wasn't happy with her answer. There was something she wasn't telling me.

It was mid-afternoon by the time I made it to see David Baker. He was in Richard's office. All Richard's personal effects – photographs, papers and so on – were in two cardboard boxes. David was busy loading his stuff into two large crates, probably the same ones he had unpacked the day before. With Richard's photographs taken down, and the window switched off, the office looked bare indeed.

'I saw the message you put out on e-mail,' David said. 'I thought it caught just the right tone.'

'Thank you.'

'But it might have been a good idea to have talked to me about it first. As you know, customers are my responsibility,' he smiled as he said this.

'I'm sorry,' I said. 'It mostly went to Rachel's contacts. People we're collaborating with on projects, rather than actual customers. I didn't think of asking you.'

'I think it's better if I'm involved in all external communications,' said David. 'It's important for the company to have a consistent image with the outside world. I've done a lot of work on improving other people's perception of us in the VR community, and I'd like to do what I can to build on that. Richard was very supportive of the initiative.' He was still smiling, his voice reasonable.

Although I had avoided corporate politics at Harrison

155

Brothers, I had watched it in action. Many investment bankers are motivated as much by power as by greed. They are also aggressive. I had often thought that it was a good thing that the Harrison Brothers junta found themselves in an investment bank rather than a third-world dictatorship; at least the knives in the back were all metaphorical.

I knew what David was doing. He wanted to slide me gently into what he considered to be my proper place – I was the temporary figurehead, and he was the man who was really going to run the show.

Except that wasn't the way it was going to be.

There was no point in being subtle. This man had been trained at IBM and Harvard Business School. He knew all the political games anyway.

'I know you wanted to be managing director, David. But it didn't happen. I have that role, at least for a few months. So I make the ground rules.'

'Oh yes? And what are they?' There was just a trace of sarcasm in his voice.

I softened my tone. 'You and I need each other, David. I need you, because you're the only commercially adept person in this company. Walter Sorenson thinks a lot of your abilities. I don't want to lose you, especially now.'

'Well, that's nice to know.' The sarcasm was still there.

'You need me, because my father and I control almost half the company. I'm only going to be here for three months, and when I'm gone, the field will be wide open for you.' I stopped short of promising him the position of managing director after I had gone. I needed to find out a lot more about David Baker before I did that. 'So, all you have to do is be patient, and help me. I'll be happy to listen to all the helpful advice that you can give me. I'm sure I'll end up taking most of it. But *I'll* take the necessary decisions. This company is my responsibility, and believe me, I'm going to do my best with it. It's in your interests as well as mine to make sure it survives. And then prospers. So, will you help me?'

David had listened in silence, his fingers propping up his

chin. When I had finished, he waited, considering his choice of words.

At last he spoke. 'Have you ever run a company before?'

'No, I haven't.'

'Have you ever sold a computer? Or any industrial goods?'

'No.'

'Have you ever drawn up budgets, sales forecasts, production schedules?'

'No.'

'How many people have you managed?'

'Look, David,' I said impatiently. 'We both know I have no experience. But I pick up things quickly. I work hard. I have common sense. And I have good people around me who understand these things. One of whom is you.'

He paused again, weighing me up. He was trying to embarrass me, but I was determined he wasn't going to succeed. 'OK. I'll help you,' he said at last. 'But you have to understand that the VR business is a very difficult one. It's not for amateurs. I have a lot of personal capital invested in this company, and I don't want to see it all blown away. I know how to steer this business through the next few months, so you had better listen to what I have to say.'

'I'll listen, David. But, remember, I take the decisions.' We stared at each other. This was not going to be easy. 'Right, then. Tell me about our customers.'

David ran through everything professionally. And it was a professional operation, especially for a small firm like FairSystems. There were some big-name customers: the US military, NASA, DEC, Framatome, Deutsche Telekom, Sears Roebuck, the RAF, the Metropolitan Police, and a scattering of large corporations around the world. But, as Sorenson had pointed out at the board meeting, they only bought a handful of systems each. None seemed about to put in the orders for hundreds of machines that would make FairSystems really take off.

I mentioned this to David.

'You're right. That's the next big challenge. But we have laid a good foundation. I think it's an outstanding achievement for a

157

young company like ours to have put together a customer list like this. Especially with only six salesmen. Once we have the product at a sensible price, we'll sell thousands. You've got to get Rachel and her boys to come up with something that costs less than twenty-five thousand dollars, and then see what we can do.'

It was true, he had done a good job.

'But even with the product at current prices, I'm sure we'll see strong sales growth,' David continued. 'For example, I'm putting together a deal with Onada Industries that should earn us big royalties over the next few years.'

'Who are they?' I asked.

'They're a Japanese electronics company that's just getting into entertainment. They have their eye on catching up with Sega and Nintendo. Now, entertainment is an area in which we're very weak. We developed a system with Virtual America, but that's it. There are only a couple of dozen of our systems out there. A company called Virtuality in Leicester have a stranglehold on the world market at the moment. This is our chance to break it.

'So, I'm negotiating a deal where we work with Onada to help them develop a virtual reality entertainment system of their own that will wipe the floor with Virtuality and Sega.'

'Great,' I said. 'Sounds like a good opportunity. Well done.'

'I hope I can close the deal soon. They'll be here next week to discuss it.' Once David said this, I could see he regretted it.

'Oh good. I look forward to meeting them.'

'Oh, I don't think you need bother.'

'If Onada are about to become our biggest customer, I want to meet them. And I'd like to see documents on the negotiations so far.'

David sat back in his chair.

'You know Richard would have wanted to be involved,' I said. 'All I want to do is follow what's going on. I won't interfere.'

David wasn't happy, but he gave in. 'OK. The meeting is at nine next Monday.'

'Good.' I stood up to go. David stopped me.

'Oh, Mark?'

'Yes.'

David forced a smile. 'I was meaning to ask you. Would you like to come round to dinner on Saturday night? I'm inviting Rachel, and Willie too. I hope you can make it.'

I, too, forced a smile. 'Thank you,' I said, seeing my weekend in London with Karen disappearing. I couldn't refuse David's hospitality, even though I suspected it was politically motivated. I really had to go. 'I'd be delighted to come.'

It was six thirty, and I was tired. But there was one more thing I wanted to do before I went home. I went back upstairs to Software. Everyone was still there. Rachel was talking to Andy, the man-boy I had seen coming out of the Project Platform room. He saw me and hurried off. He had developed dark bags under his eyes, his hair was tousled, and his shirt-tail was hanging out. His mother would not have been pleased.

'Rachel?'

'Yes?' She looked straight at me, defying me to ask some more about Project Platform.

That could wait.

'I want to learn as much as I can about programming and virtual reality,' I said.

'Oh yes?' said Rachel, trying not to smile. It was a difficult thing to ask. But I knew that there were many managers in the computer business, David amongst them, who knew very little about how computers worked and were programmed. I was determined not to be one of them, even if I risked some humiliation at the start.

She looked round the room. 'These people have spent years on software design. It's not something you can pick up over a wet weekend.'

'I know that,' I said. 'But there must be some books I could read. Something that would tell me how you go about writing a program. How you organise the programmers, what's possible, what's impossible, that sort of thing. And anything you have on the background to virtual reality would be very interesting.'

159

Rachel looked at me sceptically. 'Are you serious?'

'Yes. It's important.'

She thought for a moment. She pulled out a couple of books from her bookshelf: *The Art of Computer Programming* by Knuth, and *Virtual Reality Now* by Larry Stevens. 'Start on these. When you've read them, we'll talk.'

It was strange. Since the age of fourteen, if not before, I had steadfastly refused to show any interest in mathematics or computing. That was for 'computer freaks', nerds like my father and brother. Sure, I had learned how to draw up spread-sheets, but that was only because it was an essential tool for trading the markets. But that evening I found reading the books Rachel had given me stimulated parts of my brain I didn't even know I had. I resolved to borrow some software and a computer from Rachel to try out programming for real.

David was true to his word, and I was able to move into Richard's office the next morning. I put his photographs of the prototype VR machines back on the wall, and worked out how to switch on the electronic window. It showed the view of the Firth of Forth from Kirkhaven. The Isle of May, with its two lighthouses, was clearly visible to the east. The sea moved gently, and small fishing boats chugged in and out of the harbour. Over the course of the morning, I saw the sun move across the sea, from left to right. I liked it, and decided to keep it.

I looked around the office. It was small, but it was all mine. I had never had my own office before. It felt a bit claustrophobic and lonely; I was used to having a hundred people within my field of vision. I paced around for a minute or two, and then opened the door wide.

Susan, Richard's secretary, and now mine, came in. She was about thirty, with permed brown hair, and a motherly look about her. 'Can I get you a cup of tea or anything?'

Having spent most of my working life in a trading room, where secretaries are a rare sight, I wasn't used to being waited on. 'No, let me get you one.'

160

In the end, we both made our way to the machine which dispensed tea.

'It's good to have someone in that office again,' said Susan as we walked back. 'Especially Richard's brother.'

'Had you worked for him for long?'

'Three years. He was a good boss, although he worked much too hard.'

'Everyone seems to do that round here,' I said.

'Ah ha. But they do it because they want to.'

'You miss him?'

'Yes, I do,' she said, biting her lower lip. 'The place has had an awful feel about it since he died. I mean his personality used to be everywhere, it lit up the whole factory.'

'Well, I know I won't be able to replace him,' I said, 'but I will do my best for the company and the people in it. For his sake, as much as anything else.'

'I'm sure you will. You know, you look quite a lot like him,' Susan said, eyeing me up and down. 'And don't underestimate the goodwill towards you here. We all feel for you, and we'll all do our best to help.'

'Thanks.' I smiled, and took my cup of tea into Richard's office. FairSystems felt a bit like a family, and if it had been Richard's family, it was my family now.

I sat down at the smooth black desk, and thought about the company. David Baker bothered me. He was clearly very good at his job. And he clearly didn't like me being around. Somehow I would have to run the company without alienating him so much that we lost him. We couldn't afford that. I wondered what had been the cause of the big argument he had had with Richard.

Rachel, too, was impressive, and I was much more confident of being able to work with her. Technologically, it was clear that FairSystems was very strong. We just needed that breakthrough she had spoken about; the high-volume production and mass-marketing that would bring down the price of VR systems so that everybody could use them. That would involve significant risk even for a company as big as IBM. For a company of FairSystems' size and financial position, it seemed impossible.

I was still intrigued by Steve Schwartz's theory that a buyer was accumulating FairSystems' stock at low prices with the connivance of Wagner Phillips. Well, I had a perfect opportunity to find out more about that. Willie and I were having lunch with Mr Wagner himself that very day.

I turned on my computer. It beeped and told me I had an e-mail waiting for me. With a small smile of gratification that my presence in the company had been noticed by the computer as well as everyone else, I clicked on a couple of menu options to call up the message.

The smile disappeared.

Give Up. Go home. FairSystems is fucked.

Doogie

12

Scott Wagner was smooth. He looked good. Broad shoulders under a well-cut suit. Tanned face with a square jaw. Blue eyes that held mine steadily as he talked. Immaculately groomed thick hair. A fit thirty-five-year-old body that emanated well-controlled energy.

He sounded good too. A soft spoken, pleasing American voice. Diction that was clear, slow and measured. Sincere. Powerful, but in a low-key way.

He was in the UK for three days to check out a possible candidate for flotation on NASDAQ, and wanted to meet Willie and me. Willie was obviously in awe of him, alternately flattered to receive his attention, and scared to be in his presence. As he sat at the conference table, he reminded me a little of David Baker, but he was altogether a classier act. He represented what David wanted to become.

We were in the restaurant of the Balbirnie House Hotel, which had been the local laird's residence when Glenrothes had been no more than an estate between villages. We were the first in the elegant dining room; Wagner was anxious to catch a three o'clock flight from Edinburgh airport.

The waiter came, and Wagner ordered smoked salmon, followed by a salad. No wine, just still water. I thought I would get stuck into some venison, and yes I would like some of the Pomerol, thank you very much.

'I had a fascinating meeting with Scottish Enterprise this morning,' Wagner said.

'Oh yes?'

'Do you know how many things were invented by Scotsmen?'

'The haggis? The kilt? The caber? McEwan's Export?'

Wagner smiled. 'Much more than that. The telephone, the television, radar, Tarmacadam, penicillin, chloroform, the pneumatic tyre. Even the adhesive stamp! What I can't figure out is why this country isn't as wealthy as California.'

'Because they all left Scotland before they invented any of this stuff?'

'I guess that must be it. But I still think there's a great opportunity here for firms like ours which know how to finance young companies.'

'I hope you're right,' I said. 'Tell me a bit about Wagner Phillips. You have quite a reputation in small-company stocks. But you haven't been going that long, have you?'

'We're coming up to our fourth anniversary. Dwayne Phillips and I set the operation up with half a dozen of our old colleagues. We now employ a hundred people. We've had a good few years. The breaks have come our way.' Wagner's voice was tinged with pride.

'Very impressive. Where did you all come from?'

'Drexel Burnham. I'm sure you remember them, you're in the business.'

'I certainly do.' Drexel had risen from obscurity to become one of the most powerful investment banks on Wall Street. It was Drexel which had organised the biggest leveraged buy-out in history, when Kohlberg Kravis and Roberts had purchased RJR Nabisco for twenty-five billion dollars. They had achieved this through the financial genius Michael Milken, a maverick who had broken all the rules, and ended up in jail for it. Drexel's excesses eventually caught up with them too; they'd gone bankrupt in 1990.

'You've probably heard some bad things about Drexel,'

164

Wagner said, 'and there's no doubt that towards the end, some in the firm went too far. But there were some exceptionally talented people there, real entrepreneurs. It struck me that that culture would be well suited to financing young growing companies with equity. So, we set up Wagner Phillips to do just that.'

'And it worked?'

'It sure did. We've done over a hundred initial public offerings since we started out. That's a hundred companies that have raised finance from the stockmarket to develop new ideas and create jobs for America.' Wagner hesitated, and then grinned, 'And Scotland too, of course.'

'And who buys these shares?'

'Oh, a range of institutions and individuals. We're not afraid of risk, and neither are the investors we talk to. They're often entrepreneurs who have been successful in their own right. They trust us. We look after them.'

Ah, stuffees! Every broker likes to have stuffees, investors who will buy whatever the broker stuffs down their throat.

'So you have a lot of discretionary money?' I asked innocently.

Wagner smiled. 'Let's just say we like to feel that we have created a little community of investors and companies with similar goals and ambitions. In my view, that was one of the things Mike did very well at Drexel. And everyone benefits.'

'And FairSystems is part of this community?'

'Sure,' said Wagner smiling. 'And I know we're going to be right there for you as you grow.'

I wasn't at all sure I wanted FairSystems to be part of Wagner's little coterie. He was right that Michael Milken's success had been built up on a network of clients, all of whom had owed him favours of one sort or another. This network had done wonders for Milken; it had given him the power to frighten the largest corporations in America. True, it had also worked well for many of his clients, but many more had ended up either bankrupt or in jail.

The food came, and we tucked into it. Wagner seemed to

have little enthusiasm for his salad, but I liked the venison. The wine was good, too. I looked around me. The dining room was filling up with businessmen, and a few wayward American tourists who had wandered a little off the beaten track and ended up in Glenrothes.

'Tell me about the share placing last November.'

'We were very pleased with it,' he said. 'We achieved an excellent price of ten dollars, and of course the shares traded up to a twenty per cent premium in the first couple of days. We attracted an excellent investor base, the shares are broadly held. Quite a result.'

And one that had cost FairSystems more than one million of the eight million dollars raised, I thought.

'Take me through the share price movements,' I said. 'After that initial leap, the shares stuck at twelve dollars for a couple of months, and then slid down to six, didn't they?' They had fallen further since Richard's death, but that was hardly Wagner Phillips' fault.

'Yes, that was disappointing. But you know, the company wasn't coming through with what it had promised in the prospectus.'

I wasn't going to let him wriggle out of it. 'But the company didn't release any information at all before the price fell, or indeed until my brother died.'

'The American markets expect quick results, Mark.' Wagner was polite, but there was an edge to his tone that implied I didn't know what I was talking about and I should leave it to the experts. Not enough to be rude, but enough to cause me to feel unsure of myself.

'I've watched the share price closely,' I said. 'And something else must be going on to drive the price down, especially given the high volume of shares traded. What is it?' I knew I sounded aggressive, but I thought the direct question would demand a direct answer.

It demanded but didn't receive. 'Gee, I guess the markets just act strange sometimes. We all have to live with it.'

'What are you telling your customers about us?'

Wagner paused a moment. 'I guess we're being a little cautious right now. Not negative, just cautious.' He saw my frown. 'You have to understand, Mark, that our analysts must be free to take their own view on a stock. I'd like it if they were a lot more positive, but I can't tell them what to think.'

Like hell he couldn't. He had told his sales people and analysts to bad-mouth FairSystems, and the share price was going down as a result.

'So, who's been buying?'

'I'm afraid I can't say.'

'You can't say? But aren't you our broker?'

'It's a difficult situation,' Wagner said apologetically. 'But our clients expect us to keep their dealings confidential. We have to respect that.'

'Is it one buyer, or many?'

'I'm not sure,' said Wagner. 'I guess it would be a number of buyers.'

I didn't believe him, but it was clear he wasn't going to tell me more.

'I was really sorry to hear about Richard,' Wagner said, picking at his salad. 'He was a neat, neat guy. How are you finding stepping into his shoes?'

'Interesting,' I said.

'It must all be a little daunting.'

'Not really,' I lied. 'There are good people here, especially on the technology side. We'll do fine.'

I could see in Wagner's eyes that he didn't believe me, but he wasn't going to challenge me. 'Uh huh. Well, if you find things get a little hairy, I may be able to find you a buyer.'

Sneaky. I knew he already had a buyer. But he wanted to get me to retain him to find one. More fees, no doubt.

'Yes, Richard mentioned that you have a prospective buyer. Who is it?'

Wagner's eyes widened slightly; he hadn't expected that Richard would have told me this. He recovered quickly. 'I'm sorry, I can't say at this time. They're very eager to retain their anonymity.'

'But you're our broker,' I said again. 'Don't you have a duty to tell us?'

Wagner smiled and shrugged. 'My hands are tied.'

'What price will they pay?'

'Well, the share price is at four and a half dollars today, and still drifting down. I'm not sure you could get more than a thirty per cent premium. So, six dollars, I guess.'

Six dollars. That was a lot less than the ten dollar flotation price. But I now owned almost four hundred and eighty thousand shares, so that represented over $2.5 million for my total holding. Selling out for six dollars might end up being the best offer we would get. I would have to keep Wagner sweet. For a moment I regretted being so aggressive with him.

I tried to be civil. The rest of the meal passed in the useless chit-chat of international finance: airlines and airports, the direction of the markets, and a struggle to find obscure mutual acquaintances. Finally Wagner paid the bill, and we left. Outside the hotel, a driver in uniform stood by a smart black Ford Granada, waiting to take Wagner to the airport. Willie and I shook Wagner's hand, and he sped away.

I was beginning to regret recommending Wagner Phillips to Richard. I hadn't really known much about them beyond what Karen had told me: that they were an aggressive, fast-growing firm with plenty of high-tech clients. True, they had succeeded in raising money for FairSystems in difficult circumstances. But at what cost? I had a nasty feeling I had yet to find out.

I turned to Willie. He had been silent throughout the meal. 'What do you think?'

Willie screwed his face up into a frown, considering what to say. He plucked up his courage. 'I may be havering,' he said, 'but I don't like him at all.'

I laughed. A good man, Willie.

'How's it going?' asked Karen.

'Pretty well,' I said into the receiver. 'I'm having to learn an awful lot very fast, but it's interesting stuff. And I had my first brush with investment bankers from the other side of the table.

That was fascinating.' I told her about my lunch with Scott Wagner.

'Sounds like he'd go down brilliantly at Harrison Brothers.'

'I think he would be too much even for us. Anyway, what's going on in London?'

'Big news.'

'What's that?'

'Jack fired Sally.'

'Oh, no! What a jerk!'

'Wait. It's not so bad,' Karen went on excitedly.

'Why? What happened?'

'Well, as you can imagine, I was pretty upset about it. One minute she's sitting right next to me. The next minute she's been disappeared. She didn't even get a chance to say goodbye.'

'Yeah. I've seen it before.' We all had.

'So, I went to talk to Bob Forrester about it. I said that in my opinion Sally would make an excellent sales person if we just gave her a chance. I said I would spend more time with her, and I would take the responsibility if it didn't work out. And then, guess what he said.'

'What?'

'He said that there would be a big reorganisation over the weekend, and on Monday, Jack Tenko wouldn't have a job.'

'Hurrah!'

'Exactly. He told me to ring Sally at home and tell her to take the next few days off, and to come in to work as usual on Monday.'

'Well done!' I said. 'I'm proud of you.'

'I'm quite proud of myself, actually.'

'And what are they going to do with you?'

'They're going to keep me on in London, and probably give me more responsibility, Bob said. Bob asked me to keep an eye on his own portfolio for him.'

'Sounds good.' I was impressed. Karen was much better at politics than I. I wasn't at all surprised that she was going to come out of all this ahead. I should probably get her up to Scotland to deal with David Baker. Which reminded me.

'I've been invited to a dinner party on Saturday in Edinburgh. Do you want to come? It would be great to see you.'

'I'm sorry, I've agreed to go to the ballet with that guy Peter Tewson. I can't blow him off now. He's a client.'

'Oh, come on Karen,' I pleaded.

She hesitated. 'No, it's not just that. Now I've said yes, I haven't the heart to stand him up. I'd really better not.'

I sighed. I did miss her.

'Oh well. Speak to you later.'

'Bye, Mark.'

13

I spent Saturday morning at the factory. There was a whole stack of papers and e-mails to go through. People wanted decisions: Jock wanted to hire two more assembly workers to meet increased demand, which would have been fine if we'd had the cash to pay them. Our suppliers of keyboards were always delivering late; should we get rid of them, or give them another chance? The sales team's entertainment expenses were running consistently over budget. Once again, even minor overruns could screw up our cash position.

At two, I went through to Software to pick up Rachel. We were going to see her brother, Alex. She was sitting by Andy Kettering's desk with Keith Newall. Keith was lounging back in his chair, his long legs propped up against a bin.

He was unhappy, and talking fast. 'This is turning into a gangbang, Rachel. You let me and Andy work together, and we'll come up with something cuspy. If you have half the code-grinders in Scotland working on it, we'll still be fixing bugs at Christmas.'

Rachel sighed, and turned to Andy. 'Have you got the time to deal with this without help?'

Andy was calmly listening to Keith's tirade. He thought a moment. 'I suppose so,' he said. 'Who needs sleep anyway? And you'll be around if I get bogged down, won't you?'

'Yes, I will,' said Rachel. 'OK, Keith, we'll do it your way. But you've only got four days. I want results by then.'

Keith smiled, and relaxed suddenly. 'You'll get 'em.'

Rachel turned to me. 'We've still got a couple of problems with the software for FairRender.'

'Is it serious?'

'It's always serious,' she said. She saw the look of alarm on my face, and laughed. 'But don't worry, we always solve it, don't we guys?'

'Always,' said Keith.

'Are you ready?' Rachel asked.

'Whenever you are.'

She stood up. 'OK, let's go. I'll just get the kit.'

She disappeared into her office and returned with a large hold-all full of equipment. We dumped it in the back of the BMW, and headed for a small hospital on the outskirts of Edinburgh.

'What happened to your brother?' I asked.

'He had a rugby accident six months ago,' she answered flatly. 'He damaged his spine. He's paralysed from the waist down.'

'Oh, no. I'm sorry. Is it . . . permanent?'

'We don't know. They're going to try some fancy surgery in a couple of months' time. There is a chance he may recover completely, or he may just stay as he is.'

'How old is he?'

'Twenty-two. He had just started with a firm of accountants. He used to play rugby for Edinburgh University, and he'd just joined Watsonians. He was injured in his second match for them.'

'Poor guy.'

We drove through some iron gates, and up a short drive to the hospital. Three wheelchairs were gathered under the shade of an old chestnut tree, which dominated the large lawn surrounding the building. We walked in through the reception area and along a corridor to her brother's room. Rachel knew the way well.

172

He was sitting in a wheelchair, next to french windows that opened out on to the garden. He was reading a book. The room was small, with a bed, a TV, a couple of chairs, and a portable computer. The bed was surrounded by complicated medical equipment.

His face lit up when he saw Rachel. She bent over and kissed him. 'Alex, this is Mark, Richard's brother.'

He bore some resemblance to Rachel, but his chin was squarer, and his hair, though naturally curly, was cut short. Despite the wheelchair, he looked young, fit and tough. I could believe he was a good rugby player.

'What position do you play?' I asked, careful to keep the question in the present tense.

'Flanker. Do you play?'

'I used to play number eight at university, but I haven't touched a rugby ball since then.'

'I'm sorry about your brother.'

'And I'm sorry about your back.'

Alex smiled, and turned to Rachel. 'What have you got for me?'

'It's a new game Virtual America have developed. It's called Manhunt. I thought you could play it with Mark.'

Alex sized me up. 'I'd be glad to. Is that all right with you?'

I nodded, surprised at being roped into a computer game. 'That's fine.'

Rachel took out two small headsets and a couple of 3-D mice and plugged them into the computer. She also attached a compact disc drive, and slotted a CD into it. She tapped several keys and a map of an island appeared on the screen.

'OK, this is how it works. You, Mark, have landed on the shore of this island. You have to get to a secret cave, find an ancient scroll, and get back to your boat. You, Alex, have to find him and stop him. Alex won't know where you've landed, nor where the cave is. You'll both be armed with cutlasses. Mark, you'll be able to move faster than Alex, but I warn you, Alex is good at these games.'

Alex smiled. It was only a computer game, but I could see he wanted to win. I felt my own competitive instincts rising.

Rachel spent a couple of minutes explaining details of how to move about in the virtual world, and then told us to put on our goggles.

I saw a map of the island. My location was marked on a sandy beach. I could also see a cave in the side of the mountain, where the scroll was hidden. Between the two points were a jungle, a river, and a plain.

I switched to the view of the virtual world. Now I was actually standing on the beach. I looked down and could see my bare feet beneath ragged blue trousers. I was wearing a billowing white shirt, and as Rachel had promised, I was carrying a cutlass. I could hear the breakers all around me. In front was thick jungle, behind the sea and a tiny rowing boat bobbing in the waves.

I set off along a path into the trees. It was much darker out of the sunlight. The jungle noises, birds and a thousand insects, pressed in from all sides. I could only see a few yards ahead of me along the path. I pressed ahead warily.

Where was Alex?

I heard a hissing sound, and looked down. There was a cobra ready to strike, it's tongue darting in and out. I leapt back and brought my sword down in one movement. I caught the snake just as it lunged, and it fell to the side of the path, dead.

'Nice reactions,' said Rachel in my ear. I smiled, took a deep breath, and walked on.

Although I had only been in the virtual world for a few minutes, the island was already beginning to feel real. I had more or less forgotten that I was in a small hospital room in Edinburgh. And with that came the fear of the hunted. I turned my head to look from side to side as I walked.

There was a bend in the path by a large tree draped with vines. I rounded it, and saw Alex jogging towards me. He was dressed as a pirate too, in a red shirt, with a patch over one eye, and a cutlass in his hand. I panicked, and turned and ran. I had a real sensation of speed, if I looked down I could see my feet

174

flying along the path. The jungle rushed by on either side, and the world moved up and down in time with my legs. As I neared the beach I realised that soon, with my back to the sea, I would have to turn and fight, so I darted off the track, into the jungle.

I slashed my way through the undergrowth. I could hear Alex behind me, catching up fast. I slashed harder. He was only a couple of yards away from my exposed back when I emerged into the open. The river was in front of me, and beyond that the plain leading off to the mountains.

I leapt into the river, and much to my relief, swam across. Once again the sensation was remarkably lifelike. I could hear the sound of the water rushing past my ears, and the splash of someone jumping in behind me. I pulled myself out on the far bank, and ran, my eyes focused on where the cave should have been.

It only took a minute of running at full speed to reach it. I turned round to look. Alex was nowhere to be seen. He knew I was faster than he, so he hadn't followed me. He was lurking somewhere, watching.

The cave was dark. I stumbled through the gloom, looking for the scroll. It was a creepy experience. Creatures scurried across the cave floor, and bats flew into my face when I disturbed them. Eventually, I found it in an old chest.

Now, how to get back to the boat? Alex was out there somewhere, waiting for me. I decided to rely on my superior speed, hoping that he wouldn't be able to move through the jungle fast enough to cut me off. I ran back to the river, heading for a point a couple of hundred yards to the left of where I had crossed earlier. I swam across, and plunged into the trees along a narrow path. I couldn't see Alex, but I kept running. My own breathing was heavy in my ears, and my speed was decreasing. I was tiring. I slowed to a walk; I might need to conserve my energy for a sudden sprint. I reached the sea about a hundred yards from the boat. The beach was empty apart from some driftwood and coconuts. I jogged towards the boat looking to the right along the line of trees.

I caught something out of the corner of my eye. I turned to look ahead. There he was right in front of me, standing in front of the pile of driftwood, sword at the ready. Damn! He must have been hiding there.

He swung at me, and I just had time to jump back. I lunged at him, but it was all over in seconds. I was surprised, and Alex was very quick. I soon saw the sand tumbling up to meet me, and then everything went black.

I took the virtual glasses off. 'Phew!' I said. My heart was beating rapidly, and I felt damp from the sweat. I had played the odd computer game before, and had been mildly diverted, but never had I experienced anything quite like that.

Alex took his headset off too. He was grinning broadly. 'Nice effort.'

'I told you he was good,' said Rachel to me. 'How did you like it, Alex?'

'Not bad at all,' he said. 'I like that one. The running is especially realistic. Yeah, it's good. Can I keep it?'

'Sure,' she said.

We stayed all afternoon, and didn't leave till seven. We were going straight on to David Baker's dinner party.

'Jesus,' I said once we were both in the car. 'He's so young! It must be horrible for him. And for you.'

Rachel nodded. 'I do what I can with the VR. I think it helps. I don't know. I just hope so.'

So did I.

David Baker's flat was in an elegant crescent in Edinburgh's New Town. It was one of a pair of flats on the second floor of an imposing Georgian building. David himself opened the door.

'Ah, so you came together,' he said, casually. 'That makes sense.' I wondered if he was concerned about an alliance of Rachel and me against him. But if he was, he showed no sign of it. 'Come in, come in. Can I get you a drink?'

The flat was decorated well, and furnished with the kind of odd bits that a couple gather together in their first years of marriage, plus one or two better pieces that are given pride of place. In the Bakers' case, this role was taken by a beautifully polished antique dining table, which was now laid for six.

Willie was there, and two women whom I didn't recognise. 'Let me make the introductions,' said David. 'This is Annie Granger . . .' I nodded at the thin, gawky woman with glasses and a wicked smile who was sitting next to Willie. My immediate thought was, Is this Willie's girlfriend, or just a date for the evening? I couldn't decide. Willie sat awkwardly near her, but then he would have done that whatever her status.

Since Karen hadn't been able to come, I was alone. So was Rachel. Did she have a man somewhere? Interesting question.

'And this is my wife, Pat.'

Pat was tall with long red hair and green eyes. She was wearing a long skirt, and a blue silk shirt over a white T-shirt. No make-up. Not at all the sort of wife I would have expected David to have come up with. She shook my hand. 'Hello. Dave's told me a lot about you,' she said in an English accent. 'And I'm very sorry about your brother.'

'Thank you,' I said.

She kissed Rachel on the cheek, and the two of them began to talk like old friends.

I spoke to David, Willie and his date, Annie. Annie had a wry sense of humour, and a way of gently mocking Willie that he thrived on. David was altogether more relaxed in his own home than in Glenrothes.

I sat next to Pat at dinner. 'So how do you like the weird world of virtual reality?' she asked.

'It's stimulating,' I said, smiling.

'It sounds like it. Dave's told me a fair bit about it, although I've never been in one of the machines.' She shuddered. 'It seems very strange to me. Creepy, really.'

I thought of Doogie's tirade against virtual perverts. 'It can be. But on the other hand it can also be genuinely useful.' I described my afternoon with Rachel and Alex.

Pat listened with interest. 'I wish Dave would tell me about these things. All I usually hear about is sales targets, meetings and deals.'

'Does he talk much about work at home?'

'Yes, he does. It's very important to him. He thinks about it all the time.'

That seemed to be a condition that affected everyone at FairSystems, I thought. Even I was in danger of catching it.

'So what do you do?'

'I help run a hostel for homeless people over at the top of Leith Walk.'

'Really?' I was taken aback.

'Yes. Well, they're not all homeless. But they're all helpless. Many of them just can't manage to run their own lives.' She saw my expression, and laughed. 'It's not that extraordinary, you know.'

'No, I know it isn't,' I replied in confusion. 'But it's just – '

She interrupted. 'You can't imagine Dave's wife doing that sort of thing?'

'I suppose not,' I admitted.

'Well, there's probably a lot you don't know about Dave,' she said.

'Oh yes?' I was curious.

'Yes. We met in Uganda about nine years ago.'

'What were you doing there? What was he doing there?'

'Dave was doing some work for the World Bank, and I was a volunteer working for Oxfam. That whole region was suffering from terrible drought.'

'I didn't know David worked for the World Bank.'

'Oh yes. He was very idealistic. He'd just done a master's in Development Economics at Sussex University. He was convinced that if the developed world just thought hard enough about third-world poverty, it would go away. And he wanted to show them how.'

'Quite an ambition.'

'Yes. But a noble one.'

'And you? Why did you go out there?'

'I just couldn't sit about while people starved,' she said,

smiling shyly, as if embarrassed by the simple sentiment she was expressing. 'I still can't.'

There was a brief lull in the conversation at the other end of the table. David overheard what we were saying.

'Is she telling you about Africa?' he asked, also looking a little embarrassed.

'Yes,' I said. 'I'm impressed.'

'Well you shouldn't be,' said David. 'I was an idealist then. I thought I could solve the world's problems. Now, I know there's no point.'

'There must be some point, surely?' I protested.

David shook his head. 'Aid goes on three things: weapons, bribes, and expensive lifestyles for aid-workers. Hardly any of it gets through to the poor, and when it does, they just spend it on booze and food and forget all about growing their own crops. It's depressing.'

I looked at David's wife. She showed no reaction; she had obviously heard it all before. David followed my eyes.

'Don't get me wrong, you always need aid-workers. Pat has saved more lives than I've sold computers. Someone has to deal with the victims of society's failings. But you can't change things. So the important thing is to go out and get what you can for yourself.' Here was Harvard talking. I had heard it before. 'Well that's what all you guys in the City do, isn't it?' David said defensively. 'Play with money. Earn big bonuses. Spend them.'

He was, of course, right. I had no business criticising him.

There was an embarrassed silence. Pat got up to get the next course. Annie asked Willie where his Porsche was. A sore point, that. He had given up his Price Waterhouse Cavalier to join FairSystems, and had had to content himself with a six-year-old Renault 5 since then.

Pat returned with a delicious stew. It took me a few minutes to notice that there wasn't any meat in it. I suspected David's vegetarianism had gone the way of his other ideals.

A lively conversation had started between David and Annie. I took the opportunity to try to find out more about him.

179

'How do you find life as a corporate spouse?' I asked Pat, quietly.

She smiled. 'I try to avoid corporate entertaining,' she said. 'This is the first time for a while.' She sighed. 'The whole corporate thing was difficult to adjust to at first, especially when Dave was at IBM. But basically I lead my life and he leads his. He has always been very single-minded. He wants success badly, and I'm sure he'll get it.'

There was no trace of bitterness in her voice, just honesty. I wasn't sure why she was prepared to be so open about her husband to his boss, however temporarily I might hold that role, but I wanted to take advantage of it.

'Did David like my brother?'

Pat didn't answer straight away, and I thought for a moment I had gone too far.

'I liked him when I met him,' she said. 'In fact you two are quite alike.' She paused, choosing her words carefully. 'I think Dave respected him. He thought Richard was going to go all the way, and Dave wanted to be there with him. Dave took a big risk going to work for FairSystems. With his record at IBM and his MBA, he could easily have taken a much better job at a more prestigious company. But I think he sees FairSystems as his ticket to making a million or two. And he would hate it if that opportunity slipped away.'

'I hope he's right,' I said.

Pat took a gulp of wine. 'Well, I honestly couldn't care.'

She lowered her voice. 'When Dave wants something, he gets it. He's the most determined person I've ever met. I suppose it's one of the reasons I fell in love with him.'

'Is that a warning?' I asked.

She ignored the question, stirring the stew in front of her. 'Anyone want some more?'

We were in the car, heading back to Glenrothes. Annie had tempted Willie off to a club somewhere in Edinburgh.

'Did you hear what Pat said to me?' I asked Rachel. She'd

been sitting opposite me, and I was sure she had kept half an ear open to our conversation.

'Ah ha.'

'I wonder why she told me so much about David?'

'I don't know. She's always struck me as quite an open person.'

'But he's her husband.'

Rachel sighed. 'Their lives have headed off in different directions. She never acts as though that bothers her, but I bet it does. I bet she hates it. I'd say she doesn't completely trust her husband, and she wanted you to know it.'

'Do you know what he and Richard were arguing about before he died?'

'No,' said Rachel. 'There were a few tense moments between them earlier on this year. And then the day before he was killed, they had a huge argument. You could hear it all round the factory. David stormed out. David insists it was about the direction of the firm. He says he wanted to cut prices and Richard didn't.'

'And you don't believe him?'

'No. I mean it's quite possible that they disagreed over pricing strategy. But Richard wouldn't have got worked up over that. It would just have been another problem he would have calmly analysed. No, I'm sure it was something else.'

'But no idea what?'

She shook her head. 'Sorry.'

We carried on to Glenrothes. Rachel's flat was the top half of a grey terraced house five minutes from the factory.

She got out of the car. 'Thanks for the lift.'

'Rachel!' I called after her. She paused. 'Thanks for taking me to see Alex.'

She smiled quickly, and she was gone.

I spent Sunday alone with my brother in the quiet Scottish fishing village that was his home. When I sat in his sitting room, reading about computers and virtual reality, I felt him standing behind me, looking over my shoulder, ready to explain

181

a point I didn't understand. It wasn't an unpleasant feeling, in fact I enjoyed it, in a bitter-sweet kind of way. I felt closer to him then than I had since he had died. Although I was more or less living in his house, I still felt like a visitor. I slept in the small spare room at the back of the house, and I had moved few of Richard's belongings.

After lunch, I walked across the bridge to the little churchyard where I was going to bury him. I spent an hour sitting there, listening to the Inch rushing down to the shore, and hearing underneath it the muted power of the North Sea. The daffodils were dying off, but the trees that lined the burn were budding. The May sun warmed my face weakly, the breeze ensuring that I kept my jersey on.

I remembered the beach in Cornwall that we'd gone to each year as children. It was a secluded cove, nestling amongst towering, jagged cliffs. The shoreline was exciting, rock pools, great boulders to climb, even caves. Richard and I would spend as much time clambering around on the rocks as swimming in the sea.

One day when the tide was out, I had ventured out of sight of the beach round the shoulder of the cliffs along a narrow strip of sand. I discovered a wonderful cave hidden amongst the rocks, and spent half the afternoon exploring it. When I turned to go home, my path was blocked. The tide was coming in, and waves were crashing against the cliffs which I had skirted round a couple of hours earlier. The narrow strip of sand had disappeared. I panicked. I screamed and cried and felt utterly alone. In the end I just curled up in a ball as high up on the rocks as I could get, and watched the sea crash in ever closer.

Then I heard my name, and a scrabbling sound from the cliff above. It was Richard! I shouted back and he heard me. In a few minutes he was down beside me. He put his arm round me. The panic lifted. I was safe. It was tricky climbing back up the cliff, even dangerous, but I wasn't scared any more.

Now, without him again, I was alone. And once again I was scared.

'Hello, Richard,' I muttered into the wind. 'Are you OK, wherever you are?' I felt silly, self-conscious, talking to him, but somehow it helped. 'I miss you. I wish you were coming back.' I tried to keep my voice even, to stop the tears.

'What can I do for you, Richard?'

As I asked the question, I knew the answer. I could find out who had killed him, and make sure he was punished. And I could look after FairSystems for him.

The cosy beer-laden fug hit me as I pushed open the door of the Inch Tavern. A murmur of unintelligible conversation came from the group clustered round the bar; I recognised most of the faces. I was pleased to see the trim figure of Sergeant Cochrane leaning against the bar, nursing a pint.

Jim Robertson was welcoming, and he asked after my burn. It was almost two weeks since the fire, and I was no longer wearing a bandage. There was a raw splash of red over the back of my left hand, as my body began the process of repairing itself. I bought a pint and caught Cochrane's eye. He nodded, and we walked off to the quiet table away from the bar.

'How are you getting on?' I asked.

'Badly,' said Cochrane. 'We haven't got a single firm lead, as far as I know.'

'How's Superintendent Donaldson taking it?'

'Och, he's a very patient man. He'll just keep going.'

'So you haven't pinned anything on Doogie Fisher?'

'No. We tried. But nothing.' Cochrane took a large gulp of beer. 'Have you got anything for me, son?'

I thought hard before answering. I was quite prepared to share any concrete information with Cochrane, but I didn't have any hard facts.

'Not really,' I said. 'I'm getting a much better feel for how things work at FairSystems. And I've spoken to Doogie Fisher myself.'

'And?'

'Well, Doogie and Richard certainly were enemies, and

183

Doogie admitted he would do anything to stop the development of virtual reality.'

'Right. He's got a pretty impressive record as well.'

'I know he's been in prison.'

'He did a two-year stretch for GBH. And there's a thick file from Special Branch. They've been watching him for years. He's been seen with a lot of unpopular characters. Although he just has the one conviction, our boys think he's dangerous.'

'I can believe that!' I said. 'And then there's David Baker. I don't think he liked Richard much either, although he won't admit it.'

'Aye, they had that row, didn't they? We haven't been able to find out what it was about. Baker said it was over the strategic direction of the company, and wasn't serious.'

'Well, I'm not sure that's quite right.'

'Do you know what it was really about?'

I shook my head, and drank some beer. 'David's very ambitious, you know.'

'So?'

'Yes, you're right,' I sighed. 'So what? I can't work out why he would have wanted to kill Richard.'

'But you have a hunch?'

'It's not even that strong,' I said in frustration. 'I've never met a murderer, I don't know what one looks like. It's just I can't work out who else close to Richard might have done it. I probably shouldn't have mentioned it.'

'No, no. Every wee bit helps.'

'So can you tell me something?'

'Maybe.'

'Where were Doogie and David when Richard was killed? And when the boathouse was burned down?'

Cochrane stared into his beer for a moment. 'I'll tell you, but don't let anyone know I did. Donaldson would have my arse. We need some sort of a break here, and who knows, you might just give it to us.'

'I'll help you if I can.'

'Good. Now, Doogie has an alibi for the Saturday your

brother died. He was in his flat talking to some of his pals on a computer network. The Internet, I think it's called. We checked with the network, and they confirmed it.'

'And David?'

Cochrane leaned forward. 'David Baker's a bit more interesting. He was at home all day on Saturday. He says he was preparing a presentation most of the day, and then went for a run. His wife was at work herself till five, so she can't corroborate what he says.'

'Interesting,' I said. 'And what about at the time of the fire?'

'Well, that was three in the morning. Everyone was tucked up in bed, weren't they? Anyone could have put on a pair of slippers, and gone lighting bonfires.'

I thought that over for a moment. 'But David's married. I've met his wife. She would have known if he'd left the house.'

'That's where you're wrong, laddie,' said Cochrane.

'Why?'

'Because they sleep in separate bedrooms.'

14

I cast my eyes quickly over the legal document in front of me. Twenty minutes in which to read thirty pages. I should just about have time, although I wasn't sure how much would sink in. Damn David! Why couldn't he have given it to me on Friday as he had promised?

The basic deal was simple. We would license our simulation management software, FairSim 1, to Onada Industries for them to develop virtual reality games for the massive world entertainment market. We would earn a small royalty on each game sold. I took a gulp of strong black coffee, and checked my watch again. A quarter to nine. Onada would be here in fifteen minutes. I read on, my eyes flicking down the pages.

Whoa! My eyes jarred to a halt. I read and reread the paragraph. I didn't like what I saw.

We were going to give Onada Industries the source code to FairSim 1.

This seemed to me to be a big mistake. Once we had released our code to Onada then the power in the relationship would be squarely with them. In a year or two they would come up with a different, if similar code, and we would be history. This was dangerous. The source code to FairSim 1 represented the total of FairSystems' knowledge to date on how to build virtual worlds. It was the heart of the company.

And we were giving it away.

Ten to nine. I picked up the document and strode over to David's office. He wasn't there. I called to Susan.

'Have you seen David?'

'He's in,' she said. 'I saw him half an hour ago. Isn't he in his office?'

'No. Can you phone around and try to track him down. I need to find him urgently.'

I went back to my desk, and waited, tapping my fingers impatiently. What was David thinking of? Had he deliberately given me the papers late in the hope that I wouldn't spot the clause? Or was I blowing this out of proportion. Was it in fact a fair price to pay for access to the entertainment market? In the short-term, maybe. In the long-term, no.

Eventually David strolled into my office. It was a couple of minutes past nine.

'Susan e-mailed the whole company looking for me. What's up?'

'I've just looked through this,' I said, holding up the Onada agreement.

'And?'

'It gives away the source code for FairSim 1. We can't do that.'

'We're not giving it away, we're selling it,' said David patiently. 'We'll get a big royalty stream from Onada. It's a great deal for us commercially.'

'But then Onada will have all our knowledge about VR. They'll be able to use it to develop all sorts of stuff of their own. We'll lose our lead in VR technology.'

'Look, Mark, don't worry,' said David. 'We'll still own the code itself. I've thought all this through, trust me. This is the product of six months of negotiation, and Onada have brought over a big honcho from Tokyo to close the deal. They're waiting for us now. Shall we go?'

I clenched my teeth. 'David, I said I'm not happy with us giving away our source code.'

David was losing patience. 'Look, Richard and I worked on

187

this for months. This deal could save us financially, and get us a powerful new partner. We can't afford to let this opportunity slip,' and he walked out of my office towards the board room.

I followed him in two minds. He was the marketing director, I ought to trust him. Especially since he had conducted these negotiations with Richard.

But I was being bounced, and I didn't like it.

They were arrayed along the other side of the board-room table, four Japanese in a row. Dark blue or grey suits, white shirts, wild swirling ties. The ties had intricate patterns of leaves, peacocks, bright suns. The effect was spoilt a little by the fact that all four were wearing them. Conformity in rebellion.

The pecking order had been made clear during the introductions. 'The big honcho from Tokyo' was the smallest and oldest. A squat man with closely cropped grey hair, he seemed permanently on the verge of sleep as he watched the proceedings from heavily hooded eyes. He didn't speak any English. He was referred to as Mr Akama.

His deputy was much younger, probably in his thirties. His name was Yoshiki Ishida, but we could call him Yoshi. He spoke in a flawless American accent. He explained that he had a master's degree from MIT and had just spent three years with Onada Industries' US subsidiary in California. He was now General Manager of Onada Industries plc in London. He was clearly intelligent, very intelligent. He did all the talking, and occasionally spoke rapidly and deferentially to his boss, who would give a curt response, and resume his semi-sleeping position.

The other two Japanese didn't say anything, and were quickly forgotten.

David and I were on the other side of the table. I left all the talking to him.

He was good. He spoke with respect and without any of the condescension with which some westerners address the Japanese. They took out the draft contracts and began working through them.

188

I have to admit I was intimidated. I had come across the Japanese before in the bond markets. I had always dismissed them as the dumb guys with all the money and none of the sense. Someone has to buy at the top and sell at the bottom for the rest of us to make an honest buck, and more often than not it was the Japanese.

But these men were different. Onada Industries was a medium-sized Japanese electronics company, and as such was bigger than any British company in the same sector. The Japanese reputation in electronics was formidable. It was difficult to believe that once they got their teeth into virtual reality, a company like Onada wouldn't swat the likes of FairSystems to one side.

And we were just about to give away the code for FairSim 1 to these people.

But what did I know? A twenty-eight-year-old whose experience of virtual reality was measured in weeks rather than years. David knew much more than me about this sort of stuff. And Onada would not be happy if we tried to change the terms of the contract now. They could be a powerful enemy.

Yet I had always had faith in my own judgement. It had seen me through many difficult situations at Harrison Brothers. I remembered my first few months as a trader. I was working for Gus, at thirty an old man of the markets who was a legend in his own lunchtime. We were trading 'perpetuals', or 'perps'. These were extraordinary bonds that never matured. Apparently, this didn't matter, since investors could always sell the bonds if they wanted to. Hundreds of millions of these bonds were traded every day, and they were treated as the next best thing to cash.

This bothered me. It seemed to me that all this only made sense if someone else was always around to buy the bonds. What if the market for perps disappeared? Then you would be stuck with these things for ever.

I explained my concerns to Gus. He explained to me that I was an ignorant trainee, and went off to lunch.

Well, the price of these perps began to slide, bit by bit. Gus thought this was great. Perps were cheap; ship 'em in, shag!

One afternoon, he rang the office from the White Horse to say that he was going to take the afternoon off. I was worried, the perps were falling again, and we were getting hit with bonds. 'Ship 'em in,' he slurred. 'The market will bounce in the morning.'

Well, I didn't. I sold every perp we had, the market crashed off a point and never recovered. Gus went crazy and wanted me fired. I was moved up to settlements instead. But a week later, it became clear that perps were just that, perpetuals. Gus was gone, and Bob Forrester gave me his job.

Since then I had trusted no one's judgement but my own. I took a deep breath.

'I'm not comfortable with this,' I said, pointing to the offending clause.

They were the first words I had spoken during the meeting. Yoshi's eyes darted towards me. David looked at me furiously. Mr Akama's lids moved up perceptibly. I wondered if he truly didn't understand any English.

'I'm afraid FairSystems will not be able to release the code for FairSim 1,' I went on. 'Can I suggest instead a similar approach to the one we use with our other partners, where we work with them on the design of each application?'

Subtle this was not. David's jaw dropped. He was too stunned to say anything. I felt almost sorry for him. He had had his legs taken out from under him by a boss who was five years his junior in front of his major client. Tough. I just couldn't let the contract go ahead. And he shouldn't have tried to bulldozer it through.

Yoshi stared at me for several seconds, his cheeks slowly reddening. Then he turned to Mr Akama, and spoke rapidly to him. Mr Akama was now well and truly awake. He spoke fast and angrily, darting black looks my way as he spoke. Yoshi couldn't get a word in, but simply nodded his head, barking 'hai' at regular intervals.

Finally the tirade stopped. Yoshi turned towards us. He took

190

a few seconds to calm himself down. 'Mr Akama would like to thank you for your time,' he said, with extreme politeness. 'Unfortunately, Mr Akama feels that these negotiations are unlikely to reach a conclusion that is acceptable to both parties. I hope you will excuse us, we will have to hurry to catch our airplane.'

The Japanese all stood up, bowed with varying degrees of inclination, and we escorted them out to the black stretch Mercedes that had driven them to the factory from Edinburgh.

'What the fuck was all that about?' shouted David, as soon as the limousine had turned safely out of the car park. 'I thought we'd agreed we'd go ahead. Onada would have been our biggest customer. That deal could have been worth two million dollars a year!'

'If we give away FairSim 1, we give away the company,' I said calmly. 'And we didn't agree anything.'

'If we don't give them FairSim 1, they don't do the deal!' shouted David in exasperation. 'I've spent six months working on that deal! Six months down the drain!'

'They'll be back. If they want to launch a virtual reality entertainment system, which they do, they'll be back. They have nowhere else to go.'

'Like hell they will!' shouted David. 'You've just screwed up the best deal this company's ever had!' He stormed off back into the factory.

I looked around. A couple of engineers had heard us. The receptionist looked on, open-mouthed. I had no doubt that details of our argument would be all round the factory before the day was out.

What would Richard have done, I wondered, as I walked back up to my office.

I suddenly had a thought. 'Did Richard keep a file on Onada Industries?' I asked Susan.

'Oh yes,' she said. Within thirty seconds it was on my desk. I looked through the last few documents in the file. There was a draft of the contract dated 17 March, just over a month before Richard had died. I looked for clause 4(a) which referred to

191

FairSim 1. There it was, heavily scored out in black pen, and NO was scrawled next to it in Richard's writing. Then there was a brief fax from Onada Industries that said that since Fair-Systems would not agree to clause 4(a) as drafted, all discussions would be terminated.

I was shocked. As soon as Richard had died, David had reopened negotiations with Onada, reinserting a vital clause that Richard had explicitly rejected.

Suddenly, I didn't feel so sorry about humiliating him.

15

The sun shone brightly on Richard's funeral. The minister was more than happy for his church to be used for the event. It turned out that Richard had even been an occasional visitor on Sundays, something that had surprised me. The service was simple and meaningful, no long eulogies. Looking out to sea, I thought this was the right place to lay Richard, and the right way.

I had finally prevailed upon the procurator fiscal to release Richard's body. He had insisted that Richard should be buried in case any future defence lawyer might want the body exhumed for further examination. The thought of that eventuality was unpleasant, but at least it was good to know that he was no longer lying in the mortuary.

I hadn't made a big fuss about the funeral, but there were about fifty people there. I recognised most of them. David, Rachel, Willie, Susan and half a dozen others represented Fair-Systems. Jim Robertson was there, and Sergeant Cochrane. Walter Sorenson had been able to organise a trip to Britain to coincide with the funeral. Thankfully, Karen had flown up as well; it was good to have her with me.

But one person grabbed all my attention. I tried to ignore him through the service so that I could devote my thoughts to

Richard and his memory. Afterwards, there was no escaping him.

My father.

I was shocked to see how much he had changed. His hair had thinned, gone greyer. There was a slight stoop. His face was creased with wrinkles. And he looked tired and pale.

Clinging to his arm was a woman. She was in her mid-thirties, slight, and just as pale as he, although she had dark hair and dark eyes. She looked familiar. With a shock, I realised that she reminded me of photographs I had seen of my mother when I was very young.

I wanted to avoid him. Not out of spite. I just couldn't trust myself to keep my temper with him, and I didn't want to start an argument over Richard's grave. But I couldn't ignore him completely at my brother's funeral. So I took Karen by the arm, and led her over to where he and his wife were talking to Sorenson.

Sorenson saw me coming and approached me. I introduced him to Karen.

'We've met,' he said. 'Last time was at a Harrison Brothers' conference at Boca Raton. Do you remember?'

'Oh, yes,' said Karen. 'Nice to see you again.'

'And you,' he said smiling at her. 'Well, I'll drop in to Fair-Systems this afternoon, Mark, if you'll be around?'

'I will be,' I said. 'See you then.' He walked off.

'Perhaps I'll join him,' Karen said, tactfully. 'Leave you to it.'

I nodded, and turned to my father.

'Hello, Dad.' I waited for a word, a reproach, some stiff small talk.

Instead, his chin shook, and he put his head in his hands, sobbing deeply. The woman next to him looked at me quickly with a mixture of confusion and embarrassment, detached herself from my father's arm, and drifted off towards Sorenson and Karen. We stood there for several minutes while the other mourners departed.

I put my arm round him. Finally, he straightened up and said, 'I loved him. I loved both of you.'

I felt a turmoil of emotions, sorrow for Richard's death, sympathy for my father's grief, guilt that I had ignored him, memories of that other funeral eight years before, but still, underlying it all, anger.

'Come back to Richard's house for some tea,' I said.

Dad looked round and caught the eye of his wife ten yards away, watching him. She nodded and smiled weakly. She pointed to the gate of the churchyard. 'OK,' he said, and walked back to the house.

The kitchen was warm and cosy. I put the kettle on. Dad looked frail and worn, sitting on the chair at the kitchen table. The air of authority about him that I remembered had mostly disappeared. We had so much to say to each other, and so little desire to say it.

'I came up to see Richard a couple of times last year,' my father said. I raised an eyebrow. I hadn't known that. 'There's some interesting birdlife in these parts. It's an important landfall for migrants, and occasionally you can get some very rare sightings. We even saw a bee-eater once by the cliffs to the east of here.' He sighed. 'He loved this place. He told me it gave him a chance to think. He was a great thinker,' my father chuckled. No mean intellect himself, he had always said that Richard had the better brain.

My father continued. 'When he first left Edinburgh to set up FairSystems, I was disappointed. Richard could have been a great scientist. But when I talked to him about the company last year, I began to appreciate why he'd done it, and even to admire him for it.'

I listened in silence.

'In science, big breakthroughs are made and problems are solved through a lengthy process of publication in scientific journals and peer review.' Dad's words had become precise again, professorial. 'The problem Richard was addressing couldn't be solved in that manner. He wanted to be the man responsible for introducing virtual reality into the very fabric of society. That's not just a problem of electronics and software design. It's a problem of management, of marketing, of product

195

development, of strategy, and of finance. And that makes it harder. Richard thought he was nearly there. One more year . . .'

I knew Richard had done great things technically. But I had a financial training, and the thing about finance is that everything can be quantified. The famous bottom line. Measured financially, I was not at all sure how successful Richard's company would prove to be.

My father turned to me. 'We have to see it through, Mark, for his sake.'

I stood up and went over to the window. A fishing boat was manoeuvring its way into the harbour. 'It would make more sense to sell,' I said.

'More financial sense perhaps. But Richard didn't want to sell out.'

'I know. But believe me, FairSystems is only just hanging on. We might not have a choice.'

'Well, do what you can.'

'I will, Dad.'

'Thank you.' My father sipped his tea. Neither of us said anything.

He cleared his throat. 'About your mother . . .'

I held up my hand. 'No Dad. Not now. Maybe not even some other time.'

He gave me a quick nervous smile. He pushed his tea to one side, and stood up to leave.

'Are you going straight back down to Oxford?' I asked.

'We're having lunch with Walter. Then we're catching the plane back to Heathrow this afternoon.'

I could have invited him to stay, but I really didn't want to. And his wife was waiting outside. I was relieved that I had avoided her.

He stood by the door. 'I'm glad we talked today.'

'So am I.'

Did I mean it? I didn't know.

He left. A couple of minutes later there was a knock on the door. It was Karen. She looked sombre, but her eyes were dry.

'How are you doing?' she asked, putting her arms round me.

'I feel like shit.'

'How was your father?'

'Oh, I don't know. He's obviously upset about Richard. He's also worried about selling FairSystems.' I stared at the floor for a minute or so. Karen kept quiet, her arms still round my neck.

'It was strange seeing him. It felt good at first. But then I think about what he did to my mother . . .' I just managed to control the emotion that was churning in my chest. I put my hand on her waist. 'I feel so alone, Karen. With Richard gone, my mother dead, and my father . . . impossible to talk to.'

'You could try to talk to him.'

'No,' I said quickly. 'I can't do that. That would be letting my mother down.'

Karen didn't say anything, but just put her head on my shoulder.

'Do you really have to go back this afternoon?' I asked.

'Yes,' she said. 'Sorry. But it was hard enough to get today off. I've definitely got to be at work first thing tomorrow morning.'

'OK,' I said, disappointed.

Sorenson arrived at my office at about half past three. Karen had eaten some soup with me for lunch, and I had dropped her off at the airport before driving back to Glenrothes. The emotional strain of the morning was still with me.

Sorenson was strong, and full of breezy good humour. Richard's funeral was behind him. 'How are things going here?'

'We're struggling on,' I said. 'I think I'm getting to grips with what's going on pretty well. But I had a bit of a run-in with David yesterday.'

'Tell me.'

I told him about the disastrous meeting with Onada.

'That sounds strange,' said Sorenson. 'You were right to stop the deal going ahead, but it's a shame it had to be done in front of the Japanese. I can't think why Baker would want to give away the code.'

197

'He thinks it's a good trade. He says we could make two million from the deal. But I checked the files. Richard specifically threw out that clause in March.'

'Did he?' said Sorenson, thoughtfully. 'How has Baker been performing otherwise?'

'I'd have to say he's done very well,' I said. 'There's been very little fallout from Richard's death. He's put together a great customer list very professionally. He works hard and gets results.'

'Well, do your best to patch things up. We can't afford to lose him right now.'

'I'll try.'

'Have the police got anywhere with Richard's murder?'

'No. Though they've asked plenty of questions.'

'I know,' said Sorenson. 'They even got the FBI in Chicago to check that I really was speaking there that day. And they've asked my stockbroker for my trading records. Of course they didn't find anything.' He got up to leave. 'You're doing well. Keep it up. And call me or send me an e-mail if you need any help.'

I pulled out a grey suit the next morning, one with a thin blue stripe. I hesitated, and held it up to the light. After a moment, I stuffed it back in the wardrobe, and put on some cotton trousers and a thick casual shirt instead. I just didn't want to look like David Baker.

I didn't leave home until eight thirty, and didn't get to Glenrothes until just after nine. I enjoyed the drive through the rolling East Fife countryside. How many times had Richard driven along this road in the morning? What radio station did he listen to on the way? Did he wonder, as I did, about the people who lived in the large gloomy house a couple of miles outside St Monans? Or did he just concentrate on FairSystems and its problems?

The funeral had made me feel a little better about him. It had acted as a focal point for my grief, and the grief of all those there. If I wanted to think about him, I now had somewhere to go. Just that knowledge blunted the pain.

But, as I drove under the Victorian railway viaduct at Markinch, which acted as a sort of ancient industrial gate for the town of Glenrothes, the anger was still there.

There was a crowd of people in the factory car park. They were pacing round in a tight circle, carrying placards that I couldn't quite read. A dog darted in and out between their legs. A television crew was watching them, as was a group of four or five journalists clutching notebooks.

I didn't venture into the car park, but drove the BMW up on to the kerb fifty yards or so from the factory. I considered trying to sneak round the back, but I was pretty sure they would see me, so I chose the bold approach. As I neared the protesters, I could read their placards. 'VIRTUAL REALITY – VIRTUAL HELL', 'VIRTUAL REALITY – THE HEROIN OF THE PEOPLE', 'JUST SAY NO', 'SAVE OUR KIDS' MINDS'. As I walked nearer, I heard them chatting away to each other. It looked more like a nice day out than a protest.

I was within twenty yards of the doors when they spotted me. I heard cries of, 'That's Mark Fairfax!', 'There he is!', 'Stop him!'

I quickened my step to just short of a run. Two men sprinted over to me, and placed themselves squarely between me and the entrance. One was quite slight but the other was a big bastard. I hesitated. I could push past, and maybe start a fight. I could call the police. Or I could stay and talk. I was very aware of the TV crew's film rolling, and I could hear the snap of camera shutters.

'Fairfax! Just a moment Fairfax!' I recognised Doogie's voice, clear above the cries of his fellow protesters. I decided to push past the two men. They jostled a moment but let me through.

Then, suddenly, Doogie's face was inches from mine. It was a hard face, an angry face. A dangerous face. He was tense, the veins in his neck bulged. The front of his skull beneath his hairline was sprinkled with little droplets of sweat. I could smell him, his sweat, his anger.

'Listen to what I have to say, Fairfax,' he said in a calm,

199

threatening voice, low, but clear enough for the journalists to hear.

My first instinct was to hit him. He was so close, invading the square yard in front of me that was my space. Then I thought of the TV cameras, shoved my hands deep in my trouser pockets, and concentrated on controlling my anger.

Suddenly, the protesters were silent. Doogie paused to let the press get closer. 'Listen to me, Mark Fairfax,' he said again, but this time in a loud stage hiss. 'I have here a letter that you and your brother have both seen. Neither of you did anything about it.'

He pulled out some papers. My heart sank. I recognised the heading on the notepaper.

He held the letter up in the air. 'This letter is from the lawyer of the family of a young man. A young man who was so disoriented after using a FairSystems virtual reality machine that he crashed into a tree on his motorcycle and died.'

I could hear the scratch of pencil on notebook from the pressmen behind me. 'There is more,' Doogie said. 'Richard Fairfax went to great lengths to persuade the boy's family to keep quiet about the accident. They are scared. So scared that they don't want their identity to be made public. But virtual reality kills people! You can't cover it up for ever!' He waved the letter triumphantly. There was a rustle of papers as the protesters handed out press releases to the journalists. 'What have you to say about that?'

I took a deep breath, and counted to three. 'Nothing,' I said, as calmly as I could. 'Now, if you've finished, can I get to work, please?'

A voice piped up from behind me. 'Are you aware of this accident?' I looked to see who it was. He was a tall thin man in his twenties, pencil poised over the classic reporter's notebook. Doogie stayed quiet to let him speak. It must have been pre-arranged, I thought. All the more reason to be careful.

'No comment.'

'But you must have a comment, this is a question of public safety.'

'I said, no comment.'

'Can we see this letter?' It was a different reporter this time, a woman with an English accent.

'I'm sorry, I can't release it,' said Doogie. 'I promised the family I would protect their identity.'

'Do you deny that this boy was killed after using a Fair-Systems virtual reality machine?' The thin journalist again.

I could see this was going to get difficult. He wasn't going to give up. His high-pitched accusing questions were getting on my nerves. The press of people round me, and especially the television cameras a few feet from my face, made me claustrophobic. I decided to cut and run.

I pushed through the crowd. 'I'm sorry I can't help you, I must get to work now.'

'Mr Fairfax! Mr Fairfax!' the journalist shouted after me.

I was out in the clear, when a hand pulled at my arm. I spun round. It was Doogie. He was smiling. 'Take my advice. Go home,' he whispered.

I turned and walked into the factory.

'When I say it can't be done in two weeks, it can't be done in two weeks!' Keith was pacing round the table waving his arms. David, Rachel, Andy and he were all crammed into my office. The meeting was heating up.

'We promised the market we would release FairRender on the first of June,' said David icily. 'It's the seventeenth of May today. That means you've got less than two weeks.'

'But I'm telling you, man, this is non-trivial. I mean we're talking about two months, not two weeks.'

David was clearly frustrated, but he kept his cool. 'You mean you could miss the deadline by two whole months?'

'I mean we've got to forget about deadlines altogether. Anyway, this deadline was your idea, not mine.'

'Are you sure you'll ever solve this problem?' asked David.

'Yeah, yeah, of course I'm sure. The chips are fine. It's just the software driving them that's the problem. If we release it now it'll work, but not well. We'll just be storing up trouble for the future.'

David looked at Rachel. 'Can't you put more people on to it?'

Rachel knocked the ash off her cigarette. 'Not really, David. It's a question of figuring out the best way forward, and then following it. Brute force won't work. Andy and Keith probably will.'

'So what can we do?' asked David.

'How many customers have you promised FairRender to?' I asked David.

'Five or six.'

'And are any of them desperate to have it right now?'

David hesitated. 'No, I suppose not right now.'

'Well, let's just tell them it'll take a little longer to release than anticipated. We're only talking, what, a couple of months. Is that right, Keith?'

Keith nodded.

'But when Richard was around, we always delivered on time,' David protested.

'And I suspect we were the only company that did,' I said. 'Look, I'm sure they'll understand, given what's happened. And you have to agree, quality is the most important thing. We can't ship a product that doesn't work.'

David shrugged, and nodded grudgingly. 'OK. We can probably get away with it this once, but we'd better not make a habit of it.'

'Marketroids,' Keith muttered under his breath.

'Cool it, Keith,' I said. 'And you and Andy had better have something good by the middle of July.'

'OK, boss,' said Keith, and smiled. The meeting broke up, and they left the room.

'David?' I said. 'Have you got a moment?'

David hesitated, turned round, and sat down again, his arms folded.

'I checked Richard's files,' I said.

'And you found that he had vetoed that clause in the Onada agreement.'

202

'Well?'

Baker didn't say anything for several seconds. He leaned forward with his elbows on the table, thinking. Choosing his words. Giving them more weight. Some trick he had picked up somewhere.

'I've given up a lot to come and work here,' he said. 'I could have gone all the way at IBM. I came in the upper quartile of my class at Harvard. I could have walked into any job in a big company anywhere in the world. But I came here.'

I watched and listened.

'Do you want to know why?'

'OK. Why?'

'I believe this company can make it. I believe virtual reality is one of the few true growth industries around. This is one of the leading companies in the world in that field. And I want to get in at the ground floor. Now, I have friends from B-school who are working for McKinsey, Bloomfield Weiss, General Electric. They wonder what I'm doing pissing around with a company like this. And I'll show them.

'But this company has to be run professionally. Richard did a great job, but he was an inventor at heart. He was more concerned about building bigger and better VR machines than making money. You know I'm right, don't you?'

I knew he was right, but I was damned if I was going to admit it.

He looked down his long nose at me. 'We had some ex-traders at Harvard. Good guys. Smart guys. But they took quick decisions. And once they had taken them, they stuck to them, whatever. Great in the pressure of a dealing room. Disaster in the real world.'

Ouch! He was right there too. But even so I was sure that what he'd been planning to do with Onada was just plain stupid. And no matter what he said, I would back my own judgement. For better or worse.

'I'm here to take decisions,' I said. 'You may not like them, but you will have to live with them. And to take decisions, I need to have the facts. You hid the fact that Richard had vetoed

203

the Onada agreement. This company will not function if you carry on behaving like that.'

He slapped his hand on the table. 'This company will not function at all if it's run by a bunch of amateurs! We're facing bankruptcy, for God's sake. A deal with Onada is the only way out.'

I kept my cool. 'David, I do not want you to withhold information from me again. Is that understood?'

David turned on his heel and walked out.

I felt isolated, stewing in my office. After a few minutes' trying to concentrate on the figures in front of me, I got up and walked off to Software.

Rachel was in her office, chatting with Keith. He scarpered when he saw me coming. God, being the boss took some getting used to!

Rachel looked tired. Her face was pale, and her eyes were darkened under her glasses. I thought she was wearing the same black jersey she had worn the day before, but it was hard to tell. I was already beginning to realise it took a lot to make Rachel look tired. She must have been working straight through the night.

'Did you see the demonstration this morning?' I asked.

'No,' she said. 'I must have missed it. But I did overhear something about a crowd outside. Of course, in this building you can't just take a peek out of the window and have a look.'

'Well, Doogie was there, and a mob of protesters from BOWL. And the press, and television. Doogie told them all about the Bergey accident.'

Rachel suddenly seemed to wake up. 'No!'

'It's not going to do our reputation much good.'

Rachel frowned. 'No, it isn't.'

I sighed. 'We really didn't need this.' I glanced at Rachel. 'And I do want to know what really happened.'

'All right. I'll check it out next time I go to California, I promise.'

'Do you go to California a lot?' I asked, surprised.

'Sometimes.'

'And who do you go and see?'

'Oh, different people.'

Rachel's evasiveness was deeply frustrating, especially today.

'OK, well next time you go, check out what happened. And make sure next time is some time soon.'

She nodded. 'David told me what you did on Monday.'

I tensed.

'I think you were dead right,' she continued. 'We can't let anyone get that code, whatever they pay us.'

'Thank you.' I did appreciate her support.

'But I think David is pretty pissed off. You've hurt his pride, and he has a lot of that.'

'Yeah, I know. We just had words about it. But he didn't seem too pleased with your people this morning, either. What was all that about it taking two months to sort out the software for FairRender? I heard you three talking about four days.'

Rachel hesitated. A small smile flickered across her face. 'Actually, we cracked it at six o'clock this morning.' That explained the dark semicircles under her eyes, neatly framed by the lower rim of her glasses.

'Oh?' I said. 'So why did you tell David it would take two months to fix?'

'Because we can't release FairRender on the first of June.'

'Why not?'

Rachel was looking very uncomfortable now. She stubbed out her cigarette in an empty cup, and immediately lit another one.

'It's to do with Project Platform. And Jenson Computer.'

'I see,' I said, feeling the irritation rise in me. 'And you can't tell me anything about it.'

'No, I'm sorry.' She hesitated, as if deciding whether to say something. In the end, she spoke. 'He's coming in today.'

'Who is?'

'Jenson.'

'What! Carl Jenson himself?'

'Yes. Carl Jenson. That's right.'

Even I had heard of Carl Jenson. He was a legend of

corporate America. His company had been one of the first to imitate the IBM PCs in the early 1980s, and within five years he had built Jenson Computer into a business with sales of several billion dollars. He had achieved all this with style, and was one of the favourites of *Business Week* and *Fortune*. And, of course, Jenson Computer was FairSystems' most important customer. Our survival depended on him.

'Why didn't you tell me earlier?'

'I didn't think of it.'

Of course she had thought of it. 'Come on, Rachel.'

She straightened up and looked me in the eye. 'Well, the thing is, he didn't want to see you at all, but I told him it was a good idea, and he really ought to.'

That made me feel about two inches high. It said a lot for my standing when the boss of our biggest customer didn't even want to see me.

'What's he got against me?' I asked.

'You're from the City. He hates the City. Actually, he hates Wall Street, but what's the difference?'

None, really. 'Why?'

'Well, Jenson Computer made it big in the eighties. Jenson was a hero. But in the last couple of years the price of PCs has continued to fall to the point where even Jenson Computer is losing money. He was caught in a squeeze by IBM and Compaq price-cutting from above, and the Taiwanese and Koreans shipping volume from below. He bought a chip manufacturer two years ago, but that acquisition hasn't worked well. It's hard to say what's going to happen to the company. So the share price has gone down.' She tapped ash into her coffee cup. 'And so Wall Street want Jenson's head. He's yesterday's man. A has-been.'

'And he doesn't like it?'

'You can say that again. Carl's ego is massive. He doesn't want to be a has-been before he's forty.'

'So why is he here?'

'To talk about a few things we're working on together.'

'Like Project Platform?'

Rachel knew there was no point in denying it. She nodded.

'Rachel, what the hell is Project Platform? I have to know.'

'I can't tell you,' said Rachel. 'I'm sorry, but I just can't. Carl Jenson specifically told me not to. He's worried about your City connections, and the fact you're only here for three months. He's paranoid about secrecy. You have to trust me.' Her deep brown eyes were pleading. 'It's best for all of us that I don't tell you.'

I looked closely at her face, partially obscured by dark curls. I did trust her.

'OK,' I said. 'Does David know?' It was childish, but I didn't want David Baker to know any secrets that I didn't.

'No. He knows it exists, but he doesn't know anything about it. The only people who know are me, Keith, Andy and Sorenson.'

'Sorenson knows?'

'Yes, I think Richard told him. He cleared it with Jenson first.'

'And you can't clear me with Jenson?'

'I told you. I tried. He wouldn't have it.'

I sat back in my chair for a moment and thought. Not knowing about Project Platform irritated me. But I had never let emotion get in the way of my trading judgement, and I wouldn't now. I trusted Rachel. I believed that her reluctance to tell me was because she was afraid for the success of the project. And although I didn't know what Project Platform was, I knew we needed it to work. Nevertheless, it was going to be hard to manage the company knowing nothing about its most important contract.

'OK,' I said. 'But see if you can persuade him to trust me. If I'm going to run this company properly, I need to know what's going on in it.'

Rachel smiled. 'Good. I knew you'd understand. And I will try to get him to change his mind about you.' She got up to leave. She paused, and glanced at my shirt and trousers. 'Oh, by the way, I'm glad you're not wearing a suit today.'

I had to laugh. The scruffily dressed woman in front of me

was just about to meet one of the legends of computing, and she was giving me advice on my clothes. The funny bit was, she was probably right.

I sat in my office waiting. Rachel had said she and Jenson might come by any time after three. It was half past five. For two and a half hours I had sat at my desk achieving very little. Ed had left a message earlier, but I didn't feel like talking to him. Harrison Brothers seemed a very long way away.

I fielded calls from a couple of journalists asking about BOWL's allegations. All I said was that we had received a letter from someone considering pursuing a claim but that they had chosen not to proceed, and that I had no further comment. I wanted to give them as little as possible to go on.

I called Karen.

'Harrison.'

'Hi. It's me.'

'Oh, hi. What's up?' She sounded hurried.

'Can you just check FairSystems' stock price for me?'

'Hold on.' She was back a few seconds later. 'It's three dollars! What's happened?'

I explained about the BOWL demo.

'Hang on, I'll see if there's a story on Reuters. Yes, here it is.'

She read it to me. It was only a couple of lines, and mentioned 'unconfirmed reports' of a fatal accident after a virtual reality session.

'It sounds pretty vague,' she said.

'If Wagner has seen it, he'll have plenty of ammunition to scare his clients with,' I said gloomily. 'And it's a great opportunity for whoever is accumulating the shares to buy more.'

'Looks like it,' said Karen. 'I've got a client holding. I've got to go.'

'OK. Thanks anyway.'

'No problem. See you.' She hung up.

Three dollars! Oh God.

And now all I could do was wait for Jenson. I was nervous. I was alternately angry that I knew nothing of Project Platform, and scared of frightening off Jenson by letting him think that his confidentiality had been compromised.

So, he thought I was a Wall Street jerk? Well, I would try hard not to act like one. I was glad about the suit, although I couldn't help feeling naked facing a high-pressure business situation without one.

There was a tap at the door and Rachel showed Carl Jenson in to my office. He bustled in and immediately the room was filled with his presence.

If ever a man exuded wealth and power, it was he, but he did it in a way that was totally unfamiliar to me. He was a short man, running a little to fat. He was dressed in a red and white checked shirt which was tucked into immaculately pressed chino trousers. A gold chain nestled in the matted hair just below his neckline. He had a puffy face, topped with a mop of curly dark hair, tied back into a little ponytail. What set him apart from ordinary mankind was his eyes.

They were small, black and deep-set. They darted from object to object. In the two seconds that they alighted on my face, I felt a powerful intensity of intelligence and energy. It was a relief to see them dart off again round my little office.

'Mark, good to meet you. Carl Jenson.'

'Good to meet you.' He placed his hand in mine, squeezed it rapidly, and sat down at my small table. Rachel followed him in, and sat next to him.

He took charge of the conversation. I felt as though I was racing after a runaway truck, just managing to cling on.

'I was real sorry to hear about Richard. He was a true genius. In ten years' time people will be calling him the grandfather of this industry. It's a shame he won't be there to hear it.' His eyes rested on mine for a second. He meant what he said.

'Thank you,' I replied.

Jenson moved on. 'Rachel tells me that you're running this show for three months. Is that right?'

'That's right.'

'Know anything about virtual reality?'

'Not much,' I said.

209

'Rachel says you work in financial services. That right?'

'Yes.'

Jenson studied me for an instant. 'You don't look like a banker to me.' It was a compliment.

I shrugged.

'Those investment bankers are assholes, all of them. Whenever I want to buy a company, once the bankers find out, the shares go up. And they think I don't notice!' Jenson slapped the table. His words were really speeding up now. 'They don't understand the first thing about my business. All they care about is quarterly earnings per share. I don't give a shit about quarterly earnings per share. I care about the future.'

'And what is the future?'

Jenson stood up and walked over to the electronic view of the Firth of Forth.

'That's cute,' he said. 'I like that.' He turned to me. 'You ever heard of Sun Tsu?'

'Wasn't he a Chinese general?' I asked.

'Yeah. Fifth century BC. But what he said then makes sense now.'

'And what did he say?'

'He said that the army that chooses a battlefield that suits its strengths will win without having to fight.'

'I see. I think.'

'Well at the moment there's a war going on out there. And we're all taking casualties, from IBM to the cheapest Malaysian manufacturer. The reason is, personal computers are a commodity. Any bozo can make them, provided they got a chip. It's the chips that are the brains of the computer, and most of those are made by Intel.'

He began pacing, bouncing round my little room, talking rapidly.

'So, a couple of years ago, I bought my own chip maker. A company called Intercirc. Now I make chips as good as Intel's, and put them in my own computers. So I got the weapons I need in this war. But I'm still not making money. Intel makes all the money. Everyone follows their designs, people buy their chips first, they got the biggest plants. They got the high ground. So, what am I gonna do?' He stopped and leaned over the table, eyes boring into me for a couple of seconds. 'I'm gonna choose my own battlefield. Virtual reality. In the virtual reality marketplace, I can make the computers and the peripheral hardware and the chips better than anyone else. Better than IBM, or Intel, or the Japanese or the goddamn Koreans.'

'But there isn't a mass virtual reality market yet.'

'There will be,' said Jenson. 'Fifteen years ago I was the one who foresaw what would happen to PCs. I was twenty-four then. Well, now I can spot the next wave. And it's virtual reality.' He held my eyes for a full five seconds, burning this insight into my brain.

'This isn't something for arcade freaks, or perverts. This is going to be part of life for all of us in the next century. And those fuckwits on Wall Street can't see it!'

I thought for a moment. 'So you hope that with our technology you can open out the VR market? You manufacture the FairRender graphics chip and assemble our computer systems.'

Jenson didn't answer. He just kept pacing.

This was interesting. Rachel had mentioned that for a mass VR market to develop, systems, and particularly the chips inside the systems, would have to be manufactured on a large scale. Jenson seemed willing to contemplate doing just that. He was an important customer indeed.

'And Project Platform has something to do with all this?' I asked.

'Maybe,' said Jenson. 'But I wouldn't expect a Wall Street kid to understand it.'

I ignored the dig. 'I know Project Platform is very confidential. I can assure you Rachel has told me nothing of the details. She says that you've insisted that the project be kept secret.'

'Damn right.'

'Well,' I continued reasonably, 'I would be grateful if you yourself could tell me what Project Platform is about. That way I can make sure that we do the best possible job for you. It's

211

very difficult to run this company without knowing anything about it.'

'Hey. I'm sorry you're finding it difficult to run FairSystems. But that's your problem, not mine.'

I decided not to rise to the provocation. And it was obvious that to ask more questions about Project Platform would just lead to confrontation. But it annoyed the hell out of me that he wouldn't tell me.

He stopped pacing and sat down. 'How're you coping without Richard?'

Ah. This was a difficult question, but I had been asked it before by other customers, and come up with satisfactory answers.

'Everyone has been hit by his death, naturally,' I began. 'But as you know, we have very good technical people here. Rachel was aware of almost everything Richard was doing technically. And David Baker has good relationships with our customers.'

'And what about leadership? Every company has to have a leader.'

'That's down to me. And I've been very pleased by the support I've received from everyone working here.' And I had been. Although there were countless problems, I thought I had done well with the people. Already they seemed to trust me, and accept my authority.

'Uh huh.' Jenson wasn't convinced. He leaned back. 'Richard ran a great operation here. I hope you're not going to screw it up.'

'I won't,' I held his gaze. 'Everything will carry on as normal.'

There was silence for a moment, then Jenson stood up and made his way to the door. 'Well, it was great to meet you, Mark. And to see you, Rachel.' He smiled to her. We showed him out to Reception. He paused at the door. 'I passed through some kind of demo outside earlier.'

I tensed.

'They were shouting about some kid who had gotten himself killed using VR. Do you know about that?'

212

I nodded. 'They have no proof that VR actually caused his death.'

'Good,' said Jenson. 'Because if they did, that would be very bad publicity for all of us, don't you think?'

With that, he left.

'Phew,' I said. 'Is that man crazy?'

'Kind of,' said Rachel. 'There is a debate in the industry about whether it's clinical or not. He won't allow any psychiatrist near him for long enough to find out.'

'And what was all that about Sun Tsu?'

'Carl's always up on all the new hip ideas. He comes from New York but he fancies himself as a Silicon Valley entrepreneur. Despite all that bullshit, though, he gets things done.'

'I can believe it. Will he pay up?'

'Yes, he'll pay. We're on time.'

'Good. Look Rachel, whatever this Project Platform is, please make sure you get it right.'

'Och, we'll get it right,' she said.

I was tired as I drove home. Tired and worried. The BOWL demonstration and the latest plunge in the share price were hardly good news. And although Jenson seemed to be committed to putting resources into a mass virtual reality market, I still felt a bit of a fool after the meeting. What the hell was Project Platform?

It was dark by the time I drove down through the narrow streets of Kirkhaven and along to the end of the quay. I parked the car and got out. Although there was a breeze that evening, the corner of the road just outside Inch Lodge was sheltered. I locked the car and fumbled for my house-keys.

Behind me I heard a rapid pattering sound. It was coming closer, fast. I turned round just in time to see a dark brown body hurl itself against my chest. I was thrown back against the wall of the house, and on to the pavement, the wind knocked out of me. As I lay on the ground, gasping for air, I heard a low growl inches from my ear, and felt hot breath on my face. I looked up.

213

I saw teeth, tongue and saliva. I kept absolutely still, trying to control my breathing.

'Hannibal! Stay!'

I couldn't take my eyes off the dog, but I recognised Doogie's voice. 'Get up, Fairfax!' he said, and I felt a kick in the ribs.

I pulled myself to my feet.

The dog stood foursquare in front of me. It was only about two feet off the ground at the shoulder. But it was strong, and powerful, and I didn't want to mess with it.

Doogie pointed to my groin.

The dog moved closer, its muzzle an inch from my trousers, still growling in short low bursts. It's saliva dripped on to my knees. I pushed my back as hard as I could into the wall, and inched my hands forward to protect me.

'Don't do that!' shouted Doogie. 'You'll lose your fingers!'

Slowly, I moved them back by my sides.

'You saw our demonstration today,' said Doogie. I took my eyes off the dog for a second to glance at him. He was standing loosely on the balls of his feet. His voice was calm, but menacing. 'Virtual reality has to be stopped, and we're going to stop it. Whatever it takes.'

The dog growled. I looked down. A strand of saliva was hanging down from its lips.

'Now some people are going to get hurt. FairSystems, for example. We're going to destroy FairSystems. Do you understand that?'

I didn't say anything. I just kept my eyes on the dog.

'So if I were you, I'd just forget all about it and piss off back down to London. And don't go crying to the police about any of this, eh?'

I wasn't watching Doogie, so the punch took me by surprise. It was a quick movement, a rapid blow to the solar plexus. Once again I fell to the ground, and this time I couldn't breathe in. I opened my mouth but the air wouldn't come. The surface of the road went black around the edges. Then, finally, the air rushed in, and I took huge gulps of oxygen. I felt sick.

I lifted my head up from the pavement and saw Doogie's feet retreating down the road, Hannibal's paws trotting along beside them.

16

The morning papers all carried something about the demonstration, but in most of them it was tucked away in the middle. They were careful about Doogie's allegations. Like Reuters they talked about 'unconfirmed reports'. There was a small article in the *Financial Times*. According to Susan there had been a clip on *Scotland Today*, the regional news programme. She said my confrontation with 'that Doogie' was quite dramatic. It seemed that within the company Doogie wasn't remembered very favourably.

Rachel came into my office at about eleven.

'You're looking a lot better this morning,' I said.

She smiled. 'It's amazing what twelve hours' sleep can do. But did you see the papers?'

'Yeah. It's not good, is it? Still, it could have been worse. At least they couldn't confirm the story.'

'Ah ha. I wonder why Doogie didn't show them the letter?'

'You don't believe that bit about the family wanting to remain anonymous, do you?'

'No. That was crap.'

'You know I saw him last night.'

'Where?'

'Outside Inch Lodge. With his dog. He said he would destroy FairSystems. He told me to go back to London.'

'Why should you?'

'He and his dog were quite persuasive.'

'Ooh.' Rachel winced. 'Did you tell the police?'

'He warned me not to, but I did. I saw Sergeant Cochrane this morning. They'll give Doogie a hard time over it. But there weren't any witnesses, so they can't actually prosecute him. And according to Cochrane, Doogie seems actually to enjoy being questioned by the police. The harassment gives him some sort of legitimacy as a true revolutionary. Apparently, he's an expert on his rights. And his dog's.'

'Are you going to take any notice of him?'

'No,' I smiled. 'I don't like being threatened.'

'Good. But be careful. You never know what Doogie will do.'

'I will be, don't worry.'

Rachel turned to leave. Her way was blocked by Susan. 'Carl Jenson's here again. He wants to see you.'

'Jenson?' I looked at Rachel. She shrugged. 'OK, send him up. Can you stay for this, Rachel?'

Within a minute, Jenson had rushed into my office.

'Hey, Mark. Rachel. How're you doing?'

I gestured to a chair, but he ignored me. 'I like that,' he said, pointing to the electronic window. 'I see the sun moves across the sky depending on the time of day. But does the day shorten in winter?'

I had no idea.

'No,' said Rachel. 'It's May, all the year round.'

Jenson nodded to himself. 'Cool. I gotta get one of those.'

He took a seat, and leaned forward. 'I'm worried about your company, Mark.' Straight to the point.

'Oh yes?'

'Yeah. You're shortly going to be a key supplier for us. And we need to know you're going to be around for the next couple of years. Are you?'

There it was, the question that had been dogging me since Richard's death, asked baldly.

'Well, I have been reviewing the figures with Willie Duncan, our finance director, this morning, and – '

'I don't want horseshit,' barked Jenson. 'I want to know. Will FairSystems still be here in two years' time?'

'I think so.' Despite myself, my voice cracked.

His eyes bored into me. 'Oh yeah? Well I think you might not be. I've seen a lot of companies fold in my time, and you're showing the signs. Falling stock price, threat of litigation, rumours of a cover-up, original founder replaced by a financial chief executive. I've seen 'em all.'

'I can explain,' I protested. 'You can hardly blame us for Richard's death. Technically things are still progressing fast – '

'Cut the crap,' said Jenson. 'You're in the shit and you and I both know it. And you can't handle it. You told me yourself yesterday that you're finding it hard to manage FairSystems.'

I reeled. If he was trying to goad me, he was succeeding. But worse was the sudden rush of panic I felt. He's going to take away the Project Platform contract. Without it, we're definitely sunk. I glanced over to Rachel. Even she looked rattled.

'Don't worry, I'll keep Project Platform with you,' said Jenson. 'I just think it would be best to withhold the advance payments until September.'

No! We needed that five hundred thousand pounds desperately. There was no way we could wait until September for it. I recalled the numbers Willie and I had pored over earlier that morning. The company would be out of cash by the end of June.

'Mr Jenson,' I said. 'You know how important cash flow is to a small, growing company like ours. It would be very disruptive if we didn't get the cash you owe us on time. That would be a breach of contract, and we may have to halt the Project Platform work entirely.' Of course I didn't know what was in the Project Platform contract, but I had to bluster.

'Hey kid. You'll complete the Project Platform project. You have to, or you got no future.'

I was in a corner, struggling. Try a compromise.

'Perhaps you could pay us two hundred and fifty thousand now, and the rest in July?' I suggested.

'No.' Jenson was firm. 'I'm not about to lose three-quarters of a million bucks and screw up a major project because you go under next month. That would be stupid, and I'm not stupid. If you can survive till September, then I know you'll be around for the long-term, and you'll get paid. If not, it's been nice knowing you.' He gave me a quick smile. 'You're a finance guy. You'll find the money. Just give your Wall Street buddies a call.'

'Carl, you can't be serious,' said Rachel.

'I am serious,' he said. 'Sorry, Rachel.'

'If you refuse to pay us the money you owe us, we'll cancel Project Platform,' I said, 'and then we'll sue you.'

Jenson held up his hands. 'If that's the way you want to play it. You think about it. I'm flying back to the States now. Call me tomorrow and tell me whether you want to go ahead.' He sprung up from his chair. 'Be good,' he said, and he was gone.

I put my head in my hands. Oh shit. This was it. This had to be the end. There was no way in hell FairSystems was going to make it now. It was less than two weeks since I had taken over Richard's company, and already it was finished.

I sat up. Rachel still looked stunned. 'Did you expect that?' I asked.

'No. It doesn't make sense. We're too important to Jenson for him to dump us.'

'Well, that's what he's done.'

'Do we carry on with Project Platform?' Rachel asked.

'Do we hell!' I said, angrily. Then I thought for a moment. 'Well, maybe you should keep working on it. Just don't give Jenson anything new. Is that possible?'

'I suppose it is.'

'Good. I'd like the project still to be alive if Jenson changes his mind so we can respond quickly. I hope I never have to deal with him again, but we may have no choice. He's right; it's our only hope. Now, I suppose I'd better tell the others.'

A couple of minutes later, David and Willie had joined us. I told them the news.

Willie sucked in through his teeth, and muttered 'dear dear' to himself several times. David didn't seem bothered at all. In fact, he seemed quite pleased.

219

'What do we do now?' asked Willie.

'How long do you think we can last without the Jenson money?'

Willie pulled out his projections. 'We might make it through the next four weeks. I doubt we'll make the June payroll.'

It was 19 May today. FairSystems paid its employees on the fifteenth. We had less than a month.

I returned to Kirkhaven that night depressed. I drove slowly along the quay, but didn't see any sign of Doogie. Or, more importantly, his dog. I walked out along the harbour wall, and sat down to think; or rather to brood.

I had failed. There was no other word for it. I had let down all the people for whom I most cared. Karen. My father. Richard. His company would be lucky if it survived him by two months.

I knew it wasn't all my fault. But I was used to winning, to having luck on my side, to making money. Secretly I believed that you made your own luck, and only losers failed because of 'circumstances beyond their control'.

The truth was that I knew nothing about virtual reality, and nothing about running a business. I had done my best to ignore this fact, trusting to my own intelligence and common sense to overcome all problems, but my initial self-confidence had reached a low ebb. Sorenson's trust in me had been totally misplaced.

And I still had no idea who had killed Richard.

I looked out to sea. The wind blew against my cheeks. It was cold. I couldn't see the sun behind the layers of cloud. Suddenly I felt moisture against my face; it wasn't spray but rain. I huddled beneath my jacket.

What the hell was I doing here?

It was probably seventy degrees in London right now. I could be drinking a beer on my terrace, waiting for Karen to come home. Suddenly the hubbub of the Harrison Brothers trading room beckoned, like a large family painfully missed. Greg, Ed, the other traders, the screens, the buying and selling.

And then there was Karen. I felt a long way away from her. It might have been my imagination, but I felt that the physical distance between us was affecting our relationship. Well, if that was true, what was I doing up here, piddling about with a lost cause? I should have been spending more time with her, not less.

So, I arranged to spend the weekend with Karen, and Monday at Harrison Brothers.

'Tell me about it,' Karen said. She was curled up on the sofa with a glass of wine. She looked lovely, her fine blonde hair rested lightly on her shoulders, which were turning light brown under the first showing of May sunshine. Her slim calves were seductively tucked up under a blue summer dress.

We had spent the afternoon racing at Sandown. It had been a good day. Busker's Boy had run for the first time in a two-mile flat race, and I'd put a hundred pounds on him to win. I had lost it when he had come second by a length, but he had run well, and I didn't feel a complete fool. And Karen had managed to pick three winners by betting on yellow. She was fifty pounds ahead, and that had put her in a very good mood.

I had cooked supper, and we unwound in each other's company. Until now, Karen had stayed clear of the subject of Fair-Systems, and I had been grateful.

But now I was eager to talk. 'I think FairSystems is going bust,' I said.

'Well, if the shares are down to three dollars, it must be bad.'

'Oh, I don't think the market knows how bad it really is. That fall was on worries that VR systems kill people. Which is bad enough. But what's worse is that we've just lost our biggest customer.'

I told her all about Jenson, and what I knew about Project Platform. I also told her about Doogie's threats.

She listened sympathetically. 'It's not your fault.'

'Of course it is,' I snapped. Karen looked startled. 'Sorry,' I said. 'But I've let you down, I've let everyone down.'

'Bullshit. There was nothing you could have done. Where's

221

this famous trader's detachment? You're getting emotionally involved.'

'Of course I am! It is my brother's company after all!'

'OK, OK,' said Karen. 'Mark, I know FairSystems is important to you. But you've tried and done your best. There's no more you can do. No more anyone can do. Face it, you've got this trade wrong, but there's still time to get out with something. Take your losses.'

Her words cut through the clouds of worry and despair like a ray of common sense.

'How long have you got till the cash runs out?'

'A month, maybe less.'

'That still might be enough time to sell the company. You mentioned there were buyers about. Sell out and salvage what you can. Forget FairSystems. Forget that nutcase, Doogie. Come back to London.'

I thought through what she had just said. Nothing short of a miracle would keep the company afloat now. If it went bust, it wouldn't help anyone. At least if it were sold, the workforce would keep their jobs and Richard's technology would live on. Dad might not like it. Rachel might not like it. But there was no choice.

'You're right,' I said. 'I'll sell the company.'

We made love that night. It had been a while. I had missed Karen, and we had had a good day together. But once again it didn't quite work.

Was it me? Was it her? I didn't know.

Afterwards, I asked, 'Is anything wrong?'

'No,' she said. 'Everything's fine.'

Puzzled, I rolled over and went to sleep.

It was amazing how, once I had taken the decision to sell, my mind cleared. I still felt bad about it. I had failed. I felt guilty that I was betraying Richard in his wish that FairSystems should remain independent. And I had let down my father.

Also, I had failed completely to find out any more about

Richard's death. I was sure it was tied up with FairSystems in some way, but I had no idea how. And if fifty of Fife's finest couldn't work it out, how could I?

Karen was right. I was in a losing position. There was nothing I could do to make it better. I should take my losses, get out and move on to the next opportunity.

One thing I didn't like was giving Doogie the idea that he had scared me into running away. But that was only pride. And, truth be told, it would be nice not to see that bloody dog again.

I called Sorenson on Sunday evening, and told him my decision. He was supportive, encouraging even. He had been unable to produce a miraculous solution when I had told him about Jenson's withdrawal of the advance payments. He didn't seem to blame me for what had happened, and he agreed wholeheartedly with my decision to sell.

He said he would talk to my father, who rang me half an hour later.

'Walter's spoken to me,' he said.

'I'm sorry, Dad. But we have to sell.'

He sighed. 'Yes, I know. It's a shame.'

Silence.

'Walter told me this had nothing to do with you,' he said. 'Thanks for trying.'

'That's OK.' They were kind words, but I still felt I had let him down. And, to my annoyance, I cared.

I plunged into the familiar buzz of the Harrison Brothers trading room. I strode towards my desk with anticipation. According to the weekend papers, the trade that Ed and I had put on the previous month was finally coming right.

I got to my desk and turned on my machines. 'Hi, Ed,' I said as I tapped in the page number for the US treasury market. He was on the phone, but he gave me a wave.

I was right! The spread between the two- and ten-year US treasury bonds had tightened from 1.40 to 1.28 per cent. I did some quick calculations in my head. That was nearly a point profit on a hundred million dollars, or just under a million bucks! Not bad.

Ed finished his call. 'Look at this!' I called over to him. 'Did we get it right, or did we get it right?'

He winced and scratched the back of his head. Something was wrong. I looked at him and thought.

'We have still got the trade on, haven't we?'

'Not exactly,' said Ed.

'What do you mean, not exactly?'

'I took it off last week.'

'Oh. How much of a profit did you lock in?'

Ed was writhing in his chair. He had developed a devastating itch behind his shoulder blade, which he rubbed as he screwed up his face.

'It was more like a loss. A two hundred and forty thousand loss, to be precise. The market had a hiccup at the long end for a couple of days last week. A big account sold ten years and bought three years. The trade moved against us, so I cut it. Then it came right back.'

I couldn't believe it. I had told Ed to leave the trade on. How could he possibly have lost that much? I felt a complete fool for having trusted him. The guy must be a total moron.

Ed read my expression and winced in pain again. 'Etienne told me to take it off.'

'Etienne? What do you mean?'

'Well, he's been looking over my shoulder every day since you left. As soon as the trade went underwater, Etienne noticed and told me to cut my losses.'

'Why didn't you call me at FairSystems?'

'I did, but you weren't there.' I remembered receiving a message that Ed had called. I had ignored it; I'd been too preoccupied with what was going on at the company. 'Besides, Etienne told me to take it off right away. Two hours after I sold the position the trade started to go our way.'

I was furious, but not with Ed. I was mostly angry with myself. And I wanted to kill Etienne.

'OK, Ed, don't worry about it,' I said, and I stood up to discuss the matter with Etienne.

Ed picked up the phone, cowered in his chair, and kept his eyes glued to the screen.

'Etienne, may I have a word,' I said moving over to where he was standing next to Greg.

'Not now, mate, I am busy,' said Etienne in his strange French bond trader accent. His English was very good but there were certain words that mixed cockney and Parisian. The effect in one so smooth was bizarre.

'Yes, now,' I replied. 'Why did you tell Ed Bayliss to sell my treasury position?'

'I said not now. I said I am busy,' Etienne answered, without looking at me. He picked up Greg's phone.

I pulled it out of its socket. Etienne turned to me, anger flaring in his eyes.

'We could have made a million dollars from that trade, instead of losing two hundred grand!' I was aware that the trading room had suddenly gone quiet.

'The trade was too big for Ed to handle,' he replied, his voice a barely controlled growl. 'He is only a kid. He had lost two hundred thousand. How long should I have waited? Until he lost half a million?'

'I was in control. You could have called me.'

Etienne turned to look at me. 'How many times did you call in in the last two weeks, *hein*?'

I was momentarily at a loss for words. 'Uh, well . . .'

'None!' shouted Etienne. 'You leave a kid with three months' experience a four hundred million dollar position to manage in the most dangerous markets we have seen for years, and you don't even call in! You are dangerous, mate. Bloody dangerous.'

I didn't say anything. If Etienne had just let Ed handle it we would have been well on the way to making back the $2.4 million. I was angry with Etienne, but also angry with myself. I knew that in a way he was right, I should have checked in. If only I had answered Ed's call.

But I forced myself to turn on my heel and walk the five paces back to my desk. Ed cowered next to me.

Etienne disappeared out of the trading room in disgust, and Greg strolled over.

'Guess that trade didn't work too well, huh?'

'Piss off,' I said.

He leaned against my desk. 'How are you doing, buddy?'

'I've been better,' I muttered.

'How's it going in Scotland?'

'Not good. I think I'm going to have to sell FairSystems.'

'Too bad,' Greg said. 'But that means you'll be back here soon?'

'I expect so.'

'Good. We've missed you.' He nodded to Ed. 'This guy's been doing well without you. I'm sorry I couldn't stop Etienne taking that trade off. But Ed's pointed out some great opportunities for me on that Bondscape machine.'

'Good for you.'

'No, seriously. He's done well.' And with that Greg sauntered off towards the coffee machine.

I turned to Ed. 'OK, I made a mistake. From now on you don't take a trade off without checking with me first. And I will call in regularly. OK?'

'OK.'

'So what do we do now?' I asked. 'The ten-year two-year trade hasn't got much left in it, so there's no point in putting it back on. But I'm determined to make back that money we lost last month.'

'I have an idea,' Ed said, looking at me nervously.

I relaxed. Greg was right. Ed was a bright kid. If he had a good idea, I didn't want to scare him off. 'OK. Let's hear it,' I said in as encouraging a voice as I could muster.

'Take a look at this,' he gestured to the Bondscape glasses lying beside him. Bondscape was now permanently installed at his desk, adding to the considerable clutter that was already there.

I moved my chair next to his, and put on the glasses. I was

transported into the Bondscape world of gently rolling green hills and scattered buildings. There was something both thrilling and restful about it. Thrilling because you felt yourself literally surrounded by the world's billions of financial instruments. The sheer size and might of the global capital markets pressed in all around you. When the markets moved rapidly, it was scary, you felt you would be crushed by the sliding buildings, which grew and shrank above and below you.

But on quiet days like today, the buildings languished peacefully in the virtual sunlight as they rested on gently sloping hills. The eagle wheeled serenely overhead.

I found myself at the foot of a very tall building surrounded by a cluster of much smaller ones. Italian flags flew above each of them. The tall building covered a large area. This suggested it was a big Italian government issue, and it had a much higher yield than other similar issues.

'It's the CCTs of August oh-one,' said Ed.

The bonds he meant were the Certificati di Credito del Tesoro maturing August 2001. They had the full backing of the Italian government.

I checked the roof of the building for the yield. 'It's two and a half per cent over LIBOR! That's ridiculous,' I said. Two and a half per cent over LIBOR meant it would be possible to borrow money, buy this bond and lock in a profit of two and a half per cent with little risk. That is what is technically called a 'free lunch'.

I took the glasses off. 'Why is it so cheap?'

'All sorts of reasons. The Italians have just decided to levy withholding tax on CCTs, so everyone has been dumping them. Then, in their wisdom, the Italian treasury decided to launch their biggest CCT issue ever.'

'And it was a flop?'

'A total disaster. It's at a price of ninety-five, and it should be trading at ninety-eight.'

'Where's the catch?'

'There isn't one,' said Ed.

227

I spent half an hour running through the details of the bond with him. He was right. No catch.

So we bought a hundred million dollars of the CCTs, and I went back up to Scotland.

17

'We have no choice but to sell,' I said. 'I've spoken to Walter about it and he agrees. I'll call Scott Wagner this afternoon and get him to work on it.'

I looked for reactions. Willie was relieved. David just smiled. Rachel didn't like it.

'Are you asking us or telling us?' Her voice was cutting.

'I'm afraid I'm telling you,' I said. 'But we can put it to a vote if you like.' I sensed that Willie and David were on my side.

'Can't we persuade Jenson to change his mind?'

'I tried. He was pretty adamant.'

'What about banks? You should have contacts in the City. Can't you arrange something?'

'No bank in its right mind would lend us money in our current state. It would be pouring money down the drain.'

'Well, I'm against it,' said Rachel. 'We all know Richard would never have sold out, so I don't think we should, just because he's . . . dead.' Rachel was getting quite upset. Colour had rushed to her cheeks, and her voice was wavering. It took us all aback. We weren't used to Rachel getting emotional about anything.

'If we find the right parent, then you can carry on your work,' I said gently. 'You can still bring virtual reality out into the world.'

'Don't patronise me!' shouted Rachel. 'I can't believe you're doing this! You've seen how hard we've all fought to get this far. Richard, me, Keith, Andy, Terry, David, Willie, even you. All those seven-day weeks. The twenty-four-hour days. All those impossible problems solved.' Her face was bright red now, and the words were tumbling out. 'And we're so close. So bloody close. And now you're going to throw it all away, ignore everything your brother believed in, all he worked for!' She stood up. 'Well, you can do it without me!' she shouted, and stormed out.

We all sat there, stunned. 'She'll come round,' said David. 'She doesn't have any choice. All geniuses are entitled to a tantrum every now and then.'

I sighed. 'OK, I'll get in touch with Wagner Phillips and see what buyers they can come up with. One month should give us just enough time if we move. But we must stretch every last penny.'

David and Willie left. I sat and pondered Rachel's reaction.

I had suspected she would be against a sale, but I hadn't anticipated the strength of emotion in her response. David was wrong. It was most unlike her to have a tantrum. And without her the company would be worthless.

I was tempted to leave her to cool down. But something made me go after her. There was something wrong, something that she knew about and the rest of us didn't. Now was the time for her to tell me what it was.

The blinds in Rachel's office were drawn so I couldn't see in. Keith, Andy and the others stared as I walked past them to her door. I knocked.

No answer.

I pushed the door open, crept in, and closed it behind me.

Rachel was sitting, her head in her hands, her hair falling down in front of her face to the desk. She was sobbing quietly. She didn't look up.

'Rachel?'

She still didn't look up. The sobbing stopped and was replaced by sniffs.

I sat down in the chair in front of her desk and waited. Her weeping made me uncomfortable, but I decided to stay. I knew that if she wanted me to leave she would tell me.

She didn't.

After a minute or so, she sat up and threw her hair back from her face. Her cheeks were blotched red and shiny with tear stains. There was a drip on the end of her nose, which she wiped with a sleeve.

We sat in silence.

Then she said, 'You know this is the first time I've cried for him. He's been dead nearly a month, and this is the first time I've cried.'

She tried hard to control her voice, breathing deeply, talking slowly and deliberately, but it didn't work. She sobbed, and hung her head in her hands again.

I didn't say anything. I wanted to say something like 'there, there,' but it seemed so weak I thought it better just to sit and listen.

'God, I miss him,' she said. 'He was a wonderful person. A truly great person. And I can't accept that he's gone.

'Sometimes, late at night, when I'm in here working, I feel that he's here with me. That we're worrying over a problem together. I can be working here for two or three hours with him. And we come up with ideas, with solutions. Together.'

She had controlled her sobbing, but she wanted to talk. 'I worked with him for so long on all of this. I was often the only person in the world who could follow where his brain was going. I felt privileged, special. And now there's so much going on in here,' she pointed to her head, 'and no one to share it with. Sometimes I think it will drive me mad.'

'Did you love him?' I asked.

She stared at me for several moments deciding how to answer. She wasn't shocked by the question. I was sure it was something she had worried over during those long nights.

'I don't know. I don't know what love is. Do you?'

Did I? Of course I did. I loved Karen, didn't I? Didn't I? I wasn't sure.

Then I thought of Richard.

'I loved him,' I said.

She gave me a small smile. An acknowledgement that she understood. That she respected my love for my brother.

Then her face darkened. She took a deep breath. 'And then you talk about selling out, selling everything that he worked for. And it's like you're killing him again. Don't you see?'

'I understand,' I said. 'But there's nothing I can do.'

'You don't understand.'

That hurt, but I didn't want to argue. I shrugged my shoulders.

Her eyes rested on mine. Beneath the moisture and uncertainty, raw intelligence stirred. She was thinking. She came to a decision. 'You don't understand, because you don't know about Project Platform.' She stood up. 'Come on.'

She shook out her hair, smoothed her jersey, straightened her shoulders, and walked out. I followed her.

We crossed the room to the door marked Project Platform. She took out a Chubb key and unlocked the door. I raised my eyebrows.

She gave me a weak smile. 'The guys back there could break into almost any modern access system known to man. But none of them is a locksmith.'

The room was small. It contained a Silicon Graphics workstation, and two Jenson PCs. All three had FairSystems virtual glasses linked to them. There were also the tell-tale spoors of Rachel, an empty wine bottle, a full ashtray. One wall held a large white board. Rachel's small neat handwriting covered it. It was a work schedule for Project Platform.

We sat down. Rachel turned on one of the Jensons. 'Try this,' she said, passing me the virtual glasses, and handing me a wand.

I put the glasses on. I found myself in a plush office. Rachel was sitting opposite me at a well-polished mahogany table. Behind her was a terrific view of a modern city under a cloudless sky.

'Hi,' said Rachel. It was a good image of her, almost as good as a photograph. And she moved naturally. 'Although in reality I'm sitting right next to you, I could just as easily be hundreds of miles away.' She smiled. 'Both you and I could be working from home, and need to talk to each other. This way we can have a realistic meeting without ever leaving our homes.'

'But can't you just talk over the phone?'

Rachel smiled. 'You can, but face to face is better. Body language is everything in social interaction. Sensors in the virtual glasses can detect a range of expressions that are then replicated on the virtual image you see in front of you. Besides, meetings are better than the phone when there are more than two of you. Let me get Keith to join us, and I'll show you what I mean.'

She paused and a few seconds later Keith walked into the virtual room, wearing his uniform of black jeans and T-shirt. 'Hi, Rache, what's up?' His eyebrows raised when he saw me. 'Who's this?' he asked.

'It's Mark,' Rachel said. 'Don't worry, I had to tell him about Project Platform.'

Then she turned to me. 'To us, you look like Mel Gibson. That's why Keith didn't recognise you.'

'Mel Gibson?'

'Yes. He's our default male. My choice. Once you've been body-mapped, then you'll look like yourself in the virtual world. Of course, there's nothing to stop you choosing a totally different image for yourself, if you want to. You'll notice that Keith has managed to put on a fair bit of muscle.'

It was true. Keith's normally skinny frame had filled out, his pectoral muscles clearly defined under his T-shirt. I laughed.

'Now, let's say we all wanted to look at some figures together. Boring, but one of those things people do in real life.' She pulled out a piece of paper from under the table, and passed it over to me. It was one of Willie's forecasts. 'See that figure there?' she said, pointing to the cash balance. 'Try to change it.'

'Happily,' I said. 'What do I do?'

'Just point to it, say "change", and then the number you want.'

233

I changed the number to one million. The whole forecast changed, and FairSystems ended the year solvent.

Keith laughed. 'Easy, isn't it?'

It was strange how quickly I could get used to the virtual world. Within a couple of minutes it did take on its own reality. And it was true that it was much easier to talk to three people in a virtual office than over a phone.

'Do you mind if I go now?' asked Keith.

'No, thanks for joining us,' Rachel replied. The virtual Keith walked out of the office.

'Now, do you want to buy a house?'

'All right,' I said, not knowing what to expect.

In a moment we were outside an ordinary suburban semi-detached house. 'Follow me,' said Rachel.

I didn't do anything, but the virtual me followed Rachel inside. We walked through an empty hallway into a living room. There was a garden through the french windows.

'Now, virtual representations of furniture have been saved in a database. Let's see how they fit in the house.'

Rachel pointed and clicked, and soon a sofa, table, bookcase, desk and armchair were all in the room. She tried different configurations. 'Wander round,' she said. I found that I could now move around the house. I looked in the kitchen, walked up the stairs, and checked out the bathroom.

'You see?' Rachel said. 'It certainly makes buying a house easier. The rooms can be fed into the computer from drawings, or even measurements, and the furniture uses a database of four hundred different pieces. You just select those which are most like your own.'

We were back in the office. 'As you know, some of the biggest applications for computer programs are databases. Well, VR can help you see data in an entirely new way. Most databases can only be viewed in two dimensions on a record card. With VR, you can watch data in at least three dimensions. In Bond-scape, there were eight dimensions. Let me show you a much simpler database.'

We switched to a map of Britain, dotted with a series of

columns, each made up of a number of blocks piled one on top of the other. 'Assume you're a salesman, covering customers throughout the country. This database shows you all your customers. Take a look at Leeds.'

I pointed to Leeds, and clicked. I was standing on a station platform, next to a sign saying Leeds. Beside me rose a large column of blocks. Each had a name, address and telephone number.

'These are stacked in order of when they were last seen,' Rachel said. 'The blocks at the top are those that you saw most recently. Or we can reshuffle them.' The blocks blanked, and then stood out in a different order. 'Now the blocks at the top are your biggest customers. Let me find out which buy widgets and which gadgets.' Suddenly the blocks were coloured in, red for widgets, blue for gadgets.

'It's possible to get all this information on an ordinary database, of course, but in VR you can analyse it much more clearly. This is an example of how, when you begin to use VR, you suddenly see old information in a new light.'

We left the database, and went back to the office. 'There are all kinds of other things you could use this system for,' she continued. 'Booking a holiday. You could see the area you were staying in, and the hotel. Shopping. You could buy anything from tins of beans in a supermarket to a car. You know from playing Manhunt with my brother how experiencing a game in virtual reality is much more fun than watching it on a screen. And the computer games market is huge.

'Then there is social communication. We're in an office here, but people will soon be able to communicate over the phone wires using VR. Once people are used to it, then voice or text messages just will not be enough.'

She shut the machine down. 'With this system, VR will move from specialised, expensive applications, to the sort of everyday uses that an ordinary individual in a business or at home might want.'

'Phew,' I said. 'Can we really do all that?'

'We have the technology to do it, yes,' said Rachel. 'Of course we need communication systems to improve, but once fibre optic cable reaches most homes and offices, VR will follow.'

'Who designed all these applications?'

'A whole range of software companies. They all used our software and graphics chip.'

'It's very impressive. But can't you do much of this on standard computers?' I asked.

'You can do the calculations. But display is all important. Once you've used VR, then a flat screen will seem primitive. Businessmen, Internet surfers, games players, they'll all want it.'

'And we'll do all this with Jenson?'

'Yes. We use our graphics chip, our simulation manager, and our headsets. Jenson manufactures them all in volume. The price comes down to two thousand dollars a system.'

'Two thousand dollars?'

'Yep.'

I thought it through. There was still a big problem, the problem that had dogged us all along. 'We still don't have a mass market. How do we create one?'

'That's where Project Platform comes in,' said Rachel. 'Look at this.'

Rachel clicked some buttons on her computer. Windows came up. Windows is the operating system used on eighty per cent of personal computers.

'OK?' I said.

'Look at the bottom row, on the right.'

I did. There was a little picture, or icon, of a person wearing a pair of virtual glasses.

'You mean our system is going to run under Windows?'

Rachel grinned. 'Yes. Project Platform is the codename for the alliance between us, Jenson and Microsoft. Our system will be bundled up with every copy of Windows sold. If anyone wants to use a VR application under Windows they'll have to use FairSystems' simulation management software, and the FairRender graphics system. And it will be right there, on everyone's computer, just waiting for them to try out.'

'How much do we charge for this?'

'Not much,' said Rachel. 'But it will give us a tremendous advantage in developing new software. And even a couple of dollars is a lot on tens of millions of computers sold.'

'And Jenson makes money on selling the computers.'

'Right. He gets a head start over the competition in making virtual reality PCs. What's more, if anyone wants to make a PC that will use VR, they'll have to buy a FairRender chip, made by Jenson.'

'So we all make money. How about Microsoft? What's in it for them?'

'They get the use of the most advanced VR system for PCs in the world, and they kick-start a whole new market.'

'Wow,' I said. 'If this works, our royalties could be worth millions.'

'It's more than that,' said Rachel. 'This is a revolution in computer technology that is about to happen, almost as great as when IBM introduced the PC in 1981.'

'You're right. And we're IBM.' I thought about the IBM PC, and how many millions had been made during the 1980s. Soon companies like Compaq and Jenson had learned how to clone them. IBM had made good money for ten years, and so had the others.

'No,' she said patiently. 'Jenson Computer is IBM.'

Then it came to me.

'Microsoft.'

Rachel nodded.

I saw the weedy image of Bill Gates staring up from the book Richard had left open on his sofa. Bill Gates' firm, Microsoft, owned DOS and Windows, the operating systems that drove most of the millions of personal computers used round the world. In less than fifteen years, Microsoft had grown from nothing to be worth more even than the mighty IBM. And the reason was that the Microsoft operating system had become the standard. Just as IBM had promoted Microsoft with its personal computer, so Microsoft would promote FairSystems through Windows.

237

In the new world of mass market virtual reality, FairSystems would own the standard operating software.

I remembered Microsoft was worth more than thirty billion dollars.

And I was considering selling FairSystems for ten million dollars or even less.

No wonder Rachel didn't want to do it. No wonder Richard had been so keen to avoid a sale at all costs.

Richard had been right all along. He was on the brink of building a company that would change the world. And it wasn't just pretty technology. This company could be stupendously successful in terms that I understood: turnover, profits, market capitalisation.

My trader's mind began churning. This would be the trade of the century if I could pull it off. Sure, the odds were against it. It still looked like FairSystems would go bust before Project Platform hit the streets. But if I could manage to keep the company alive for the next four months . . .

I took a deep breath. 'OK,' I said. 'We don't sell. We'll get through to September somehow.'

Rachel's face lit up. She jumped out of her chair. 'Yes!' she shouted, and leaned over and gave me a quick, triumphant kiss on the lips.

Surprised and elated, I said, 'Let's calm down and work out how to do it.'

We talked through the options. There weren't many, but neither of us was downhearted. Although there was no obvious solution, I was confident that I would find one somehow.

'Given what you've told me, Jenson's decision to ditch us seems completely crazy,' I said. 'He's shooting himself in the foot.'

'I know. I can't figure it out.'

'I wonder what Microsoft think? Have you any idea?'

'No. The negotiations for that end of the deal were all done by Jenson. He's a big customer of Microsoft, and he has a close relationship with them. I think Richard met them, but no one else in FairSystems has. Apart from a couple of their software people who I've spoken to, that is. Why? Are you thinking of talking to them?'

I rubbed my chin. 'I don't think so. I don't want to scare them into going somewhere else. We should carry on as if nothing has happened. Jenson's bluffing, I'm sure of it. What I'm not sure of is why?'

'I could go and talk to him,' Rachel said. 'I need to go to California anyway to check out the motorbike accident. Maybe I could find something out at Jenson. Until last week, he and I got on quite well.'

'It's a good idea. Try it.' I frowned. 'But we certainly can't rely on those payments from Jenson. We need to get some cash from somewhere. And quickly.'

I had to wait till two that afternoon to call Scott Wagner. It was six a.m. in San Francisco, but he was already in the office. You have to get up early if you want to play the financial markets from California.

'I want to talk to you about the possibility of raising some new equity,' I began. 'We have some very interesting projects coming up, but we'll need some more money if we're to finance them properly.'

'How much?' Wagner asked.

'Oh, five million dollars would cover it,' I said casually.

'When do you need it?'

'A month.'

'That's too fast.'

'Couldn't you just go to existing investors for more cash? It would significantly improve the value of the whole company.'

'No point.'

'Why not?'

'They're not too impressed with your track record so far,' said Wagner. 'The shares are down to three dollars from the ten they invested at. They're not going to throw good money after bad. If you need finance, why don't you just face reality and sell to a stronger company?'

'We have a real future as an independent – ' I began.

Wagner's voice hardened. 'Mark, you don't understand.

There is no possibility of raising any money for FairSystems at this time. The track record sucks, and it looks like the company is falling apart since your brother died. Your only hope is to sell. I control the shares, and I am telling you to sell.'

I was shocked by his tone. 'I've decided to run this company independently.'

'I don't care what you've decided. I'm telling you to sell. So sell.'

'Who owns the shares?'

'In effect, I do.'

'If you're acting in concert to threaten me, aren't you breaking SEC rules?'

'Look buddy,' said Wagner. 'You've fucked up bad. Your shareholders don't like it. They want you to sell up and get out. I've given you an offer you won't refuse. So take it.'

'Who is the buyer?'

'I can't tell you yet.'

'How much?'

'Four dollars a share. Eight million dollars for the whole company. Take it. You've got no choice.'

'Fuck off,' I said, and hung up.

So that was how Wagner's little community of investors and companies worked. He had done us a favour by raising equity, and now we owed him a favour. He controlled the equity, so he controlled us. I hated being beholden to Wagner. What really annoyed me was the obvious pleasure he got from exercising his power. Well, I would call his bluff, and see what trouble he could stir up.

Where else could we get money? I tried some of the banks we had asked earlier, but got emphatic 'Nos'. We would just have to press on and hope something turned up.

With a sigh, I rang my own bank manager, or rather my 'Personal Account Executive'. Since he had seen my bonus cheques he had been falling over himself to offer me assistance. Well, now he had a fine opportunity.

He was encouraging but cautious. I was a valued customer to the bank, but he would have to see the details before agreeing to the loan I was suggesting. I hoped we wouldn't get to that stage.

David put his head round the door.

'How's the sale going?'

'It isn't.'

'What do you mean, it isn't?'

'I mean we're not going to sell the company. I want one more try to get new money in.'

'What? You can't be serious!' He came into the room and stood squarely in front of my desk.

'I am.'

'And who decided this?'

'I did.'

'Jesus, Mark! We don't have time to muck around. If you don't start the process now, we'll go bust before we close a deal!'

I was tired of being pushed around. 'David,' I said. 'Leave it to me. All right?'

'You're doing your best to ruin this company, Mark. And I won't let you do it. I've got too much riding on this. If you don't do something, I will.' He turned on his heel, and swept past Rachel coming in, clutching two cups overfilled with coffee.

'Ow!' she cried, shaking her hand. 'That's hot! Here,' she passed me one. 'Black, isn't it?'

'Thanks,' I smiled. She sat opposite me.

We sipped our coffee in silence for a moment. 'Why is he so keen to sell?' I wondered aloud. 'He seemed positively to be smiling this morning.'

'I think he sees he has a good future in this company if it's taken over,' said Rachel. 'He'd get your job.'

'A buyer could always put their own man in,' I said. 'It would be the natural thing to do.'

'What's to stop him doing some sort of deal beforehand?'

'What, you mean he delivers FairSystems to a buyer and in return the buyer makes him MD?'

'Maybe.'

It would be just the sort of thing David would do, I thought. I would have to watch him very carefully. 'So who's he done a deal with?'

'I don't know,' said Rachel. 'Who's the buyer that Wagner has lined up?'

'Wagner Phillips is broker to a whole range of Californian high-tech companies. It could be any one of them.'

'Including Jenson Computer?'

'I don't know.' I followed Rachel's logic. 'But it's a thought. Jenson might have frozen our payment in the hope of forcing us to sell out cheaply to him. And he's using David Baker to help him, to provide an inside track.'

'Maybe. If Carl Jenson wants something, he gets it.'

'Why doesn't he just offer to buy us directly?'

Rachel shrugged. 'You're the investment banker. Perhaps he thinks he can get us cheaper this way.'

'If he can close a deal quickly, then Project Platform continues, and he owns the technology as well as manufacturing the product,' I said. It made sense. It made a lot of sense. 'See what you can find out when you get to California.'

I called Karen quickly. She looked up Jenson Computer on her Bloomberg screen. Their broker was Wagner Phillips.

It looked as though my marketing director, my most important customer and my broker were ganging up against me. This was not going to be easy.

Rachel flew out to California the next day, Wednesday. It would be a quick visit, she would be back on Saturday morning. I hoped she would be able to change Jenson's mind. She stood a better chance than I did.

I decided to tell as few people as possible that I had reversed my decision to sell. Telling David had been a mistake. I would stall Sorenson and the board, let them think that I was trying to do a deal.

The phone rang. It was Steve Schwartz.

'Mark, you know you asked me to find out who's buying your stock?'

'Yes.'

'The rumour is it's Frank Hartman.'

'Frank Hartman? Who's he?'

'I've never met him, but I've heard of him. He's an Ivan Boesky lookalike. He runs a hedge fund out of New York. Or at least it's called a hedge fund, because that's the fashionable name for these things. In the old days he would have been called an "arb". He buys stocks, and miraculously a little while later they go up when the company is taken over. Investors in his fund do very well.'

'Is he a crook?' I asked.

'You know there isn't black and white in this business. Only shades of grey.'

'And what shade is Hartman?'

Steve laughed. 'Charcoal.'

A question popped into my mind. 'Does he have any connection with Jenson Computer?'

'None that I know of. Why?'

'Oh, I don't know. I was just wondering. Thanks a lot, Steve. If you hear anything else, let me know.'

I called Karen to ask her what she knew about Hartman. Sally answered her phone and said she was out, but she would be back at lunchtime. I didn't leave a message. I'd call her that night.

I checked in with Ed. The Italian trade was half a point in the money, and moving up steadily. There had been no signs of interference from Etienne. Ed said Bob had spent half an hour with him, looking at Bondscape. He was almost convinced.

It was interesting to see how much Ed's self-confidence had developed in the last few weeks as he had been left by himself. I was surprised to feel myself threatened. He was clever and he learned very quickly. How long would it be until he learned all I knew? One year? Two years? It was a sobering thought.

There was a knock at my door. It was Keith and Andy. They looked agitated. Trouble, I thought.

'You got a second, Mark?' asked Keith.

'Of course.' They sat down. They made a strange couple, the loquacious, gangly chip designer, and the cherubic programmer,

243

who looked half the former's height and half his age. They both appeared worried. 'What's up?'

'There's a lot of talk around the factory,' Keith began.

'Oh yes? What about?'

'The rumour is we only have enough cash to see us through till July. Is that true?'

I couldn't lie to these people. 'Yes.'

'And is it also true that you're trying to sell the company?'

I hesitated. I had decided to keep my strategy to myself. But these two had invested so much of their lives in FairSystems. They had a right to know.

Before I had a chance to speak, Keith was talking. 'Because if that's what you want to do, you're wrong, man.'

I tried to interrupt, but he waved me to be quiet.

'If you'd been here the last three years, you wouldn't want to give up now. I mean, I've worked for big successful companies before, but this is different. We've got a great team here. The work we've done over the last few years, the problems we've overcome, the solutions we've found, it's been amazing. We eat sleep and dream this stuff.'

He leaned forward, eager to explain more. 'Take FairRender. Two years ago, I had an idea of how we could build this revolutionary new graphics chip. I told Richard. At first it seemed like it would take two more generations of chip design before it would be practical. So we put it on one side and tried something else. But I couldn't let it go. I was determined to find a way of fitting this system on one of today's chips.'

His hands were waving about now as he demonstrated what a big idea it was and what a tiny piece of silicon it had to fit on. 'I couldn't stop thinking about it. Eating, sleeping, watching TV, the problem was always there, you know, somewhere in my head. Then it came to me. I was on the bog. I stayed there over an hour.'

He leaned back triumphantly. 'And now FairRender is ready for production.'

I couldn't help smiling. 'But if we sell out, FairRender will still be produced, just by a bigger company,' I said.

'That's not the same thing,' said Andy. 'We're Richard's team. We're going to get Project Platform out his way. Or not at all.'

'You could lose your jobs.'

'We can get other jobs,' said Andy. 'But we can't recreate what we've got here.'

'What do the others think?'

'They're all with us,' insisted Keith.

'It'll be more difficult for some of them to find new work,' admitted Andy. 'But they'd hate to sell out now, believe me.'

Keith cleared his throat. 'Me and Andy have four thousand quid we can put up if it'll help.'

I smiled. 'We need a lot more than that. But I appreciate the gesture. You should keep your savings in the bank, you may need them.'

They both watched me in silence.

Eventually, I spoke. 'I've been impressed by the dedication I've seen in everyone in the factory. It's taken this company a long way. You've all worked hard to make FairSystems into something more than just a dream, and I'm not going to be the one to sell out just before we get to wherever we're going.'

'So you're not going to sell?' asked Keith, holding his breath.

'I'm not going to sell,' I said smiling.

'Hey!' said Keith, and he turned to Andy and grinned.

'It's a big risk I'm taking,' I said. 'And it's your jobs I'm risking.'

'That's fine with me,' said Andy.

'Yeah,' Keith grinned. 'We're nearly there. Let's not quit now.'

'Thanks for all your help.'

'No problem,' said Keith, 'Thank you for being straight with us. We'll make it. You'll see.' They both got up to leave.

As the door closed behind them, I looked at the photographs on Richard's wall. They were the first VR machines he had rigged up. They were strange contraptions. What was now a compact pair of virtual glasses, was then a massive helmet, hooked up to a metal arm, linked to a mini-computer. That was how Richard had tracked the movement of the head before

245

electromagnetic sensors had been developed. For some highly accurate applications, the old method was still used.

The company had come a long way since then. It represented so many different things. As Rachel and my father had said, it was all that was left of Richard. It was the manifestation of his dreams, and his achievements. It was also an opportunity to make or lose millions of pounds. And it was the livelihood of sixty people. I was risking sixty pay cheques.

But talking to Keith and Andy, I realised that FairSystems was more than a job to them, too. They hadn't put in all those hours just for a pay cheque. It was an adventure, an attempt to achieve what no one had ever achieved before, and for them, too, a chance to do something for Richard.

I wasn't going to let them down.

I called Karen that evening. I wanted to talk to her, and I was eager to find out about Hartman. She wasn't in. I tried later. Still no answer. I had one last go at a quarter to twelve. Nothing.

The next morning I called her at six fifteen. It should have been a good time to get hold of her. Her alarm clock was permanently set at six fifteen.

No reply.

OK. I admit it. It wasn't strictly necessary to ring her that early. I just wanted to see whether she had spent the night at home.

I rang her at work, at about ten.

'Hi, Mark, how are you?'

'I'm OK,' I said. 'I tried to ring you last night.'

There was the briefest of pauses at the other end of the line. 'Well, you missed me then. I had a late-afternoon meeting in Amsterdam, and it went on a bit. I missed the last flight home, and had to stay at a hotel at the airport. But I got the first plane to London, and I was only a few minutes late for work.'

'Oh, I see,' I said. 'Steve called me yesterday. He said that FairSystems' shares are being accumulated by someone called Frank Hartman. Do you know him?'

'No,' said Karen. 'I mean I've heard of him. But Harrison Brothers won't deal with him. He's supposed to be a bit dodgy.'

'He must be very dodgy if Harrison Brothers won't deal with him.' Our employers were not very particular about whom they dealt with, as long as it brought in a quick buck. 'Can you find out a bit more about him? You know, ask around?'

Karen hesitated. 'I'd rather not. I mean, I wouldn't like to be seen to have anything to do with him, even if it is only asking questions.'

'Can't you just make a few discreet enquiries?'

She hesitated. 'OK, Mark. I'll see what I can do. I've got to go now. There's someone on the other line.'

I put the phone down and thought.

So Karen had been stuck in Amsterdam. But hadn't Sally said that she would be back at her desk in London at lunchtime? Could she have left her desk after lunch, and got to a late-afternoon meeting in Amsterdam? Possibly. Possibly not.

I shook my head. I was probably just imagining things. Being away from Karen had made me more sensitive than usual.

18

It was good to see Rachel striding through the small crowd at the arrivals gate at Edinburgh airport. She smiled broadly when she saw me. Despite her protests, I took the shapeless black canvas bag off her.

'It's not heavy,' she said.

It was.

'Sorry I'm so late. Did you get my message? We took off three hours late from San Francisco, so I missed the connection at Heathrow.'

As I walked towards the black BMW lurking in the car park, I felt a touch of embarrassment. I looked across to Rachel as she opened the door. Did I imagine a slight wrinkling of her nose as she stepped in? The moment passed as I switched on the engine and pointed the car north towards Fife.

I asked Rachel about Jenson.

'I told him that we had suspended work on Project Platform, and we wouldn't start again until he paid us,' she said. 'He said we were fools, but it was our choice. I asked him why he wasn't paying us. I said this business about testing us sounded like crap to me.'

'Subtle.' I smiled. 'What did he say?'

'Same thing. He'd been burned before by suppliers letting him down, and he didn't want it to happen again.'

'Did you believe him?'

'No. I think it's bullshit. I think he's trying something on.'

'Did he mention anything about buying us?' I asked.

'No, he didn't. Nothing at all.'

'And he won't pay us?'

'Definitely not.'

'Damn!' I slammed my hand down on the steering wheel. 'It's obvious what's happening. Jenson's going to wait till we're desperate, and then buy us cheaply. If we go into receivership, then he'll put an offer in to the receiver the next day. The closer we are to bankruptcy when we give up, the lower the price will be. Once he's bought us, he'll be both the Microsoft and the IBM of the virtual reality business. He's got us by the balls.'

I shook my head. 'No wonder Hartman's buying a stake.' I told Rachel what Steve Schwartz had discovered. 'He probably knows what Jenson's up to, and wants to get in first.'

We slowed down at the tollbooth for the Forth Road Bridge, and crossed the estuary into Fife.

'Did you find out anything about the motorbike accident?' I asked.

'Yes, I did,' said Rachel. 'It was very interesting.'

'Tell me.'

She pulled out a cigarette. 'Do you mind if I smoke?' she asked.

'I'd rather you didn't.'

'You'd rather I didn't? But you wouldn't mind too much if I did?' She was smiling.

'I would a bit,' I said, trying to hold firm, but not really succeeding.

'Only a bit? Well, I need a cigarette a lot. A lot a lot,' said Rachel lighting up. She took a deep drag. 'Oh, that's much better,' she said. 'Thank you for being so understanding.'

I couldn't help smiling. 'So, tell me.'

'Oh yes. Well, I flew down to Los Angeles yesterday morning. Jonathan Bergey came from Santa Monica, which isn't too far from the airport. His parents live in a nice middle-class neighbourhood. They were both in when I got there. Bergey used to be a schoolteacher, but had to retire when he was traumatised by a killing in the classroom. He said he had received a settlement from the school system. Apparently, the metal detector hadn't picked up the gun the kid carried to school.'

'So he sued?'

'I suppose he must have done,' said Rachel, thoughtfully. 'Anyway, he says that his son had been playing our virtual reality system in an amusement centre all evening. He rode back that night on his motorbike, and wrapped himself round a tree.'

'Was there any evidence that the machine had anything to do with it?'

'Not really,' said Rachel. 'One of the kids with him said he seemed woozy afterwards. An attendant at the amusement centre said he saw Jonathan stagger a bit just before he got on the bike.'

'Could he have been drunk?'

'Apparently not. They don't serve alcohol on the premises.'

'So, what happened then?'

'Well, Bergey said he knew a good lawyer, who wrote us a letter. Then, a week later, another lawyer called Todd Sutherland showed up. He said he was acting for FairSystems. He put pressure on Bergey to drop the case. I told Bergey we didn't know any Todd Sutherland. I asked him what sort of pressure this man had used.

'Bergey wouldn't tell me. But he said a couple of weirdos from a group called BOWL had been trying to persuade him to take up the case again.'

'BOWL, eh? Still, it's hardly surprising they followed up that letter. But how did this Todd Sutherland get Bergey to drop the case?'

'I think I found out later,' said Rachel. 'What really bothered me was that our systems posed a health and safety threat. After all the testing we've done, there really shouldn't be that sort of problem.'

'Quite right.'

'So, I asked in a local shop where the nearest high school was. I went there at lunchtime, bluffed my way in, and sort of mixed in with the students. I asked about Jonathan. It didn't take long to find out – the story was well known around the school. Jonathan liked to play virtual reality games when he was high on LSD.'

'I see,' I said. 'So this Sutherland character found out that Jonathan Bergey was stoned when he crashed his motorbike, and told his father that?'

'I think so,' Rachel said.

'Poor guy,' I said.

'What, the dad? Yes, he seemed pretty angry about it. I felt bad talking to him.'

'That would explain why Doogie took his time to publicise the letter. And why he never wanted to show the details to journalists. It wouldn't have taken them long to find out what really happened.'

'That's right,' said Rachel. 'But Doogie was gambling that Richard wouldn't know the full story. He was bluffing. Rather than publish the letter straight away and have it discredited, he hoped he could use it as leverage against Richard. And then you.'

'But it didn't work.'

'No. So eventually he ended up making the allegations anyway, but without the evidence to back them up.'

It made sense.

'So, how can we find out who Todd Sutherland is?'

'Done it,' said Rachel smiling. 'I thought I'd heard the name before. I spoke to David yesterday, and he confirmed that Sutherland does legal work for one of our customers.'

'Jenson Computer?'

'No,' said Rachel. 'Onada Industries.'

'Onada?' I shook my head. 'This just doesn't make sense.'

We were getting close to Glenrothes, but I didn't want to drop Rachel off yet. There was a lot I wanted to talk to her about.

'Do you fancy a drink?' I asked.

'Do I ever.'

'Do you know any good places around here?'

She directed me to a pleasant pub with a garden, and I ordered a pint of bitter for me, and a glass of red wine for her.

We sat at an outside table with wooden benches. The beer tasted good. 'What's going on here, Rachel?'

'I don't know. I thought about it a lot in California. You know, I hoped that distance would give me a better sense of perspective.'

'And did it?'

'Not really. I mean, I can see lots of the pieces, but none of them seem to fit together.'

'I know,' I said. 'But let's go through them. It seems pretty clear that Jenson is trying to get control of FairSystems somehow or other. And we do know that Hartman has been buying our shares.'

'Is there any connection between Jenson and Hartman?'

'None that Steve knew of.' I thought a moment. 'But then of course Hartman has been buying shares through Wagner Phillips. And they are Jenson's broker. Maybe Scott Wagner is co-ordinating it all?'

'Do you think David's involved?' Rachel asked.

'Could be. What do you think?'

'I think it's highly likely. He's just too smug about our position. He wants FairSystems sold.'

'And then there's Onada. They want our source code, and we won't give it to them. And they tried to shut up Bergey. Do you think that's all they're doing?'

'Who knows?' said Rachel, draining her glass. 'Can I get you another one?'

'Just a half.'

She was gone a couple of minutes. It gave me some moments to think.

She returned with my drink. 'Thanks.' I took a sip of the beer. 'You know, Rachel, there's something else we can't ignore.'

'What's that?'

'Richard's murder.'

Rachel flinched.

'Look, I know you'd rather not think about it,' I said. 'But his company was the only thing in his life, it *was* his life. We're not just talking about someone taking over FairSystems. We're talking about someone killing Richard.'

Rachel's bottom lip quivered. She took a couple of deep breaths. 'I know you're right. And you're also right that I haven't been able to bring myself to think about his death. It's just too . . . horrible.' She wiped a tear from her eye.

'Sorry.' I touched her hand.

'No. I've got to face up to it some time.' She sniffed. 'I'm OK. Carry on.'

She didn't look OK, but I continued anyway. 'If we're right, and Jenson is trying to get control of FairSystems, you can bet Richard would have done his best to block him. So Jenson might have had a motive to get rid of him.'

'But was he even in the country?'

'I don't know. But he wouldn't have to be. He could have got someone else to kill him.' I groped through the possibilities. 'David Baker, perhaps. Sergeant Cochrane said David didn't have an alibi for that Saturday.'

Rachel shuddered and shook her head. 'I can't believe any of it. OK, maybe Carl Jenson is obsessive, and maybe David Baker is a weasel, but I can't imagine them actually killing anyone. I've worked with both of them for years.'

I raised up my hands resignedly. 'I know what you mean. But murder does happen, and the murderers don't wander around with a label on their foreheads.'

We fell silent, thinking. 'There is one man who's crazy enough to kill somebody,' Rachel said.

'You mean Doogie?'

'Ah ha.'

'I can believe he's capable of it.' I crossed my legs as I remembered my last meeting with him and his dog. 'But it doesn't look like it. Sergeant Cochrane says that he was hooked up to the Internet all morning.'

Rachel frowned. 'How do they know that?'

'I think Cochrane said that they checked with the people who run the network. I don't know. Presumably he would have to log on, and that would be recorded somewhere.'

'Yes, it would,' said Rachel. 'But that would be the easiest thing in the world to fake. Especially for someone like Doogie. He could get one of his Internet buddies to log on to his machine under his name whilst he was out doing whatever he was doing. And you'd never find out.'

'Are you sure?'

'I'm sure.'

'So it could have been Doogie after all.'

'Ah ha.'

'Well, whoever it is, I'm determined they're not going to get away with it. They've taken Richard's life, and there's nothing I can do about that now, but they won't take his company. I won't let them!'

Rachel looked up, surprised by the anger in my voice. Suddenly, she looked worried. 'Mark?'

'Yes? What is it?'

'If you're right and Richard was killed because he got in the way of someone's plans for FairSystems . . .'

'Yes?'

'Well. They might go after you next.'

She was right. The thought had occurred to me, but I had tried to ignore it. I didn't want to let it scare me. It just goaded me on.

We sat in silence a while. The anger slowly subsided. It was a warm evening, and other drinkers were beginning to join us outside at the tables. A sudden breeze swept through the garden, sending paper napkins flying, and blowing Rachel's tangled hair across her face. As she pulled it out of her eyes, she smiled at me. Her concern for me had been quite touching. I was growing used to her company. I even enjoyed it.

I thought of Richard and Rachel. He had, I supposed, mentioned her before, but what he had said about her had never sunk in. I wondered if he had appreciated what an extraordinary woman she was. I imagined them talking together about the wilder shores of virtual reality, his eyes calm and steady, listening to everything she had to say. Had she been cool, unsmiling, calculating with him, I wondered. Or had that broad smile I had sometimes glimpsed shone through? I could see her staring at him in admiration with those warm eyes.

I was curious about her. I asked her about her family. She was happy to talk.

'I was brought up in Hillhead, a "nice" part of Glasgow. My parents taught at the local school. Physics and mathematics, in case you were wondering. I was a real little star pupil until I hit thirteen, and then I dropped out.'

'That's a bit young, isn't it?' I asked.

'Not in Glasgow, it isn't. I skived off classes, smoked, drank. By the time I was fifteen, I was into drugs. I got five O grades, but that was only because my mother begged me to show up to the exams.' Rachel drained her glass.

'When I was sixteen, I started taking heroin. Injecting it. I took it a couple of times. I thought it was great.' She sighed. 'Just then my best mate collapsed. She'd been doing heroin for a year or so. Her parents took her off to a clinic. I went to visit her there. It was a horrible sight.

'Suddenly, I could see clearly what I was doing to myself. I stopped the drugs. And I started listening in some of the maths classes. Despite myself, I found it fascinating. The school had some computers, and I began to mess around on them. I didn't have anything to do with the other computer nerds of course, but I thought if I was interested in the machines, why shouldn't I learn about them? My mates thought I was mad.

'I did pretty well in my Highers, went to Edinburgh to study Computer Science and then went on to the Department of Artificial Intelligence. That's where I came across Richard and virtual reality. The rest, you know.'

'What made you do it?' I asked, fascinated.

'Drop out, you mean?' Rachel shrugged. 'I've asked myself that many times. I don't know, it's not like I hated my parents or anything. I was just bored, I suppose. I found school boring, I found my parents boring, Hillhead was boring. I wanted a bit of excitement. And I wanted to make my own way.'

She nodded to the empty glass of wine. 'And I'm not completely reformed now.'

'You drink a lot, don't you?'

'Ah ha,' she said. 'I always have done. And I've been drinking more since Richard died. Mind you, I drink steadily. I don't get drunk. I find it relaxes me. Helps me get through the night.'

She saw the way I was looking at her. 'You're right, I do drink too much. I definitely smoke too much. And I have a lousy diet and I don't sleep enough. It'll be a miracle if I make it past thirty-five. And I don't really care.'

'I do,' I said without thinking.

She glanced at me in surprise.

'I mean, you ought to look after yourself.'

She shrugged. 'Maybe.'

We sat in silence, watching the other drinkers in the garden. A group of six or seven young men sat down, each with glasses brimming with beer, laughing loudly at each other's jokes.

'Did you have many boyfriends?' I asked.

She laughed. 'I did when I was young. I don't know how many boys, and men, I had before I was sixteen. I was dead lucky not to get pregnant. But then I sort of lost interest. I had other things to think about.

'There was a boy called Ewan at Edinburgh, but he couldn't handle me. He was too nice.'

I gave voice to the question hanging in the air. 'And Richard?'

'Richard . . .' she smiled to herself. 'No, nothing happened with Richard. Our relationship was much too important to risk with sex.'

I supposed that made some kind of sense. She was a strange woman, Rachel. Despite her screwed-up background and her solitary existence, she had somehow managed to achieve a sort of self-contained serenity. She led her life in her own way, and she was happy with it. I admired the way she had managed to pull herself back from teenage self-destruction.

'So, tell me about you,' she said.

'Well, my father is a maths teacher too, though at university.'

She was smiling at me. 'I know,' she said. 'Richard told me.'

It should have occurred to me that over the years Richard would have told her all about our family, but somehow it hadn't. With a start, I realised that Richard may well have spoken about me. I wondered what he would have said. The guilt came back in waves. Perhaps he had told her about that last argument we'd had. I hoped not.

Rachel was watching me. She knew I was thinking about him. 'You're quite different, you know,' she said.

'What do you mean?'

'Oh, you and Richard, you're very different. I mean I can tell you were brothers, but you are more, I don't know, sympathetic. You care more about people.'

'Richard cared about the people who worked for him, didn't he?' I said. 'And he cared about me, I think.'

'Yes, he did.' Rachel smiled. 'He talked a lot about you. But he was so coldly single-minded in everything he did. Sometimes he was more like an automaton.'

'Hold on,' I protested. 'I'm a trader. I'm supposed to be cold and dispassionate about things.'

Rachel just laughed.

I smiled. 'Oh well, I hope you don't mind.'

'No,' she said. 'I like it.'

I took her back to her flat in Glenrothes. She offered to cook some supper, and I accepted. As we walked up the stairs I was suddenly curious to see where this strange woman lived. She went straight to work in the small kitchen, and invited me to look around. I did just that.

The flat was small and simple: a living room, a bedroom, a bathroom, and a kitchen. The living room was filled with books, which surprised me. I wondered when Rachel found time to read. I quickly scanned the shelves. The black backs of the Penguin Classics were much in evidence. There were also textbooks and journals on computing. And there was a whole bookcase full of poetry. Much of it I recognised – Yeats, Auden, Tennyson – but there were three shelves containing poets of whom I had never heard.

Next to the bookcase was the inevitable computer, perched on a tidy desk. The walls were dotted with prints of abstract paintings, a huge Jackson Pollock sending the wall above the small gas fire into confusion.

I went back into the kitchen. A bottle of Valpolicella was open on the table. Rachel gestured to it. 'Try some,' she said. I poured a glass, took a drink and felt the strong dark liquid warm the back of my throat. I wondered how Rachel managed to drink so much of the stuff without getting a headache.

We ate at the small table perched at one end of the living room. The pasta was good, the sauce surprisingly tasty. We talked long after supper as the summer twilight crept into the room. Then I asked her about the poetry I had seen on her bookshelves, all the names I didn't recognise.

'Oh them! They're all Americans. I quite like them, actually.' Rachel seemed embarrassed.

'I would never have imagined you reading poetry,' I said.

'Oh, I don't really. Not very much.'

I smiled at her. 'Of course you do, or you wouldn't have all those books. Don't be shy about it.'

Rachel looked at me, interested. 'Do you read poetry?' she asked.

I wanted to say yes, but that would have been a lie. 'I'd like to. It just doesn't mean anything to me. When I read it, I just see the words. For some reason, my brain doesn't separate the sounds.'

'Then you should read it aloud,' said Rachel. 'Poetry should be listened to, not read.'

'So read some,' I said.

'Oh no.'

'Go on. I'll listen. I'd like to listen.'

'OK,' she smiled nervously. She went over to the bookcase and pulled out a couple of volumes. She curled up on the floor and began to read. I sat in an armchair and listened and watched.

The poems were by someone called James Wright. They were about simple things: a man lying in a hammock, two Indian ponies. Rachel read them beautifully. Her low, husky voice with its gentle Scottish accent brought out the atmosphere of each poem. She had clearly read them all many times for her careful delivery picked up nuances that a casual reader would have missed.

When she had finished with Wright she picked out Lawrence Ferlinghetti. I ceased following the words, but was lulled by Rachel's voice. Her face glowed a soft golden brown colour in the yellow light from the standard lamp beside the bookcase. Her dark eyes glistened as they darted back and forth across the page. Her slim hands occasionally brushed aside the strands of dark brown hair as they drifted in front of her face.

I watched her, bewitched.

19

The wind bit into my face as I looked across at the fishing village slowly waking up. It was grey and cold. A stiff breeze whipped up the waves against the harbour wall. I shivered and stuffed my hands deep into my jacket pockets. My brain was tired and confused.

I had returned to Kirkhaven after midnight, and had slept fitfully. Waves of conflicting feelings washed over me as I lay in bed until, at half past five, I could stand it no longer. I got up, pulled on some clothes, and walked down past the burned-out boathouse to the small patch of sand by the sea.

I had spent a long day with Rachel the day before, and felt I had got to know her much better. She fascinated me. To spend time with her was to communicate with another human being in a way that was completely new to me. And I was beginning to realise that, physically, she was beautiful. It was a beauty that was carefully hidden behind an array of defences: the baggy jerseys, the blank stare at meetings, the hours spent behind computer screens. But watching her the night before, I had seen a beautiful woman with a graceful body, a torrent of dark hair, clear golden skin, a wide smile, and those deep brown eyes that could express emotion, understanding and intelligence all at the same time.

I could feel myself slipping towards something. I didn't know what, but it both excited and scared me.

I trudged along the shore, keeping just out of reach of the impatient waves spreading over the new yellow sand of early morning. What was I doing? What was I thinking of? Rachel might fascinate and intrigue me, but she was a strange woman. Part of the unreal world I had entered over the past month, a world bathed in this grey northern light, a world of virtual reality machines, of murder, of a company that could either be worth hundreds of millions or nothing. I had been under a lot of pressure recently. I was in danger of losing my sense of perspective.

I struggled to get a grip, to remember who I was. A successful young trader at Harrison Brothers with excellent prospects. I had a beautiful girlfriend. I had worked hard over the last year to achieve a stable, happy relationship for both of us. Sure, the last few weeks had been difficult, but that was mostly my fault for opening up the whole can of worms that was FairSystems. I trusted Karen completely, and I knew she trusted me. I couldn't betray that trust and still keep my self-respect. It would be a stupid, foolish thing to do.

I would have to make sure Rachel realised there was nothing between us, nor was there likely to be.

I waited till ten to call Karen. When she answered the phone her voice, full of sleep, sounded very sexy.

'I'm sorry to wake you,' I said. 'I thought you'd be up by now.' I could quite happily stay in bed till eleven on a Sunday morning, but Karen was usually up at eight.

'Oh, Mark, morning. No, I just thought I'd have a lie-in this morning.' Her voice sounded tense.

'What did you do last night?' I asked.

'Nothing,' she said, a hint of anger creeping into her voice. 'I stayed here and watched TV. Why do you ask? Are you checking up on me?'

Whew, she was tetchy this morning. I backed off. I had just

wanted to ring for a chat, but things had not started out well. 'No, I was just curious. Just making conversation.'

'Well, I watched TV. What did you do?'

Oh God. I had asked for that. I meant to tell her the truth. After all, I had nothing to hide, and that was the whole point of ringing her. But somehow I didn't.

'I just read some poetry.'

'Huh? You read poetry? Are you OK, Mark?'

'I read poetry sometimes,' I said defiantly.

'Oh yeah? Like when.'

It was true that in the year since I had been with Karen I hadn't read any.

'There's something in the air here that made me want to do it.'

'Very romantic,' said Karen flatly.

She was silent. I had called. I should say something.

'Did you find anything out about Hartman?' I asked, more to break the silence than anything else.

'Is that what you called me about? You ring me at ten o'clock on a Sunday morning to ask about that crook Hartman? Well, Mark, I didn't find out anything about him because I didn't ask anyone. Nor am I going to. You and Richard got yourselves all worked up over nothing. And I'm not going to threaten my reputation in the market over imagined conspiracies.'

This conversation was going nowhere fast. I had called Karen to tell her, and myself, how important she was to me, and I had ended up in the middle of a row.

'OK,' I said. 'I'm sorry. Let's just leave it.'

'Fine.'

'I'll call you later.'

'Good. Bye.'

The phone clicked in my ear.

Although it was Sunday, I went into work. There was a lot to do, as there always was. I should think half of the workforce was there.

There was a knock on my door. It was Rachel.

'Hi,' she said, as she entered. She wore a broad smile, and it may have been my imagination, but her face seemed to glow. She looked delectable.

'Oh, hello Rachel.' I smiled weakly, and tried to stop my heart pounding.

She sensed there was something wrong. Her smile faded. 'I, um, wanted to see if you had any ideas about what we should do with Jenson.'

I picked up my pen. 'There's not very much we can do right now, is there? Perhaps we can discuss it later.'

Her smile was completely gone now. 'OK,' she said as she turned to leave.

'Rachel?'

'Yes?'

'About last night.'

'What about last night?' she asked, avoiding my eyes as she lit a cigarette.

I wasn't sure how to go about this. I had to make certain that she realised I didn't want to become involved with her. I felt I needed to make a definitive statement, a restraint on myself as much as on her.

I cast around for some words. 'I, er, spoke to Karen this morning.'

'Oh, yes?' said Rachel, blowing smoke up to the ceiling in that dismissive way I recognised.

'Yes.' Now what? Rachel's eyes finally met mine. Cold and aloof, she stood there, impassive, waiting. 'Yes. I hope she'll come up to Kirkhaven soon. I'd like to introduce you.'

'That would be nice.'

'Yes. Dinner, or something?'

'I like dinner.'

'Good. OK,' I said, and picked up a sheet of paper in front of me, and pretended to read it. It was instructions for the photocopier.

Rachel looked down and saw the title. 'Well, I'll leave you to it,' she said without a hint of irony, and walked out.

Ten minutes later I walked past her office. She had the blinds drawn.

I had a few pints that night. A few more than I had intended. But it was warm in the Inch Tavern, the company was friendly, and became friendlier as the evening progressed. I enjoyed losing myself in the affairs of Kirkhaven, and what was on the telly.

It was late when I left. The night air was crisp against my face. I stood still and craned my neck upwards. I could see stars. Lots of them. They were lovely.

Kirkhaven was a lovely village. A friendly place. I could feel at home here, I thought, as I slowly made my way downhill from the pub. It was nice to go out for a proper drink. I was taking life too seriously these days.

I paused at the little stone bridge over the tumbling Inch. And looked down. You could see flecks of water reflecting white in the moonlight. The eddies danced and changed according to some irregular pattern. My father would have had fun with that. The chaotic motion of the Inch Burn. I chuckled at the thought.

I stood up and crossed the bridge. I had only walked five yards, when I heard a low moan. I stopped and looked around. I couldn't see anyone on the road behind me.

There it was again.

It was coming from the bushes down by the stream. It was dark down there. Perhaps someone had fallen off the bridge.

I scrambled down the side of the little gully until I was standing on a stone, peering into the gloom. I waited hoping that my eyes would adjust to the darkness.

I heard a rustle behind me, and felt a crashing pain on the back of my skull. Then everything went black.

I awoke to feel the cold stone under my cheek. My head hurt like hell. I tried to get up, but it was difficult. I lay back for a couple of minutes to regain my strength. When I did stand up, I swayed uncontrollably. The beer swilled in my stomach and

I was sick. I stood still, breathing deeply, and then pulled myself up the bank of the stream. I staggered home, and collapsed on to my bed.

I ignored the alarm and slept through till eleven. When eventually I did wake up, my head hurt like hell. I rang Sergeant Cochrane, who came round straight away. I told him all that I could remember, which was precious little.

'We'll make some inquiries to see if anyone saw any strangers around the time you were attacked,' he said. 'Especially anyone who looked like Doogie Fisher. And I'll inform Inspector Kerr.'

I nodded.

'But, laddie, if I were you, I'd be very careful. I don't know if whoever it was meant to do permanent damage, but they could easily have done. And they may try again.'

He looked round at the windows in the kitchen. 'You should get some locks fitted. This place would be a doddle to break into. In the meantime, I'll give you a lift to the surgery.'

The doctor chastised me for not calling out an ambulance immediately after the attack, and told me to stay in a darkened room for the rest of the day. He would check up on me later that evening.

I did as I was told. The combination of the knock on the head and the hangover was extremely painful. I slept as much as I could.

I felt much better the next day, although my brain was fuzzy round the edges. I went into the factory first thing in the morning. An appreciable pile had built up on my desk during that one day away.

I switched on the computer and scanned the e-mails. One instantly caught my eye. The title was 'Warning'. It was dated Monday, the day before.

I clicked on it:

You could have been killed last night. You will be killed next time. Remember what happened to your brother.
    Go back down to London. Forget all about
FairSystems. Stay alive.

It was unsigned.

I looked for the sender's address. All e-mail over the Internet has an address. It was 34254877@anon.penet.fi.

Uh?

I rang Rachel.

'Are you OK? I heard you were attacked on Sunday?'

For a moment I was pleased to hear the concern in her voice. But I didn't let it show. 'Oh, it's nothing,' I said coolly. 'Just a tap on the head. But can you come up and take a look at something? I've just received a weird message.'

She came right up. After a quick glance to make sure I was still in one piece, she avoided looking at me. I showed her the message.

'Nasty,' she said.

'Who's it from?'

She looked at the Internet address. 'Someone in Finland.'

'Finland?'

'Yes. It's almost certainly an anonymous server.'

'What's that?'

'It's a way of sending messages anonymously over the Internet. They're supposed to be for people who want to contact support groups for things like AIDS or alcoholism, or for dissidents in oppressive regimes. But you can use them for virtually anything.'

'But why would anyone in Finland want to kill me?' I was confused.

'The sender could come from anywhere in the world. It's just the server that's based in Finland.'

'And presumably whoever runs it won't tell us who sent this message.'

'No. That's the whole point.'

'What about the police?'

'I imagine even they would find it difficult. The people who run these services feel they're defending a basic right.'

'Well, I'm sure Kerr will try.' Then I asked the question they, and I, were most interested in. 'Who do you think it was? Doogie?'

266

'I don't know,' said Rachel. She was still sullen.

'The last one he sent was signed.'

'Ah ha. But after what happened to you last night, he'd be foolish to send you another one with his name on it. He would certainly be capable of using this service. But then so would anyone who knew a bit about the Internet.' She looked at her watch. 'I've got to go now. There's a lot on at the moment.'

As she closed the door behind her, I rested my sore head in my hands and thought.

Once again someone was pushing me around. Trying to get me to abandon Richard and his dream. And once again I wasn't prepared to give up.

But this time was different. This time I had nearly been killed. This was getting much more serious.

Was it worth it?

It was very important to me that Richard's life had not been in vain. So important that I would risk my own to ensure that his dream would be realised.

And maybe I was suffering from that innate overconfidence of the trader. The belief that in the end I could always outwit the market. Whoever this guy was, I believed I would get him before he got me.

David Baker came in to see me that afternoon to discuss a new contract. We walked over to the machine to get a couple of cups of coffee.

'Are you still determined to hang on?' he asked.

'Yep,' I said. 'More determined than ever.'

'Have you found any more cash?'

'No. We're going to have to do this from internal resources.'

'We haven't got any.'

'Minor point, David,' I smiled.

He looked grim. 'We don't have long now, Mark. Less than three weeks.'

'Well, I'll worry about that.' I wondered why he hadn't mentioned the attack. He must have known about it. Wouldn't it be the natural thing to do? Maybe. But our relationship was hardly natural. 'Now, what have you got for me?'

David pulled out some papers. 'I think we're finally getting somewhere with ARPA. It looks like they're willing to sign up with us.'

'Great!' And it was good news. ARPA was the US Department of Defense's Advanced Research Projects Agency. It was the chief source of largesse for small virtual reality companies, and hence an important customer. But it was difficult for us as a UK company to get contracts from them. David had done very well to get to this stage.

'When will we get paid?' For companies in the sort of cash-flow situation that we found ourselves in, the first question was always when? The second was how much?

'Not till January one,' said David. 'If we're still here, of course.'

I ignored the comment. I knew that the moment any of us ceased to act as though we were around for the long-term, it would all be over.

'That'll be a good start to next year,' I said. 'Now, let's see what you've got here.'

The issues at stake were complex, and David and I worked on the deal for two hours. I was impressed by his grasp of the problems, and also pleased that he had decided to consult me. There was still no love lost between us, but if we could at least talk to each other on business issues, that was good for FairSystems.

We had just finalised the deal we would offer ARPA, when the phone rang. It was Scott Wagner. He was to the point.

'I have some good news for you,' he said. For a moment, I thought he might have decided to sponsor an equity issue after all, but it wasn't that. 'There's been heavy trading in FairSystems stock early this morning. The price is up two to five dollars on good volume. This could be a good opportunity to sell.'

My relief to see the price moving up was tempered by suspicion. 'We'll see,' I said. 'Who's behind this? Frank Hartman?'

'I honestly don't know,' said Wagner.

I didn't believe him. 'OK, tell me if you see any more buying.'

'And what about my client, the guy who wants to buy the whole company?'

'We'll see.' I hung up.

David Baker looked at me enquiringly. I told him what was happening to the share price.

'Wagner's right,' he said. 'This is the time to sell.'

The phone rang again.

'Hi, Mark, Carl Jenson. How are you doing?' His voice boomed down the wires from Palo Alto.

'Fine, Carl.' I tensed, waiting for what he had to say.

'Good. I'm calling out of courtesy to tell you something you should know. Today we're filing a thirteen D with the SEC to inform them that we've built up a stake of over five per cent in FairSystems.'

My heart pounded. Was Jenson finally showing his hand?

'Are you going to make a bid for the whole company?'

'It's a neat little company. I'd just like to own some shares, that's all.'

I seized my opportunity. 'So will you reconsider your decision to cancel the advance payments on Project Platform?'

'Hey, Mark. I just called out of courtesy, you know? I don't want to start renegotiating something we've already agreed. Bye.' And with that he was gone.

I put the phone down, took a deep breath, and sat up straight in my chair.

That was it. FairSystems was in play.

'In play' is merchant banking jargon. It means that a company is vulnerable to takeover and a potential predator has publicly signalled his interest. It means that if anyone wants to buy the target company, they had better declare themselves. It is an apt term. Big companies and Wall Street arbitrageurs play with the target company's stock price, and ultimately its future. It is very rare for a company in play to remain independent.

But that is what I was determined FairSystems would do.

I told David what Jenson had said. I called Rachel and Willie into my office, and told them too. I told them I was determined to keep FairSystems independent. Rachel nodded, Willie looked worried. David just smiled. That disconcerted me. It meant he didn't think I stood a chance.

I called Sorenson in California. His secretary said he was actually in London on business, and gave me the number of the Hyde Park Hotel where he was staying. Fortunately, he was in when I called. I told him the news.

Sorenson took it in his stride. His deep American accent powered down the lines, unruffled, in control. 'Good. This is just the opportunity we've been looking for. It will move the stock price up. Let's tell Wagner Phillips to get a move on. If they can find us a buyer now, we can keep control of the process and find the best price and the best fit.'

It made sense, but I wouldn't do it. I couldn't stall Sorenson any longer.

'No.'

There was a pause. When the line came to life again, Sorenson's voice was still calm. 'Why do you say no, Mark?'

'Because I want to keep the company independent.'

'I'd like that too,' said Sorenson reasonably. 'But it just can't be done. There comes a time when you've got to punt. FairSystems will be history in three weeks unless we do something. At least this way we stay in the game. Really, Mark, we have no choice.'

'My father and I can block a sale,' I said. 'I will not sell out.' My voice was as firm as I could make it.

Sorenson sighed. 'Is that your last word, Mark?'

I suddenly felt wary. Sorenson's voice was not threatening, but nonetheless he was warning me not to cross him. 'Yes,' I said.

'OK, I'll call you tomorrow. I'm disappointed in you, Mark.' He was gone.

I wondered what would happen next.

20

The answer was waiting on my desk the next morning.

It was a fax from Burns Stephens, FairSystems' lawyers. It announced that an extraordinary general meeting was to be called the next Tuesday at the offices of Burns Stephens in Edinburgh. A motion to remove myself as managing director would be put forward. The letter said that it was in all the shareholders' interests to sell the company as a priority, and I had declared myself completely opposed to this course of action. It was signed by Walter Sorenson as chairman, and the only other non-executive director, Nigel Young.

Attached to it was a form waiving the shareholders' rights to twenty-one days' notice of an EGM with an explanation that such a delay would not be in the best interests of the company, whatever the result of the meeting.

I called Willie and Rachel into my office, and asked Willie to bring the company's articles of association.

I showed them the fax. Willie's ever-present frown deepened.

'Can he do this?' asked Rachel.

I raised my eyebrows at Willie.

He burrowed through his papers. 'I think he can. We had to change the articles of association when we did the Initial Public Offering last year. It gives the non-executive directors powers to call an extraordinary general meeting to remove executive directors if they believe those directors are acting against the interests of public shareholders.' He stopped at a page, and scanned it quickly. 'Yes, here it is.'

'And what's this waiver?'

'Technically, there should be twenty-one days' notice before an EGM is held. Here they're asking for only six. But if enough shareholders object then they will have to wait the three weeks.'

I thought about that for a moment. Sorenson was right. If there was going to be uncertainty over the management of the company, the sooner it was resolved the better. 'No, six days is fine,' I said. 'But what happens at the EGM?'

'The motion is put to shareholders, and they vote. A simple majority will suffice for the motion to be carried. Most of them will vote by proxy, of course.'

'So as long as I can count on just over fifty per cent of the vote, then I keep my job?'

'That's right,' said Willie. 'I've got a list of major shareholders. Shall I go and get it?'

I nodded, and Willie scurried out.

I looked at Rachel. 'This is not going to be easy,' I said.

She gave me a half smile. 'I appreciate you trying.'

'I want this company to remain independent as much as you do.'

Another half smile touched her lips.

Willie returned with a summary of the shareholding. It ran as follows:

Mark Fairfax	23.75%
Dr Geoffrey Fairfax	20.0
Walter Sorenson	4.0
Karen Chilcott	3.75
Rachel Walker	3.5
David Baker	2.0
William Duncan	1.0
FairSystems employees	2.0
Publicly held	40.0
Total	100%

I pointed to the publicly held figure of forty per cent. 'What do we know about these?'

'Not much more than when you asked me last time,' said Willie. 'Except, of course, that we know Jenson has five point seven per cent according to the thirteen D he filed yesterday. All the others are nominees.'

'Frank Hartman chief among them,' I muttered.

'Who's he?' Willie asked.

'An arbitrageur who's been accumulating our stock.'

Willie grimaced.

'Now, how does this stack up?' I grabbed a piece of paper and wrote two columns: SALE and NO SALE.

I put Sorenson, Baker and all the publicly held stock in the SALE column. I was sure Wagner would recommend a sale to his clients, and I saw no reason why Jenson, or Hartman or whoever else owned the stock would think differently.

In the NO SALE column I put myself, Rachel, my father and Karen.

'Put the employees there too,' said Rachel.

'Really?'

'They'll back you, you'll see,' she said.

'OK.' I wrote them in. 'Willie?'

He was plunged into deep, deep confusion. 'Ooh, I don't know, Mark. I mean I'd like to support you. But Walter is right about the cash situation. It's very risky not to sell. I don't know.'

I looked at him and smiled. It was unrealistic to expect Willie to take the high-risk option, and he didn't really owe me any personal loyalty. So I put him in the SALE column.

He saw what I was doing, looked embarrassed, but didn't stop me.

Rachel totted the numbers up in her head. She sighed with relief. 'Well, we're all right then. I make it forty-seven per cent for a sale and fifty-three per cent against.'

I wasn't so sure. 'It depends on him.' I pointed to my father's name.

'He'll support you, surely. He's always been against a sale, hasn't he?'

'I don't know. We're not exactly close. And he puts a lot of store by what Sorenson says. I'll have to talk to him.'

'Well, if he's with us, we're there.'

They left me. I wasn't concerned that Willie wanted to maintain his neutrality. As finance director it made sense. And I was sure of Rachel's support.

I wasn't so sure of my father. Unless I had his support, I couldn't count on fifty per cent.

So, I called him. He had indeed spoken to Sorenson the previous night, and agreed with him that the company should be sold. He regretted that I would be removed, and his regrets sounded genuine. I said I wanted to talk to him face to face. He said I was welcome to try to persuade him, but it wouldn't make any difference. We agreed to meet at the King's Arms in Oxford at twelve the next day.

Sorenson called that afternoon. He said that he didn't hold anything against me in person, but as chairman he had to act in the best interests of the shareholders. If I changed my mind, he would be happy to recommend keeping me on. He said he would see me in Edinburgh for the EGM. I was polite, but said my views hadn't changed.

On my way out, I bumped into David Baker. He was coming the other way down the corridor. He couldn't avoid me.

'You must be pleased, David,' I said, unable to keep the bitterness from my voice. 'A chance to become MD at last.'

David held his hands up in a gesture of innocence. 'Hey, I didn't ask for it. It was Walter's suggestion. But, frankly, it's the only course of action that makes sense.'

He frowned and pushed past me. The arrogant sod!

I spoke to Karen that night. Our phone conversation on Sunday still rankled. Also, the effects of my day with Rachel hadn't worn off. I wanted to straighten things out, to make up. She seemed to feel the same way.

I told her about the meeting Sorenson had called to oust me as managing director.

She was sympathetic. 'Oh, Mark, that's awful. But you're the biggest shareholder. Can't you just vote against him?'

'I've done the sums. It's not that easy. I need my father to vote with me. When I spoke to him today, he didn't sound too positive about that. In fact, I'd say he sounded quite negative.'

Then I asked the question that had been nagging at me ever since I had gone over the voting numbers with Rachel and Willie. 'You'll vote for me, won't you?'

'Of course I will.'

I was hugely relieved. 'Thank you. I knew you would, but it's just good to be sure.'

'Don't worry.'

'How about coming up to Kirkhaven this weekend?'

'I'd love to, Mark, really I would. But I'm playing tennis with Heather on Sunday morning.'

'Karen, I really think you should come,' I said firmly. 'We haven't spent much time together recently, and it's bad for us. I would like you to come.'

There was silence for a moment. 'Yes, why not? I can cancel Heather.'

'Great! Get the ten o'clock shuttle. I'll meet you at the airport.'

I didn't tell her about getting my head bashed in. With the EGM looming, I didn't want her worried about my safety.

There is a quiet bar at the back of the King's Arms at the end of Broad Street that is frequented by dons and college porters. They usually drink alone, sometimes exchanging a couple of words, enough to show comradeship, not enough to disturb a pleasant pint and a smoke. I knew that my father had been an occasional visitor many years before.

I bought myself a pint of bitter, and him a half, and we sat facing each other across a small table.

He was on edge. Nervous, but not hostile. He was paler than when I had last seen him. He didn't look any better than he had at Richard's funeral. Underneath the nerves, his eyes seemed listless, almost dead.

'Thank you for seeing me,' I said.

He held up his hand. 'No, no. Thank you for coming down.'

He paused, looking down into his beer. He sighed. 'I'm sorry about the vote next Tuesday. Please don't take it as a lack of support for you. I just know when to give up. Walter went through the options, and basically there are none. We have no choice. We're beaten.'

And he looked beaten. Grey-faced, shoulders slumped, he looked six inches smaller than I remembered him all those years before, and twenty years older.

'You yourself said that FairSystems was all that was left of Richard. That we owed it to him to keep it going,' I urged.

Dad nodded. 'Yes, I know I did. But that was just a romantic notion.' He spoke slowly, his voice beaten down by despair into an expressionless drone. 'Richard is dead now. There's nothing we can do about that. If FairSystems has to be sold, so be it. Neither you nor I can fight it.'

'Yes we can,' I said, with an intensity that startled him. I leaned forward. 'Did Richard ever tell you about his dreams of a virtual reality system on every desk?'

Dad smiled wanly, remembering. 'All the time.'

'Do you know how close he was?'

'He always said he was very close.'

'Well he was. Only four months away, in fact.' I ran through Project Platform. It was still very confidential, but I needed to use everything I could to persuade my father. He may be an other-worldly don, but he's intelligent. He picked up on the consequences right away. I thought I detected a gleam in his eye that had not been there before.

Then it disappeared. 'It's a shame Richard isn't alive to see it.'

'But I am, Dad, I am!' I grabbed his arm, willing him to follow me. 'If you won't do it for Richard, do it for me. This is so important to me. It's the most important thing in my life just now. Please support me. Please.'

He glanced up at me. I saw in his eyes a whole mixture of emotions: indecision, uncertainty, mistrust of a son who had rejected him for ten years. He was also assessing me. What he saw, and how he felt about it, I could not tell.

'About your mother . . .' he began.

276

'Not now, Dad.'

'Yes, now!' he said, his voice suddenly full of urgency. 'You want me to do something for you. Well, I want you to do something for me. Let me talk about her. You've never given me a chance to explain.'

I stared at him. He was right, I supposed. I sat back in my chair, arms folded, reluctantly ready to listen.

'I loved your mother. She was so vital, so passionate, so alive. But she wasn't always easy to live with. You must remember the rows we had?'

I nodded. I did. And I had to admit that the majority had been started by her. But they had been over quickly, and she had been sunny, warm and loving again. My father had just brooded for years.

'I tried so hard,' Dad said, 'but we never got anywhere. And then I met Frances and we fell in love.'

I wasn't impressed. This was my mother he had abandoned. 'And then Mama died,' I said.

Dad flinched. 'Yes, she died. And, yes, I did feel guilty. And I had done wrong. I knew it at the time, and I know it now. But can't you forgive me?'

'Why?' I said, arms crossed. Of course I had thought about forgiving him many times in the past. I had been tempted. But each time I had turned away from it. It would have been dis-loyal to my mother, and that was quite simply something I was not prepared to be.

My father hesitated, looking down into his drink. He coughed. 'There's something I feel I ought to tell you, Mark. It's not very pleasant, but it's something you ought to know.'

I waited, listening.

'Your mother wasn't always faithful herself.'

The anger leapt inside me. 'Dad! You can't say that!'

He nodded sadly. 'It's true.'

'I don't believe you.'

'It happened at least three times that I'm aware of. Once with someone you know.'

'Oh yes? Who?'

'Walter.'

'Walter Sorenson? Don't be ridiculous!'

'I'm not being ridiculous! It was when we were at Stanford. You were just two.'

'So you think Sorenson had an affair with Mama?'

'I'm sure he did. He used to do that sort of thing quite regularly. I think he still does.'

'But you and he are best buddies.'

My father nodded. 'That's right. Or at least we are now.'

'But what about what he did to you?'

I looked at my father in confusion. He didn't answer right away, but I saw it coming.

'It took a long time, but eventually I forgave him.'

My mind was doing somersaults. I felt the certainties behind my hatred for my father being shaken. How could my beautiful mother have been unfaithful? My father was the monster of the family. Yet I knew he was telling the truth. I saw the broken old man in front of me, and I felt a rush of sympathy for him.

Sympathy was followed by guilt. He had forgiven the man who had taken his wife. And yet I hadn't forgiven him, my own father. Then the old certainty came back. He had abandoned my mother to die. Now he was trying to manipulate my feelings. Well he wouldn't succeed, I couldn't let him. I had to leave. Now.

I put down my glass. 'OK, well, thank you for seeing me,' I mumbled. 'I've really got to go now.' I stood up, avoiding his eyes. 'Bye, Dad,' I said and stumbled out of the pub.

I met Karen at Edinburgh airport at 11.15 on Saturday morning. I was looking forward to the weekend. She had only been up once, and that was for Richard's funeral. It had been a mistake not to let her see this side of my life properly before. I wanted to show her Kirkhaven and the factory at Glenrothes. I tried to put last week's attack out of my mind, and convince myself that we would be safe. I certainly didn't want to tell her anything about it; it would hardly help boost her confidence in my staying on at FairSystems.

I had returned from Oxford on Thursday night depressed. It would have been worth travelling all that way for a half hour conversation if the result had been that my father would vote for me. But now I thought that unlikely. The whole thing had got caught up in that discussion about my mother that had left me agitated and confused. I suspected it had left my father disappointed.

Still, I forgot all that as I saw Karen hurry towards me. She hugged and kissed me, and shivered in the crisp Scottish air. 'OK, let's go,' she said.

She settled comfortably into the BMW. 'I do like this car,' she said. 'It's a shame you keep it up here now. I miss it.'

We drove out of the airport and north across the Forth Road Bridge, past the mine-scarred landscape around Cowdenbeath and Kirkcaldy, and on towards the East Fife coastline. An hour later, we nudged down the narrow streets of Kirkhaven, and pulled up outside Inch Lodge.

'We're here,' I said, and showed her into the house.

'Can I have a look round? I didn't see very much of it when I was up for the funeral.'

'Of course.'

She wandered round making appreciative noises. 'You're right, it is a nice place. It has a good feel to it. Quiet. And friendly.'

I smiled. 'I'm getting quite attached to it.'

'I'm hungry,' she said, and we headed back to the kitchen.

I warmed some soup for lunch, and we ate it at the old oak table, looking with dismay at the rain driving in from the sea, beating against the windows. I had planned a walk for the afternoon, but instead I decided to show Karen the factory. She said she was curious, she had never seen a factory before.

We drove through the grey outskirts of Glenrothes, negotiating the series of unnecessary roundabouts with spurs leading off to nowhere. Karen was clearly disappointed. 'Glenrothes is such a romantic name. I expected something more than this.'

'What, moors, and lochs, and monarchs of the glen?'

'Yes. I haven't seen a single man wearing a skirt yet.'

279

I laughed. 'You probably won't. Most of the inhabitants come from around Glasgow. They've come here to work, and work they do well. And believe it or not, this place is actually greener than Glasgow.'

It was difficult to believe, with the rain lashing down on the road surface, and bouncing off the roofs of the grey modern factories.

We pulled up outside the FairSystems plant. Even though it was Saturday, there were a number of cars in the car park. I showed her round the factory, explaining how each part fitted into the FairSystems whole. I was fluent and surprised myself by how much I had absorbed about the company.

We paused outside the Project Platform room. Without being specific, I told her a little about it, and how FairSystems and Jenson Computer would change the world. To my disappointment, she seemed unmoved.

'Don't you see?' I said. 'This is a great opportunity for FairSystems to dominate the world virtual reality market into the next century.'

Karen sighed. 'It's a good story. But you're beginning to sound like Richard. We both fell for it once, but we shouldn't fall for it again.'

'But look what happened to Microsoft!'

'Oh, Mark,' Karen shook her head. 'Microsoft makes software for computers. Everyone has computers. Computers are useful. FairSystems makes toys. Don't you understand that Mark? This is a toy company, and a tiddly one at that. Let it be bought by a bigger toy company, and come back to the adult world.'

'These are not toys – '

Karen interrupted. 'Mark, you're becoming obsessed, just like your brother. It's all hype, and the sooner you come back down to earth the better.'

'But, Karen, I thought you agreed with me that we shouldn't sell out.'

'I said I'd support you,' Karen said, a touch of exasperation in her voice. 'But I never said I agreed with you. You have to keep a sense of perspective. Maybe it's just easier for me to do, since I'm not so closely involved.'

I saw further argument was pointless, and led her out of the building. We passed Rachel's office. Rachel was in there working. She looked up and saw us walking past.

I hesitated for a moment, confused. Would it look odd to introduce them, or would it be odder still if I didn't? Karen solved my dilemma. 'Who's that staring at us?'

'That's Rachel Walker, the technical director. I've told you about her. Come and meet her.'

So we went into Rachel's office. She had obviously spent the night there. There was an empty bottle of wine on her desk, and two ashtrays, both full. She was smoking as we came in. She looked even more of a mess than usual; her hair was tousled and in her eyes, and she was wearing a black shapeless jumper over jeans with holes in.

Karen edged reluctantly in. She disliked tobacco smoke, and she extended that dislike to all who produced it.

'Rachel Walker, this is Karen Chilcott.'

Rachel stood up. 'Pleased to meet you,' she said, with only a touch of coldness. 'What do you think of the place?'

Karen looked down over her wrinkled nose. 'It's different to what I expected. I thought there would be more machines, and conveyor belts and things.'

'Yes,' said Rachel. 'You're absolutely right, we ought to have more conveyor belts, don't you think, Mark?'

Karen looked at me sharply. I changed the subject. 'Can you tell Karen what you're working on?' I regretted it as soon as I had said it.

'Certainly,' said Rachel smiling sweetly. 'Put these on.' She gestured to the virtual glasses that were plugged into her computer. I wanted to stop Karen but I was too late.

Rachel quickly tapped a few keys. Suddenly, on the screen in front of her was a shiny mass of grey, green, brown and red. Karen let out a yelp. 'You are now inside a patient's liver. You see that there,' Rachel said, pointing to a giant solid grey-white ball covered with thin tendrils, 'that's a tumour, and it must be

281

removed. This is a program that will allow a surgeon to use an endoscope to examine a liver prior to an operation. It's a terrific breakthrough. Take a look around.'

The image began to swell and spin. It made me ill just watching on a flat screen, it must have been horrible for Karen. She put up with it for about five seconds, and then tore the glasses off. 'Yeucch,' she exclaimed, looking rather green herself. She got up from her seat. 'Thank you, I think I get the picture.'

'Oh, I'm sorry,' said Rachel. 'It's so realistic it does take a bit of getting used to. I've got another one that doctors can use to diagnose cancer of the colon. Do you want to see that?'

'No thanks,' said Karen, as I propelled her out of the office, glowering at Rachel over my shoulder.

Rachel just repeated her sweet smile. 'Bye now. Thanks for dropping in,' she called out after us.

'Whew, what an awful woman!' said Karen. 'God, I pity you having to work with her. Get me out of here!'

We drove back to Kirkhaven in silence. I was angry. Angry with Karen for refusing to see how important FairSystems could be, and angry with Rachel for having pulled such a stunt. What had she been thinking of?

The rain abated as I cooked supper, and the evening sun emerged, pale and watery, flickering in pink and gold on the surface of the still disturbed sea. The meal went down well, and we walked over to the Inch Tavern for a drink afterwards.

The pub was warm and snug, and Jim Robertson gave us a friendly welcome. Karen relaxed. Her cheeks had picked up a pink glow from the walk, and her yellow hair and white teeth glimmered in the subdued light of the pub.

'I saw Dad on Thursday,' I said.

'Oh yes? How did it go?'

'Not good.'

'He won't back you at the EGM?'

'I don't know. He didn't say. But I doubt it after our conversation.'

'Why? What happened?'

'He said my mother had an affair with another man when she was young.'

'Really? Do you believe him?'

'I'm inclined to,' I said.

Karen wrinkled her nose. 'Why do you think he told you this?'

'Because of who the other man was.'

'Who?'

'Walter Sorenson.'

'No! You can't be serious!'

'I am. His point was that he's forgiven Walter. And so I should forgive him. But I won't.' I felt the anger rise in me again. 'He's manipulating me, and I don't like it.' I took a sip of beer. 'Did you ever forgive your father?'

I looked up at Karen, and was surprised by what I saw. Her eyes ignited. Anger flashed in them. 'Will you shut up about my father! And all this stuff about men running off with bimbos! Can't you see I don't want to talk about it?'

I stretched my hand out towards her. 'Karen, I'm sorry.'

'Don't touch me!' screamed Karen. 'Just keep off me! I don't have to put up with you any longer. Now leave me alone!'

She pushed herself away from the little table in the pub, blinking back the tears, and rushed past the gawping drinkers for the door. Reddening under their stares, I followed.

Outside the pub, it was raining hard. Karen stood on the pavement, breathing deeply, her hair turning dark as it soaked up the rain.

'Karen, come home. Let's talk,' I said, putting my hand on her shoulder.

'I will not talk to you!' she shouted, tearing my hand away with such force that it hurt my wrist. She trudged off up the hill into the rain. I watched her hunched body disappear round a corner, and then turned back to Inch Lodge.

I waited for her, brooding over what she had said, what she had done. I had seen her angry and hurt before, but I had never seen that anger directed at me. And I didn't like it at all. My mind was a jumble of indignation, incomprehension and worry.

At about midnight, I heard a knock at the door. She was soaking wet, water streaming from her nose, her chin, her hair and her clothes.

'Karen – '

'Don't even think of trying to get into bed with me,' she said, pushing past me, and rushing up the stairs. After a couple of minutes I heard the bath running.

I sat in the sitting room, waiting until I heard the slamming of the bedroom door. Then, slowly, I climbed the stairs, and pulled myself into the bed in the guest room.

Karen came down late the next morning. She had dark rings under her eyes, and she was sniffing from the beginnings of a cold. I hadn't slept very well myself, and I was tense as I sat with a cup of coffee and a newspaper spread out in front of me.

I waited.

'I'm sorry, Mark.'

She walked over and we embraced. 'I don't know what got into me. I'm really sorry.'

'It's OK,' I said, brushing the hair from her face. 'Don't worry about it.'

But it wasn't OK. We tried to be polite and friendly to each other all day, to pretend that nothing had happened. But it had.

The day was a disaster. The wind and rain came back with a vengeance, hammering against the windows of Richard's house. We spent most of the day inside, reading the papers or watching television, talking little. When it was finally time to take her to the airport, and I saw her heading off for the departure gate, I was relieved. So, I suspect, was she.

I was in a dark mood as I drove back to Kirkhaven through the unrelenting rain. My hopes for the weekend had been dashed. Karen was unimpressed by Kirkhaven, and had become quite negative about FairSystems. But her explosion really unsettled me.

Half of it I understood. I knew how raw the pain of her father's walking out on her remained. I had seen how remembering her abandonment could affect her. But, in the past, this anger had been directed anywhere but at me. I had always been able to join her in her misery, to help her through it. That was really the basis upon which our relationship had come about.

Now her anger had been directed at me. Full blast. That, I was not used to.

What had I done? What had changed?

21

We were in a large board room at the offices of Burns Stephens in Edinburgh. The walls were wood-panelled, and a chandelier sprawled down from the ceiling. A worthy Victorian advocate glowered at the small group of people in the room. Although Burns Stephens was less than ten years old, they had acquired impressive offices in a Georgian building in Drumsheugh Gardens, within walking distance of Charlotte Square, the elegant financial centre of the city.

The board was lined up on one side of a long table, facing four rows of reproduction regency chairs. In the centre was Walter Sorenson. I was seated on his right with Rachel next to me. On the other side of Sorenson was David Baker, then Nigel Young, the urbane merchant banker, looking at ease in the surroundings. Next to him were Willie, and Graham Stephens, FairSystems' lawyer, who both presided over neat piles of papers.

In front of Rachel was my sheet of paper dividing share-holders into SALE and NO SALE. We needed fifty per cent to win. By our calculations, as long as my father and Karen sided with me, I would make it with fifty-three per cent of the vote against forty-seven per cent. But I wasn't at all sure that was the way it would go. I had run over my last conversation with my father a dozen times, and each time had come to the conclusion that he would vote against me.

The worst thing was that now I couldn't be sure how Karen would vote. When I had asked her the previous week, she had clearly said that she would support me, but had things changed over the weekend? I just didn't know.

I had been furious with Rachel on Monday.

'Why did you go through that charade with the liver?' I demanded. 'It was hardly going to persuade Karen to support us.'

'I wanted to show her how powerful virtual reality can be,' Rachel answered with a straight face.

I snorted. 'It was just petty jealousy.'

'Jealousy?' repeated Rachel, raising her eyebrows. 'And just why would I be jealous? Why should I care if you go out with an ignorant merchant banker?'

'Oh, quit playing games,' I muttered in frustration. 'You've probably put her off FairSystems for ever.'

'But I thought you said she was firmly behind you,' said Rachel.

'Well, now I'm not so sure,' I said, stalking off.

Here we were, sitting down doing the sums, with only five minutes to go before the vote, and I could tell Rachel was not so certain she had done the sensible thing. She was biting her bottom lip, and frowning down at the sheet of paper in front of her where she was drawing never-ending rings around Karen's name.

'Is there any chance that some of the public stockholders won't vote? We might scrape by then.'

I shook my head. 'I very much doubt it. Scott Wagner seems to have total control of the stock. I'm sure he can persuade them all to vote with him.'

I caught Wagner's eye amongst the small group of people sparsely scattered through the room. He saw me, smiled, and winked. Damn! He looked so confident. I was even more sure that he had tied up the public stockholders' votes.

It was interesting that Wagner had come all the way over

from San Francisco. It was important to have representatives from his firm there to deliver the proxy votes and to watch what happened, but there was no need for the head man himself to be present. I suspected that he had a deal in his inside pocket, and he would be ready to show it to Sorenson and David as soon as I was removed.

I hoped he had flown five thousand miles for nothing.

I looked out for Carl Jenson, and Frank Hartman, but they were not there of course. I recognised most of the small crowd. There was Wagner and a sidekick, my father, Keith, Andy, Terry and a dozen other employee shareholders of FairSystems grouped together at the back, and two other men, sitting uneasily three empty chairs away from each other. One was short, tanned, with a moustache and a lime-green polo shirt. The other was a tall man with glasses, a white button-down shirt, and a dark grey suit. They both looked American.

My father had chosen to fly to Edinburgh to cast his vote, when he could quite easily have done so by proxy. He wanted to be there at the end, I thought morosely. There was no sign of Karen, nor did I expect her. There was no need at all for her to be present.

Sorenson cleared his throat, and called the meeting to order. Immediately his deep voice imposed its authority on the room. With his square shoulders and upright posture, he dominated proceedings.

'First of all, I would like all the shareholders present to identify themselves. Willie Duncan will check proof of identity and any powers of attorney. Please state whether you will be voting in person, or whether you have already sent in a proxy vote. Since this is a small gathering, why don't we go one by one? You sir.' He pointed to the short man with a moustache and a polo shirt.

'I'm Darren Polona from Jenson Computer. I will be voting in person on behalf of my company.'

Sorenson nodded as Willie scurried over to check his papers. He pointed to the tall besuited man a couple of chairs away.

'Martin Woodcock of the International Secure Fund of

Bermuda,' he drawled. I was right, he was also an American. 'We have already filed our proxy.'

I leaned over to Rachel. 'I bet that fund is one of Hartman's. He's probably here keeping an eye on things for him.'

The others were all straightforward. Within a couple of minutes Willie had all the papers he needed, and Sorenson moved on.

'We only have one item on the agenda today,' he began. 'This is the following resolution:

"That Mark Enrico Fairfax be removed as managing director of FairSystems and that he be replaced by David Anthony Baker."

'Enrico?' Rachel whispered in my ear.

'It comes with the Italian mother.'

'Before taking votes from the floor, I will ask Willie to read out the result of the proxy votes.'

This was it. It should be easy to tell which way Karen had gone from these votes. Rachel had the numbers in front of her.

There was total silence in the room.

Willie stood up, coughed and stammered. 'Oh come on Willie,' I murmured under my breath.

Finally, he got it out. 'Votes for the resolution, seven hundred and sixty-one thousand. Votes against, thirty-two thousand, three hundred and twenty.'

My heart sank. I looked over to Rachel for confirmation. 'The bitch,' she hissed.

Karen had voted against me. My own girlfriend had voted to have me fired.

Rachel leaned over. 'Seven hundred and sixty-one thousand is thirty-eight point oh five per cent,' she whispered. 'That's basically all the public shares except Jenson's plus Karen's three point seven five per cent. The bits and bobs against the resolution were those employees who aren't here and voted by proxy.'

'So they only need another twelve per cent to win?' I asked.

Rachel nodded. I looked down at her piece of paper and then along at my fellow board members. Jenson had 5.7 per cent,

Sorenson had four per cent, David had two per cent, and Willie had one per cent. They would all vote for the motion. It added up to 12.7 per cent or 50.75 per cent in total. They would win, no matter which way my father voted.

I saw a smirk on David Baker's face, and a broad grin on Scott Wagner's. They knew.

I felt a rush of bitterness sweep up inside me from somewhere in my gut. It felt acidic, like bile. I wanted to retch. I had fought so hard for this company over the last few weeks. I had anticipated how things might have gone wrong: bankruptcy was always a possibility that I had taken seriously. But somehow this wasn't.

And to be forced out by Karen!

My thoughts were interrupted by Walter Sorenson. 'Thank you Willie. I now call upon those shareholders present to cast their votes. All those in favour of the resolution?'

The Jenson Computer man raised his hand sharply, but no one else from the floor moved. I was aware of a row of hands being raised along the board table to my left, but I didn't focus on them. My eyes fixed on my father. He sat there, immobile. Sorenson repeated, 'Any more in favour?' I quickly glanced at Sorenson, who was staring at my father, but to no avail.

I felt the tears well in my eyes. I was touched. Dad had listened after all. He had supported me when I'd needed him. It wasn't his fault that his support was not going to be enough. After the way I had ignored him over the last ten years, I had no right to expect his backing; following Karen's treachery, it was especially moving to receive it.

'All those against?'

I raised my own hand, as did Rachel, and my father. The FairSystems people at the back waved their hands up and down. Keith even raised two hands in a typically childish attempt to even the scores.

I looked over to Willie for the result.

My heart stopped.

He was rocking back and forward on his chair, his face ravaged by contortions of anguish. His hands were pushed firmly into his lap, and he was leaning on them in an attempt not to let them escape.

My God, I thought, hadn't he already voted for the resolution? I realised I hadn't actually checked to see how the board had voted.

David Baker was staring at Willie too. Within a couple of moments everyone was.

Willie reddened. He hasn't voted yet, I thought. But he needed to vote against the resolution for me to win. An abstention wouldn't do.

Willie's agony was harrowing to watch. I thought at any moment he would collapse, or simply run out of the door.

There was a cry from the far end of the room. I recognised the voice. It was Terry, the big hairy Yorkshireman. 'Come on, yer great poofter! Stick yer 'and up!'

This was met with cries of agreement from the others at the back of the room, Keith most vociferous amongst them.

Something clicked in Willie. His face cleared, he smiled at the rabble, and raised his hand to a huge cheer.

'Thank you, ladies and gentlemen,' said Sorenson, unmoved. 'Perhaps you could give me the results when you're ready, Willie?'

Willie put his hand down and shuffled through bits of paper. After a long minute, he handed a small sheet to Sorenson.

'Votes for the resolution, nine hundred and ninety-five thousand. Votes against the resolution, one million and five thousand. Therefore, I declare that the resolution is defeated.'

A cheer came from the back of the hall. I turned to Rachel. Her eyes shone, and she smiled broadly at me. 'Well done,' she said. We shared our success for a moment, before we were surrounded by the FairSystems rabble. They had been courageous, I thought. They had chosen the risky path, which could easily lead to all of them losing their jobs. I was thankful for their loyalty. I would remember it.

I looked over their shoulders into the room. The Jenson representative gathered up his papers, and left alone. Hartman's man was impassive, and wandered over to Scott Wagner, who chatted to him, throwing bitter glances in my direction. Nigel Young walked past, paused briefly to nod stiffly at me and murmur 'Well done', and then left, embarrassed. He was followed by a red-faced David Baker. He glowered at me with a mixture of savaged pride and pure hatred. I had never seen him so angry.

There was a flurry of backslapping as the FairSystems people, Keith and Terry prominent among them, mobbed Willie. It was as though he had scored the winning goal in the cup final, which in a way he had. He had a lop-sided smile on his face. He looked bewildered by the attention, but obviously enjoyed it.

'Why did you do it?' I asked, shaking his hand.

'Oooh, I don't know. I suppose I just didn't want to see you lose. I must be mad. Why did I ever leave Price Waterhouse?'

I smiled. 'I don't know, Willie, but I'm very glad you did. Thanks,' I said, and meant it.

The small crowd dispersed. I saw my father talking to Sorenson. Sorenson noticed that I was free, and walked over to touch my arm. 'Can I see you in Graham's office in a few moments?' he asked.

I nodded, and as he walked off, I turned to my father.

There was a lot I wanted to say to him, but I still didn't feel comfortable saying it. In the end, all I could manage was, 'Thanks, Dad.'

He grinned at me, his face full of pride. 'You were right to come and see me in Oxford. And this isn't something I did for Richard. I did it for you. God knows how you'll keep Fair-Systems alive, but I trust you to do it. Good luck.'

I couldn't say anything. But I knew he could tell from my smile what I felt.

Once again, he had put his trust in me to save FairSystems. And I would do the best I could. For me, for Richard, and for him. For our shattered family.

He took a deep breath. 'Come and see me in Oxford for lunch one Sunday. Bring your girlfriend,' he said. He glanced up at me, waiting for an answer.

I paused for a moment. My mother was dead. Richard was

dead. My family was standing right in front of me. I needed him. Everything has to be forgiven sometime.

I nodded. 'That will be nice.'

He tried to contain his smile as he said, 'See you then,' and walked out.

I searched out Graham Stephens' office, and found him in there with Sorenson. Stephens left us to it, congratulating me and saying, 'Use the office as long as you like. Let my secretary know when you've finished.'

Sorenson sat on Stephens' sofa, and beckoned me to sit in his armchair. He was a lot like Bob Forrester. Both men enjoyed successful careers, and were full of energy and authority. Although older, Sorenson was if anything bigger than Forrester, and fitter. He had an easier charm.

But he had just tried to fire me and had failed. I wondered how this encounter would go, what I should do. Fresh from my vote of confidence, I didn't feel overawed, and I was sure I was quite capable of standing up to him. Would he try again to persuade me to sell out, I wondered. Perhaps this was just the beginning of a board-room war.

Sorenson began in calm tones. 'Congratulations, Mark. You have just won a very important vote. As you know, I differ with you on the right way forward for the company. But I must respect the views of the majority of the shareholders, even if that majority is a narrow one.'

I nodded, wondering where this was going.

Sorenson continued. 'I would be more than happy to carry on as chairman of FairSystems. I think we can both agree that the company has a difficult period ahead of it. As I told you at the time, my proposal of the resolution to remove you was nothing against you personally. I genuinely thought the sale of the company was in the best interests of the shareholders. But I quite understand if you feel that you're unable to work with me in future. So I'm happy to tender my resignation as chairman, if you want it. It's up to you.'

I didn't reply immediately. I was surprised at first by Sorenson's proposal. But as I thought it through I realised he was right to suggest resignation right away. The company was not going to survive if its chairman and managing director were at loggerheads. He was willing to make peace. As he said, it was up to me.

'No need to answer right now if you don't want to,' Sorenson continued. 'But it would be a good idea to let me know in the next day or two.'

'No, that's all right, I've made up my mind.' I was pretty sure that Sorenson was genuine when he said he would support me. And the company would need all the help it could get over the next few weeks. I didn't feel anything against him, he had been very open with me at all times. 'Please do carry on as chairman, at least until the end of the year, if we get that far. We should have a better idea what's happening then. But you'll have to accept that I'm not going to sell out, whatever the circumstances.'

Sorenson smiled. 'Good. I shall be happy to continue. And I kind of got the message about you not being wild about selling.

'Now, I want to spend today and tomorrow in the company. I think it's important to preserve morale, and to show that the board isn't split over this. I'll call Nigel Young and make sure that he'll give you his support as well. I'm sure he'll agree. I'd also like to talk to you and Willie about how exactly we're going to get through the next few weeks. You have these horrible insolvency laws in this country that make directors liable if a company trades while insolvent. FairSystems must be pretty close to that now. I don't mind sailing close to the wind on this one, but I don't want to end up in jail.'

'Fine,' I nodded.

'Also, you've got to try to keep the management team together. Can you rely on them?'

'Rachel, yes. Willie, yes. David, no.'

Sorenson nodded. 'That's not going to be easy. This little episode won't have helped much. But you badly need someone with general business expertise. I admire your guts, but you haven't got David's experience. I'll talk to him, and try to persuade him to stick around.'

I wasn't sure I wanted him to stick around. I wasn't at all sure about David. Whenever I thought about the constantly shifting swirl of enemies that surrounded FairSystems, David Baker was always in there somewhere. My victory at the EGM had dealt with an immediate problem, but there were people out there who wanted to see FairSystems ruined or sold, people who had wanted Richard killed, who at that moment might even be planning my death. And I still didn't know who they were.

David was a link to these people. Perhaps it was wise to keep him where I could watch him.

'OK,' I said. 'He stays.' I looked at my watch. It was twelve o'clock. 'I'm going back to the factory now. Shall I give you a lift?'

'No thanks,' said Sorenson. 'I'm having lunch with your father, and I've hired a car. I'll see you about three.'

And he did. The whole factory felt his presence. Despite the predicament we were all in, the result of the EGM had raised spirits throughout the company. Sorenson's enthusiasm, and visible support for me simply raised them further. Even I began to feel confident that we would get through.

True to his word, Sorenson spent a long time poring over the figures with Willie and myself. We worried over Jenson's delayed payments. I told Sorenson that I thought Jenson was just trying to weaken us so that he could force us to sell out.

'That's typical of Carl,' he said, grimly. 'He sure knows how to play it tough. And there's not a whole hell of a lot we can do about it. I tell you what, when I get back to California, I'll give him a call. I'll try to persuade him to give you at least part of the advance payments he originally promised. I can't guarantee it'll work, but it can't hurt.'

We all worked late that night. Finally at nine thirty Sorenson left for his hotel, Balbirnie House. Willie was going to meet him for an early breakfast the next morning to go through more figures.

I headed for Kirkhaven, tired but exhilarated by the day's events.

When I got home, there was one telephone call I still had

295

to make that evening. The phone rang ten times before she answered.

'Hello?'

'Karen? It's Mark.'

'Oh. Hello Mark.' She was expecting trouble.

She got it.

'Why did you vote against me?'

'Because you're wrong,' said Karen, coldly. 'You're carried away with FairSystems, just like your brother was. You can't see straight. It's in a mess. You should sell it.'

That riled me. 'It's up to me to decide whether to sell or not. It was my brother's company, I'm the managing director. I can't believe you could be so disloyal. You, of all people, should have supported me!'

There was silence at the other end of the line.

'Karen? Karen?'

'I don't have to listen to you shouting at me,' she said, and hung up.

I called back and let the phone ring and ring. But she didn't pick it up.

We were all three of us bunched round the small table in my office, Sorenson, Willie and I. We were looking at Willie's daily cash-flow projection, in particular the column headed 13 June. That was two days before pay day, the day when the cash figure went from positive to negative. Negative forty-five thousand pounds to be precise.

'I'm sorry, Mark, but this figure really bothers me. Graham Stephens has explained to me my duties as a director under Scottish Company Law. It's illegal to allow a company to continue in business if you know it's not going to be able to meet its creditors. And it looks like we'll be in that position in less than two weeks' time.'

'We'll find the cash,' I said.

'Where from exactly?'

'There are a lot of options. We'll do it somehow.'

Sorenson looked at me closely. He knew I had no idea where

the cash would come from, but he knew I would try hard, and, as he himself had said, he knew I had guts. He came to a decision.

'OK. I'll give you until next Wednesday. Seven days. If I don't have concrete evidence of some cash coming in by then, I'll call in the receiver.'

I coughed. 'One of the options is for you to put up some of your own money.'

Sorenson sat stock still. I could feel Willie cringe in the chair beside me. But it was a fair request. And Sorenson must have had some spare cash.

'You told me that you frequently backed companies you believed in.'

He breathed in through his nose. 'Mark, as you know, I already have a sizeable stake in this company, and of course I'm at risk for my director's fee as well. More importantly, my reputation is on the line here, and that's my greatest asset. I would remind you that my preferred strategy is to sell out. Given that, it would be illogical for me to buy in, wouldn't it?'

I wasn't sure his stake was that 'sizeable' given his net worth, but he had a point. 'OK,' I said, disappointed.

'Now, you have my support for the next seven days.'

I was still hopeful that somehow I would get hold of some funds. And if all else failed, there was still my bank, although I wanted to avoid that if at all possible.

Just then, David popped his head round the door. Sorenson had been as good as his word, and had secured an assurance from David that he would carry on working for FairSystems, and accept my continuing role as managing director. I wasn't too sure what that assurance was worth, but I was willing to do my part.

'I just had an interesting phone call,' he said.

'Oh yes?'

'It was from Yoshi. He said he happened to be in the country and wanted to fix up a meeting with us.'

'Fine,' I said. 'When?'

'Today. He says he's going to fly up this afternoon. He suggested four o'clock.'

'Today! They don't waste their time, do they? Do you want to come, Walter?'

'Gee, I'd sure like to. But I've got to catch the four o'clock flight from Edinburgh if I'm going to make my connection back to San Francisco.'

'Shame. It would have been good if you could've made it. Is it just Yoshi? Or is he bringing his boss?'

'Just Yoshi, I think,' said David. 'It must be a spur-of-the-moment thing.'

'OK. Thanks, David. We'll see what he has to say.'

When David had left the room, Sorenson asked, 'Who's Yoshi?'

'Oh, I'm sorry. That's Yoshiki Ishida from Onada Industries. They're the people we've been talking to about licensing our software for the entertainment market. You remember, the ones who would only deal if they got the source code to FairSim 1.'

'I certainly do,' said Sorenson. He looked thoughtful for a moment. 'There's something I feel I ought to tell you,' he said.

'Yes?'

'You know I had breakfast with Willie at the Balbirnie early this morning? Just after we'd finished I saw David come into the dining room. I don't think he saw me.'

'And?' I asked, curious.

'And he went to join a Japanese business man. Youngish. They seemed to know each other well.'

'Yoshi?'

'I don't know who this Yoshi is, but it sure looks like it could have been him, doesn't it?'

He was right. It did.

It was two minutes to four, and I was staring at the afternoon sun reflecting on the sea through my electronic window. Around this time a fishing boat always nosed its way into the harbour. I had found the regularity of the picture comforting at first, but it was beginning to irritate me. I would have to get it changed.

I was confident Yoshi would arrive at exactly four, and I would get a call at one minute past. I was curious to see what would happen at this meeting. I hadn't been surprised to hear that David had met Yoshi earlier for breakfast. That stuff about Yoshi just happening to be in the country made no sense; Yoshi had said that he was based in London. Obviously David had planned the meeting before the EGM, on the basis that I would be out of the way, and he would be MD. He just couldn't wait to give away that source code, I thought.

I called Keith. Andy picked up his phone.

'Is Keith ready?' I asked.

'Yes,' said Andy. 'He nipped out a quarter of an hour ago with his camera. He should be in his car now, waiting.'

'Good. Thank you.' I put the phone down.

Sure enough, it rang again at one minute past. I gave them a few minutes to stew, and then wandered off to the conference room. Yoshi was polite and friendly, almost casual. Without his boss and cronies around, he had decided to assume his American persona.

'Welcome,' I said.

'It's great to be here again,' replied Yoshi. 'Thank you for seeing me at such short notice. It's a shame I have to rush in and out like this. I like it up here. And I don't even get time for a round of golf.'

'Do you play?'

'Oh, sure. All the time. And I hear there are great courses around here.'

'There are, I believe,' I said. 'Although I don't play much. How about you, David?'

I was curious to hear what David did with his spare time.

'I haven't played for a long while,' said David. 'There's too much to do around here.'

Of course, macho MBAs didn't play golf. That was for the dead wood. For the first time since I had moved up to Scotland, I thought about taking it up.

299

I sat next to David, with Yoshi opposite. 'Now, how can we help you?'

'I wanted to touch base with you on a couple of things,' Yoshi began in casual American. 'First of all, I want to update you on how we are progressing our strategy in the virtual entertainment market. It only seemed fair that we should keep you in the loop, given our earlier discussions.'

He paused, looking at me. I motioned for him to continue.

'We have linked up with a small outfit in Japan who are developing a VR simulation manager that we can use as a basis for our virtual entertainment software. It's not quite as good as yours, but it's close. It will certainly be adequate for our needs.'

He's bluffing, I thought. He wouldn't be here if he wasn't. But I would play along. 'So, you no longer need to deal with us?' I said evenly.

'That's right, Mark.'

'Well, I'm glad you've found a suitable solution to your problem,' I said with no trace of concern. 'But, in that case, I don't understand why you're here.'

Yoshi looked at me closely for a few moments. He had clearly hoped for something more from me. He knew we were in trouble, and he was trying to use that as leverage. But I wasn't going to let him. It was pride as much as anything else. And I thought he was bluffing. 'We know that FairSystems is in play,' he said at last, 'and that Jenson Computer is building a stake.'

He glanced at me for confirmation. I didn't give him any.

'It's likely that you will lose your independence soon,' he continued. 'The reason I'm here is that I want to make an offer for your company. We could discuss a friendly deal of course, with continuing involvement for yourself and all your people should you wish it. We feel that FairSystems and Onada Industries would make a great fit.'

So there it was on the table. The predators really were showing themselves now. Yoshi was looking for a reaction. He got it.

'No,' I said.

He pressed on. 'The arbitrage community is getting involved,

300

Mark. FairSystems' days as an independent company are numbered.'

'No,' I said again.

Yoshi took a deep breath. 'There would be many synergies between our companies. With your VR software and our hardware technology, Onada could soon overtake Sega in the electronic entertainment business. They have nothing close. Think about it.'

'No.' I was beginning to enjoy this.

Yoshi tried a different tack. 'I can assure you, you'll be much better off as part of a Japanese group than falling for a US company. American companies fire people and cut costs. The Japanese invest for the long-term. That's why Japanese companies dominate the world electronics industry.'

'No.'

Yoshi sighed. His eyes flickered towards David, who hadn't said anything, and who wore a perfect poker face.

'OK,' he said. 'I get the message. But our offer won't be on the table for ever. Once we hook up with this other company, we won't need you. It will be too late. And either you'll go bankrupt, or Jenson Computer will suck you dry of all your technology, and close your factory down. You don't have much time to choose.'

He stood up to leave, and we shook hands. 'I'm sorry you've wasted your journey,' I said.

'Think about it,' said Yoshi, and David Baker saw him out.

I closed my eyes. Jenson Computer and now Onada Industries. I wondered how many other companies there were whose biggest customers were their biggest enemies.

22

I loitered in the corridor for David. I had to wait at least ten minutes. He and Yoshi obviously had a lot to talk about.

He tried to turn back when he saw me, but he was too late. I pulled him into the conference room. He shuffled impatiently from foot to foot.

'Why did you lie to me, David?' I began.

David's eyebrows shot up. 'Lie?'

'Yes, lie. I know you had breakfast with Yoshi at Balbirnie House this morning. Walter Sorenson saw you.'

For a moment I saw anger in David's eyes. He didn't like to be caught out. Then he pulled himself together. 'I'm sorry I couldn't tell you about that,' he said coolly.

'And why couldn't you?'

'Yoshi said he wanted a meeting with me alone this morning. I couldn't really argue with him, since he's such an important customer. He was adamant that you should know nothing about it.'

God, David was smooth. And quick on his feet. 'And what did he want to discuss?'

David was in his stride now. 'He told me Onada Industries were about to make an offer for FairSystems, and he wanted to know my reaction.'

'And what was your reaction?'

'As you know, I've consistently been in favour of selling the company. I told Yoshi that, but I said your response would probably be negative.'

So far, so plausible. Yet it was much more likely that David had arranged this meeting with Onada believing it would fall the day after the announcement of his appointment as managing director. That shouldn't have been too embarrassing to admit to. But David didn't look embarrassed. He was brazening it out. He was hiding something, I was sure. What?

Then I remembered the thought Rachel had had when David had been adamant that we should sell the company. We had been suspicious of Jenson Computer then, not Onada, but the thought might still prove to be correct.

'David, have you done a deal with Onada?'

Got him! David's eyes flickered for a moment, and then his face took on a pose of puzzled innocence. 'A deal? No. What sort of deal?'

'Oh, I don't know. A deal whereby you deliver FairSystems to Onada Industries, and in return they make you managing director.'

'No!' said David, with too much righteous indignation.

'You bloody well have, haven't you?' I moved closer to him. 'Haven't you?'

Suddenly we were no longer two business rivals, but two men staring each other down. I was taller than David and stronger. And he suddenly thought I would use that.

He knew I knew.

He backed off, or rather pulled away. He walked to the far corner of the room, and turned round. 'So what if I did? This company would have a real future with Onada. The Japanese will dominate virtual reality in five years anyway; if they set out to do something, they always succeed. You're only an amateur manager, you have no idea what you're doing. The firm would be much better off with me running it. It's obvious; certainly to the Japanese.'

'So how much have you told them about the company, David? Do they know about all our development plans?' Suddenly I was very glad that David didn't know the details of Project Platform. I felt total contempt for him. 'You make me sick! You've betrayed everyone who works here. You're fired. Now get out of the building!'

'Fuck you! I was just doing what made commercial sense. If you and Richard didn't like it, then that's your problem!'

Richard didn't like it. Richard? I remembered the big row David had had with Richard the day before he'd died.

'Richard knew you were negotiating with Onada behind his back! He talked to you about it, didn't he?'

David was quiet now.

'I bet he fired you that afternoon,' I went on. David's face was impassive. I thought I caught a flicker in his eye. 'But he never got a chance to do anything about it before he died. That was convenient, wasn't it?'

David just looked at me.

'Did you kill my brother?' I asked quietly.

'Don't be ridiculous,' said David scornfully.

'You heard me. Did you kill my brother?' I repeated.

'I don't have to listen to this,' he muttered, and pushed past me.

I grabbed hold of his sleeve. 'Hold on, David. Answer my question!'

David turned to me. 'No, I didn't kill your brother. I don't know why he was killed. But I can guess. He got in the way of someone who wants to own this company. Now you're in the way. And when you get killed, I won't shed any tears, believe me.' With that, he pulled his arm away, and pushed through the door.

I watched him go, breathing heavily. I was sure David had betrayed FairSystems to Onada. I had been right to keep him on, if only to make certain of that. But had he killed Richard? I couldn't tell from his response. It was possible.

I slumped into my chair. A cold feeling crept over me. I had never completely trusted David, but I hadn't really imagined that he could have been so contemptible. And if he had killed

304

Richard . . . Then again, had he been threatening me in that last outburst?

I didn't know.

I went to Rachel's office. 'We won't be seeing much more of David,' I said.

'Why?'

'I fired him.'

'You what! Why?'

'You were right. He had done a deal to deliver FairSystems in return for being made MD. But it was with Onada, not Jenson Computer.' I explained all about our meeting with Onada. 'And my guess is that Richard discovered this just before he died.'

'Jesus!' said Rachel. She thought it through. 'Oh my God. Do you think he killed Richard?'

'I don't know. Maybe.'

'Well, be careful, won't you. I've been scared about you since you were attacked and you got that sick message. I mean, if David did kill Richard – '

'He wouldn't be stupid enough to kill me as well.'

Just then Keith popped his head around the door.

'Did you get the pictures?' I asked.

'Yeah. I'll get them developed now. You should have them this evening.'

Rachel raised her eyebrows. 'I just wondered whether anyone at the Inch Tavern would recognise our friend Yoshi,' I explained.

'Now that would be interesting.' Rachel shook her head. 'I still can't believe David did that deal with Onada.'

'Well, he did. And he's gone now. And we'll make Onada regret it, too. What do you think about this Japanese company with the new simulation manager?'

'It's bollocks.'

'Are you sure?'

'They're bluffing. Yoshi said the simulation manager was in development, did he? If that's the case, it could be months away from final testing. Maybe even years. If there was a Japanese company with a better product than ours ready now, we'd never hear from Onada again. And I would have picked up the rumours by now.'

'So we hold all the cards?'

'For a change, yes, we do. They need a simulation manager that works right away if they're going to launch a credible product.'

'Good,' I said. 'Let's make them sweat then.'

I liked talking to Rachel. At that moment my girlfriend, my chairman, my colleagues, and my customers all seemed to be turning against me. She, at least, was an ally. Since our victory at the EGM, she had been a lot warmer towards me. Once again, I found I looked forward to talking to her. The snide comments had stopped, and she didn't mention Karen at all. She was throwing herself wholeheartedly into saving the company, and she was enjoying it.

Kerr looked, if anything, more tired than usual. He arrived with a note-taking detective constable.

'OK. Tell me what happened.'

I ran through what David had said to me. They wanted his exact words. As I spelled them out, it became clear that he hadn't admitted to anything more sinister than having breakfast with Yoshi without my permission. But Kerr was grateful for the lead.

'This will give us something new to work on. And by God we need it. Doogie Fisher's not going to crack. In fact the harder time we give him, the more he enjoys it. The bastard likes to feel he's persecuted.'

'Do you think David might have killed Richard?'

Kerr gave a world-weary sigh, and stretched. 'I don't know,' he said. 'But we'll ask the questions.'

It had been a long, tough day. I was pleased David had gone. And it was good to have my position as managing director unquestioned. But there was still a lot to be done.

I went for a pint at the Inch Tavern, taking the photo of Yoshi with me. That gave the regulars something to chat about. Once again, the friendly atmosphere did its work. I left at about ten. It was just getting dark. I walked down the hill to the little bridge over the burn.

The bridge was poorly lit, and shadows reached out across the road. I could hear the stream gurgling mysteriously under the stone arch. I looked behind me. There was no one around. The nearest house was thirty yards away, and had no lights on.

Suddenly, I felt afraid. I stopped. What was I doing here? Was I mad? I had nearly been killed at this very spot. I should have driven, or walked back to my house with someone else.

I had been drunk then; I was sober now. I could walk back to the pub and ask for an escort. No. That was ridiculous.

Someone was playing with my life. Someone had killed Richard. Someone was trying to ruin FairSystems. Someone was thinking hard about killing me.

Was it David Baker? Doogie? Someone I didn't even know?

Whoever it was, was he going to scare the hell out of me from now on?

No, he wasn't.

I looked across the bridge. There was almost certainly no one there. And if there was, he was hiding in the gully of the stream itself. If I walked rapidly across, I'd hear him, and I would be able to run before he reached me.

What if he had a gun?

Ridiculous. People just didn't carry guns in Kirkhaven.

So, I took a deep breath and walked rapidly across the bridge. Nothing moved. All I heard was the sound of the sea and the burn.

If someone was trying to scare me, he was succeeding.

I had half a dozen e-mails waiting for me the next morning. Two were interesting. One was from Susan saying Steve Schwartz had called. He didn't want me to call him back, but he wanted me to be sure to drop in to see him when I was next in London.

Intriguing.

The second was from Sorenson.

I find it incredible that David really has been involved with Onada in the manner you describe. But if he has, you are right, he has got to go.

He leaves a serious gap in management. Given his departure, I am even more worried about the solvency of the company. I have spoken with Graham Stephens who shares my concerns. So, if you can't come up with some more funds by next Wednesday, unfortunately, I will have to appoint a receiver. I hope this won't be necessary.

Good luck.

I sighed deeply. There was no escape. It was Thursday, and no miracle was going to happen in the next six days. I dialled my Personal Account Executive.

I told him I wanted to draw down the loan we had spoken about. Ninety thousand pounds. It would mean taking out a mortgage again on Inch Lodge. And taking the borrowing on my own house up to the limit. With my existing mortgage, it added up to a hefty monthly interest bill. I reassured him that I had more big bonuses from Harrison Brothers to come. The funds would be available within a week. The documentation I had given the bank for the original mortgage was still recent enough for him to work on.

I put the phone down and closed my eyes. I knew I was making a classic trader's mistake. Betting everything on a trade that was going wrong.

According to Willie's cash flows which were etched on my brain, the ninety thousand pounds would, with luck, buy another month, giving us until July's pay day, and it might even take us into August. We were expecting some money in from two customers in the last week of June, which would help. God, I hoped the bastards paid up on time!

I was betting everything, but I didn't mind. This had long ago ceased to be simply a large-scale trade. I was emotionally, psychologically and financially wedded to FairSystems. I would either live or die with it. And that knowledge gave me the grim thrill of the chronic gambler.

I went to Willie's office, and got him to draw up a subordinated loan note issued by FairSystems plc to me, maturing in six months' time. The amount was ninety thousand pounds.

'Are you sure you want to do this?' he asked, looking at me as though I were mad.

Well, I was mad. I nodded. He wasn't really surprised.

Back to more immediate problems.

Onada Industries.

So, Onada were going to acquire FairSystems, were they? They thought they had all the cards, that we would flee the evil Americans and fall into their arms? Well, they were wrong.

For once in my brief career at FairSystems, I had the upper hand, and I was going to make full use of it. If I was lucky, I might find a longer term solution to FairSystems' cash-flow problem as well. By longer term, I meant three months, rather than three weeks.

I sought out Rachel.

'Now, you're sure Onada don't have any alternative to Fair-Sim 1?'

'Not if they want to succeed in the entertainment market,' she said. 'And believe me, they want to do that.'

'Good. Then help me draft a couple of faxes.'

They went to the top two electronic entertainment companies in the world: Sega and Nintendo. They mentioned that we had been in discussions with Onada, but that these had fallen through, and we were looking for another Japanese partner. I asked for an early response if either company had any interest in talking further. I wasn't looking for anything concrete. Just enough to scare Onada. Then I called Yoshi at his London office.

'Hello, Yoshi. It's Mark Fairfax.'

'Oh. Good afternoon, Mark,' he said. He didn't sound too pleased to hear my voice.

'I've been thinking about our discussions yesterday.'

'Yes?' Yoshi was wary, but I detected a flicker of interest.

'Yes. I'd like to meet early next week to discuss ways we can work together. Say Monday? Your offices?'

There was silence on the line as Yoshi thought. I didn't break it.

'OK. Monday morning at eleven. Here. Will it be just yourself attending?'

'No, I'll be bringing Rachel Walker, our technical director.'

'OK. I'll see you then.'

He hung up. He didn't even ask about David Baker.

I pulled the photograph of Yoshi that Keith had taken the day before out of my briefcase. The regulars at the Inch Tavern had had no problems in identifying him as the oriental man who had had a drink with Richard the night before he'd died.

It would be interesting to see what Yoshi thought about that.

I worked very late that night, until way past midnight. The pile of papers on my desk grew faster than I could whittle it down. But they all had to be dealt with. The day-to-day operations of the company had to continue smoothly if FairSystems was going to survive. It was hard going; I was very tired.

I opened my eyes with a jolt. My computer was still whirring, and papers were strewn all over my desk. My neck was stiff. I looked at my watch; it was half past three! I had fallen asleep. I looked in dismay at the pile of work still to be done and decided there was no way I could concentrate on anything now. Time to go home to bed.

I looked in on Software on my way out. The lights were still on, and I was curious whether anyone would be working at this hour. The room was quiet and still. Through the electronic window, trees waved in the wind against a full moon. It was eerie. I could just make out Rachel's silhouette through the blinds of her office at the far end of the room. She was sitting at her computer. I debated whether to go in and say good night, but I was just too tired, so I left.

I didn't get in to work until ten the next morning, but even so I was still exhausted. I was just taking my first sips of black coffee, when Rachel knocked on my door.

'Nice lie-in?'

'I don't know how you do it,' I said. 'If I work past ten at night, I'm dead the next morning.'

Rachel grinned. 'You're just lacking in stamina. I find it works best to take great chunks of sleep when you can. I got ten hours last night.'

I laughed. 'You can't fool me. I saw you.'

Rachel looked puzzled. 'Saw me?'

'Yes, at half past three this morning. You were still working.'

'You were dreaming.'

'What do you mean? I saw you. Through the blinds.'

'But I went to bed early last night. It must have been one of the others.' She paused, thinking. 'I wonder what they were doing in my office?'

We went through to Software.

'Were any of you guys working late last night?' she asked.

There were blank looks all round.

'Not really,' said Andy. 'I was last out and I left at about ten.' Ten o'clock in the evening was early for these people.

'You didn't see anyone in my office?'

'No,' Andy shrugged.

'You're sure about that? There was no one else here?'

Andy held up his hands. He looked a little hurt.

'Sorry, Andy. I wasn't accusing you of anything. But Mark said he saw someone in my office at three o'clock last night.'

'Well, it was no one here,' said Andy.

Rachel gave me a worried glance. We looked into her office.

'Has it been disturbed?' I asked.

Rachel looked round, examining everything closely. She moved over to a computer in the corner. I recognised it as Richard's Compaq. 'This has been touched. I'm sure I left the keyboard on the side here. It's now right in front of the machine. Someone was in here!'

'Who would want to break in?'

'Doogie!' she exclaimed. 'Could it have been Doogie?'

I tried hard to recall the exact shape of the silhouette, but it was difficult. I'd been very tired, and I had been expecting to see

Rachel. 'It might have been him,' I said. 'But quite honestly it could have been anyone.'

'Christ!' said Rachel. She rushed out of her door. 'OK, everyone,' she cried. 'Stop what you're doing. Doogie was in here last night. I don't know where exactly he's been, or what he did, but I want everyone to check their computers carefully for any viruses. And no one should transfer any files until we've cleared everything. No e-mails, nothing. Keith, let everybody else in the building know what's happened. Andy, you check the servers, and the firewall.'

There was a stunned silence from the programmers, and then they all broke into movement. Many of them looked worried. 'God knows what we've lost,' said Rachel. 'No wonder the guys are scared.'

We went back into Rachel's office, and she powered up Richard's computer. I sat watching as her fingers flew over the keyboard, her eyes focused on the screen. After twenty minutes, she leaned back. 'I can't find anything here. It looks clean. Now, let's try my machine.'

'Doogie broke into our systems once before,' Rachel said, logging on to her own machine. 'But he did that by dialling into our network from outside. So we tightened up our security. We have something called a firewall machine through which all communications with the outside world flow. It makes it much easier to guard against a remote attack on our system.'

She paused to stare at her screen for a moment. 'But if he breaks in to the building itself, that's a different thing entirely. Then he can pass files around the network from the inside.'

'What might he have done?'

'Oh God, who knows? He might have planted a virus that replicates itself from file to file in our network, and then takes the whole system down at some point in the future. That's probably the worst case. Or he might have been searching our files looking for information. Or it might be something much more harmless than that. Last time all he did was produce a silly display hack.'

'Display hack?'

'Yes. The screen disappeared in flames and the words VIR-TUAL HELL rose out of them. It was Doogie's idea of a joke. He just wanted to show us he'd been into our system. It scared the shit out of us.'

Morning stretched into afternoon. People rushed about checking this and that, and passing round anti-virus disks. But no one found anything. A team of policemen arrived, Kerr among them. They couldn't see any sign that the locks to the building had been forced. The front door was secured by a standard Chubb lock and an electronic access system. I arranged to have the lock changed, and more added. Keith became very worked up about how we could change the codes on the access system, but I took no notice. Anything electronic I assumed Doogie could break into. Steel, cylinders and tumblers I had more confidence in.

I looked in on Rachel at three. She pushed back her chair from the machine, and sighed.

'Find anything?'

'Nothing,' she said. 'We've checked for every virus known to mankind. Of course, Doogie might have invented one himself, and that would be much harder to find.'

'Perhaps he was just copying files.'

'Maybe.' She shook her head. 'I wondered how he'd got hold of the Bergey letter that he used to blackmail Richard. Perhaps he just broke in then, too.'

'So, do you think the network is OK?'

Rachel drew on her cigarette, thinking hard. 'No. If Doogie got into my computer, he would leave something on it, even if it was just a display hack like the last one.'

'But it looks like he hasn't?'

Rachel shrugged.

I wondered what Doogie would want to do. Cripple Fair-Systems' computer system was the obvious answer, but we had checked and found nothing.

'Is there anything Doogie could have done to make his path into our system easier?'

'What do you mean?'

'Well, it must be a real pain to physically break into the factory every time he wants to gain access to our computer. Is there any way he could have opened a path into our network past the firewall machine? So that he could just call in whenever he wanted without us knowing?'

Rachel's eyes lit up. 'You mean introduce a back door?'

'Do I?'

'Yes, you do,' she said, and turned to her machine with renewed enthusiasm.

Two hours later, she came into my office with a broad smile on her face.

'You were right! He installed a sophisticated packet sniffer!'

'A packet sniffer?'

'Yes. A packet sniffer can eavesdrop on all the information going around our network. Doogie's was looking out for someone logging on as a super-user to the firewall machine. The packet sniffer would pick up their user ID and password. It would then use this information to set Doogie up as a super-user himself.'

'And what's a super-user?'

'A super-user is someone who controls the computer. At the moment, Andy and I are the only two super-users on the firewall machine. If Doogie became a super-user as well, then he'd be able to bypass the firewall machine into our network without alerting anyone. He could look through our computers at his leisure.'

'I see. Have you destroyed this packet sniffer?'

'Andy's dealing with it right now.'

'So we're safe?'

Rachel winced. 'I hope so. But we can never be sure. And of course we don't know what files he copied, if any.'

'And he did waste almost a whole day of everyone's time whilst we tried to work out what he'd done,' I said.

Just then Kerr came in.

'Find anything?' I asked.

'No. Nothing yet. And I'm not hopeful. All we've got is your ID, for what it's worth.'

'I saw him!' I said.

Kerr rubbed his eyes. 'No. You saw a figure who you thought was Miss Walker. That's not going to go very far in court, believe me.'

I believed him. 'So aren't you going to bring him in?'

'Oh aye. We've got a team waiting outside his flat now. And when I've got him, I'll find out what the hell he's up to.'

'Any luck with our friend David Baker?'

'He's almost as bad as Fisher,' said Kerr. 'He's got a lawyer. He won't answer any questions. His excuse is he's putting together a wrongful dismissal case that you'll be hearing about shortly.'

He collapsed into a chair. 'I don't know. Fisher's still my favourite. If only he hadn't been logged on to the computer network at the time of your brother's murder.'

I looked at Rachel. 'That's easily faked,' she said.

Kerr sat up. 'But he showed us passwords, addresses, everything.'

'Believe me,' said Rachel. 'Doogie and his friends could fake that. If you show me what you've got, I'll show you how.'

Kerr rubbed his hands. 'I'll do that. You know,' he said, smiling for the first time, 'I think we're getting closer.'

The Fife Constabulary's eye was now firmly on Doogie Fisher.

Just after Kerr left, my computer beeped at me. It was an e-mail.

Hey Fairfax!
   I've got you now. With what I know, FairSystems is fucked.
      So long!
      BOWL

Shit! Doogie had turned up something after all.

23

The factory was buzzing. Everyone worked over the weekend, even though they knew the chances of overtime pay were negligible. I was there Saturday and Sunday, too. There was a lot to do. And I was glad of an excuse not to see Karen in London.

I spoke to her briefly on the phone; we were polite but cold. I decided not to tell her about my meeting in London. I hoped I would be able to get down and back in a day, and avoid spending the night with her. I was still angry about her vote at the EGM.

I spoke to Kerr. They'd arrested Doogie and searched his flat, including his computer. They had found nothing incriminating. They'd kept him in the police station for twenty-four hours, and then they'd had to let him go. The evidence was just too thin, even for a charge of breaking and entering. Kerr sounded even gloomier than usual.

We received no reply from Sega, but a fax arrived from Nintendo on Saturday morning. It said they wanted to talk, nothing more. I hoped it would be enough.

Rachel and I flew to Heathrow early on Monday morning. I wanted to catch Steve Schwartz before our meeting with Onada. It was good to have Rachel with me; I needed an ally.

We took the tube into the City. When we arrived at Harrison Brothers' offices I talked the security guard into giving Rachel a visitor's pass and took a lift up to the trading room on the second floor. I looked over to Karen's desk. Fortunately, her chair was empty.

Jack Tenko's chair was empty too. So was his desk. All his papers and belongings were gone. As Karen had said, he was history.

Steve was absorbed in his graphs, and didn't take any notice of me for five minutes, beyond a brief wave of his hand. He was using a mouse to draw a web of support and resistance lines on the graph of one of the stocks in which he had a big position. Steve didn't believe absolutely in what his charts told him, but he always wanted to know what they said nonetheless.

Rachel watched fascinated. I could see her brain whirring, trying to work out exactly what Steve was doing.

When he had finished, I introduced him to Rachel. He smiled politely, and was immediately bombarded with questions on what he'd been doing and why, and whether he was doing any non-linear analysis, and if not, why not.

Steve seemed to enjoy the interrogation session, and I realised it would go on all day unless I put a stop to it.

'You said you had something for me, Steve.'

'Oh, yes,' he said, bringing his mind back to me. His face clouded and he leaned forward, looking over his shoulder. No one was taking any notice of us.

His voice fell to a whisper. 'It's about your friend Hartman. It looks like the SEC are after him.'

'That doesn't surprise me.' The SEC was responsible for tracking down securities fraud and insider dealing in the United States. From what I had heard of him, Hartman would be a natural target.

'No, I mean they're really close. There's a guy I know at Bloomfield Weiss who's been subpoenaed to provide information on all his trades in Futurenet with Hartman and a bunch of obscure offshore funds. The word on the street is, stay clear of dealing with the guy. None of us wants to get implicated in this sort of thing after the Boesky business.'

'What's Futurenet?' I asked.

'It's some company involved in communications software in Seattle. It was bought by Jenson Computer last year. It was obvious that there was something funny going on in the stock before the takeover announcement.'

'I've heard of them,' Rachel said. 'They do software for wide area networks. But we don't use them.'

'Keep all this to yourself,' Steve whispered.

'OK,' I nodded. 'Thank you.' I turned to Steve's screens. 'Can I have a look at a graph of our share price.'

'Sure.' Steve tapped a few keys, his computer's guts whirred and ground quietly, and a graph of the FairSystems share price action appeared.

'It's firm,' he said, 'Look.'

And indeed it was. The price had reached six dollars at the time of the EGM and then slipped to five. Since then it had risen back up to six. Tall thin bars under the line of the graph indicated that this movement had been on the back of decent volume.

'Someone's still accumulating stock,' said Steve. 'I'm sure of it.'

'Jenson Computer?'

'Could be. You'll soon hear about it if it is them. They have to tell the SEC. Unless they're buying through untraceable nominees. Or through Hartman's network.'

'You said it was Jenson Computer who bought Futurenet?'

'That's right.'

'And what happened to Futurenet afterwards?'

Rachel answered. 'They fired a third of the staff. They had just opened a factory in Greenock, which was closed down. A lot of their best people left of their own accord. Not a happy place.'

'Well, that's not going to happen to us,' I said with determination.

I asked Rachel to stay with Steve for a couple of minutes, and nipped over to the far side of the room. There was a flurry of activity; Harrison Brothers was just launching a new eurobond issue. I realised how much I missed the buzz, the restrained excitement, the feeling that anything could happen at any time. Greg was on the phone, and waved to me as I walked past. I had a quick chat with Ed. The Italian trade was going well; the bonds were up to ninety-seven and a half. Ed gave me a quick look at the monthly P&L numbers. We were already over two million dollars up! Very satisfying.

Bob Forrester strolled into the trading room. He noticed me, and came over. 'Good to see you here, Mark. I'm glad you haven't forgotten us,' he boomed.

'Things seem to be going pretty well here without me,' I said, nodding at the P&L.

'Yeah, Ed's doing well. But we need you back, Mark. We're behind budget for the year, and I can't afford to have you out of action much longer.'

'I thought I had until the first of August.'

'I'm sorry, Mark. I need you back next week.'

It was a statement, not a request or even an order.

'I can't do it. FairSystems is in a delicate situation. I really can't leave it.'

Bob looked at me closely. I held his gaze. He knew I wasn't going to back down.

'OK,' he said. 'Three weeks, and I want you back at your desk, or you'll find someone else sitting in it when you do show up,' and he turned on his heel and walked out.

That was all I needed! Especially with the extra debt burden I had just taken on. If I lost my job, it wouldn't be so easy to get another one. Being out of the market for even a couple of months would make a difference.

Well, I didn't have time to worry about that now.

Onada Industries' UK headquarters was just off Hammersmith Broadway. The building was small, square, and very modern. Inside, everything was square and very modern as well. Most of the employees seemed to be young English men or women with polite, efficient smiles. I sighted one Japanese hurrying down a corridor in the distance.

We were shown up to a conference room. It was sparsely, but

expensively furnished in cherry and light oak. The lighting was indirect, reflecting off the glowing white walls. One wall was made of glass, and provided a one-way view of the reception area. From the outside it had seemed to be green and smoky. Rachel and I sat down.

Rachel was looking smart, at least for her. Her jeans were black, not blue, and didn't have any holes in them. It was probably her best jersey, lambswool, and not nearly as baggy as her others. For once it was possible to see her slender legs and full figure; in fact, it was impossible to miss them. Her hair was tied back from her face, revealing her ears, and slim neck. The dim, indirect lighting of the room made her skin glow in a way that reminded me of that evening in her flat in Glenrothes.

My thoughts were interrupted by the opening of the door. Mr Akama entered with Yoshi and the two acolytes.

So, Akama was in town? I wondered if he had made a special trip for this meeting, or if he was just passing through. I smiled to myself. Rachel was right; we were important to Onada.

Akama bowed to me, nodded minutely at Rachel, and sat down. I nodded back. A line of elephants marched from left to right down his tie towards his trousers.

We meandered through some small talk. Mr Akama had not taken any English lessons since we had last met. He was stiff, barely smiling. I doubted he had recovered from the insult of me overruling David's deal with them. Or perhaps he was embarrassed that I had found out how they had used David as a spy within FairSystems. Mr Akama had a number of reasons not to like me very much. Sitting there, watching me through half-closed eyes, he looked a powerful enemy.

Finally, Yoshi fell silent waiting for me to talk.

I didn't. I simply passed across the fax we had sent to Sega and Nintendo. I waited a few moments for Yoshi to whisper to Akama, and then flicked across Nintendo's reply.

It did the trick. Mr Akama reddened, and rattled sharply to Yoshi. Yoshi turned to me.

'Mr Akama is most upset that you have chosen to treat your business partners in this way. He says that you must know that

Onada and Nintendo are business rivals, and it is most insulting for you to betray our trust.'

I laughed. 'Tell Mr Akama that I'm upset that he's done a deal with my marketing director to betray me.'

Yoshi paused for a moment and then passed on the message to Akama, who had regained his composure, and simply left his eyes resting, impassive again, on my face.

'I have a proposal,' I said, clearing my throat. 'We will make FairSim 1 available to Onada Industries on a non-exclusive basis, but we will not reveal the complete source code. We will make our people available wherever necessary to adapt Onada applications to FairSim 1. We will do this at industry rates, but we will require an advance payment of two hundred thousand dollars against this programming time.'

'We have no interest in this arrangement,' said Yoshi with impatience. 'We thought you were here to discuss the sale of your company.'

'Well, I'm not.'

Yoshi thought for a moment. 'Why should we go along with your proposal? We would want exclusive use of FairSim 1, at least in the entertainment sector. Why should we pay you anything when others can use the same system?'

I would have to tell them more. I had expected it. I hoped Jenson wouldn't find out. I would just have to trust in the Japanese obsession with secrecy.

'What I'm about to tell you must be in strictest confidence, OK?'

'Sure,' said Yoshi. I thought Akama's head moved in a slight nod, but I couldn't be certain.

'FairSystems is about to produce FairSim 2, which will be considerably more powerful than the current version. But, more importantly, we have developed a totally new graphics system for it to run on. This will allow computers to perform VR calculations much faster than ever before. We hope that this will become the industry standard. It will be available to everyone, including Onada Industries.'

'Then why should we pay you anything in advance for it?'

'You won't be paying for the system itself, but for the programming expertise. Our people understand this system better than anyone. They will be able to adapt your applications programs much faster, and to a higher standard, than any of your rivals. Within six months, you'll have the most efficient virtual reality programming in the world. Of course what you do with it is up to you.'

Yoshi was listening. He understood exactly what I was saying. So, I was sure, did Mr Akama.

He frowned. 'What is to stop Nintendo or Sega from coming to a similar arrangement with you?'

I had thought of that. 'Good point. We would be happy to provide our programming expertise on an exclusive basis for entertainment applications for a six-month period.'

'Six months? That's nothing!'

'It's long enough for you to build up a worldwide lead. It's also long enough for your people to pick our people's brains. Think, Yoshi. Two hundred thousand dollars for world leadership! It's got to be worth it.'

He thought about it. He turned to Akama, and they talked for five minutes.

Finally, Yoshi breathed deeply through his nose, and said, 'Thank you for your proposal, Mr Fairfax. We will discuss it in Tokyo and perhaps we will talk more soon.'

'Ah. I forgot to tell you. I want agreement in principle before I leave this office, or else I'll talk to Nintendo.' I was really pushing it, I knew. Expecting a Japanese company to make an instant decision was almost expecting the impossible. But there was only one right answer for them. What I was suggesting fitted right into their strategy, and they could not risk me going to Nintendo.

And we needed the cash quickly.

More debate. 'We need to call Tokyo,' said Yoshi.

'We'll wait,' I said.

And we waited. At one, they brought us some sushi for lunch. Yoshi popped in to check we were all right.

'We're fine,' I said. 'Are you getting anywhere?'

Yoshi sucked through his teeth. 'It's very difficult. It's nine o'clock in the evening in Tokyo now. But we are trying.'

He moved to leave, but I called after him. 'One moment, Yoshi! There are a couple of things I want to talk to you about.'

He hesitated. I pointed to a chair. 'Have a seat.'

He thought it over, and decided to sit down. He looked wary. As well he might.

'Todd Sutherland is your lawyer, isn't he?'

'He does some work for us, yes,' said Yoshi, looking puzzled.

'Why did you send him to shut up Jonathan Bergey's father?'

'Jonathan Bergey?'

'The boy who died in a motorbike accident after playing on one of our VR machines. And taking LSD.'

Yoshi was silent, thinking.

'It would have been very bad for the whole VR industry if that story had got out,' he said eventually. 'Especially for VR entertainment. In fact, the link with LSD and VR could have been just as bad as the accident itself. You know how important the VR entertainment market is to Onada Industries. We couldn't allow a public lawsuit.'

'How did you find out about the accident?'

Yoshi shrugged.

'David told you?'

Yoshi just shrugged again.

It sounded plausible. Yoshi stood up to go.

'One more thing,' I said. 'Look at this.' I pushed across the photograph Keith had taken of Yoshi in FairSystems' car park. He picked it up and frowned.

'I showed this to Jim Robertson, the landlord of the Inch Tavern in Kirkhaven. He told me that he recognised you as the man who was having a drink with Richard the night before he died. The man who checked in to the Robbers' Arms as Hiro Suzuki.'

Yoshi's frown deepened.

'Why were you there, Yoshi?'

'I don't have to answer your questions.'

'But if you have nothing to hide, why don't you?'

Yoshi stared at the picture in silence.

'Perhaps I should ask Mr Akama what you were doing there?'

Yoshi sighed. 'OK. I'll tell you.' He paused for a few seconds. Collecting his thoughts? Or making something up?

'I came up to Scotland to play golf that weekend. Richard had recommended Kirkhaven as a good place to stay. While I was there, I called him to ask him out for a drink. It was purely social. He and I got on quite well.'

Suddenly I remembered that drink with Richard and Greg in the Windsor Castle. Richard had mentioned that he had spent the day trying to negotiate with a Japanese company. I thought he had said that they were tough, but he quite liked the man he was negotiating with. That must have been Yoshi.

'You didn't discuss business at all?'

'No,' said Yoshi. 'Obviously, I was anxious for Richard to change his mind about doing a deal with us. But we didn't discuss that directly. I just wanted to develop my relationship with him.'

'That's funny. The locals said that you had an argument with him, and he stormed out.'

Yoshi thought for a second. 'Perhaps he was in a bad mood.'

'And was he in this bad mood because he knew that David Baker was your mole in FairSystems?'

Yoshi shook his head. 'I can't speculate as to why he was in a bad mood. I just don't know.'

Like hell he didn't. But there was still something that interested me. 'Why didn't you want me to mention this meeting to Mr Akama?'

Suddenly Yoshi looked very uncomfortable. 'He doesn't know about it. I would be very grateful if you didn't mention it.'

He had answered most of my questions, so I owed it to him to keep quiet. 'OK. But I might have to pass this on to the police.'

Yoshi's discomfort rose. 'You don't have to do that do you? As I said, it was all perfectly innocent.'

'We'll see.' I had got him where I wanted him. Insecure.

'Well, if you do talk to them, please ask them to be discreet.'

I didn't answer and he left the room.

'What do you think?' I asked Rachel.

'I don't know. I think he's telling the truth.'

'Mm. But I'm not sure he's telling the whole truth. He's hiding something.'

We waited there all afternoon, and ordered a pizza for supper. I was happy to wait. I could tell Onada weren't stalling, they wanted to take a decision.

The time wore on. Rachel's imagination was fired by her discussion with Steve that morning, and she questioned me about the markets and how they worked. She was very quick to understand what I was talking about, and I enjoyed explaining it to her. She obviously found finance more interesting than she had expected. When I suggested this to her, she denied it, muttering something about how the City was a parasite on British innovation. Perhaps she was right.

Finally, at eleven o'clock in the evening, or seven o'clock in the Japanese morning, Yoshi came back in the room, looking tired.

He held in his hand a one-page letter, signed by Mr Akama, agreeing in principle to the terms I had demanded. I shook his hand and smiled. 'It's been a pleasure doing business with you, Yoshi,' I said, only half-ironically, and Rachel and I left the building.

I was elated as we walked out on to the streets, and so was Rachel. It felt good finally to outwit one of the many predators who had been circling us for the last month. And it was a great deal for FairSystems. Not only would we get the two hundred thousand dollars just when we needed it, but we could secure software sales into a market in which we had previously done nothing.

A good result, and well worth the waiting.

'What now?' asked Rachel. It was twenty past eleven. We had intended to go back to Edinburgh that evening, but it was now too late.

325

'There's a hotel round the corner,' I said. 'We can try that for you.'

We walked a hundred yards to the huge concrete Novotel I had spotted on the way to Onada that morning. It was full.

We could have spent all night trying to find Rachel a hotel. 'Come back to my place,' I said. 'I have a guest room. You can sleep there.'

Rachel raised her eyebrows. 'What will Lady Karen think?'

I blushed. 'She should be asleep when we get there. But if you meet her in the morning, just be polite will you?'

'I'll try,' Rachel smiled. 'Let's go.'

So we hailed a cab, and headed for home. To my surprise, I rather enjoyed returning home in a cab with her, rather than Karen. I did feel more relaxed and comfortable with her around. With Karen I was always on edge for some reason or other. Something was always wrong, a problem between us was just dying down, or a new one was looming on the horizon.

And I still couldn't believe she had let me down at the EGM.

We spilled out of the taxi, and I unlocked the front door. It was almost midnight. I hoped Karen would be in bed. I'd have to wake her up of course, but I hoped I could leave her encounter with Rachel till the morning. We climbed the stairs to the first floor, and I showed Rachel the guest room. She stopped, and listened. I listened too.

I could hear music, very low, coming from the sitting room upstairs. It was the music from *Twin Peaks*, one of Karen's favourite CDs.

Damn, I thought. She was still up. It didn't sound as though she'd heard us.

Rachel crept into her room, and closed the door behind her. She was quite happy to avoid Karen. I decided to wait a few minutes before going upstairs to talk to Karen so as to give Rachel time to get into bed and out of the way.

I went into our bedroom. It was a bit of a mess, which was odd. Karen usually liked to keep things very tidy. The bed was unmade, and some of her clothes were sprawled about the place. Maybe she just tidied up for me, and left to herself was a slob. A nice thought, but unlikely.

I hung up my suit jacket in the wardrobe. I wasn't looking forward to talking to Karen. I hadn't had a chance to confront her face to face about her vote at the EGM, and after midnight was not the best time to do it.

I picked up some of her clothes on the floor, and put them on a chair. A skirt, a bra, a blouse.

A wine glass caught my eye. And another.

Two wine glasses!

I stood up, looking at the scene around me in revulsion.

A rush of anger flowed through me. I closed my eyes and clenched my teeth. Then I turned, and ran up the stairs.

I threw open the door of the sitting room. Karen looked up in surprise. She was sitting in the armchair, wearing nothing but a dressing-gown. She had a full glass of wine in front of her. My eyes raced round the room. Whoever he was wasn't there.

'Poured yourself a new glass, did you?'

She was speechless. Her face went white.

I took a couple of steps towards her. 'Karen. Why are there two used wine glasses in our bedroom?' I asked quietly.

She stood up. Our eyes met. She composed herself in front of me. Her face clenched up, her brow furrowed, her lips became a short thin line. She stared back at me, defiantly.

'Where is he?'

'He's gone.'

'Did you . . .?'

Karen smiled.

'I can't believe it! How could you? In my house!'

'With you likely to ring up any time of day or night, we had to.'

'You mean when I called you from Scotland he was here? With you?'

'Sometimes,' she nodded.

There was no sign of shame. She knew she was caught, and she was admitting it, challenging me to accuse her.

'Who is he? What's his name?'

She didn't answer. Her eyes held mine, defying me.

'Get out,' I whispered.

'Mark,' she said. 'I love him. I always loved him. I always will love him.'

'Get out!' I shouted, and pointed to the door.

She was gone, passing a white-faced Rachel at the head of the stairs.

I collapsed into the armchair. It smelled of Karen's perfume. I kicked it with my heel, and moved over to the big windows.

I should have known. I should have seen it coming. No wonder she had seemed strange recently. Of course she hadn't really wanted to see much of me when she could have been seeing him. I thought of how distant she had seemed when we were making love. I bet she was different with him. How could she do it? How could she string me along like that?

Now I thought about it, I had been strung along from the very beginning. 'I always loved him.' Those were her words, thrown in my face, and they were true. I knew she used to love this jerk, but I thought she hated him now. And I had hoped over time she would grow to love me. What a fool!

I felt a nudge on my shoulder. Rachel handed me a tumbler of neat whisky. She was holding a glass of red wine in her own hand. I took the whisky, unable even to acknowledge it, and drained it, handing the empty tumbler to Rachel. She brought it back a moment later.

She sat in a small upright chair in the corner, bottle of wine next to her, and watched me. I was suddenly very aware of her presence, but I couldn't talk to her. I sat down in my own chair, leaned forward, and stared at the rug.

Who the hell was this guy, anyway? What did I know about him? He was an older man. He had known Karen for several years.

Bob Forrester! Maybe. Hadn't that jerk Jack Tenko said that he had the hots for Karen? She'd been sucking up to him like crazy this last couple of months. How come I hadn't seen it? And I had spoken to him myself, just a few hours before!

But if it was him, why was he so keen for me to return to London?

My brain functioned incoherently for a long time. The first flush of anger was dulled, but still there. My mind darted rapidly from scene to scene with Karen: dinners we had been to together, watching her flirt with a customer on the phone, seeing her face glowing in the Inch Tavern. All these images that I had held so fondly now were black-edged.

Rachel finally said something. 'You should go to bed.'

I nodded, stood up, and stiffly made my way down the stairs. I turned at my door, smiled weakly at Rachel, and let myself in.

But I couldn't sleep in that bed. I grabbed a blanket, and headed for the sofa upstairs.

Rachel and I flew back to Scotland in silence. Rachel let me think; I had a lot to think about.

I had lost Karen, although I wasn't sure I had ever truly possessed her. I felt foolish, and I felt used. I also felt angry. My pride was hurt. What could she see in that big oaf Forrester? Or whoever it was. The more I thought about it, the more I realised it could be anybody.

But at the same time I was surprised to feel a sense of relief. Karen had never been easy to figure out. I had worked hard at the relationship, and although that had seemed worthwhile when things were going well, it was good not to have to worry about her any more. I had my own problems to think about.

I sat in my office and stared at the electronic sea. Richard's death had sent me reeling. I wasn't going to let Karen's betrayal do the same thing. I felt at times like a tiny piece of driftwood, pushed this way and that by waves swirling round the rocks. Onada, Jenson, Hartman, Baker, Doogie. They were all messing me around, messing my company around. Someone, probably one of them, had threatened to kill me. It would only be a matter of time before they carried out that threat.

All I had been able to do until now was react to events.

That was going to change.

I told Rachel what I was going to do. She was enthusiastic.

329

First, I called Hartman. I arranged to meet him at his offices in New York on Thursday.

Then I called the SEC in Washington. I said I wanted to meet them to discuss information I had relating to insider trading in my company. They too agreed to meet me in New York.

Then Jenson Computer. Friday in Palo Alto.

Baker and Doogie I wasn't sure about. I had better leave them to the police. And I should tell Kerr about Yoshi's visit to the Inch Tavern. I was about to phone Sergeant Cochrane, when Susan told me that Detective Inspector Kerr was downstairs.

'Send him up.'

Kerr looked tired and serious. He was trailed by a younger man in a smarter suit.

'This is Detective Inspector Morland of Edinburgh CID.'

'Afternoon, inspector. Would you like a cup of coffee?' I asked. 'You look like you need it.'

'Aye, I do that,' Kerr said. 'White. Three sugars.'

Morland shook his head.

I slipped off to the machine and came back with two cups. 'What can I do for you?' I asked.

'Doogie Fisher's dead,' Kerr said. 'Murdered.'

'What?'

'He was found in his car at the bottom of a cliff. A walker spotted it at low tide. It looks like someone strangled him, and drove his body there to dispose of it.'

'When did this happen?'

'Some time last night. He was last seen at eleven o'clock in a local pub with some friends. He said he was going off to meet someone. Apparently, he was looking forward to it.'

'Do you have any idea who did it?'

Kerr sighed. 'No. Not yet, at any rate. But Inspector Morland and his colleagues are working hard on it.'

'Do you think there's a link with Richard's death?'

'We don't know yet. But it's obviously worth checking. Doogie's dog was shut in his bedroom, which suggests that he might have met someone in his flat, and then left. He may even

330

have been killed there. So far we haven't been able to find a note of any appointment. There's nothing in his diary.'

'No one saw anything?'

'There are a lot of people wandering around that area of Edinburgh at night, and it's quite a transient population. No one would think anything of seeing a stranger. We have vague descriptions of about six different people from a girl of fifteen to a man of fifty-five. Oh yes, and a young man of about thirty, tall with dark hair.'

'Oh, I see. That's why you want to talk to me?'

Morland cleared his throat. He had listened disapprovingly as Kerr had rattled on. To him, at least, I was a suspect.

'Where were you last night, sir?'

I winced as I remembered. Creeping into my own bedroom, to find my girlfriend's underwear all over the floor.

'I was at my house in London. I flew back up to Edinburgh this morning. Hang on, I've probably still got my boarding card.' I fished it out of my pocket, and showed it to Morland, who peered at it closely.

'Thank you, sir. Do you have any witnesses we can talk to, just to confirm that?'

'Yes. Rachel Walker was there. And so was my ex-girlfriend, Karen Chilcott.' Kerr raised his eyebrows at this. 'Inspector Kerr has already met her.'

Kerr nodded to Morland.

'Have you any idea why Doogie Fisher was killed?' Morland asked.

I shook my head and glanced at Kerr. 'No, none. No more than Inspector Kerr and I have discussed. Wait a moment.' I dug out the printout of the e-mail BOWL had sent me the day after the break-in. 'Have you seen this?' Morland nodded. I had sent a copy to Kerr. 'By the way, did you get round to charging him with that burglary?'

'No,' said Kerr. 'There wasn't enough evidence. But frankly we were more interested in linking him to your brother's murder.'

'He could still have done it,' I said.

331

Kerr scratched his ravaged nose again. 'Maybe. Maybe not. You have no idea what he's referring to here?' he asked, looking at the e-mail.

'No, none. Although by the sound of it, it's pretty damaging to FairSystems.'

'Well, whatever it is, it must be important. And I wouldn't be surprised if Doogie was murdered for possessing it. We still don't know why your brother was killed. But we think his killer was someone he knew. Perhaps your brother had the same information as Doogie. Perhaps he was murdered by the same person.'

It sounded possible. Plausible.

'There is something else I should tell you,' I said, suddenly feeling very uncomfortable.

I pulled the photograph out of a drawer. 'This is a picture of Yoshiki Ishida. He works for Onada Industries, the Japanese company that recruited David Baker to help them take over FairSystems. The regulars at the Inch Tavern identified Yoshi as the Hiro Suzuki you have been looking for.'

Kerr grabbed the photograph. 'How long have you had this picture?'

'About a week.' I could feel my face reddening.

'And why didn't you show it to us earlier?'

'I wanted to show it to Yoshi myself. He says he was just up for the weekend to play golf. I think there's more to it than that.' I couldn't have given it to them earlier. Their questioning of Yoshi might have endangered our negotiations. That was something I couldn't risk.

Kerr was angry. 'Listen, sonny. When you get information like this, you tell us right away, OK? We'll ask the questions.'

I held up my hands. 'OK, OK. I'm sorry. I won't do it again.'

Kerr got up to go, taking the photograph with him. 'Someone killed Richard and Doogie because they got in his way. It seems to me you're getting in a few people's way, yourself. So you'd better take this seriously.'

'I will,' I said.

332

As the two policemen reached the door, I called after them. 'Have you spoken to David Baker about Doogie?'

Kerr turned and scowled. 'He's legged it. He had a row with his wife and left home two days ago. We don't know where he is. But we'll find him.'

24

We were crushed into the metal box twenty feet underground with at least a hundred other human beings. It was rush hour. Rachel and I had arrived in New York the night before. Our plane had been four hours late, so we had checked into an airport hotel. We took the subway into the city to save on expenses.

There was silence in the carriage as it lurched along. My head was jammed six inches away from a banker who had eaten something very spicy the night before. The air-conditioning was fighting a losing battle with the heat; it was boiling in there. Even in my lightest summer suit, I was sweating hard. Rachel stood about a yard away from me. She was looking good in a tight black top and trousers. No bra. Her summer clothes, I supposed. I hoped Hartman would appreciate them.

Her eyebrows suddenly shot up, and she reached down behind her. 'Excuse me!' she said in her loud, clear Scottish accent. The press of people drew away from her. Oh oh, another weirdo. 'Excuse me! Does this belong to anyone? I found it on my backside!'

She held up a hand. The hand was attached to a besuited arm, which was in turn attached to a small man with glasses, a *Wall Street Journal* and a briefcase. He looked like he wanted nothing to do with the offending item.

'Ah, it's yours sir. Please keep it in your own pockets in future. It will do less damage there.'

The man went bright red, and everyone in the subway car cracked up. He scurried off at the next stop.

Hartman's offices were in a nondescript tower block near the Rockerfeller Center. He had one floor, the twenty-sixth. The name on the door was Hartman Capital.

We waited in reception, watched over by an elegantly dressed black woman. On one side was a door labelled 'Hartman Capital Employees Only'. People scurried in and out. As the doors swung open we could catch a glimpse of a small trading room, maybe twenty desks. But just a glimpse.

After twenty minutes a man in his mid-forties thrust his way through the doors. He was tall and spare, balding, with what remained of his hair close-cropped. He walked straight up to us, and, ignoring introductions, said, 'Come through.'

He took us through the door opposite the trading room, into a small conference room with a view of the flanks of the next-door skyscraper.

'Sit,' he said, gesturing to some chairs. He walked round to the other side of the table, pulled a chair back, and sat with an ankle crossed over his knee. He stared at us through black framed glasses, the pyramid he made of his fingers tapping his chin. In most people this might appear a relaxed pose, but not in Hartman. He was listening, hard.

There was silence for a moment. 'You wanted to see me. I only have ten minutes, so you had better get to the point.'

I did. 'Mr Hartman, I know you have a stake in my company.'

'Hartman Capital has a small stake in FairSystems, yes. One point two per cent, I believe.'

'We think that when you add in the stake of companies associated with you, your stake becomes much larger.'

Hartman's brows narrowed slightly. 'My other financial interests are none of your concern, Mr Fairfax.'

335

'They are when in total they own a big chunk of my company.'

Hartman just snorted. I waited, hoping to lure him into saying something. But he waited too. He wasn't going to say anything.

'I know that you, through your various investment interests, voted against me at the recent Extraordinary General Meeting. What I want to know is, what are you doing with my company?'

Hartman smiled a thin smile. 'Nothing. It's just an investment like any other. The company makes no sense by itself. It should link up with another partner that's financially stronger. When it does, the share price will go up. I'll make some money and sell out. Easy.'

'And what happens to people who get in your way?'

'If they're doing the wrong thing for shareholders, and there's a move to remove them from the board, then I'll support that, naturally.'

'What about other ways of removing them?'

'What do you mean?'

'You know my brother Richard was murdered?'

'Yeah. I heard. Bummer.'

He was goading me. I didn't respond.

He stirred himself. 'Fairfax, if you think I killed someone over your chicken-shit little company, you must be crazy.' He pointed back towards the way we had come, back towards his dealing room. 'I have two billion dollars under management through there. Your entire company is worth, what, fifteen million tops? Why am I going to get a guy killed over that? Even if I am into getting guys killed, which, by the way, I'm not.'

I sort of believed him. I tried another tack. 'You have a reputation for being extremely well informed about companies in which you invest.'

Hartman laughed, a short sharp bray. 'I like the way you put that. Yes, I am well informed. I do anything I can to get as much information as I can, legally. It pisses off some people. But it's good for the markets.'

336

'Oh yes?' I said.

'Oh yes. You ever hear of the lead steer?' I had, but there was no stopping him now. 'The market is like a herd of cattle in a stampede. Except they've all got to follow someone. Some smart beast has got to be in front deciding where to run. And that's me. I'm the lead steer. I get the information first, and show the other guys which way to go. They need me.' He was really animated now, waving his arms. 'These securities laws are all bullshit. Someone's always going to know more about stocks than the dumb widows and orphans. Hell, no one knows more about FairSystems than you, and you're allowed to buy and sell shares, aren't you?'

'Well, not till two years after the initial placement,' I corrected him.

'OK, OK. Detail. But after that? You can buy and sell shares all day long to guys like me who are trying to figure out what the hell is going on. Who can blame us if we try to get an edge?'

'Even if it's against the law?'

Hartman calmed down a touch. 'No, I don't break the law. But what I'm saying is, they should change the fucking law.

'Anyway, you wanted to know what I want from your company. It's simple. I want you to quit screwing around and sell it. Then I can take my money and go find something a bit more interesting to invest in. Got it?'

'I'm not going to sell,' I said.

'Jeezus!' exclaimed Hartman. 'Another one of these fucking freeloaders! Anything to keep your job! It's management like you that brought this country to its knees, until we investors got smart and started demanding some shareholder value from our companies. You just want to keep your fucking job. Well, tough shit!'

I ignored the fact that I was English with a good job already and we were talking about a Scottish company. It was obvious that Hartman already had clear ideas on this issue. Still, at least I knew where he was coming from. I'd got what I wanted.

'There's no point in continuing this discussion any further,' I said. 'Goodbye, Mr Hartman.'

'Yuk,' Rachel exclaimed, when we were safely out of the building. 'Talk about a capitalist monster! People like him should be lined up against a wall and shot. Where's Lenin when you need him?'

'Maybe. But I don't think he killed Richard, do you?'

'No,' she admitted. 'I wouldn't put something like that past him in a mega takeover. But FairSystems is just too small.'

'You know what the worst thing is?' I said.

'What?'

'When Project Platform comes off, and the shares jump to a hundred dollars, that bastard is going to make a fortune.'

'Oh yeah,' said Rachel sadly. Then she brightened. 'Still, at least we can help the SEC with their inquiries.'

'That will be a real pleasure.'

We emerged from Chambers subway station into Foley Square, beneath the imposing columns of the Federal Courthouse. We made our way behind it, past a row of fast-food kiosks to a small scruffy plaza littered with bored-looking cops, just hanging out. Opposite a large ugly red sculpture was an even uglier brown block, the office of the United States attorney. It was from here that much of the work that had led to the convictions of Ivan Boesky, Dennis Levine and Martin Siegel had been carried out. The convictions had brought tremendous publicity to Rudolph Giuliani, the former US attorney. He was now mayor of New York.

When I had called the SEC in Washington, I had eventually been put through to a lawyer called Adele Stephenson who had agreed to meet us at these offices.

We were escorted through a range of narrow corridors to a conference room. There, four people were waiting for us. As we entered they all sprang to their feet. One of them offered his hand.

'Good morning, Mark. My name is Adele Stephenson. We spoke on the phone.' She was about forty, with a lively, intelligent face. 'This is my fellow attorney from the SEC in Washington, Mike Lavalle. And this is Tony Macchia, and Dan Gilligan from the US attorney's office here in New York. We're co-operating on this investigation. Please have a seat.'

Rachel and I sat down. It was interesting that both the SEC and the US attorney's office in New York were involved. Steve was right, this clearly wasn't just another routine investigation. But it wouldn't have surprised me if the current US attorney had developed a special interest in financial crime, after the success his predecessor had made of it.

'Thank you for seeing us,' I began.

'Not at all. It's good of you to come all this way. And believe me, we're very interested in what you've got to say.'

'As you know, I'm the acting managing director of Fair-Systems. As you may also know, my brother was murdered a couple of months ago.'

'Yes, we had heard about it from the police in Scotland. I'm sorry.'

'Thank you. I'm not sure how much you know about Fair-Systems?'

'Assume we know nothing. Tell us from the beginning.'

So I went through FairSystems' history since my brother's death, and the interest shown in the company by Jenson, Onada and Hartman. I told them I was sure that the activity in the shares showed that illegal stakes were being built up by Hartman and possibly by Jenson Computer as well. I also told them of Richard's suspicions that the stock price was being manipulated and about his murder.

All four listened. All four took notes.

When I finished, they were still scribbling. 'Does this fit with what you know?' I asked.

'Pretty much. What you've told us will be very useful. We need to build as strong a case as we can before we make a move.'

'I heard a rumour that you are investigating Frank Hartman?'

Adele winced. 'Yes. We've been trying to keep it quiet. We've been investigating Hartman for two years now. Since Boesky was put away in 1987, insider trading hasn't stopped, it's just

339

gone underground. People were blatant before, careless. And it still took us years to nail them.

'Well, now they've wised up. We can tell from stock-price action that people are still trading on inside information; indeed, we've developed sophisticated computer programs to detect it. But it's very hard to work out who is behind it, harder still to prove it. Nevertheless, the name of Frank Hartman is involved a statistically significant number of times. So we set out to catch him.'

Stephenson was leaning forward in her chair. She looked earnest, and very determined. 'We want to take our time, use the same techniques that pinned down Boesky in the end. We pick off the weak links in the chain. Offer them immunity if they agree to pass on information to us and testify against Hartman eventually. Over the last two years, we've turned three little insider traders.

'Then, in April, we received a call from your brother, Richard. He was suspicious about trading in FairSystems' stock. He'd put together a complicated analysis that he claimed backed this up.'

'So Richard got in touch with you? I never knew that.'

'Yes. It was just one phone call shortly before he died.'

'And his analysis made sense?'

'Our own systems didn't pick anything up in FairSystems' trading. But our analysts thought your brother might be right.' She smiled. 'In fact they've incorporated some of his ideas into our own system. Anyway, from then on we watched the company closely. As you've discovered, Frank Hartman has been trading illegally to build up a stake.'

'Can you prove it?'

'Difficult. It's going to be hard to prove that all the offshore funds that have been buying your stock are related. Nor can we show that Hartman has any inside information. Is there anything he could know about FairSystems that isn't public knowledge? Something that might cause the shares to rise?'

I thought a moment. 'There are two possibilities.'

'Yes?'

'The first is a takeover bid by Jenson Computer. Although they haven't formally made an offer for the company, Jenson has bought five point seven per cent, maybe more.'

'We're aware of that. He made the appropriate filings. But we don't know whether Hartman knew of this beforehand.'

'He might have done. I'm pretty sure Wagner Phillips are acting for Jenson Computer, and of course they're the brokers who helped Hartman accumulate his stock.'

'We have our suspicions about Scott Wagner, too. We're watching him closely. But you mentioned something else?'

'Yes. There's some new technology that FairSystems is just about to announce. Actually, it's more like a new set of alliances. I'd rather not give you the details, but the code name is Project Platform. Anyway, if this project is as successful as we think it might be, then FairSystems could be worth many times its current share price.'

Adele Stephenson leaned forward with interest. 'Who knows about this Project Platform?'

'Just a very small group of people within FairSystems. And a similarly small group in Jenson Computer, including Carl Jenson himself. Come to think of it, there must be some people in Microsoft who know as well.'

Macchia interrupted. 'So the leak could have come from anywhere, if there is one?'

'I suppose so,' I admitted.

Macchia picked up a sheet of paper.

'We've learned a bit about Hartman's methods,' he said. He was slightly built, with a dark complexion and a small moustache under a large nose. He was probably a couple of years younger than Adele. They were clearly working together as uneasy equals. 'He's set up a tangle of offshore funds, controlled either by himself or by people he cuts into his network. This means that any stock buying he and his friends do seems to be spread over dozens of purchasers.'

'I see.'

'This is a list of eight companies which we believe Hartman has been involved with.'

341

'Can I look?'

He pushed across the table a white sheet of paper with the names of the companies, their eventual acquirors, and the date. No title, no headed paper, no signature.

Rachel and I glanced down the list. I only recognised one. Futurenet, eventually acquired by Jenson Computer in September 1992.

'Does he always use Wagner Phillips as a broker?'

'No,' said Adele, eager to take control again. 'He uses a range of brokers, all the big firms that will still deal with him. Of the smaller firms, Wagner Phillips is probably the one he does most of his business through, especially anything high tech.'

'Were they involved in the Futurenet transaction?'

'They certainly were. They were acting for Jenson Computer, the acquiror. And Hartman did a number of his trades through them.'

I wasn't surprised. 'May I keep this?' I asked, raising the sheet of paper.

'You should know that we sent a copy of this list to your brother. After he was killed, the British police got in touch with us. Like you, they were concerned that his death might have had something to do with his suspicions.'

So Donaldson had done his follow-up. And drawn a blank, presumably.

'Have they discovered any connection?'

'No, they haven't. I spoke to Superintendent Donaldson when I knew you were coming to see us. He said he was happy for us to give you this information.'

That was big of him, I thought. But I knew that Donaldson had been suspicious of me when he had first questioned me about trading in FairSystems' shares, so I was glad I now seemed to be off his list. I wondered who was on it now that Doogie was dead.

Adele Stephenson nodded towards the piece of paper in my hand. 'It looks like FairSystems is next. We'd like to gather enough evidence to prosecute on this one. Anything you can find will be much appreciated.'

342

Rachel and I got up to leave. The four lawyers stood up and shook our hands.

'Oh Mark,' Adele said as I opened the door.

'Yes?'

'Be careful. When these guys are in a corner, they can get dangerous.'

We caught an American Airlines flight from La Guardia to San Francisco that afternoon. The plan was to drop in on Walter Sorenson the next morning, and then go on to see Jenson at his factory in Palo Alto. A taxi took us to a hotel in Menlo Park, at the northern end of Silicon Valley. It was only six p.m. San Francisco time, but, of course, it was way past the middle of the night in Scotland. It had been a long day, and it looked as if the next day would be just as long.

I looked across at Rachel. She was staring out of the window of the taxi, watching San Francisco Bay race by. We made a good team. Although we had very different backgrounds, somehow we had a similar way of thinking. I smiled as I remembered that evening in her flat in Glenrothes when she had read to me.

We reached the hotel and checked in. The clerk at the desk tapped some keys on her computer. 'That will be a double room?'

I was just about to correct her when I stopped myself. I looked at Rachel. She looked at me. The corner of her mouth twitched upwards.

'Yes, a double,' I said.

The question had been innocently put, but the clerk was quick to pick up on the pause. She couldn't help smiling to herself as she clattered the computer in front of her.

'OK, here's your key card. Your room is on the third floor. You're all set.'

We rode up in the lift together. Suddenly, I felt nervous, and excited. I gave Rachel a small smile. She smiled back at me. We didn't say anything.

When we reached the room, I dumped the cases on the floor. 'It's nice,' said Rachel, wandering around the small space. She opened the cabinet where the television was hidden, and checked out the minibar. Then she disappeared into the bathroom.

I wasn't sure what to do with myself, so I stood at the window, looking down at the hotel car park, and the busy intersection below. My heart quickened in anticipation. I tried to keep perfectly still, to keep calm, to wait for her.

I heard the bathroom door open and shut behind me, and felt Rachel's presence next to me. 'Not much of a view.'

'No.'

I turned to her. She looked up at me. For once she had lost all her aloofness and self-confidence. She blushed, a warm glow spreading up from her neck. I brushed her hair away from her face, and touched her cheek.

She smiled, a sweet smile of happiness, nerves and confusion. She lifted her big brown eyes to mine. I bent down and kissed her. Our lips touched gently, and then she pulled me down to her, and kissed me hungrily.

My hands reached up towards her chest. She pulled away from me, and lifted her top over her head. It was a struggle, and we both laughed. I held both of her full firm breasts in my hands, and the nipples stiffened beneath my fingers.

'Come here,' she whispered hoarsely, pulling me towards the bed.

We made love in a rush of urgent fumbling, neither of us familiar with the other's body, both of us eager to fulfil our desire. Later, she curled up in my arms, her hair a mass of tight black curls on my chest. I stroked it, gently.

We lay there a long time in comfortable silence. Then Rachel stirred. 'I'm thirsty,' she said. She pulled herself out of bed and padded over to the minibar. I watched her. She looked natural and relaxed without clothes on. Serene. She took out a bottle of wine and poured two glasses. She gave me one, and sat next to me cross-legged. She reached for her cigarettes, and was just about to light one when she paused.

'Do you mind?'

'No, that's fine,' I said.

'Are you sure?'

I smiled at her sudden concern. 'No, go ahead.'

She lit up, and took a long drag.

I looked down at her black top and trousers on the floor.

'I like your summer clothes,' I said. 'Even if it was difficult to prise you out of them.'

Rachel laughed. 'I should hope so. I selected them specially.'

'What? For me?'

'Yes, for you.'

'I don't know,' I laughed. 'Women are so manipulative.'

'Oh no. It's just men are so easy to manipulate.'

I smiled. I liked the idea of Rachel trying to tempt me. She did have a great body; I couldn't deny that when she had finally revealed it, it had had an effect.

'Can we do this again?' I asked.

'What, now?'

'No, not now. Tomorrow. The next day. Next week.'

'Yes please,' said Rachel, grinning broadly. 'But what's wrong with right now?'

I thought that there was nothing wrong with right now, and we made love again, slowly, gently, getting to know each other.

Afterwards I fell asleep.

I woke several hours later. The red numbers on the alarm clock said it was 4.15 a.m. That was of course lunchtime in Scotland. I watched Rachel as she lay next to me, breathing gently, her lips slightly open, her face untroubled in sleep, surrounded by a mass of dark hair.

I felt relaxed and elated at the same time. I had no qualms about Karen, I didn't miss her at all. It was good to be with someone as straightforward as Rachel, a woman who knew what she wanted, and what she wanted was me.

Rachel's eyelids flickered, she opened her eyes, and for a moment didn't seem to know where she was. Then she saw me and smiled. 'Hi,' she said.

'Hi,' I said and moved over to kiss her.

25

Sorenson's house was in Los Altos Hills, a town about five miles from Menlo Park, on the other side of Stanford University's campus. The community seemed to consist of large low residences, spaced well apart, set in woods of oak, pine and eucalyptus. Many had swimming pools and tennis courts.

We drove along a quiet road that wound uphill through the trees. The houses seemed bigger than most we had seen. The road eventually came to a dead-end next to a mailbox labelled 'Sorenson'.

His house was a rambling, one-storey wooden building surrounded by oak trees and exotic shrubs. We rang the bell, and Sorenson himself came to the door. 'Mark, Rachel, come in.'

The interior was entirely open plan. The hallway merged into a large living area, which was dominated by a huge picture window, stretching the length of the wall.

'Go take a look,' said Sorenson.

We walked over to the window. There was a tremendous view over the trees and low buildings of Palo Alto to the San Francisco Bay, shimmering in the sunshine. Beneath the house, a large lawn stretched down to a tennis court. Just outside were a wooden deck and a cool blue swimming pool. Somehow I didn't think any of this came cheap.

'Lovely,' said Rachel. 'How long have you lived here?'

'Oh, five years. It's a great location for the Valley. And we kind of like it here. But, of course, I spend a lot of time on the road.'

'You can say that again, dear. You spend half your life in Europe these days.' There was a noise of quick light footsteps as someone walked into the room behind us. I turned and saw a thin, well-groomed woman aged anything between forty and sixty. She had blonde hair and a tight, lightly tanned face. I wasn't sure how much was real, and how much was artificial, but from her cheekbones and bright blue eyes you could tell she must have been beautiful once. She was still good-looking now.

'This is my wife, Shirley. Shirley, this is Mark Fairfax and Rachel Walker. Mark is Geoffrey's son.'

'Oh, it's so nice to meet you,' said Mrs Sorenson, holding out her hand. 'It was simply horrible about your brother. How's your father taking it?'

'It's difficult for him,' I said.

'Well give him my love when you see him, won't you. I think he's such a sweetie.'

I wondered how the four of them had fitted together, all those years ago. My father, my mother, Sorenson and his wife.

'Can I get you some coffee?'

We said yes, and in a moment she was in the kitchen clattering about with cups.

'So, how did it go in New York?' Sorenson asked.

I told him all about our conversations with Hartman and the SEC. He listened with great interest.

'It looks like Richard uncovered quite an operation,' he said. 'Do you think the SEC are close to making an arrest?'

'Not quite yet. But they'll get there. They seem pretty determined to me.'

'But so far they've found nothing that connects all this to Richard's death?'

'No. I asked the SEC how Donaldson was doing. It seems the Scottish police investigated that line pretty closely, but didn't come up with anything. And of course there are other possibilities.' I told him about Doogie and his death, about Yoshi's

347

presence at the Inch Tavern, and about David Baker's disappearance.

'It's difficult to say, but I'd guess it has something to do with the Japanese,' Sorenson said. 'That guy Yoshi pops up in all sorts of strange places. And I think you were right all along about David Baker. We should have gotten rid of him earlier.'

Mrs Sorenson came in with the coffee. She was about to sit down, and then Sorenson glared at her. It lasted less than a second, but she noticed it, and for an instant anger flared in her eyes. It was one of those moments when you catch a glimpse of the true state of a marriage behind its carefully maintained façade.

'I'll just leave you to it,' she said, smiling again. 'I'll be out on the deck.' She left the room.

'So, do you have any theories?' Sorenson asked.

'No. But I think we're getting closer. The SEC gave us a list of suspicious companies that they know Hartman was involved in. I've got it here.' I pulled out the list and handed it over to him. 'Recognise any of them?'

Sorenson frowned, thinking. 'Well, I've heard of some of them,' he said. 'Futurenet makes network software, I think. A couple of the others are familiar.'

'But there's nothing that you know of that links them all together?'

Sorenson thought a moment. 'Sorry. Nothing I can think of. Have you got any ideas?'

'Not yet. But we'll check them out when we get back to Scotland.'

Sorenson drained his coffee, and poured another. 'Do you want some more? It's decaf.'

Rachel looked shocked at the word 'decaf', but then recovered herself, and shook her head. I held out my cup.

'You're going to see Jenson now?' Sorenson asked.

'Yes. Our appointment's at eleven.'

'And what kind of deal have you got for him?'

We discussed strategy for the Jenson meeting for half an hour and then left, saying goodbye to Mrs Sorenson before we went.

348

She was sitting in a deck chair reading a Jackie Collins novel, the Santa Clara valley stretching out into the distance below.

The sun shone down on the gleaming structures that lurked on either side of Page Mill Road. There was not a house to be seen; every building was dedicated to the mighty computer. It was nothing like Glenrothes; these edifices were bigger, sleeker, more mysterious. The vegetation was lush, and to my eyes exotic – palms, eucalyptus, the odd redwood pointing straight up towards the sky.

On the left was the Stanford University campus, and on the right we passed the impressive entrance to Hewlett Packard's facility. HP was a role model for Silicon Valley. The company had started in a garage, but now had its headquarters in this elaborate and sprawling complex. Jenson Computer's plant was a little farther on, just off El Camino Real, the backbone of the Valley. It was difficult to see much from the road; tall shrubs and a discreet security fence provided an effective barrier. We presented ourselves to the guard at the gate. He was armed, and he took his duties seriously. He wanted ID, and phoned through before he would let us pass.

Finally the gate was raised, and we drove into a parking lot in front of a six-storey, white hexagonal building. Two huge flags fluttered outside: the stars and stripes, and the Jenson Computer flag, green lettering on a white background. Behind these nestled two large grey structures, like the hulls of spaceships, sleek, silent, with the promise of great power within their walls.

I parked in a visitor's space outside the white building, exchanged glances with Rachel, took a deep breath, and entered. It took ten minutes, and two more security checks before we found ourselves in Jenson's office.

It was large but bare. Jenson bounced out of his leather chair and ran round the desk to greet us. His chino trousers and green polo shirt were immaculately pressed. His eyes alighted on each of us. 'Mark, Rachel, how you doing? Sit down, sit down.' He ushered us to a round glass table, and we all sat.

The office was dominated by Jenson's huge curved desk.

There were a phone and two computers sitting on it, one of them attached to a pair of virtual glasses, and nothing else. Not a shred of paper to be seen. Behind his desk was wall-to-wall glass. The office was on the ground floor, and opened out on to a close-cropped, well-watered lawn and a small wooden building that looked like a Japanese temple. The walls were decorated with abstract art of the straight-lines-and-white-spaces type.

'So. What do you guys want?'

'We wanted to talk to you about Project Platform,' I said.

'Oh, so you know about that now, do you?'

Rachel answered. 'I thought it was OK to tell him, given the position we found ourselves in.'

'I guess that's fair. But my understanding was that you had stopped work on the project?'

'No, we're still working on it,' I said. 'In fact, we're ready to implement our part of the deal.'

'Great! I knew you guys wouldn't give up.'

'But first we need to come to some sort of arrangement. Something that makes sense for both of us.'

'Sure, sure. We can talk about that.' He began to pour us mineral water from the bottle on the table. 'But let me tell you, we've been busy too. It's all coming together,' he put the bottle down after pouring only half a glass. 'We're definitely going to ring the bell on this one. The operating system is testing real well on the new machines. This thing is more powerful than even I imagined.'

Rachel smiled quietly.

'This woman's a genius, Mark. A true genius. No, really. None of our guys could do anything like this, and we have some of the best in the industry.'

'I don't doubt it,' I said.

'Come and take a look.' Jenson leapt to his feet, and bustled quickly out of his office. We tried to keep pace, sweeping past security guards who were lucky to get the barest glance at our visitors' passes. Jenson spoke rapidly as he walked, but I couldn't catch what he said. A phone at his hip chirped. He snapped an answer, and within fifteen seconds the conversation was over.

We belted over the tarmac to one of the sleek spaceships, labelled 'Building A'. We were let in through a port at the side. More security men cowered in Jenson's path. We walked down a short corridor, and entered a large space, filled with benches, plastic and metal. It looked much like the production floor of our own factory in Glenrothes writ very large, a thought that comforted me somehow. But there was some very expensive-looking equipment dotted around the floor.

Jenson explained. 'We design, assemble and test here. All the components are manufactured by other people, often in the Far East. Apart from the chips. They come from our Intercirc plant just a few miles down the road. This room is where we design the computers. Come and look at this, Rachel.'

He pulled us over to where a young man in a black T-shirt was bending over the guts of one of the computers. He smiled in recognition as Rachel approached, and they discussed the results of the tests he had been running. Rachel seemed pleased. Jenson moved us on to meet another group of engineers who were talking excitedly about graphics chips. The conversation was way over my head, but not over Jenson's. His people treated him with deference, he seemed to emanate an almost godlike aura as he moved through the plant. But there was also respect. He knew his stuff.

After twenty minutes or so, he dragged us back towards his office. As he strode on ahead, Rachel whispered to me, 'He's right. It's all coming together. The FairRender system is working really well in their new model. There are still some bugs, but nothing major.' Her eyes were shining; she was as excited as Jenson.

We returned to Jenson's office. 'So, what do you think, Rachel?'

'It's good. Once we add in our improvements to the software interface, the system will work brilliantly. But, of course, you won't be able to use the FairRender chip without our permission.'

'Hey, I know that.'

'Shall we talk about a deal, then?' I asked.

Jenson didn't answer. His eyes briefly touched my face. 'There's something else I want to show you. Come on.'

He pressed a switch, and the glass windows behind him opened. He led us out on to the lawn. The grass was wet underfoot; it had recently been sprinkled. He took us over towards the intriguing wooden structure I had spotted before.

We came to some steps, and Jenson kicked off his shoes. We did the same. He then placed his tiny mobile phone next to them. He raised his eyebrows at us. We shook our heads; we were unarmed.

The building was designed like a Japanese temple. We walked over tatami mats to the other side of the cool wooden room, which opened out on to a tiny, intricate garden of trickling water, ferns and moss.

'Sit,' ordered Jenson.

We sat, Rachel cross-legged, Jenson in the lotus position, me with my legs bent uncomfortably under my body.

'I saw a guy a few years ago,' Jenson said. 'He told me to slow down, or I'd wind up dead. Said I should meditate every day. So I do. And it works.' He closed his eyes. 'Now, let's be quiet for a few minutes.'

So we were quiet. Jenson breathed deeply, in through his nose and out through his mouth. His chest and stomach rose and fell. It was strange to see this bundle of energy at rest. I had no doubt that it was good for Jenson to slow down for a few minutes each day. And it didn't surprise me that he pursued relaxation as manically as everything else.

After a few minutes, the quietness and the running water began to soothe me, too. I found a more comfortable position for my legs. The small trickle, and the ferns brought back thoughts of a damp Scottish hillside.

Finally, Jenson moved. He took one last deep breath, and turned towards us. 'That's better. Now, are you going to sell me FairSystems?'

Straight to the point. I suddenly began to wonder whether

this bizarre ritual was some kind of negotiating technique. I was in Jenson's home territory, my guard was down, he would swoop.

If that was what he was trying, it wasn't going to work.

'No,' I said simply.

'Hey, you got no choice. You don't sell to me and the bus leaves without you. You sell, and you get to join in on one of the best parties in town. Am I right, or what?'

'Um,' I said. 'I don't think it's quite that simple. You see we've just negotiated a deal with a Japanese company, Onada Industries. We've agreed to give them access to our simulation manager and our graphics system. And they'll give us enough cash to keep us going.'

Jenson waved his arm dismissively. 'But they're not tooled up to make the chips yet, are they? And that's just the games market, I'm talking about penetrating all the VR markets worldwide.'

'You're right, Carl. We would be better off working with you. I just wanted to point out that we can survive very comfortably without you. We don't need you.'

Jenson was watching me closely. 'It still makes sense for you to sell.'

'Well, I hope that we can continue to work on Project Platform with you. But we need access to more cash, and I don't want to sell the company. So, if you don't help us, then I'll be obliged to do another deal with Onada, this time giving them exclusive rights to the graphics system. I'm sure they would be happy to pay well for that.'

'So, what do you want?'

'The five hundred thousand pounds you owe us would do for a start.'

Jenson's small dark eyes bored into me. For once they were still, all energy and power, all directed at me. He was focusing everything on the problem, and the problem was me.

I waited. A chipmunk scampered along the wooden steps down to the delicate garden.

'That won't do,' said Jenson, slowly, his eyes never leaving me. 'Project Platform is going to change the world, I'm convinced of that. My company's future is totally dependent on it. I don't want Jenson Computer to be reliant on a fly-by-night outfit thousands of miles away that will either go bust or do a deal with the Japanese when I'm not looking. I need some control.'

I sat still, listening.

'I want fifty per cent,' he said.

I looked at Rachel. She raised her eyebrows. It was up to me.

I felt the familiar rush of adrenalin. We were three people squatting, in jeans, in a pseudo-Japanese temple, but I might just as well have been at my desk at Harrison Brothers. A lot was at stake. Millions of dollars could be made or lost in the next minute. And I knew Jenson wanted to deal.

'Ten.'

'That's not control. That's just an accounting problem.'

'OK. Twenty per cent. Plus a slug of preference shares.'

Jenson's eyes bored into me. He knew my position and I knew his. We could take days or weeks agreeing this, or we could do it now. Jenson wanted to get on with it, I could feel it.

'Twenty-five per cent, at the current market price. Plus two million dollars in preference shares, plus two seats on the board. I'll sleep sounder if I know you have some money in the bank.'

I hesitated, thinking.

'You have a minute to make up your mind, otherwise we all go home,' Jenson said. I knew he meant it.

I used the minute. At six dollars a share, Jenson would need to put four million of new money into the company for his twenty-five per cent. That, plus the two million dollars of preference shares, was six million. That would keep Fair-Systems going for a while. And if Project Platform worked, then FairSystems' share price would rocket. The company would remain independent, and Richard's dream would be realised.

But with hostile public shareholders, I would no longer be able to rely on a majority of the votes without Jenson's support. I would have to trust him.

He had already double-crossed me once by refusing to make the advance payments under the Project Platform contract.

I thought of Richard's death. Of Hartman toying with my company from his office in New York. Of David doing a secret deal with Onada behind my back. Who the hell could I trust?

I looked at the chubby man sitting cross-legged in front of me. His motivation was clear. He was driven to make his company succeed. And he could only achieve that with FairSystems. Like it or not, we were on the same side.

'Done.'

I leaned over and offered him my hand.

He smiled, shook it, and looked me straight in the eye. 'I've got a feeling you'll be a good partner to have around,' he said. 'And, frankly, Rachel, we need your brain fast. My guys have a couple of problems that they'd like to talk to you about.'

We arrived back in Scotland on Saturday morning, exhausted. I dropped Rachel off at her flat, and went back to Kirkhaven for a bath and a doze. There was a message on my answering machine to call Daphne, Karen's mother. No chance. There was really no need for me to talk to her ever again. I smiled at the thought.

As I lay soaking in my bath, I cast my mind back over the past two days. I shared Rachel's excitement about Project Platform. It looked as though FairSystems was finally out of the woods.

But I knew everything wasn't tidied up. Far from it. I still had no idea what had happened the night Richard had died. Whoever had killed him was still out there. And I had a nasty feeling that whoever had wanted to kill him, would now want to kill me.

I spent several minutes trying again to work out who that person might be, but my brain was too tired. I got nowhere.

I went into the factory late that afternoon. Rachel, of course, had been there for hours. It was amazing how much had piled up in the three days I had been away.

At seven, I strolled round to her office. Keith and Andy were at their machines. 'Good news about Platform, boss,' Keith said, as I walked past. 'Well done!'

'Thanks,' I said, and knocked on Rachel's door.

'Come in.'

When she saw me, her face lit up in a broad smile.

'How are you feeling?' I asked.

'Fine. But there's so much to do. How about you?'

'Knackered.'

We were silent for a moment. 'I don't want to interrupt you or anything,' I said, 'but would you like to come back to Kirkhaven with me this evening?'

Rachel smiled. 'Of course I would. Let's go.'

We got into the BMW and pulled out of the factory car park. I negotiated the series of mini-roundabouts which protected Glenrothes from the south, and joined the road heading east to Kirkhaven.

I looked in the mirror for the car behind. It was a habit I had developed over the past couple of weeks. A small white Astra van with two men in it was behind us. It fell back as we drove through Markinch, but then caught up with us as we passed the giant whisky distillery in Leven.

'I think someone's following us,' I said.

Rachel turned to look. 'Who? There are lots of cars behind us.'

'The white Astra van. It's been with us since Glenrothes.'

'Well, slow down. Let's see what he does.'

I did, driving at thirty miles per hour. Car after car passed us, but not the van. It was lurking well behind us.

I sped up again. The van was still there.

'I think you might be right,' Rachel said. 'What shall we do?'

'The turn off to Kirkhaven is in half a mile, I'll stop in at the police station if he turns off too.'

I slowed down at the T-junction and indicated. The van was right behind us now. There were two large men in it. They looked like workmen.

I turned right. The van went straight on towards Crail and St Andrews.

I laughed as the nervous tension left me. 'I think we're just getting jumpy.'

Rachel sighed. 'No. You're right to be jumpy. I don't want you getting bashed on the head again.'

I parked the car outside Inch Lodge, checked up and down the quay, and let Rachel into the house. She wandered round. 'It feels weird without Richard here.'

'Maybe you shouldn't have come?'

'Oh no. I'm glad I'm here. Can I have a look upstairs?'

We went up to Richard's bedroom. 'This doesn't look familiar does it?' I asked nervously.

She smiled. 'Oh no. I've never been in here before in my life.'

Then she kissed me.

Something woke me. It was still dark. It was a banging of some sort. I looked over to where Rachel's form lay, back towards me. I smiled to myself. Then I heard it again, or a sound like it. It seemed to be coming from downstairs, not outside.

I lay in bed, listening. I thought I could hear a gentle rustling. I decided to get up and investigate.

My dressing-gown was in the bathroom, but it was warm enough in the house for me not to really need it. So I crept down the stairs, naked. I knew there was no one there, there never is when you hear bumps in the night. But I had to check.

The sitting room was well lit by the night outside. I couldn't see anything. I stood for a full minute just inside the door, listening again.

Nothing.

I checked the kitchen. Nothing.

I felt a bit of a twit, wandering around the house at night without any clothes on, looking for intruders. If someone had broken in, I would have stumbled across them by now. So I went back upstairs to the bedroom.

I stopped dead at the doorway. A figure was squatting on the bed, pinning down Rachel. A second later, I felt an arm round my neck pulling me backwards. I opened my mouth to yell, but it was smothered with a cloth backed by a strong hand. My nose was covered as well, and I smelled a strong, sweet smell.

I bucked and went down on my knees to try to trip whoever was behind me.

And that was the last thing I remembered.

26

My legs were cold. Cold and wet. And heavy, with some kind of sodden fabric. But I was very tired. I wanted to sleep.

My legs were freezing. There was a rushing sound, like a waterfall. I tried to will my eyes to open, but it was difficult. A thudding pain rushed from somewhere near the back of my head and battered me.

My legs were in water. And I was lying at an odd angle resting against something.

I forced my eyes open. It was dark. I had some sort of belt around my chest. I touched it. A seat-belt.

The adrenalin rushed through my system, and suddenly I was wide awake. I looked up. I was in a car, my BMW, strapped into the driver's seat. I was wearing the jeans and shirt I had discarded the night before. Ink-black water lapped against the car windows. Water was rushing in through the vents by the dashboard, and swirling around my legs.

It was up to my knees and rising fast.

A woman was slumped in the seat next to me. I recognised the matted dark hair. It was Rachel.

Move! I reached down to the seat-belt release next to me. It was hard to move my arms, the effect of the chloroform or whatever I had inhaled was still present. I fumbled with the release, the water moving up towards my knuckles. Finally, the seat-belt clicked open. I found Rachel's and released that. Then I pulled myself out of the driver's seat, and leaned over to her.

I shook her. 'Wake up!' No reaction. 'Wake up!'

The water continued to rush in. The car was lying nose down in some sort of river. The back was sticking up out of the water, the front was filling quickly.

Rachel wasn't going to wake up. So I put my foot against the dashboard, pulled her up out of her seat, and pushed her into the back. I crawled through to join her. The car lurched, but the rear wheels were obviously resting on something, because it remained nose down.

It was dry in the back, but the car was almost completely submerged. Outside, there was a foot or so of clear air at the top of the rear window, and I could just see a steep bank silhouetted against a starlit sky.

We had to get out quick.

I lay on the seat with my legs braced against the back of the driver's seat and one arm round Rachel's chest. I took a deep breath, pulled the handle of the rear door, and pushed.

It didn't move. The water pressure held it shut. I put my shoulder to the door, and pushed. I would only need to open it a crack, and the water rushing in would make the rest easy. But it wouldn't budge. It was no use trying the windows; they were operated by an electric switch which was already underwater.

The front seat was completely submerged now, and the water was working its way up my legs again. It would only take a couple more minutes for the whole car to fill.

I crawled up to the shelf on the back seat, so that my face was against the rear window, and pulled Rachel up with me. It was difficult, my muscles were not responding well to commands from my brain. Rachel was still unconscious.

The water was covering the back seat, which I was now kneeling on. Not long to go.

I tried to think. It was difficult. I don't know whether it was the chloroform or the panic, but I couldn't get my thoughts in order. I took some deep breaths to try to calm myself.

The water was up to my thighs.

Knock out the back window! Of course. The back window was out of the water, pointing up at the night sky, and a full moon.

I tried to hit the window with my elbow. No result. I hit it harder. Still nothing. I hit it with the flat of my hands, with my fists. I thrashed at it, flailing my arms wildly. I even tried to break it with my head. Nothing.

The panic leapt up inside me, and I scrabbled at the window more and more ineffectively, but I couldn't think of anything else to do. I just couldn't think.

The water was up to my chest now, but it looked as if it had stopped coming in. It had reached the level of the river outside. Just the very back of the car stuck out into the air. I stopped struggling, to conserve air.

I lay still, holding up the unconscious Rachel, trying to breathe slowly and evenly.

I was freezing cold.

Suddenly, I felt a sharp jolt, and the car lurched to the side. I saw a long branch of a tree hit the side of the car. I could just see the bank above the water. It was quite close, only a few feet away. Two figures were reaching out with the branch to the car, trying to dislodge it from whatever it was that was holding up the rear. The car wobbled, but remained stuck. They lunged again with the branch, and this time the car wobbled further.

I could only see the paleness of their faces. I couldn't make out their features. One was reaching out towards the car, while he was held by the other. They were both big.

There was nothing I could do but cling on to Rachel, cling on to hope, and watch, as with every blow the car shifted half an inch.

Suddenly, the two men stopped. I felt a wave of relief, but not for long. Within a minute they were back with a plank, longer and sturdier than the branch they had been using.

They placed it against the rear of the car, and held it there. Then one of them leant into it, and pushed with all his might.

I took a deep breath as the car slid under water. It turned

361

over, and I had no idea which way was up. Everything was pitch black. I was still holding Rachel under one arm, but with only one hand, I couldn't feel where I was, so I let her go. I reached for the door, and found the handle. I pushed it, and it opened. Of course! With water on the inside, the pressure had equalised. I kicked myself out of the car. I still didn't know which way was up so I tumbled, kicking my legs until I felt the bottom. Then I pushed up.

My head broke the surface, and I saw the two figures turning away from me and scrambling up the bank. They hadn't seen me.

I took a couple of breaths, and dived back down to the car. I felt for the open door, and reached in. No Rachel.

I didn't want to go back into that deathtrap, I couldn't hold my breath much longer. But I crawled into the submerged car, feeling around with my hands. Where was she? Finally, my fingers brushed her hair. I pulled. She was caught in something. I was running out of air. Why not go back up, take another breath, and then untangle her? Because she'd die, that's why. So I crawled in further. My chest felt as though it was being crushed by a boa constrictor. My ears were singing.

Her jersey was snagged on the handbrake. I pulled it free, grabbed her hair, and kicked us both out of the car. I broke the surface with a whoosh. I looked up to the bank. The two figures had almost reached the top. I knew that when they did, they would turn round. I looked around me. I wasn't in a river, but in some kind of loch. Behind me was what looked like a small island, with bushes reaching down to the water. It was only about ten yards away. I swam over on my back, trying not to make a sound, and to keep Rachel's head above water. It was hard because our clothes were so heavy, and I still had my shoes on. But I made it.

I pulled her under the bushes, just as the two men reached the top and turned to look down at the black water where the car had been. They exchanged a couple of words, and disappeared out of view.

I grasped Rachel under her armpits, and pulled her up the

bank. I laid her on her back as gently as I could, and looked down at her. She lay motionless in the damp grass. There was no time to lose. I knew the theory of mouth-to-mouth resuscitation as everyone does. But I had never tried it on a living person before. Or at least I hoped she was living. I had no idea how long someone could stay with water in their lungs before they died.

I felt her neck. I was pretty sure I could feel a faint pulse. Then I went to work. Water dribbled out from her mouth, but I didn't see any response. I tried blowing in and pressing down with my hands. Still no response. I blew harder, pressed harder. Suddenly, I felt the chest beneath me move of its own accord. Rachel coughed, and more water emerged. Her breathing came quicker, fast and shallow. Her eyes flickered.

A surge of relief. She was alive! Thank God, she was alive.

I sat next to her for a few minutes trying to catch my breath and regain my strength. God, it was cold! I could make out the form of the landscape in the moonlight. We were on an island in a loch surrounded by hills. There was no sign of habitation; the only lights were the stars. But those men must have driven the car down a track, and the track must lead to a road.

We couldn't stay on the little island all night. I had to get Rachel to warmth and a hospital. So, with trepidation, I slid back into the water, and swam across, making sure Rachel's head stayed above the surface. It was hard work pulling her up the steep bank.

I was right, there was a forest track at the top. I shuddered as I peered down into the loch for the BMW, but its black form was impossible to make out in the dark water.

I slung Rachel over my shoulder and began walking. She was heavy in her wet clothes, and I was tired and cold. At last we broke out of the forest and hit a small metalled road. I couldn't see any buildings, but there was a clump of trees about a mile away that I hoped might hide a farm, so I headed for them.

Rachel was getting heavier, almost too heavy to carry. I concentrated on just putting one foot in front of the other. Gradually, the blackness around me turned to grey, as dawn emerged.

Even in the improving light, I still couldn't see any definite sign of habitation. It took for ever, but eventually I reached the trees, which did indeed hide a stone farmhouse. It had a bell. I leaned on it, and didn't stop it ringing till someone opened the door.

27

We were in one of the administrators' offices of the Perth Royal Infirmary. I was in hospital pyjamas and dressing-gown. Kerr and Donaldson were in front of me, Kerr bleary-eyed, Donaldson looking as if it were nine o'clock on a Monday morning instead of seven on a Sunday.

Rachel was in one of the wards on a ventilator.

It turned out we had been dumped in a loch in the mountains of Perthshire. An ambulance had come all the way from Perth to fetch us.

'Now, are you sure you can't give us anything to go on? Any description at all?' Donaldson asked again.

'No,' I said, impatiently. 'They were two big men. I didn't get a look at their faces.'

'Clothes? Hair colour? Voice?'

'I didn't hear them say anything. I think one of them had short brown hair.'

'You've no idea what car they drove?'

'No, I was drugged.' Then I had a thought. 'Yesterday afternoon when we were driving back from Glenrothes, we thought we were being followed. It was two workmen in a van. But they drove on at the turn-off into Kirkhaven.'

'Now that's good,' said Donaldson. 'Can you describe the van.'

'It was a white Astra, I think.'

'Did you get the registration number?'

'No I didn't!' I was getting irritated.

'OK, OK. Well, if you do think of anything else, let us know,' said Donaldson.

'I don't think I'll bother,' I muttered.

'I beg your pardon,' said Donaldson sharply. Kerr moved his eyebrows up a millimetre.

I was tired, worried about Rachel, and my patience was wearing thin. 'All that happens is you ask me questions, I answer them, and then someone else gets killed. As I said, I don't know why I bother.'

Donaldson glared at me, and stood up to leave. Kerr stayed put.

When Donaldson had gone, Kerr said, 'That wasn't a very sensible thing to do, laddie. We're trying our best.'

'I know,' I said, resignedly. I sipped the black coffee in my hand. Kerr just sat there, waiting. There was something comforting about the world-weary policeman in the bad suit. 'Can I ask you something?'

'OK.'

'Did you ever check out Yoshi Ishida's story?'

'Aye, we did. He was telling the truth. The manager of the Robbers' Arms confirms that he was there to play golf for the weekend.'

'But that might just be a cover. I could have sworn that he didn't want Akama to find out where he was.'

Kerr chuckled. 'We checked that out too. The reason he wanted his wee trip kept quiet was that he wasn't alone. He was with the wife of one of his colleagues. That could have been very embarrassing all round.'

'Really?' I thought that over. 'It's pretty unlikely that he would take his mistress with him if he was going to murder someone, isn't it?'

Kerr nodded. 'I'd say we can rule him out.'

'What about David Baker? Did you find him?'

'We did. In Boston. He went to stay with an old friend from

366

Harvard. He says he was under a lot of strain. He'd lost his job, and he found that hard to face. His wife says they had had several rows. He had told her what he was planning to do with Onada, and she'd finally lost her temper. He couldn't have killed Doogie Fisher. And I doubt he killed your brother.'

I sighed and rubbed my eyes.

'Look, son. Whoever did this will probably try again. I'll have a man watching your house for the next few days, and I'll tell Sergeant Cochrane to keep his eyes peeled too. We can't protect you for ever, but we'll do what we can.'

'Thank you,' I said.

'Now, let me drive you home.'

Rachel was all right. They kept her on a ventilator under light anaesthetic for two days, and then she spent two more in hospital under observation. The doctor was confident that she would make a quick and full recovery.

I spent the week focusing on Project Platform, and looking over my shoulder.

The Project Platform system was ready for demonstration. The announcement was scheduled for SIGGRAPH, a trade exhibition in Florida at the end of July. The mass-production process would start just before then, when the design of the components would be finalised for manufacture in Singapore, Japan, and Taiwan. US suppliers would be cranked up shortly after that. We wanted to have product assembled and ready to ship by September.

No matter how hard I looked, I didn't see anyone over my shoulder. But I couldn't be sure. I was as cautious as I knew how.

I did receive another message on my answering machine from Karen's mother. 'Mark, it's Daphne Chilcott speaking. I am really very worried about Karen. I must talk to you about her. Please come and see me in Godalming as soon as you can. Thank you.'

I ignored it. For once, I wasn't worried about Karen. And I liked it that way.

I picked Rachel up from the hospital and took her to her flat in Glenrothes to collect some things. I insisted that she stay with me. Although we had been snatched from Inch Lodge, I was confident that she would be safer with me, now that there was a police presence. I had also installed locks on all the windows. I didn't want anything else to happen to her.

We were sitting drinking cups of tea in the kitchen.

'I've been thinking,' said Rachel.

'Oh yes?'

'Yes. About Richard's death. And the boathouse fire. And Doogie's death. I think I can guess the connection.'

'What?' I asked excitedly.

'It's to do with information,' she said. 'Richard had some information, and he was murdered for it. But the murderer left some of the information behind, so he had to burn down the boathouse to destroy it.'

'Maybe,' I said.

Rachel continued. 'Then Doogie discovered this information. And he was killed.'

'OK,' I said. 'So why did someone try to kill us as well?'

'We must have it too.'

I thought it through. 'You could be right. But what is this information?'

Rachel sighed. 'I don't know. We know it's important; Doogie said it could ruin FairSystems. We can assume we have it, we just don't know its significance.'

'What about that list of companies the SEC gave us?'

'I thought of that. We know Richard had the list. And, as you say, we've got it now. But we don't know that Doogie had it. And it's information that the authorities themselves hold.'

We sat in silence for a long while. The more I thought about Rachel's theory, the more it seemed to make sense. So what had been in the boathouse, then in Doogie's possession, and now was in ours?

I remembered the fire in the boathouse. All those papers burning. Me scrambling out with Richard's computer clasped to my chest.

'Richard's computer!' I said.

'What?'

'Whatever this information is, Richard might have made a note of it in a file in his computer. Have you looked through all his files?'

'Only some of them. I didn't have time to look through everything. There's an awful lot of it.'

'Well, I bet it's there somewhere. The fire was supposed to destroy the machine, but I saved it. Then, when Doogie broke into the factory, he downloaded the file from the computer and discovered something. He must have used it to blackmail someone else, and so he was killed. And now we have it, right there in your office!'

'Let's go!' said Rachel.

I drove quickly into Glenrothes. Rachel powered up Richard's machine. 'Hah! You were right. The hard disk has been reformatted.'

'How could that happen?'

'Doogie must have left a time bomb hidden in the machine. Everything would look normal for a period of time, say a week. Then the time bomb would instruct the computer to reformat the hard disk.'

My heart sank. 'Does that mean we've lost all the data?'

'It means that the data in there was important enough for someone to erase it.'

'But can we recover it?'

Rachel smiled, and reached into the bottom drawer of her desk. She pulled out a small cassette. 'A back-up tape.'

She disappeared, and came back a moment later with a tape-streamer, a device which would enable her to reload the information on to Richard's computer. In a few minutes, it was all there.

Rachel called up the list of directories. Half of it was gobbledygook to me. 'Let's focus on the word-processing files. We can forget the others,' she said.

Rachel called up the sub-directories in the word-processing

directory. There were six of them. Each one contained dozens more files.

'Whew!' I said. 'Have you checked all these?'

'No. Just those in the FAIRSYS and PLATFORM sub-directories.'

'Well, you can bet Doogie checked them all. Come on. Let's get going.'

We went through every file in detail. Many were boring: bill payments, letters to insurance companies, that sort of thing. Some were fascinating. Richard had had a habit of writing notes to himself on certain topics, and saving them, to be altered or added to later.

One of these was headed 'Baker'. I was right! Richard had suspected that David Baker had been working with Onada.

'Do you think that's it?' asked Rachel.

'I don't know,' I said. 'We suspected it, but it would be news to Doogie. And he could have caused us some damage with the information. He could have tried to blackmail David with it.'

'But would it have been enough to kill for?'

I thought about it. 'I doubt it. David knew we suspected him anyway. I can't see why he, or anyone else would kill Doogie for this. No. Next!'

There were a number of files relating to BOWL. Richard had obviously been worried about Doogie and his activities. Still nothing there.

One note related to the motorbike accident. It was a memo to Willie. But there was nothing really new in it. Besides, Doogie had probably seen it already when he had stolen the original Bergey letter.

I reread Richard's analysis of FairSystems share price movements. There was quite a lot of background material that he hadn't shown us before. It took time to go through it all.

After a couple of hours, we broke for coffee. Then back to the machine. The most obvious file names had yielded nothing, so we tried the others. Notes to Keith and Rachel. Negotiations over the lease for the factory. The odd letter to me. Letters to my father. Formidable to-do lists. We were beginning to give up hope.

Suddenly, there it was in black and white.

We knew. But we had to decide what to do with our knowledge. We didn't have absolute proof, and there were large gaps to be filled. I didn't want to go to the police yet. I was weary of their tendency to use information just to generate more questions. We needed to give them the answers. So Rachel and I devised a plan. It would require effort, and it would be a diversion from Project Platform, but if it worked it would all be worthwhile.

We called all the major shareholders to announce a demonstration of Project Platform in one week's time. We contacted Wagner, Jenson, Hartman, my father and Sorenson. I wanted to leave out Karen, but Rachel said it was important she was there too, for completeness' sake, and persuaded Willie to call her.

To my surprise, she said she'd come. The only refusal was Hartman. There was no point trying to persuade him.

The demonstration would take place at a virtual meeting, with the attendees in two locations, at Jenson Computer in Palo Alto, and at our factory in Glenrothes.

A dozen people, led by Rachel, worked round the clock. Keith and Andy flew over to California to prepare everything at that end.

A week later, we were ready.

28

'Please put on your headsets.'

We did as Rachel had asked. We were all sitting round the polished mahogany table in the virtual office: Jenson, Wagner, Sorenson, my father, Karen, Willie and I. The likenesses were very good. We had been photographed beforehand, with a number of different expressions, and those images had been fed into the computer. A small camera in the headset would tell the computer which expressions to use in the virtual world. The room was the same one I had seen before, when Rachel had first shown me Project Platform. It was a large office with views over a gleaming city stretching away to sea and mountains in the background.

We all looked round the room, getting the feel of the experience. For a second, my eyes met Karen's in the virtual world. Both of us quickly turned away. We had ignored each other entirely before the demonstration, and I wanted to ignore her now. I wished Rachel hadn't insisted on her coming.

'Hi, Geoff,' Sorenson waved to my father and smiled.

'Evening, Walter, or should I say good morning?' replied my father. 'What time is it here anyway?'

Good question. It was seven o'clock in Glenrothes, and eleven o'clock in the morning in Palo Alto. What time was it in virtual reality?

'Let's compromise,' said Rachel. Although no one could see her in the virtual world, we could all hear her voice. 'How about three p.m?'

There were chuckles round the table.

'What are these headsets for, Rachel?' asked Scott Wagner. 'They look like hair-dryers to me. You can't possibly be intending to use them commercially.'

'Aren't these the old models?' asked my father. 'I remember the first system Richard rigged up had headsets like these.'

'They are indeed,' said Rachel. 'The new system is particularly sensitive, and these headsets give a much better idea of the exact positioning of the head than the standard electromagnetic headsets that we normally use now. But don't worry, Scott, the modification to our lightweight virtual glasses is almost complete.'

This was a lie, but fortunately they seemed to believe it. Everyone was wearing bulky electronic helmets, which covered most of their heads. They were connected to the VR computer by mechanical arms. It was true that this style of headset was sometimes used for greater accuracy, but our virtual glasses would have done fine. In fact, unknown to the others, I was wearing a pair. They would allow me to flip from the virtual world to the real one at will.

I flipped them up now. Beside me were Karen, my father and Willie, all in their headsets, and Rachel, sitting at the computer from where she would control the demonstration. On a small TV screen next to her, I could see the conference room at Jenson Computer, where Jenson, Wagner and Sorenson were all plugged into their bulky helmets. Keith, Andy and a Jenson engineer were grouped round a computer terminal there, and I could just see a couple of security guards standing by the door.

I flipped back to the virtual office. Everyone was waiting.

I cleared my throat. 'First of all, I would like to thank you all for coming,' I looked round the table. 'We thought it important that our major shareholders could get a preview of this project. I'd like to thank Scott, in particular, as the representative of the public shareholders.'

'I'm excited to be here,' Wagner said with a virtual smile.

'We expect that Project Platform's power to bring together people thousands of miles apart in virtual meetings like this one will be one of its most popular applications. But the system includes a whole range of other features that we would like to demonstrate. Now to do this, we would like one of you to take a trip through a virtual world. Walter, as chairman, would you do the honours?'

'I'd be glad to,' said Sorenson.

'Good. When we switch to this virtual world, we'll all be there with you, seeing what you see, and hearing what you hear. But you'll be in control. You can use the 3–D mouse to navigate through the world, OK?'

'OK. I'm ready. Run it!'

'All right, Walter,' Rachel began. 'For this demonstration you start off walking through some woods. You can take it from there.'

I was switched into Sorenson's world. Through a virtual Sorenson, I was experiencing a virtual world which was under Rachel's control. So was everyone else. Sure enough, there we were in a pine forest. It was sunny, and birds were singing all around us. It felt like a spring day. Sorenson must have moved his mouse, because we began to walk along a path. After a minute or so, we came to a grey stone wall with a large wooden door.

'Can I go in?' asked Sorenson.

'Sure. Just turn the knob,' said Rachel.

I flicked up the glasses to watch Sorenson in Palo Alto on the TV screen. He looked strange, sitting in his chair, most of his head hidden by the large helmet, turning an imaginary knob with the 3–D mouse in his outstretched hand. But when I flipped down the glasses again, I saw we had entered a tunnel.

It was poorly lit, but I could just make out another door at the end. The door behind us slammed shut.

It was creepy, claustrophobic. A bat suddenly flew into my face, or our face, causing me to draw in my breath. Sorenson

374

hesitated, and then went on. I could hear things scurrying underneath our feet.

'Hey, this is really good, Rachel,' Sorenson said. 'I feel like I really am in a tunnel.'

Rachel didn't answer.

'Rachel? Rachel?'

No reply.

Sorenson paused and then went on. Eventually, we came to the gate at the end of the tunnel. He opened it, and we were pushed through with a rush. The door slammed shut behind us.

We were in a graveyard. It was dead quiet. A high wall surrounded us on all sides. Sorenson turned to go back, but he couldn't open the gate. 'Get me out of here, Rachel!'

Still no reply.

Hesitantly, the virtual Sorenson moved through the graveyard. The wind rustled through the trees, but apart from that, there was no noise. It was impossible to make out anything more than the shadows of the gravestones and sarcophagi, and the trees surrounding them. There was a moon, but it was dimmed by dark clouds.

Suddenly, I heard a grinding, creaking sound as a stone moved. Sorenson turned to look. A horizontal gravestone slowly lifted up.

Sorenson laughed, but his laugh had just a touch of nerves to it. Good.

The grave was fully open now. A figure climbed out of the ground, and perched on the headstone. It was too dark to make out the features of his face.

Sorenson slowly moved closer.

Suddenly, the wind blew the clouds away from the moon, and the figure was revealed. Sorenson gasped. 'Hello, Walter,' said the figure.

'Richard! What the hell?' Sorenson turned frantically, and then calmed down, remembering he was only in an electronic demo. 'Rachel, this is ridiculous. It's sick. Get me out of here!'

'You can't get out,' said Richard. 'You're stuck here, with me. And I would like to talk to you.'

375

A chill ran through me. Even though I knew I was listening to my own voice, cleverly altered, the figure looked and sounded just like Richard. A torrent of emotions churned inside me. I wanted to speak to him myself; I realised that was one of the things I missed most: the chance to talk to him. I felt a tightening in my throat, and a stinging behind my eyes.

God knows what Sorenson felt. 'Rachel!' he shouted. 'Mark!' The view began to shake about violently. I realised he must be trying to take his helmet off. I flipped up the glasses again and looked at the TV screen. Sure enough, he was writhing in his chair pulling at the helmet.

'Get this thing off me!' he screamed.

He tried to stand up, but couldn't. The mechanical arm attached to the helmet only allowed a small degree of movement. He pulled at the straps round his chin, but Keith had fastened them tight. He writhed and kicked but to no avail. He couldn't get out of the virtual world.

He was locked in.

I looked around the real room in Glenrothes. Willie, Karen and my father were all sitting completely still. My father's lower jaw hung open. The part of his face that I could see beneath the helmet was pale. This must be rough for him. And it was going to get worse. But there was nothing I could do about that now.

I flipped back into Sorenson's world. Richard was smiling at him. The moonlight illuminated the familiar features, and shone yellow off his hair. Richard's face and whole body had been extensively body-mapped nine months before. All his actions were controlled by Rachel, hunched in deep concentration at her computer.

'Walter, you can't escape. Let's talk.' Richard's tone was calm, reasonable, comforting. 'Talk to me.'

'I won't talk to you,' said Sorenson.

'I want to show you a few things. Come with me.'

He turned and walked down some steps into the ground from where he had come. Once again the view bucked as Sorenson tried not to follow. But there was nothing he could do; his

376

controls had been overruled. Together we were pushed down into the grave.

There were steps down to a door. Richard opened it, and beckoned to us to follow. We did.

We were in Richard's office. The pictures of the old VR machines adorned the walls, and we could see the Firth of Forth through his electronic window. Richard was sitting behind his desk.

'Hello, Walter. Thanks for coming,' he said. 'I've found something very disturbing I'd like to show you.

'As you know, I've been worried about the way our shares have been trading since February. I've talked to the SEC in America, and they informed me that a man called Frank Hartman has been building up a sizeable position in our stock. They also believe that Wagner Phillips has been manipulating the stock price to make it easier for Hartman to build up his stake at low levels. Do you know Frank Hartman, Walter?'

No answer.

'Well, the SEC has kindly sent me a list of companies that they know Hartman has been involved in over the last few years. They suspect he traded on inside information in each case. Here is the list.'

He handed a sheet of paper to us. We had no choice but to look at it.

'Do you recognise any of those names, Walter?'

Once again, silence.

'And then there's this.' Richard handed over another sheet of paper. It was a page of the documentation for the public offering of FairSystems shares, and listed Sorenson's past directorships. Five of the eight companies that were on the SEC's list were also on this second list. Sorenson's virtual hands held both lists together for easy comparison, and there was nothing the real Sorenson could do to stop them.

Richard continued. 'This is evidence that you've been providing Frank Hartman with inside information on these five companies. As a director, you would hear about future takeovers or new product launches before they were announced. You told

377

Hartman, who bought shares through nominee accounts, probably buying some for you at the same time.'

'That's bullshit!' said Sorenson.

'It looks convincing, Walter. One list comes from the SEC, and the other from FairSystems' offering documents. You can't deny the similarity. There's only one obvious conclusion, wouldn't you say?'

'I don't know what you're talking about,' protested Sorenson.

'Here, look at this graph.' Richard handed us another piece of paper, this one showing the prices and volume of trading in FairSystems shares since the company had gone public in November.

'You can see that volume picked up sharply in FairSystems shares on the twenty-first of February. That's one week after I told you about Project Platform. You told Hartman, and Hartman started buying shares. With some help from Scott Wagner, no doubt.'

If Wagner protested at this, we couldn't hear him. Only Sorenson's words were picked up. Rachel and I didn't want exclamations from the others ruining the effect.

'Now, I've drafted this letter to the SEC explaining everything,' said Richard, handing a sheet of paper to us. 'But I won't send it right away. I'll give you a week to decide what you want to do.'

'OK, Rachel, this has gone far enough. You've had your fun. Let's quit now,' said Sorenson.

'OK, let's go,' said Richard. We stood up, and followed him out of the room. We walked down a featureless corridor while Richard talked. 'We have a problem, don't we Walter?' he said in the same reasonable tone. 'If this information gets out, then it'll be very difficult to raise the money we need to complete Project Platform.

'Of course, your problem is much worse than that, isn't it? If this comes to light, then you'll be prosecuted for insider trading. That will be followed by a couple of years in jail. But a tough guy like you could probably handle that.

378

'The real problem for you will be your reputation. No longer will you be known as Silicon Valley's wonder coach. You'll be just a sad little criminal who ripped off all those young entrepreneurs he was supposed to be helping. It will be humiliating.'

Sorenson didn't say anything.

We were still walking. The corridor seemed to go on for ever.

'But, before we consider what the future holds, why don't we have a look at the past? Fortunately for you, and unfortunately for me, I was murdered.' Richard held up his hand. 'Before you protest, I know it wasn't you. You were in Chicago giving a speech at the time. We'll come back to that later.

'I was dead, but there was still that letter. You weren't safe as long as that letter to the SEC was in existence. But you knew where I kept those sort of papers. In the boathouse. So you burned it down.

'You thought the letter was destroyed. What you didn't know was that a copy of it was still on the hard disk of my computer which Mark rescued from the fire. That wouldn't have mattered until Doogie broke into the factory, and looked through my machine, which was now in Rachel's office. He couldn't believe his luck! Let's talk to him about it shall we?'

Richard turned sharp right through a narrow door. We followed. We were suddenly in Doogie's flat in Edinburgh. Doogie himself was sitting on the sofa, holding the letter.

He smiled at us as we came in. 'Well, well,' he said. 'Who's been a naughty boy, then?' It wasn't actually Doogie; it was Keith trying to sound like Doogie. To my ears that was obvious, but we had hoped it would be less clear to Sorenson who wasn't very familiar with either voice. The image of Doogie was pretty good, as he had been extensively body-mapped when he had worked at FairSystems.

'Now. Let's make a deal,' he said. 'I destroy this letter and forget I ever saw it. You make sure FairSystems doesn't last the summer.' I had no idea if this was the deal Doogie had offered, but it sounded plausible.

'But you didn't want to make a deal, did you, Walter?' said Richard.

We moved nearer to Doogie. His scornful smile disappeared. Two large hands pulled him to his feet, and encircled his neck. Doogie tried to knock the hands loose, but they stayed firmly locked around his throat. He struggled for air. His eyes bulged.

Everything went black.

For five seconds there was nothing. Then we were suddenly driving a car in the dark along a narrow lane. Headlights picked out scrappy hedges. As we rounded a bend, we saw the shimmering grey of the sea in the moonlight.

'Look behind you, Walter.' We turned round. In the back seat sat Richard, with Doogie lying on his lap. His face was pale, and his eyes were staring blankly up to the car ceiling. Sorenson quickly turned towards the road in front. Richard's voice continued, insistent, from behind our head. 'Let's stop here, shall we?'

We were driving along a rough track. It opened out into a makeshift parking spot, empty at this time of night. The car stopped, and we got out. Richard opened the car door to get out too. Below us we could hear the sea dashing against the rocks. We found our face a foot away from the back of the car, as our virtual hands pushed it towards the edge. With a final heave, it tipped up, and plunged into the dark water twenty feet below. We stared down at the agitated sea, churning against the rocks. There was no sign of the car.

Sorenson was breathing heavily, I could hear it in my earphones, but he didn't say anything.

'Very neat, Walter,' Richard said. 'Let's take a look down there, shall we?'

We ran to the edge of the cliff and dived. As the dark water rushed up to meet us, I involuntarily held my breath. We were underwater. I could just make out the shape of the car, lying on the sea-bed on rocks and sand. Richard took our sleeve and pulled us over to the driver's seat. There was Doogie, strapped into the front seat, eyes bulging, his white T-shirt flapping in the current.

I felt an attack of claustrophobic panic. The terror of those minutes spent submerged in the BMW came flooding back. I flipped the glasses up, and slumped back in my chair. I could feel the sweat cold around my body. I took some deep breaths. I looked over to Rachel. 'Bloody hell. That was just too real.'

She smiled grimly back. 'You wait for the next scene,' she said. The underwater image danced on her computer screen. It didn't look nearly as bad in two dimensions as it had done when I'd been immersed in the virtual deathtrap.

I looked over to the others. Willie, Karen and my father were all motionless. None of them would have been able to take their headsets off, even if they had wanted to. If they had tried to say anything, we wouldn't have heard it in the virtual world. I glanced at the TV screen. There was the same stunned stillness in Palo Alto.

I took a deep breath, and flipped the glasses down. To my relief, we were back in the corridor, following Richard again.

'So, Doogie was silenced, but your troubles weren't over. My brother was on your trail. You tried to scare him off by hitting him over the head and sending him that warning e-mail. But it didn't work. When the SEC gave Mark and Rachel the list it had sent me, you knew it would only be a matter of time before they discovered the link with your directorships. So you quickly organised two gorillas to get rid of them permanently.'

Rachel and I had decided not to include our experience in the loch. The last thing we wanted to do was live through that again.

'Let's go back to my murder. I know you weren't there then, but I thought you might like to see what it was like. This way.'

He opened another door off the corridor, and suddenly we were in Richard's boathouse. I saw the familiar jumble of computer equipment. It was dark, but I could hear the rhythm of the waves just outside.

Richard was standing in front of us. 'Someone came to see me that night. I let them in to the house and talked to them. Perhaps it was someone I knew. Perhaps it was more than one person. Perhaps they said they had a message from you.

'Then I took them outside to the boathouse to show them something.' He moved over to the spot near the door where I had found his body. He stood still for an age. 'Come closer,' he said. Slowly, ever so slowly, we came closer, until Richard's face was only a foot away from our own.

'Now, Walter. We die. Together this time.'

Suddenly the image changed. There was a face in front of us, a face with no features. The face of the mysterious killer.

The killer bent down slowly and picked up an axe. He raised it up above us, and held it there. We focused on the blade, grey but sharp with tiny wood chips clinging to its edge. Then it swung down right above our eyes. I flinched as virtual contact was made. I heard a scream from Sorenson. The axe was raised, blood dripping from the blade this time, and brought down again. Another scream.

I flipped up the glasses and looked at the TV screen. Sorenson was clasping his headset and screaming. It jolted violently at regular intervals. We had rigged up a piston-like device which rammed into Sorenson's forehead at every bang in the virtual world. We had set it at a level hard enough to hurt, but not hard enough to knock him unconscious. It was scaring the life out of him.

'He's closed his eyes,' said Rachel. She had installed sensors in the headset that monitored Sorenson's eye movements. Obviously, the virtual reality effect would be lost if he kept his eyes shut.

'Blast him!' I said.

'OK,' said Rachel. 'I'll turn everyone else's earphones off. Here we go!'

A bloodcurdling screech came from the speakers beside Rachel's computer.

'That's on low volume,' said Rachel. 'It's orders of magnitude louder in his headset.'

The sound was the product of FairSystems' research over the years into what noises should be avoided to prevent distress in virtual reality users. It was difficult to describe. It was high-pitched, a mixture of a baby's yell and fingernails dragged across a blackboard.

It went on for ten seconds and then there was silence. In Sorenson's world, Richard would be whispering, 'Open your eyes.'

'They're still shut. We'll try some more,' said Rachel, and the awful noise started again.

The ten seconds were nearly up, and my own nerves were fraying badly, when Rachel exclaimed, 'They're open.'

I flipped down the glasses again. Back into Sorenson's world.

Richard was standing before him, blood pouring down from a gaping hole in his forehead. 'Now tell me Walter. Who killed me?'

Sorenson was panting heavily. 'No,' he whispered. 'No.'

'Let's die again, Walter.'

Again the blade was raised above us, and again it fell. I forced myself to watch.

'I'm going to increase the pressure on the piston, and turn on the sound,' said Rachel to me. 'Don't worry, you won't hear it.'

The axe fell over and over again. Sorenson started to scream again.

'Who was it, Walter?' whispered Richard.

'It wasn't me!' shouted Sorenson at last. 'It wasn't my idea! It was her fault! She shouldn't have done it! It was stupid! Stupid!'

There was a pause. I heard Rachel's voice in my earphones. 'Right, we've got to go live here.'

Until then we had been able to use carefully rehearsed pre-programmed speeches for Richard, which I had recorded over the last few days. But now I would have to ask questions myself. My voice would be synthesised into an imitation of Richard's in real time.

'Who was she Walter?' It was strange to see my words coming out of Richard's mouth in the virtual world as I spoke them. It still seemed to me as though he was really speaking.

No reply. Just heavy breathing as Sorenson gasped for air.

'It was a woman, wasn't it?'

'I won't tell you anything. You can put me through this as long as you like, I still won't tell you.'

'Here we go again,' said Rachel. This time, Sorenson had pulled himself together. There were no screams, although I could hear the air hissing through his clenched teeth.

'Who was she, Walter?'

No response.

'Was she your wife? A lover?' I remembered what my father had said about Sorenson's weakness for women. 'Was it your mistress who murdered me?'

'Go to hell!' Sorenson muttered.

'It was, wasn't it? Your mistress. Your lover. It had to be someone who knew Richard. Who was she?'

I thought of the women who knew Richard who might also have known Sorenson. Rachel? No, obviously not.

Oh God. No. No!

'Switch us back to the meeting!'

Rachel did as I told her. The seven of us were sitting round the mahogany table again. In the virtual world, everyone had deadpan faces.

I turned to Karen.

'You killed him!'

There was silence. All eyes were on her. She looked from Sorenson to me. In the virtual world it was impossible to tell what her true expression was.

'I had to,' she said at last. 'He was going to expose Walter. It would have been the end of his career. It would have meant there was no future for us.'

'But how could you do it?'

'I didn't mean to kill him. I meant to talk him out of going to the SEC. But he wouldn't listen. And the axe was right there. It was the only way to keep him quiet.'

I was speechless. My brain was a jumble of unconnected thoughts. So her lover wasn't Bob Forrester at all; it was Sorenson. Karen had killed my brother. And even after that we had slept together, made love. It was revolting. I couldn't believe it. It was too horrible to believe.

384

I dimly heard Rachel's voice as she took over. 'And what about Doogie? And Mark and me?'

'I killed Doogie. And I arranged for those men to kill you and Mark. Walter knew nothing about it. Like he said, it was all my idea.'

'Did you know anything about this, Walter?'

'I'm not saying anything without a lawyer,' Sorenson replied flatly.

'It was worth it,' Karen said. 'It was worth it for you, Walter. Please remember that.'

The anger boiled up inside me. It came from nowhere. At one moment I was stunned, at the next every sinew of my body was filled with fury.

'You bitch!' I screamed, and pulled off my virtual glasses. I lunged at Karen, her face hidden behind the headset.

Rachel grabbed my arm and hung on. 'No Mark! Leave her! The police will take care of her!'

I pulled up short. I couldn't see Karen's eyes under the helmet. But I could see her mouth. She was smiling.

29

We stood outside the small terraced house in Jericho, a former working-class district of Oxford now taken over by students and younger dons. I was nervous. So was Rachel. I rang the bell.

Frances answered. 'Hi, come in.'

My stepmother was dark-haired and pretty, and only a few years older than me. It was a ridiculous situation.

My father was overjoyed to see us, and grinned broadly as I introduced Rachel. 'What will you have to drink?'

Rachel, Frances and I opted for beers, whilst my father had the inevitable dry sherry. He had an image to maintain. I thought he looked much better than when I had spoken to him in the King's Arms. Not so worn, not so dispirited.

Frances had prepared a traditional Sunday lunch of roast lamb. I realised it was years since I had had one, and I was looking forward to it.

'So, you decided not to stay on as MD of FairSystems?' said my father, as he cut into the meat.

'I did my best in a crisis, but I'm sure Rachel will do a much better job than I ever could. Besides, trading is in my blood.' I had persuaded her that it was something she not only could do, but should do. The idea was growing on her.

'And are you staying in the City?'

'No,' I smiled. 'I've just accepted a job with Hunter Merchant. They're a fund management firm in Edinburgh. It's a lot less money, but they have an excellent reputation. And it will be good to live in Scotland. They'll let me spend a couple of days a month at FairSystems. It should work out well.' I smiled at Rachel. I had had enough of Edinburgh airport. I didn't think much of the idea of weekend commuting.

'How are the police getting on with the prosecution?' my father asked.

'It's not easy,' I said. 'Sorenson is keeping quiet, except to deny everything. Karen says she was responsible for the whole thing.'

'What do you think happened?' asked Frances.

'I can piece most of it together. Sorenson met Karen several years ago, probably at one of the Harrison Brothers conferences. Sorenson runs American companies, Karen sells their stock, so it wasn't really surprising that they should meet. Then he chucked her, she cracked up, and I picked up the pieces.

'Sorenson got into the insider trading game through lack of money. He had an expensive lifestyle, and most of his wealth was tied up in the shares of Softouch, which went bust. He met Hartman, and started giving him inside information. It was easy money. Then Richard got suspicious about FairSystems' stock, and asked Karen and me to help him find out what was going on. Karen guessed Sorenson was involved, and contacted him to warn him. She had seen him at BGL's party just a few days before. It must have been about then that their affair restarted.'

I could hear the bitterness creeping into my voice. I remembered Karen's sudden trips to Paris and Amsterdam, her evenings spent entertaining clients. 'Karen fell for him again. When Richard threatened to expose Sorenson, she was desperate. She couldn't face the thought of losing him once more. So she flew up to Scotland to talk Richard out of it, and when he refused, she killed him.

'She must have told Sorenson what she had done. She says she was proud of it; it was a way for her to show him how

387

much she loved him.' I shuddered. 'I'm sure Sorenson had no idea what Karen was going to do. Neither did she, probably. But once Richard was dead, they were both deeply involved. They had to kill Doogie and try to kill Rachel and me to cover their tracks.' And all the time she'd kept up the pretence of our relationship. So as not to raise suspicions, I supposed. And to keep an eye on me. My skin crawled to think of it.

'It must have been Sorenson who murdered Doogie,' I continued. 'After all, Karen was still in my flat, but he would just have had time to go up to Scotland. Either one of them could have hired those men to kill us.'

'I still can't believe Walter could get himself involved in something like this,' said my father. 'He was always so straight, so above board.'

'I think that was exactly the reputation he was trying to protect,' I said. 'If he had been exposed insider dealing, it would have ruined him.'

Dad nodded. 'I can see that. He was always proud of his achievements. But to kill?'

'Once Karen had killed Richard, it probably seemed to him that he had no other option. And he's certainly a man of action.'

'She must have been a seriously mixed up woman.'

'She was,' I said. 'More than I could ever guess.'

I sighed. 'I saw her mother last week. She called me a while ago saying she was worried about Karen, but I ignored her. I had other things to think about. Anyway, she told me that Karen's breakdown when her father left was even more serious than I realised. Apparently the "other woman" 's house was burned down. Karen was ruled out as the arsonist, but only because her mother covered for her. When Karen stayed with her the night after Richard was murdered, she was in a terrible state. Although Daphne wouldn't admit it, I think she suspected her daughter had killed Richard.'

A thought struck me. 'Did you guess something, Rachel? Is that why you insisted Karen should be at the demonstration?'

Rachel smiled. 'It was no more than a guess. Just intuition, really. I had no evidence to back it up, so I thought it best not to tell you, just in case I was wrong. But I was pretty sure that if Karen was there, we would find out if she were involved or not.'

All three of them were looking at me: Frances, my father and Rachel. I answered the unspoken question. 'I just felt sorry for her,' I said. 'I knew she'd had a rough time, and that vulnerability made her more attractive, made me feel I could be useful.'

'I hope you're not going to burn down our house,' said Frances.

'No.' I smiled at her, and then at my father. 'No, I won't do that.'

The German took off his virtual glasses and leaned back in his chair. 'Wonderful. This is truly amazing,' he said, staring at the Jenson Computer in front of him. I had just run him through 'Virtual Building', a program that simulated all the details of an office block design.

'You are sure that I can put all my architects on the same network so that they can all work on the same design?'

'Quite sure. The program will work with all the major networking software. Your people will be able to walk around and work in the same virtual building, or they can try out their own variations.'

'And what about all the software we have on our PCs at the moment? Will all that run on this machine?'

'Anything that will run on an IBM PC with a Pentium chip will run on this,' I assured him. 'And you will be able to access the program directly from Windows. In time, your customers will be able to view your designs through their own computers.'

The man stood up. He worked for one of the largest firms of architects in Germany, and he was obviously impressed.

He shook my hand. 'Very interesting, Mr Fairfax. When will the system be available?'

'September,' I said. 'Shall we get in touch with you then?'

'Please do.' He handed me his card. As he walked away from the stand, he kept looking back over his shoulder at the system.

'Will he buy?'

I turned to see Rachel at my shoulder.

'Oh yes, he'll buy,' I answered.

'Come on, let's get out of here. I need a ciggy badly.'

I hesitated. The stand was crowded with eager onlookers, many of them potential buyers.

'Hey, we've been at this for four hours, we deserve a break.' She took my arm and pulled me away from the stand.

We pushed through the crowded exhibition centre, making our way towards the exit signs. Huge banners hung down from the ceiling proclaiming SIGGRAPH. SIGGRAPH was the major exhibition in the virtual reality year, and this year's in Orlando was the biggest yet. Jenson had spared no expense on the joint FairSystems/Jenson stand, and it was the highlight of the show. There were some other products that could do as much as ours, but none that was anywhere near as cheap. And none that would be bundled up in every copy of Windows sold. We really would bring VR to the masses.

It was the third day of the exhibition. Project Platform, renamed 'VR Master', had been announced on the first day and had caused an immediate stir. FairSystems' shares were already up to eighteen dollars and were still rising. Orders were flooding in, and the assembly lines in Jenson's Palo Alto factory were rolling. Richard's dream was becoming reality.

We emerged from the huge, air-conditioned hall into the early afternoon brightness. It was hot and clammy, but Rachel didn't care. She reached for a cigarette and took a long drag. We sat on the steps just outside the hall. People milled about, moving slowly in the heavy July heat. Twenty yards away, a group of a dozen or so were eating sandwiches, sprawled on a square of freshly sprinkled grass.

I glanced at Rachel's face. I knew she hadn't slept very much over the past week, but you couldn't tell. Her dark eyes still glowed brightly under her tousled hair. She saw me watching her and smiled, putting her arm round me. We sat in silence for a minute or two.

It was all coming together. Jenson was proving to be an

energetic ally, and had pushed strongly for Rachel to take the role of managing director of FairSystems. I was happy to step back and watch her, and help out where I could. The bond markets beckoned. Once you're hooked, it's difficult to give up.

Just then, the group finished their sandwiches and stood up. They moved towards us and began to march round in a circle in front of the exhibition centre. They were wearing 'Brave Old World League' badges. They shambled round, laughing and chatting, handing leaflets to anyone who would take one. Some of them carried placards: 'SAVE OUR CHILDREN', 'VIRTUAL HELL IS HERE', 'KEEP REALITY REAL'.

I watched them thoughtfully. I remembered the intense high I had felt while trading the market through Bondscape, and the extreme trauma we had put Sorenson through. Richard was right; virtual reality could do good. But I also remembered Doogie's words. What would happen when virtual reality was available to everyone, to the mentally sick, the lazy, to perverts, psychopaths, sadists?

'I know what you're thinking,' said Rachel softly. 'But it's too late now.' She stubbed out her cigarette. 'Come on, let's go. We've got some VR machines to sell.'